'*Unquiet* deceptively pr... further one treads across E. Saxey's haunting, delicate text, the closer to cracking the ice one gets. I fell through this gorgeously gothic novel and still haven't come up for air.'

CLAY MCLEOD CHAPMAN, AUTHOR OF *GHOST EATERS*

'A wonderful gothic novel rife with mystery and unease; perfect for fans of Shirley Jackson.'

A.C. WISE, AWARD-WINNING AUTHOR
OF *WENDY, DARLING* AND *HOOKED*

'Told with beguiling lyricism and compelling intensity, E. Saxey's novel *Unquiet* is an artful and complex masterwork of contemporary Gothic fiction that will leave readers unsettled and clamoring for more written by such an exciting and unique voice in horror.'

ERIC LAROCCA, AUTHOR OF *THINGS HAVE GOTTEN WORSE SINCE WE LAST SPOKE AND OTHER MISFORTUNES*

'An exquisite gothic piece. Wrap yourself up and try and decide whether it's warm like bedsheets or cold like a shroud.'

KIERON GILLEN, HUGO-NOMINATED AUTHOR
OF *THE WICKED + THE DIVINE, DIE* AND *ONCE & FUTURE*

'A brooding psychological gothic mystery, steeped in the darkest realms of folklore. Literally dripping with grief, desire, and guilt.'

ESSIE FOX, BESTSELLING AUTHOR OF *THE SONAMBULIST*

'*Unquiet* is a sly, enigmatic incantation of a book, full of mysteries and half-truths. E. Saxey creates something unique, both Gothic and quietly folk-horror-inflected, in their tale of grief, loss, unquiet spirits and outsiders.'

ALLY WILKES, BRAM STOKER AWARD®-NOMINATED
AUTHOR OF *ALL THE WHITE SPACES*

UNQUIET

E. SAXEY

TITAN BOOKS

Unquiet
Print edition ISBN: 9781803364469
E-book edition ISBN: 9781803364476

Published by Titan Books
A division of Titan Publishing Group Ltd
144 Southwark Street, London SE1 0UP
www.titanbooks.com

First edition: July 2023
10 9 8 7 6 5 4 3 2 1

This is a work of fiction. All of the characters, organizations, and events portrayed in this novel are either products of the author's imagination or are used fictitiously. Any resemblance to actual persons, living or dead (except for satirical purposes), is entirely coincidental.

A CIP catalogue record for this title is available from the British Library.

Printed and bound by CPI Group (UK) Ltd, Croydon, CR0 4YY.

To Amy Levy and her luminous writing.

TUESDAY

I needed my charms to ward off madness. Scrabbling around in the cold scullery, I hauled out every drawer in the dresser to find myself a jam jar, a candle stub, a wineglass. I'd gathered them before but the maid had tidied them away. It was vital to bring them back together, and to open a new bottle of wine.

I had been alone in the house for almost four months. I didn't regret ridding myself of my family. But it was odd to live alone, unseen and unheard, and easy to feel untethered. Impossible to recreate the family routines which had dropped away – Friday night dinner, brushing my sister's hair, trips to take tea at Whiteleys. Instead, I had made routines of my own: rising at eight, art class at nine. I had invented rituals. Between them, I kept myself steady.

So tonight, I poured myself a glass of red wine. I intended to carry it down the long, narrow garden. Our home wasn't large, having only six bedchambers, but Father had chosen it for its luxurious touches. It was the end house of a smart modern terrace, had fine rooms on the ground floor for visitors, and pillars at the front in an envious echo of nearby Kensington Palace Gardens. At the foot of the garden lay an ornamental lake. When I reached the lake, I'd spill some wine into the water, and drink the rest.

Lighting the candle wick, I dropped it into the jam jar, singeing my fingers. I was suddenly conscious that Mama would see this as a parody, in bad taste. Tonight was the first evening of Hanukkah; as I'd walked home, around sunset, I'd seen the candles in my neighbours' windows. But I didn't feel able to light our own, now Mama and my sister weren't here.

As I carried the jar over to the kitchen door, the flame jumped up (*a neighbour has gossip*) and sparked (*you will receive a letter soon*). Outside the night was dark and bitingly cold. The moonlit silver treetops thrashed in the wind, and I loved it, because inside the house, so little moved if I didn't move it. The maid, Lucy, could have helped, but she made it worse. She passed me in the hall without meeting my eyes, and everything I disturbed she put back in its place, so that it appeared nobody lived in my house at all.

The gravel path didn't crunch under my feet. Had I become weightless? No, the gravel had frozen in place. This year, December had been unusually harsh.

After a minute of walking, the path gave out into lawn. My feet crushed prints into the frozen grass. I grasped my wine and my candle. I wouldn't be sent away for a rest cure, like the classmate of mine with bad nerves.

In our childhood, my sister, Ruth, and I had performed all kinds of elaborate ceremonies in this garden. It was large enough to get lost in, or at least evade observation. I made a fine witch, with my unruly hair and my bony face. I'd cast spells, and blight every tree. Ruth, with her orderly ringlets, had played the princess. What did princesses do? Were they imprisoned in branches? Did they scry in the lake for true love? If only Ruth were here to remind me.

It was foolish to wish for Ruth because I let myself miss her. That pang multiplied, and I missed Mama, too. And – most painful, and most pointless – I missed Sam. His restless footsteps in our hall at the foot of the big staircase, his voice calling us to join him. I was hollow because he wasn't here.

Panic rattled me. I was a candle flame, wick snipped, flickering away into the night sky.

Walk the path, I told myself. *Reach the lake. Drink the wine. Go back to your room and bury yourself in your bed.*

But there was an uncanny glow to the garden ahead of me, a whiteness beyond the dark trees. I pushed branches aside to reach it.

The lake had been transformed: where dark water should have rippled, there was flat pale ice. It was fantastical. Pure white at the edges, where the lake met its border of marble kerb stones. Grey towards the centre, where the ice thinned. Dark scrapes crossed the surface – from birds, trying to land on it?

How would I draw the ice? Layers of pale pastels, scraped through to dark paper? I could imagine my oily fingertips, a blunt blade.

It put me in mind of magical changes in ballads where boulders melt or a gate opens in a hill. Your love turns in your arms into red-hot metal, or a stranger. When had the lake last frozen? I recalled Mama snapping a warning as I ran towards it, in her mother tongue of Yiddish, then explaining in English that I'd drown if I set foot on it. I must have been very young.

A movement, on the far side of the white lake, and a rustling in the bushes. Probably a fox, wanting to drink and startled by the frost. I moved closer to the edge, with my wine and candle, and waited for it to emerge.

It wasn't a fox. It was Sam.

He stood just twenty feet from me. The moon was bright. The absolute familiarity of him stamped itself on my eyes.

He waved, then he beckoned. I couldn't move, so he walked towards me, one foot onto the white ice, and then another. Walking with complete confidence, not looking down, he trusted the ice to be thick enough to bear him.

Or, no – he hadn't trusted anything. He'd mistaken the lake

for a solid surface. His foot slipped and he paused, looking down in puzzlement.

I shouted a warning.

He dropped straight down in a barrage of cracking. A fountain of moon-white water shot up from where he'd stood.

Then there was nothing left but a foaming dark hole, and jostling plates of broken ice.

I ran round the edge of the lake, as close as I could get to the hole where Sam had vanished. I threw myself down at the pool's edge, and kicked my toes into the earth to anchor myself. Stretching half my body onto the ice, I reached my arm out even further.

'Sam!'

Water pulsed out of the hole, dark green, and sucked back, and there was no sign of him.

I screamed for help, but was anyone in earshot? Lucy would be cloistered in her attic bedroom. The cold would sink Sam and the ice would trap him. He was drowned. No refusing it, no haggling.

Sam's head broke the surface. He made a great wheezing moan, dragging breath into his lungs. His arms punched out, and sliced through air and water. White foam flew everywhere around him. But his crashing was frantic, failing. He was going to sink again.

I yelled his name, stretching so far that the muscles under my arm burned.

Sam heaved himself forwards. He raised a dripping arm and reached out his hand to me.

I grabbed him. He didn't feel human. His skin was slimy and his hand slipped from my grasp. I seized the sleeve of his jacket instead. I found purchase, and I felt his icy fingers clamp around my wrist.

I tensed my agonised body and dragged him in, hearing the ice crack with every pull.

He let go, abruptly. Released, I tumbled onto the grass. Sam didn't fall back, though. He grabbed at clumps of reeds to haul himself up onto the marble kerb stones and out of the water.

On all fours on the grass, he started retching. I crawled until I was near him, but what should I do? Beat on his back? He drove the heel of one hand into his own chest, gave a horrible grating cough and then spat. His barking shaking head, his black slicked hair like fur, made him wolf-like in the moonlight.

Finally he lifted his face up to me, almost unrecognisable. I knew I must be just as smeared with filth, as open-mouthed and disgusting. One stain on his forehead looked more like blood than mud. Ruth would have reached out to it, tended it. I recoiled.

Sam's hand, strong and cold, closed around my shoulder. When he pulled, I braced myself again, but he wasn't trying to drag me closer. He was using me as a prop, swinging awkwardly round into a sitting position. When he managed to sit, he still kept hold of me.

For a long while we only breathed, both of us in ragged rasps. My lungs felt like I'd inhaled hot ashes. My arm, and my whole side where I'd thrown myself onto the ground, throbbed in pain.

But the disbelief was sharper. It couldn't be him. It couldn't be.

'Sam?'

He met my eyes. 'Judith!'

His voice was weak but it was warm. It was him.

He was back.

We hobbled up to the house together. Sam hung off me, a dead weight, his arm a vice around my shoulders. Trails of icy lake water poured from him, running down my scalp and sliding under my collar. My shoes had come off. It was so hard to trudge onwards when the gravel stabbed the soles of my feet.

As we reached the house I steered us off the main path.

'Where are we going?' he asked.

'To the conservatory.'

I yanked open the glass-panelled door and shoved him through it. The big room was chilly, but dry and out of the wind.

Sam slumped onto a wrought-iron bench. Water streamed off him and pooled on the tiled floor.

'Judith?'

'Yes?'

'Good.' His tone was relieved, even though he'd asked nothing and I'd given him no answer. He covered his face with his hands, smearing the stain on his forehead, the ooze from the broken skin. It needed to be cleaned off, but everything I could reach was covered in dirt. 'This is a mess,' he murmured. He started to shiver, so hard that the bench jittered.

I sat down on a wicker chair and studied him. The light was dim, but he was certainly Sam. His familiarity was reassuring, now, rather than shocking. But it wasn't a joyful sight, yet. I was too afraid: what if he was injured, frostbitten, waterlogged? What if he died, and this time it was my fault?

'You need clothes. Dry clothes, that is.' I didn't know where I'd find them, but it gave me a task to perform, and a reason to run away.

I peeled off my stockings in the hallway, although they clung like weeds. My legs were yellow and green with old bruises – I had developed a habit of falling – and I would have fresh marks in the morning. I pattered on clammy feet down to the kitchen. Lucy wasn't there. I'd been right: she'd retreated up to her attic for the night, thank goodness. In a cupboard I discovered old blankets, only fit for horses. I made a stack of them so high that I had to wedge it between my hands and my chin to carry it.

Back in the conservatory, I dropped the blankets beside Sam and left the room again.

He needed to be close to a fire. I was shuddering, and I'd not even been drenched, as Sam had. Our library would heat up the quickest. The large fireplace had been one reason Ruth and I had laid claim to the room, after Father had died. Entering it now, preparing it for Sam, I was conscious of how eccentric we had made the room look. We'd decorated the sober bookcases with fronds of pine, glossy holly and the heads of teasels, stencilled the walls, and hung up embroideries. And since I'd rid myself of my family, I'd been spending all my time here, covering the desk with paintbrushes and rags.

Which meant that in the big grate, under the coals, yesterday's embers would still be glowing. I screwed up paper, stacked coals and blew life into the pyramid. My wing-backed chair was already next to the fire. I dragged another, Ruth's favourite, to face it. Ruth's chair was draped with patchwork quilts that she had made, and I flung them off to keep Sam from dripping on them.

I moved back through the hall, and called through the conservatory door to Sam: 'Are you ready? May I come in?' I meant 'are you covered up', but that was an indecent question. Opening the door, I stood by it, waiting. 'I've lit a fire in the library.'

He lurched towards me. He'd wrapped the blankets round himself, and scrubbed his hair with one of them. Now he resembled a scruffy robed patriarch.

Halting at the threshold, he raised an eyebrow. He was still dabbed with slime, and my reluctance – my revulsion – was probably obvious from my screwed-up mouth. So I held out my arm, and said: 'Please do come in.'

Together we entered the house proper, and slowly crossed the hall. Sam had been our most frequent visitor, energetically pacing here under Father's paintings as he waited for my sister to descend the stairs. Now it took him an age to limp over to the library door.

Inside, Sam moved into the fire's radius and folded himself into Ruth's chair. The firelight showed up his mud-matted hair, but his hands – emerging from the blankets – were cleaner, and his long fingers exactly as they'd always been. He had dark eyes in a long face, and long hands to match.

Good news, then. I finally started to feel joy at his return, kindling in me as the fire grew. Good news? The best news! When he went missing, it had wrecked Ruth, my sister, Sam's betrothed. And it had struck Sam's brother, Toby, as well, and even taken the heart out of Mama. Two small families twisted up with loss like crumpled paper. That could be undone, ironed out. And all the horrible things that had happened since, the hundred lesser sadnesses. Sam's return would reverse all those, as well.

My sister had been so sad, for a year, that her own body had been a burden to her. Now she'd be freed. In a sense, she would never even have been bereaved.

I brought all this to mind, but I couldn't yet feel it. My heart was as numb as my hands. I needed to heat myself, then I'd feel glad.

'Good Lord. That was frightening,' Sam said. He didn't sound frightened. His voice was faint, but he sounded elated, as though we'd cheated and won. His eyes shone.

'Are you hurt at all?' I asked.

'Did I scare you?'

Had he heard me? 'Sam, have you injured yourself?'

'No, but did I? Frighten you?'

He smiled. His smile conjured one back from me. It was so typical of him to be frivolous. 'No!'

'I don't believe you. I'm still terrified! Scared myself rotten.'

I needed him to show less levity. 'Are you hurt, though? What do you need? A doctor?'

'No. I'm utterly freezing, but there's nothing else amiss.'

'Do you need…' I looked around for more coverings for him. There were only the patchwork quilts, which Ruth had pieced together out of fur and brocade, like offcuts from a coronation robe. They were more decorative than practical. 'What do you need?'

'A hot drink would be a marvellous thing. It might thaw my blood.' Sam stamped his bare feet on the hearthrug. 'Ow! That was a terrible idea.'

I hid my own bare feet under the wet hem of my dress.

'Thank you so much for all this, Judith,' Sam added. 'I suppose there's no way to clean me up a bit, before the others see me?'

I was suddenly aware of every empty room in our house. 'They're not at home now.' I didn't say more, because liars give themselves away with long excuses.

'Where?'

'Let me fetch you that drink.'

'You're very kind. Above and beyond, really, Judith.'

I didn't need Lucy to heat a pan of milk, down in the kitchen. Ruth and I preferred the rest of the house to look old-fashioned, but the kitchen was very modern. Any London cook would have refused to work over a Tudor roasting spit.

The surface of the milk was smooth. Staring at it, I stated the simplest facts to myself: *Sam's back. He's here, he's in my house with me.*

Bubbles began to pop up in the milk.

I had expected to feel joy again but it had turned to numbness.

The white circle of milk in the pan reminded me of the ice on the lake. The bubbles clustered.

Sam had asked where my family were.

The milk erupted, and the overspill scalded on the stove-top.

I cleaned up the mess, blotting stinking milk off the flagstone floor with a cloth. I poured all the liquid I could rescue into two cups, over lumpy cocoa powder, and jabbed them with a spoon until they turned rich and soothing.

When I came back into the library, the chair was empty where Sam had been. Then I saw him, seated opposite, in my chair.

'This one was out of the draught. You don't mind?' I handed over the hot cup and Sam bent his fingers gratefully around it. 'And the door?'

The library door should stay open while we were in here together, for the sake of propriety, but the draught was keen so I pulled it closed. The chair Sam had abandoned was probably cold and damp, so I crouched by the grate and pretended the fire needed tending.

'So you can't be all by yourself, all night? Can you?' He was teasing me.

'Of course I can't.' What could I tell him?

'Of course, your sister wouldn't be so careless as to leave you alone.' She'd been very careless. She'd left me alone for months. 'So…?'

'As soon as you're not drowning, you want to talk to the others.' If he could tease me, I could respond in kind. But I knew I sounded quite brittle. I picked up the bellows and puffed up the fire.

The heat finally began to lick at our faces. Leaning away, I watched Sam gradually coming to life in the warmth.

'Really, when are they back? It's late, isn't it?' He craned his head up to look at the clock on the mantelpiece. 'They can't have left you here. It can't just be you.'

'Can't it?'

'No, but is it?'

Lying and confessing were both unthinkable, and my voice failed me.

'Come on, Judith, do tell me. Why won't you? Are they where they oughtn't to be? Somewhere improper? Out watching a French revue? *Ooh la la…*'

I had to stop him talking, and that unlocked my own tongue. 'My family are in Italy.'

His smiling mouth dropped further open.

'They're most likely in Venice, right now,' I explained.

'In Italy? No! How?'

Why was he so incredulous? It was more plausible that my family were travelling in Italy than that Sam was here, in our library. My family had booked tickets, caught a boat and boarded trains. Goodness knows what route Sam had taken to get here.

'Mama and –' I made myself say her name. 'Mama and Ruth are in Italy. With your brother, Toby.'

He nodded at me slowly, as if to say *touché*, trying to understand the joke I was making.

'I should see Ruth,' he said. 'I should certainly talk to her. That's it, isn't it? I should set things straight with her.' He was sheepish, as though he'd forgotten a dinner appointment. He watched for my reaction.

'Well, you can't talk to her tonight.' It was true, but it sounded spiteful. I was too exhausted to command my voice.

'Because she's…'

'In Italy.'

'It's important, though. I have to make amends for something, don't I? Patch something up. Come on, Judith, don't be cross with me. I'll do the decent thing, whatever it is.' He was bargaining with me. He had all his usual confidence and the start of a sly smile: *just between you and me*, he was hinting, *give me a clue.*

He leaned over, clutching his blankets, to fumble with the coal tongs and add more pieces from the scuttle to the fire.

'She's in Venice! I'm not lying to you. She's gone, she isn't here.'

That stopped his smile. 'Who's staying here with you?'

He was asking after my companion, my chaperone. I couldn't be drawn into that conversation. 'There's nobody here.'

Panic welled up in my battered body. He knew what I'd done. He'd end my brief spell of freedom. His eyes wandered over me, as if seeking evidence. He must be staring at the mud on my clothes. I brushed at the worst of it, but it smeared across my skirts.

'Is that truly your dress?' he asked. 'Not some costume?'

An impertinent question, doubly so given his sodden blanket robes. 'Of course.'

'What about those velvet frocks you and Ruth always wear – have you both turned respectable?'

Ruth and I shared a passion for aesthetic dress. We'd paraded around in loose velvet gowns, looking mediaeval and (according to many men in the street) ridiculous. Tragedy had forced us both back into ordinary dresses, with stiff panels and boning that limited your movements, and made it necessary to put on an air of caution. I resented my new wardrobe, although Ruth said the clothes fortified her. I wouldn't let Sam mock me for these clothes.

'It's mourning dress. It's hardly surprising if it's dowdy.'

'Oh, damn. Stupid of me! Forgive me?'

He always wanted to be forgiven immediately. He could never bear to be in the wrong.

'Poor Judith. May their memory be a blessing…' It took me a moment to recognise the words. A phrase of consolation. People had said it to me, years ago, when Father died. People had said it to Toby, but he'd cut them off.

And Sam shouldn't say the words to me, of course. That was perverse, monstrous. He was both the only person who could comfort me, and the only one who couldn't.

'Judith – I'm so sorry, to have to ask, but – who's passed away?'

It had been so little time since I'd pulled him from the lake that I hadn't even caught my breath properly. How could things have become so strange, so quickly?

'Is it someone from your family? Not Ruth, you swear it? No! Who?'

My face scorched as the fire flared. I found the words to tell him who I mourned.

'It's you.'

My grotesque announcement set Sam off on a horrible volley of coughing, his whole body rejecting the news. I took advantage; insisting that he have a handkerchief and a glass of water, I ran downstairs to fetch them both. Busy in the kitchen, I could hear Sam choking. It put me in mind of a curse, as if snakes and toads were struggling out of his throat. I rushed back with the water, and he drank until the coughing stopped. All the while, I braced myself for his inevitable next question, which he asked as soon as I sat down.

'Judith, why on earth would you say I was dead?'

I sat in the chair opposite him, but I could only speak in fragments. 'During the Sully, the midwinter festival. In the river, at Breakwater.'

'That little village?' He sounded hazy, night-capped by recollection. 'What about it? There was a river festival?'

I tried to hold on to clarity. 'You were there, taking part in the festival, and you fell. You were carried off downriver and we thought you'd drowned.'

'You *all* thought so?' He sat up, eyebrows raised, resolutely un-drowned. 'I'd believe it of Toby, but...' As though I was too sensible. I'd made a childish mistake. It was my word against his – no, it was his whole stubborn body against my words. To justify myself, I said: 'We all thought so.'

'Oh, no. No, you can't have. You poor things...' He curled up again, face in hands, blankets closing over him. When he spoke, his voice was muffled. 'So Toby thought he'd lost me?'

I couldn't reply for a moment, because Toby's mourning had been twisted by his uncertainty. It wasn't appropriate for Toby to rend his garments while Sam might still be alive. Instead, for the whole of January, Toby had been frenetically busy: writing, revisiting the area, vigorously searching for any sign of his brother. I wouldn't relate that whole sad period to Sam.

'Yes. Toby thought you were gone.'

'Oh, no, that's simply ridiculous...' He bowed his head down again, retreated into his nest.

We'd failed Sam, clearly. We should have asked advice. But from whom? Mama had been hysterical. Ruth and I had no allies. Unimaginable, to go behind Toby's back to ask for help from his associates, or his very austere rabbi.

Sam straightened up again, reached for the coal tongs, an expensive habit. 'I'm sorry, Judith, it simply seems incredible.'

I could offer physical proof. Crossing to the high shelves where my sister and kept our favourite books of folklore, behind garlands of ivy, I dragged at the first volume of *The Golden Bough*. It toppled into my hands, and from between the pages fluttered a piece of paper, a long oblong clipping from the *Jewish Chronicle*, from late in March.

I picked it up from the floor and held it out to Sam.

'Here.' I sounded triumphant, without meaning to.

Sam read the newspaper notice without speaking. I knew what it said, more or less. Ruth knew it by heart.

> DEATHS: At Breakwater, SAMUEL SILVER, beloved brother of Tobias, in his 29th year. Deeply regretted by his family and all who knew him.

He looked at me with confusion. 'Did you think so, too?'

'Yes.' Why could he not understand? You can't be dead to a few people and not others. I could show him another clipping, where Mr Tobias Silver thanked people for 'visits, letters and many kind expressions of condolence'. That had appeared in the *Chronicle* some weeks later. Did Sam's slowness spring from his shock, or from some organic cause? My eyes fixed on the smear on his forehead, and the darkening bruise underneath it.

'Damn it! Ruth as well?' He leaned suddenly out of his nest of blankets and gripped my arm. 'How is she?'

'You were going to be married.' It was all the explanation I could bear.

'I need to talk to her right away, as soon as I can. I can't bear to think of her –' He sank back. 'There's no way to contact Ruth tonight?'

Would the police be able to send a communication? But then Ruth would be woken in the night with a wild tale, and no way to confirm it.

'We can send a telegram tomorrow,' I offered. 'First thing.'

Sam's eyes narrowed in thought. 'I shouldn't… I mean…' Or was he wincing at my suggestion? 'Has she forgotten all about me?'

An unfathomable question. 'You were going to be *married*! I should send for the doctor.' I feared he needed medical attention, but I also hoped to place the problem in the hands of some wise elder. If not a doctor, then our rabbi, or even our lawyer.

I had no idea how to send for the doctor. I could wake Lucy and ask her.

'No, no doctor.' His expression became particularly earnest, promising good behaviour. 'Please. I merely need a little sleep.'

He probably knew himself best. He could go to his own house and sleep as much as he needed.

'I have a key for Millstone,' I said. Millstone was Sam's house, next door to ours. It was one of a row of identical villas, all small but elegant. If you clambered through the hedges at the foot of Millstone's garden, you reached our ornamental lake. 'Can you walk?'

He grimaced. 'Judith, I can't go to that house.'

'But you have to sleep.' More truly, I had to sleep. But I couldn't see why he shouldn't leave. Millstone would be bitterly cold, and not stocked with luxuries, but serviceable. Toby had retained his housekeeper, a gardener and one maid to keep the place up.

'I really can't! Aren't there servants there? Who think I'm…' His voice dried up in panic.

'Oh!' None of the servants lived in, but the maid would arrive at Millstone tomorrow morning and scream when she discovered Sam in bed. What were his choices, though? Should he take a cab to a hotel? He was half undressed and covered in filth. Dukes and earls could waltz into Claridge's in such a state and demand a hot bath. I suspected that a Jewish gentleman, however respectable, would not risk it. And it would all cost money. Did Sam have any money?

It absolutely wouldn't be right for him to stay here, in this house.

Waiting for my judgement, he sank further down into his blankets. A giant foundling had delivered himself to my doorstep.

'You could stay here,' I conceded. After all, he would have been part of my family.

'Judith, that's terribly generous.'

Despite all my uncertainty, his gratitude pleased me. 'I'll ready a room for you.'

Leaving the library, I returned to the conservatory to gather up his cold and sodden clothes. There were plenty of guest rooms – we were an unusually small family – and some rooms had baths where I could deposit Sam's wet clothes. I carried the wet burden up the stairs, past the door of my sister's room. If only I could go in and find her there. But it served me right. I'd gone to such lengths to get rid of my family, I couldn't conjure them back as soon as I needed them. I pushed open the door to the first guest room.

The room was full of ghosts. White figures towered over me, brushed my face.

I flinched, then recognised them for what they were: long white dust sheets, draped to protect every piece of furniture. The maid had been very thorough. I dropped the squelching bundle of clothes in the bath, then drew the dust sheets off so that they rippled to the floor. In deference to our guests, it was a dull room, untouched by my and Ruth's magical hands: no murals, no gilded scrolls on the furniture, no patchworks. And there hadn't been a fire in the room for months. We'd had no guests since Sam died. For the second time that night, I crumpled old newspapers, propped kindling in a pyre. Then I broke three matches with my clumsy, clammy fingers. When the paper caught, though, and the blue line of flame snaked along its edges, it was beautiful. I waited for the sticks to catch, herded some pieces of coal close and hoped it would thrive.

When I returned to Sam he'd buried his face in his hands again.

'There's a room for you.' I feared he was crying, but he didn't make any sound. 'I've lit a fire upstairs.'

He raised his head at that, and gathered his ludicrous robes about him. 'You're very kind.'

We walked together up the staircase. Sam's damp feet slapped on the steps and I tried not to make a sound with my own. When we reached the top, he turned the wrong way, shambling down the opposite corridor.

'Wait!'

'What?' His hand was on my bedroom door, his eyes only half open.

'Not that room.' I was desperate for him to step away, and couldn't tell him why. He would have been mortified to know. I made a pathetic gesture to bring him back, shoo him towards the guest room. 'That door, there.'

'But this is my room.' Then he frowned, looking down. The carpet pattern, a jumble of red and green, alerted him to his mistake. 'No! Sorry! Not my house. Force of habit. So silly, so similar…'

Millstone was laid out on identical lines to my home. I would never have ventured upstairs there, so had no way to know that Sam's room was in the same corner as mine. At least he understood his mistake, now, and shuffled towards the correct door.

It felt wrong to go into my room at the same time as him, closing our doors and tucking ourselves up. Too cosy. So I turned back to the stairs instead.

'Goodnight, Judith,' he called. He used to call up to Ruth, and to me, as we climbed the stairs at the end of an evening: *Good night, ladies; good night, sweet ladies…* Always calling from the hallway below. Not coming upstairs, not yet.

'Goodnight.'

'Wait…'

He held out his hand. In it was the newspaper clipping, crumpled and dirty. Ruth would be so sad that it was ruined. No, wait, Ruth wouldn't need souvenirs any more.

'Is the date correct?'

He pointed to the top of the clipping: *March 1893.*

I nodded. He'd ask: why did Toby wait so long to make the announcement? What would I say?

'Then what month is it now? It's still cold…'

'December.'

'But that's months later.'

'Yes, of course.' But there was no 'of course' about it. I felt as though I stood on stepping stones in the middle of a dark river. I didn't dare look down to see what swirled around my feet. It was safe to go from stone to stone, question to question, as he asked them, but one of my steps wouldn't find a stone, and I'd be lost.

'I haven't been here for a long time.' His voice was puzzled. He was calculating the amount of time that had passed, marvelling at the fact. Why hadn't he known?

'Where have you been?'

Sam drew in a deep, proper inhalation. No wheezing, no cough now, thank goodness. 'I should tell Ruth first. Shouldn't I?'

'But couldn't you just tell me a part of it?' Sometimes, in myths, you need to ask three times to get an answer.

'No. I should speak to Ruth.'

He entered the room. I saw his hand move, tossing the newspaper clipping onto the fire. Then the door closed and blocked my sight.

The garden was frosty, still, but I welcomed the clarity. Pulling on a pair of boots, I had gone hunting for my lost shoes around the iced lake. It glowed white, and from the black hole in its centre a web of cracks led outwards. It was already refreezing, the dark water dimpling. It might be solid by morning. I gazed into it as though that was where Sam had come from, bursting upwards. But he'd been walking on the far side, first.

I paced around the small lake to the bushes from which Sam had emerged. By moonlight I couldn't see any broken twigs.

There was crushed grass, but I followed it a few paces, then the bushes were too thorny, and I was still chilled from the lake water. I retreated, retracing Sam's steps.

Why hadn't Sam come to the front door? Why had he ended up here? You could reach our garden from the street, if you fought your way through a narrow alley down the side of our house. Had Sam knocked at our front door, had no answer and come to find me?

I was standing back where I'd started. And here were my shoes, half buried, dirtied past recognition. I laid them by the stone bench, planning to collect them the following day. Rolling around on the grass had been the wineglass, and the jam jar with a candle stub. If I could find them and replace them in the scullery, that might close the ritual, which otherwise would hang frayed and unfinished in the air.

I stumbled around and by good fortune my foot struck the wineglass, and as I picked it up, I heard feet pacing in the garden next door. For a moment I fancied it was another person come back out of the lake, someone else supposed to be dead. But then I heard the back door of Millstone shut, and watched a weak glow move up past the staircase windows, settling in an upstairs room. Probably the housekeeper, lingering late, come out to investigate the noise of Sam's accident. It had been the right decision not to send Sam back to Millstone.

Then a sharp crack, as the back door of my own house slammed.

I spun round, expecting Sam. A pale oval face – not his – drifted down the path towards me.

'Something wrong there, miss?'

It was Lucy. Her voice had a West Country burr to it, often close to a growl of exasperation. Lucy had often played nursemaid to her younger sisters and brothers, back in her own large family. Freed from that drudgery, she took the same tone with our family: frustration and resignation, at war with one another.

I could only just make out her features, and her curly reddish hair around them. Below that, she was a lumpish silhouette, having wrapped a quilt right round herself, over her nightgown. She was annoyed at having to tramp out into the cold. I would have to tell her not to go about like that, now there was a man in the house. No, goodness, I couldn't tell her that at all.

'I heard someone in the garden,' I lied.

'Bain't nobody in the garden, miss.'

'I see that now. I must have mistaken what I heard.'

'There's nothing to hear!'

'I know!'

We were shouting at one another. Why? We weren't even disagreeing. We were always getting off on the wrong foot. She'd seen the wineglass in my hand, and she was annoyed at my tippling. Or because I made work for her by scattering kitchen items around the grounds. She was only a little older than me, but all her bones were practical.

'The grass'll die if you walk on it,' she pointed out. A dig at me as a city girl, divorced from nature. I stepped onto the gravel path rather than argue.

Lucy stalked off towards the house, too quickly, with too much risk. I needed to keep her away from the bedrooms, away from Sam. 'Use the back staircase, won't you?' I called after her.

'I always do, miss.'

She'd heard it as a reprimand, a reminder to stay in her place. Marvellous. The door slammed behind her, echoing across the garden.

To keep myself from trembling, I reached out to touch the nearest tree. The bark was obscured by ivy, tenacious stuff which thrived in our neglected garden. Insinuating my hand past the leaves, I took hold of a woody stem, and pulled myself in to lean against the tree trunk.

Poor Sam. Poor, terrified man. At least he was safe home. A line of poetry ran through my mind, a poem of which Ruth had been fond: *Home is the sailor, home from the sea, and the hunter home from the hill.*

Then I thought, quite suddenly, as though they followed on from the sailor and the hunter: *long-lost brother, prince, imposter.* Figures from folk tales, men who arrive in the night.

Sam had first arrived in our house two and a half years ago, in summer and in broad daylight.

The front bell had rung while I'd been sketching in my bedroom, and I'd scrambled down to answer it. Mama rarely invited anyone to our house. While Father was alive, we'd been part of a mishpocha, a great archipelago of families with an ebb and flow of social obligations: card parties, shopping trips, dinners and dances. But since his death, Mama had not gone much into society; her friends were few, and despite living in London for twenty years she was conscious of her accent. Ruth and I still mourned our father, but we did make visits. Father's mentors, who had helped establish him in London, treated us to tea and advice. Our friends the Isaac sisters, Rose and Leah, recruited us to play music with them, cheerfully and badly. But we hadn't been hosting, and were growing hungry for visitors.

If I could answer the doorbell before our maid, I could overrule Mama and invite the visitors into the house myself.

I ran helter-skelter down the stairs, believing the hall would be empty. Instead, I saw men, two men, complete strangers. The maid had already let them in, and abandoned them while she went to tell Mama.

A stocky young man with a neat dark beard, first of all. He scowled up at Father's wall of Pre-Raphaelite paintings. The paintings showed a parade of knights and kings, quite unfashionable, with gaudy sorceresses and sentimental half-clad mermaids. Typical bad art for a grocer like Father. But I was so fond of them, and irked by the stranger's scowl. He was very solid for a man not yet thirty, like a miniature banker. I could imagine him ten years older, but not ten years younger.

Around him paced another unknown young man, as restless as if he had stolen all his companion's vigour. He glanced up and down repeatedly, his dark fringe flopping over his bright brown eyes. (Later we would hear how his ancestors had come from Portugal, like the Mocatta family, which we found very distinguished and romantic.) He was clean-shaven, an oddity when every college man I knew at least tried for a moustache.

As I came to a halt on the stairs, the lively man stepped forwards.

He said he was Samuel Silver, and his younger brother was Toby, bachelors both. Toby turned away from the paintings to greet me gruffly but with all politeness. He kept scowling, and I realised it might not be a judgement on Father's art, but his habitual expression.

Samuel continued to tell their story: they'd sold their family concerns in Manchester, moved south to London and snapped up the house next door. His tale of adventure ended on a conventional note: 'We've come to leave our cards. Now that we're neighbours.'

I reached over to take his *carte de visite*, but he kept speechifying, gesturing. Their house would be repainted, he said, top to bottom; he mimed the top, the bottom and the paintbrush, and he wouldn't let me take the card.

I snatched the card from him. Which was fiendishly impolite, but I felt exhilarated, not ashamed.

Samuel fixed his dark, quizzical eyes on me. 'Sorry if there's any noise from the house. Or trouble.' He rolled the word 'trouble' around his mouth.

Now I was certain that he was trying to sound intriguing. But he'd hired paper-hangers, not set up a pirate den.

I looked down at the card I'd seized. It listed no profession – the brothers were not in business, as Father had been, but of a better class (as were many of our neighbours). The photograph on the card showed Samuel leaning against a marble pillar, and it caught his easy way of standing, but his features were no more than a tea-coloured thumbprint. I looked up at the original, to compare.

Sam examined me in return.

His brother, Toby, coughed pointedly, and said: 'Miss Sachs, might your father be at home?' He was embarrassed to be idling here without a proper introduction.

'My father has passed away,' I said, and saw him exchange one kind of embarrassment for another. 'But would you be able to stay and take tea, with Mama and my sister?'

Would they like us? I'd totted up the odds shamelessly. Men often liked Ruth's sweet nature. Mama, as well, was still cordial company, and her reticence at speaking to strangers only allowed Ruth to shine brighter. I didn't ask myself: *will we like them?* Sam was dashing, Toby solid. I did speculate about their provenance, but only because the coming of a new family would normally have provided conversation for weeks around the archipelago. Particularly two bachelors, of the better sort. We'd apparently trumped Mrs Leuniger, and the other matriarchs from the Upper Berkeley Street Synagogue, as the first to meet the brothers.

The newcomers did like us. We gathered in the conservatory; Sam made Ruth properly laugh, bowing her head, and coaxed Mama into conversation. Our guests didn't remark on the staleness of the cake.

I didn't know then who Sam was, what he'd been doing. I didn't know him, as they say, from Adam. He could have been travelling, swindling or murdering for ten years. Back then, my lack of knowledge was a delightful opportunity.

Now I knew Sam very well. Only a single year of his life was hidden from me. How different was this ignorance, and how much more weighty. What had he been doing? What had he seen?

WEDNESDAY

The church clock struck eight, and my head hurt as usual, but the ache had a different timbre. I felt muzzy, unsure of where I was – at home? In the cottage at Breakwater?

Into my mind's eye came a picture of the children playing in the river at Breakwater. Balancing on unsteady stepping stones to cross the river on a dare. Skipping halfway out, sure-footed, they'd then look down and lose their confidence. The river's movement would fool them that they were already falling. They'd lean over to compensate and pitch into the water. They always fell in the same direction.

Why had that scene occurred to me? Why did my room smell of river water?

I sat up in bed, saw my fingernails were grimy with earth.

I unwound myself from the mound of quilts, blankets and coats that served for my bedclothes. I used them for warmth, because coal was so costly, even though it meant I was flattened nightly by a heap of cloth, like an inverted Princess and the Pea. Extricated from my bedding, all my muscles smarted. In the dim light, the mirror confirmed a crop of new bruises, plum fingerprints on my hip and shoulder.

Moving to the windows, I hoped to see the frozen lake, but ivy blocked my view, covering the outside of the window with dark leaves. Pale stems, clinging and hairy, longed to invade my room. The gardener had neglected to hack them back. Peering between leaves and stems, all that was visible was a wall of white mist.

Sam was in my house. Sam had come back to my sister. I had to dress, and find him.

My formal frock was filthy, ruined at least temporarily, driving me to pull on an old aesthetic gown of wine-coloured velvet that Ruth had helped me to make. It would do for today. Glancing at my reflection to check I was respectable, I was surprised how well I appeared: less subdued, more purposeful. The dress fitted me as well as it ever had, its generous cut hiding feast and famine alike, and had a robe-like dignity. I hoped it wasn't obvious that it had once been a curtain, from the French windows in our library. The other curtain of the pair still hung there. The air drew deeper into my lungs without the constriction of my mourning clothes.

I closed the wardrobe door so gently it wouldn't have startled a clothes moth. I tiptoed down the staircase, and the ladies in my father's paintings regarded me with sympathy. They knew disloyalty, secrecy, the concealment of fear. Ruth and I had grown up playing at Lancelot and Guinevere, not quite understanding the details of their betrayal but feeling their dread and acting out their punishments. And red-cloaked Imogen, from Shakespeare, whose wifely fidelity had only attracted horrors. There were no contented couples in all this art. Perhaps Father had unintentionally inducted Ruth and me in romantic unhappiness. But that was all mended, now Samuel was home.

Clothed and clear-headed, my mind turned back to the insistent question. Where had Sam been?

It was right and proper that he tell his story to Ruth first, as he'd said. That was why he'd stayed silent.

No, I was his host, I'd saved him. Couldn't he hint to me, couldn't he show me the lightest sketch?

I peered into the library. Lucy had intervened: grate swept clean, patchwork quilts hanging straight, the chairs no worse for wear. No cups on the desk, no mud on the floor. She must have risen early to tidy. The longstanding cobwebs were untouched, though, as were the heaps of holly and teasels that Lucy quite reasonably refused to dust, claiming they were too prickly.

I crept on, down the back stairs to the kitchen. I was distracted by the idea of Sam, during his absence, working at interminable fairy-tale tasks to lift curses: weaving straw into gold, nettles into shirts. As I turned into the kitchen I shook them all out of my head.

A tall figure stood holding a bread knife.

'Morning, Judith! I helped myself, so I wouldn't have to disturb you.' As soon as he moved, careless and graceful, he couldn't have been anyone but Sam. And Sam was always hungry. Half a loaf lay sliced on the table in front of him – no plates. He waved the knife in lazy circles. 'Might I have something to put on the bread, dear Judith?'

I couldn't find my tongue, but I fetched a jar of jam from the larder.

'Wonderful! An excellent breakfast. You're very kind. Do you mind if I –' He started to spread the jam using the bread knife. 'Sorry, bad manners. It drives Toby wild! You know that little angry face of his. *Doesn't show respect*, he'd say. Forgive me.' His lip curled in laughter, inviting me to share his amusement. He eagerly anticipated being forgiven. 'Could I fix you a slice?'

He'd washed the mud from his hair, and his fringe fell in exactly the way I remembered. Except his forehead had a swollen lump on it crossed by an ugly scab. I was surprised how coolly I eyed it. Where was my pity for him? Where was my gladness?

Where had he *been*?

I found I was furious with him. How cruel, to disappear

without a word, and let a whole family mourn for you! To let a fiancée mourn you, and become a widow without having been a wife. Sam could be capricious – Toby told us he'd once gone to Vienna on a whim and not come back for months – but I hadn't considered seriously until this moment that he might have abandoned Ruth. Had he thought of her? Had he brushed away the thought? Brushing away guilt a dozen times a day, that was a proper fairy-tale curse-task.

My throat closed up and I had to cough before I could speak.

'So you'll be on your way back to Millstone,' I managed. 'Now that it's light.'

'Perhaps,' he said.

'You can send a telegram from the post office, at the end of the next street.'

'You mean that I should tell your sister?'

'And your brother, yes.' Was I glaring at him? I tried to smooth my brow.

'I suppose I ought.' He licked jam off the side of the knife. I'd have found it endearing, before, but now I was inclined to side with Toby. No respect.

'There's nothing to stop you. Is there?' I retrieved the jam and spooned some onto my own slice of rye bread. The things I nearly spoke were so bitter that I needed to sweeten my mouth.

'No. I don't have any other duties, being dead.'

He was trying to charm me with jokes, but severity rose up in me. '*Not* being dead, you *do* have duties.'

'I know I do!'

'Oh? If you've been alive for all this time…'

'*If?*' He spread out his hands, incredulous. 'Judith, that doesn't even make any sense.'

I kept talking, over his protests. Shouting, in fact. 'If you've been alive, I don't know why you didn't tell us, tell Ruth. *That* was your responsibility!' Sharper words were striving to get out of my mouth: *jilted*, *bolted*. I felt the absence of my mourning clothes. They would have helped to constrain me.

He slid his plate aside and leaned towards me. I pulled away. He held out his hands, as though he'd shaped an invisible explanation and was passing it to me.

'Judith, I'm teasing. Because I don't know how to explain how horrible it all is.' He let his hands fall back to his lap. 'You thought I was dead. Yes? I fell in the river at Breakwater and I never came back. A year ago.'

'Yes. And we didn't know where you were.'

'Judith, my dear, I don't know where I was, either. I don't know a single blessed thing that's happened, between that day and last night. It's a blank page, an utter *tabula rasa*.'

My disbelief felt like thin air. It dizzied me. He was spinning a yarn, trying to win me over.

'Last night you didn't say that. You said Ruth should hear about it first.'

'Last night I was bluffing! I couldn't remember. But my head was full of fuzz. I guessed it would all come right after I'd slept.' His words tumbled out. 'But when I look, there's nothing there. Nothing at all.'

I couldn't speak. I was confused because it was such a strange idea.

I was amazed because it was such a *familiar* idea.

A year ago, during those airless weeks after he went missing, my sister and I had searched for scraps of comfort. If there was a chance Samuel was alive, why hadn't he come back to us? It was ghastly to think he might be too ill to return, or kept somewhere against his will. Besides sickness and imprisonment, what possibilities remained?

Could Sam have lost his memory?

We'd pieced it together as neatly as a patchwork. Could he be living a decent life (he was still a good man), but without knowing who he was? He'd have gone downriver a long way, and been taken in by kind country folk. A blacksmith and his wife. They were simple people, practically hermits, who could hardly read and didn't take the newspapers. Sam would be happy, but as unreachable as if he'd died.

So Sam's claim to amnesia startled me. But it was also old news, it rang true. The idea of Samuel deliberately deceiving us for a year was a much more alien notion.

He smiled again. I tried to smile back. Goodness, he was a shell of himself.

We both spoke at once.

'How dreadful for you—'

'No, no, dreadful for *you*.'

'Monstrous! Really! And I've been unfair.'

He batted my words away. 'I'm so foolish.' As though forgetting a year of his life was similar to forgetting his hat.

'Did you hit your head yesterday?' I craved an immediate solution. 'Could that be to blame?'

'Maybe, maybe…'

'Or in Breakwater – as far back as that. Could that make you forget, for a whole year?' What if it had broken his brain and it wasn't healed yet? What if tomorrow he'd forget today, or next week forget this week…

'I don't know.'

'What is it like? How does it feel?'

'Like fog. It makes me sick when I bring it to mind.' I remembered the white wall of fog outside my bedroom window, and felt sick myself.

'You know, Ruth wouldn't mind!' I blurted out. 'I mean she'd mind terribly for *you*, but it wouldn't make any difference to her at all.'

'Don't tell her, will you? Don't!'

'No – I mean – *you* should tell her. Shouldn't you?' Sam

would tell Ruth. She'd be released from her tower of misery. 'And Toby.'

'Good old Toby. He'll call me a fool.'

I began to reassure him, but Toby had indeed often described Sam as a fool.

Wasn't there a folk tale about amnesia and marriage, one with a happy ending? Yes, Rabbi Jehudah had married his daughter to a beggar in rags, but the beggar regained his memory and turned out to be an equally learned rabbi. A neat reversal, and good news for the daughter.

A clock struck nine outside and I realised I wouldn't be able to attend my painting class today. My routine was broken. But did I need my routines and rituals, now? I'd adopted them because I had been lonely, and grieving. Now I needn't be either.

'So shall we go to the post office?' I asked.

Sam ran a finger round the inside of his collar, loosening it, and I suddenly noticed what he wore: his clothes from the previous day, the worst of the mud brushed off, but still filthy. His dark suit was powdered with earth. The skin of his neck had been scrubbed clean, but under a shirt that wasn't white.

'I look a wreck, don't I?' he asked.

'A bit. But you've clothes next door. As I said, I have a key. You can fetch them.' It wasn't night-time any more, and the servants might be startled to see him, but not mortally terrified.

'I hate to ask another favour, Judith, when you've been so kind, but could you fetch them for me? Just one outfit from Millstone? So I don't look so frightful when we go out.'

A scandalous idea. Go into his room, root through his clothes? 'I can't.'

'I'd simply *hate* to be arrested for vagrancy…'

'And I can't be arrested for stealing,' I said brightly, to mirror his joke.

Sam tilted his head. 'It would only take a minute. You're very deft. And I don't think I can bear to go back in that house, not just now, and frighten people.'

I reminded myself what shocks he'd endured. Nearly drowning last night, finding out his family thought him dead. I shouldn't be inhumane. And what if Toby had got rid of all Sam's possessions? That would be a horrible surprise, in his weakened condition. 'All right, I will. But—'

'Judith, you're amazing!'

'But you shouldn't wait here in the kitchen. What if our maid sees you? Or Cook?' Cook came to the house a few times a week while I was at art class to restock the pantry with rye bread and pickles, and leave stewed or fried fish for me to eat.

'Oh, naturally. I'll hide myself away.'

I hadn't needed the key to Millstone before. Toby had given it to me, in case of an emergency, and I'd kept it in a drawer in the dining room dresser. It was a long way back, under a folded white cloth. My mouth still tasted of jam as I let myself into the house next door.

Sam was comfortable. I'd have called him rich, but my friend Ella called me rich, and that made me feel uncomfortable. So, I should rather say that Sam's family had been more comfortable than ours, and for much longer. While most families moved around because of hard necessity, the Silvers had apparently relocated with more deliberation and optimism. Established in Amsterdam, they had then thrived in Manchester. Our family's home had been the largest house my father could afford. For Sam and his brother Toby, Millstone – an identical house, next door to mine – was a small place, purchased for convenience after the death of their parents. They were pruning themselves back, while my family had shot up quickly, thanks to Father's efforts. We'd appeared an equal height, but Ruth and I were rather spindly.

Sam was comfortable, but Millstone wasn't. It was uncomfortable because it was a twin of my own house, laid out identically, but stark and empty. After the Silver brothers had had the place repainted, the project of redecoration ceased. Sam had been busy courting, Toby wasn't the type. Our homes shared grand touches – oak in the library, marble in the hall – but my father had complemented these with oil paintings and carpets, and more recently Ruth and I had run amok with wall stencils, while the Millstone boys had hardly bought a stick of furniture for themselves. So now Millstone exactly resembled my own house if time had passed, and everyone was dead, and all our belongings had been sold. Or if it had been robbed.

On this visit, I felt particularly prickly, because I planned to steal from Millstone.

This was a quest, I told myself. I had to find the objects which would restore my sister's true love to her. People who undertook chivalrous quests braved more than embarrassment.

I approached the front door as a legitimate visitor would, rather than sneaking in through the garden like a burglar, but I kept my feet light on the stone steps. Turning the large key slowly in the lock, I let myself into the familiar-but-strange hallway. Just an ordinary visitor, closing the door gently, cringing when the lock clicked and the sound rang round the hall.

Only one item graced the hallway: a grey stone slab mounted on one wall, six feet square, mocking the idea of decoration. Its surface showed faint ridges and dips. Toby collected fossils with a passion. This was his best specimen: a *Coelophysis*, from America.

Toby had shown us how to read the monster in the tangle of lines: which were its legs, where were its claws. But it wasn't lively, to me. Its eye socket did not follow me as I crossed the room, not like the knight's eyes that followed me across my own hall.

I told myself there wouldn't be any servants, probably. Toby had procured jobs for most of his staff with other families. An empty house, of medium size, was not a full-time task. It would be fine – I knew the housekeeper by sight! Perhaps I could claim to be borrowing a book.

Until they caught me walking out with my arms full of Sam's clothing, like a rag-man. I stopped trying to look nonchalant, and ran up the stairs.

A folk tune came to me, a marching song, but it took me ten steps to catch the words to it: *O no sweet maid, I cannot marry you, for I have no coat to put on…* Ruth used to play it on her flute. It was the perfect musical accompaniment: I was fetching Sam a coat so he could marry my sister. A shame I couldn't sing it as I searched. But at least Sam was home, in my kitchen. Soon he'd be walking up the road in a suit that I'd stolen for him, and sending my sister a telegram to make her rejoice. That stiffened my spine.

Sam had asked me to fetch a shaving kit, too, and said there was a suitcase under his bed to load up and lug home. I suspected I knew which room was Sam's, because he'd tried to open that door yesterday evening. But the knowledge felt improper, and his mind had been muddled. I'd go room by room, as though I hadn't witnessed his confusion. The door to the first room creaked open under my hand. It was dark inside, an eerie dappled darkness. As my eyes adjusted, I saw that ivy had crawled up to cover the window, just as in my room, but higher. I quickly flipped up the bed cover and saw nothing under the bed. Kneeling down on the floor, I swept my arm into the dark space, and felt cobwebs.

The second room, another groaning door to echo along the corridor. But this room was more ruffled up, less pristine. A chair at an angle, the bed cover rumpled, the smell of rosewater. And under the bed, a case! A battered leather thing with flaking straps. I pulled it up onto the bed and opened it.

The contents sprang out. Silk scarves in crimson and gold slithered away, showing dresses and petticoats underneath. I crammed it all back in, despite the slippery layers. Squashing it sent up a scent like sweet wine. Slamming the lid, jamming down the catches with my thumbs, I felt fabric tearing. I had forced the lock mechanism right through an errant scarf.

Who did this case belong to? Everything inside it was so feminine. Was it the maid? Why would she trespass like this in a guest bedroom? Would Toby expect me to investigate, and reprimand her? She'd know someone had been here. I opened the lid a crack, and poked the ruined cloth back inside. I'd never owned any fabric that costly. The Isaac sisters had an extravagant aunt who let us wear her amber necklaces; she owned nothing like this. A maid with deep pockets and fanciful tastes. Maybe this was the trove of a fallen woman; these could be rapturous impractical gifts from a disreputable suitor. I felt appalled relief – Toby would never expect me to intervene in such a situation.

A more sober explanation succeeded that flight of fancy: it might have belonged to Sam's departed mother. I shoved the case back under the bed.

Whoever the owner, it wasn't the empty suitcase Sam had told me about, and there was no shaving kit in this room, and I was procrastinating. I knew where Sam's possessions would be, or at least where he had left them a year ago.

At the third door, I froze. In my house, this was my room. It had the same door, even the same brass plate and handle, which I would have to touch.

At arm's length, I opened the door.

It swung softly and cleanly in a wide arc. The room was empty of signs of habitation, except a mahogany box by the window which might contain a packed-away shaving kit.

It was sufficiently different from my room to let me enter.

The same size, the same windows, but the bed was in the wrong place. The window wasn't blocked by ivy, but only because the frame was open an inch at the bottom, and the tendrils snaked in and across the walls.

I prayed Sam's clothes would still be here, and that Toby hadn't tossed them away.

When I touched the carvings of the wardrobe door they felt like fur. The maids had been lazy – a year of dust had settled on them. The wardrobe swung open. Thank goodness, Toby hadn't given Sam's clothes away. All Sam's dandified garments were here together, one bright rich cloth on top of another, almost as gaudy as the hoard of women's things in the suitcase next door.

'Fetch clothes,' Sam had said, but what clothes? What did men wear? Should I take handkerchiefs, waistcoats, cravats? What parties would a gentleman, recently returned from the dead, be expected to attend? I snorted, half laughing and half panicking, and covered my mouth. I'd be heard, I'd be caught cackling to myself in the act of theft. I wouldn't be arrested – I was known, I was almost family – but I would be discovered living alone when I shouldn't be, lying to Mama.

I tried to be methodical. Sam only needed enough clothes to go to the post office. Forcing myself to grope for the suitcase beneath the bed, I dragged it out and began to fill it. Shoes, a heavy pair. A suit, carefully folded, and shirts. Then I lost perspective again, and added handfuls of everything else, certainly not looking at what they were. Sam could untangle and make sense of them.

I placed the shaving set on top of it all. The plain metal disc set into the lid had gone dull: brass? Or could it be gold? I closed the case and buckled it. Heavier than I'd expected. I had to swing it a little at each step. The swing acquired a rhythm, and the rhythm brought back my marching song: *Then up she went*

to her grandfather's chest, and got him a coat of the very, very best...
My arms ached and burned from last night's rescue.

Swaying, swinging, I maintained my balance down the stairs.
I kept up my courage by picturing my art class, and my fellow
student Ella, and imagining her scorning cowardice. The old
lizard *Coelophysis* failed again to watch or to prevent me. But I
heard the front door unlatching.

It made the same sound as my own front door, and that saved
me. The intruder would walk into the hall in only a second.
I knew where I could go to escape: straight down the back stairs,
into the kitchen.

The case was so cumbersome. Could I throw it down the
narrow staircase, to save having to carry it? So simple – gravity
would assist me! – but then I pictured it bursting apart when it
landed. So I carried it under one arm and waddled downwards.
My fingers scrabbled at the case's smooth side.

Light came from the kitchen, and a voice. 'Harold? You're
early!'

The corridor ran straight to the kitchen door, at the back of
the house. I clutched the case to my chest and hobbled at a hectic
pace. The handle turned and the door yielded. Scrambling up
the steps to the garden, I knew they wouldn't be able to see me
from inside the kitchen. Unless they followed – please, don't let
them follow...

I ran on the lawns, not the path, to soften the sound of my
footsteps. The grass was still frosted, crunchy and sage green.
Stupid of me: I'd be leaving footprints, which the servants could
track. Down to the end of the garden, seeing the frozen lake
through the bushes, grey in the daylight. Pushing through the
shrubbery, I reached the safety of my own lawns, and viewed my
house with gratitude.

It hurt to hug the suitcase, so I lowered it and held it in one
hand. This was the spot, I realised, where Sam had stood last night.

If the servants could follow my prints, could I follow his? But there were no other tracks in the grass. Despite Lucy's scolding, the grass had sprung back up, and the morning frost had dusted it over.

Limping up my garden path, I let myself in through the identical kitchen door.

I was safe, and victorious. My quest was done and I, clumsy and graceless, had robbed Millstone.

Despite my warning, Sam was still sitting, still eating, at the kitchen table. Ruth hadn't liked him coming down here, annoying our remaining servants, but he liked to sneak cake and then be scolded like a schoolboy.

I dropped the case on the floor in front of him, gasping and triumphant as Tristan showing off his trophy of the dragon's tongue.

'Here,' I said. 'You take these upstairs.' And dress yourself. 'Then we can go to the post office.'

'I've been mulling that over. I shouldn't let them know. Not yet.'

I didn't understand. My sister was sitting on an Italian terrace, with sun on her face and her heart in pieces, and Sam was saying: 'It's not right to bother them.'

'Bother?' I couldn't swallow. I wanted to spit.

Sam shrugged. 'I mean that it's not right to remind them.'

'They didn't *forget* you! They're your family!'

'Judith, I still can't remember where I've been!' He steepled his fingers. 'I must have been somewhere. What if I've been living another life entirely?' He locked his eyes with mine – an old trick he'd use on Ruth, to persuade her. I fixed my gaze on his fingertips instead, a rim of grime under each of his nails.

When I didn't answer, he continued: 'What if I was – oh, I

don't know, what's the best possible case? I was hoisted out of the river by a strong farmer.'

'Why wouldn't you have written to us?'

'Because I didn't know who I was! Don't you see? I'd forgotten I was me. I'd be very grateful but utterly clueless, and the farmer would have set me to work in his – field? Barn?'

'Someone would have *heard* about you...'

'And I'd have lived happily ever after as John Smith in the West Country. Or another country entirely! Until I remembered who I was, and came back home, and forgot *that* life entirely.'

Sam was trying to make me laugh. It was a pretty little story, and uncannily like the one Ruth and I had told one another. Had he guessed? I felt my face grow hot. I looked to see if his fingertips were calloused from labour, but he'd put them under the table.

'That's why I can't tell our families,' he concluded, making no sense at all.

'What's wrong with being a farmer's apprentice?'

'Judith. That was the best case. What if I've done other things? Terrible things?' Now he didn't smile.

How stupid I'd been! I'd scarcely seen his amnesia as an inconvenience because his forgetfulness fitted so well. I didn't know where he'd been, but neither did he, so I could pretend he'd fallen into the river at Breakwater and fetched up in my garden in London. He'd been sleeping, drifting unknowing in the river. Like King Arthur: dead, but coming back when we needed him.

But Sam spoke of *terrible things*. No wonder he hid his hands. Who knew what his hands had done? A thing so bad that he'd hidden it from himself. I told myself it wasn't likely, Sam had virtues which would survive amnesia. He would live a decent life, regardless of his name, or whether his brother was watching.

'I mean to say...' he added. 'You know what I'm worried about.'

Only one thing could give his face such an ashy shade. 'You believe you've killed someone?'

He rocked back on the dining chair and roared with laughter. 'Judith! No!'

'What, then? I have no idea what you're talking about!'

He scooped up from the floor a napkin he'd dislodged. 'Oh, much worse than murder,' he said, his face straighter. 'I might have been married.'

He was right. For him, marrying would be as cruel as violence. I'd have to say to my sister: your fiancé is not dead. Your fiancé left you and married someone else, and let you mourn him. He appeared like a stranger again, like a waxwork. A married man.

'Yes. That would be awful.'

'Yes. Your family...' He didn't say 'sister'. Sam seemed unable to say certain words, like a horse shying at high fences. But it was Ruth's suffering that would make it awful for the rest of us. 'And Toby would be livid! And now, I'd be missing for someone else, you know? Someone else might be looking for me, right now.'

I could conjure her up, instantly: a country lass, a year ago, kilting her kirtle a little aboon her knee and hiking along the riverbank, finding Samuel as a comely bit of flotsam, and nursing him back to health and love. In short, taking advantage of a sick man. Well, damn her! My sister's claim was prior, it was thoroughly earned, and I wouldn't concede it to any farmyard hoyden.

Although the hoyden could be his wife.

'So you see,' Sam said, 'I can't contact our families until I've got my memory back. And until I can tell them, I can't let the staff at Millstone know I'm – here.'

He'd shied at saying 'alive'.

'So what do we do?'

'I'll stay in the house. I won't let anyone else see me before we can tell your sister. That's the right order. And don't worry, I'll go and hide myself, stay away from the kitchen, like you said! I'll sleep, most likely. Stay out of trouble. And we'll wait.'

'Wait for what?'

'If it's a head injury, it's best for me to rest and see what comes back to me.'

As though his memories were a lost dog in Hyde Park. A very passive solution. Not bold enough at all, not good enough for Ruth.

My heart stuttered and I needed fresh air, a strenuous walk, to pacify it. I couldn't stay in the house with him all day. Better to stick to my routine.

'I need to go to my class,' I said.

'Your class?' I'd wrong-footed him. I was glad.

'Art. Painting. I'm studying painting.'

'Really?'

'Yes! Really! I've been studying for months.'

'What are you painting right now?' His question had a suspicious note, as though it was a test. That flustered me, as my current project wasn't progressing well.

'I'm drawing a golem,' I snapped. In fact, I'd been working on that weeks ago.

He gave me a look so arch it made me worry. 'Really? My word.' Perhaps there was a version of the golem story that men knew and girls didn't; perhaps it wasn't seemly. Had Ruth and I heard a rumour at school, that the first golem had been created to be someone's wife?

I stood my ground. 'I can't skip a day.'

'Absolutely not.'

'I'll be back at four. Please stay in your room as much as you can.' The room was supposed to be unoccupied, so Lucy would have no reason to enter it. I placed some coins, and the key to

Millstone, on the kitchen table in front of Sam. 'If you change your mind, Toby and Ruth and Mama are due to stay at the Hotel Raffaello, on the Via Roma.'

He shook his head regretfully. 'No, Judith.' He was sensible, he was older than I. 'Your sister has had too much uncertainty already.'

'Because of you.' A needless barb but one I couldn't hold back.

'And because of her earlier troubles. I mean, your father…'

'What?'

'He didn't make plans for you both.'

Oh, that was inexcusable. Who was he, to blame our father?

Businesses are living creatures. We'd been told this by Father's mentors, those knowledgeable men. Businesses have their fits of expansion and contraction, like respiration, and Father's business had reached a peak of expansion – and of borrowing. Being a healthy and industrious man, he'd every expectation of repaying his loans and benefiting from the growth. Another ten years, or even five, and we would have been comfortable in perpetuity. But a railway bridge in Norwood had collapsed, and our healthy father had died in the wreck, and Ruth and I had been stranded.

I corrected Sam: 'Father had many plans for us.'

'Still, I couldn't bear to make your sister suffer more.'

I imagined slapping him: how I'd need to move, how the shock would feel on my palm, how his pale cheek would redden like water reddening around a rinsed brush.

In the doorway of the attic studio, at the top of three flights of stairs, I stopped to regain my equilibrium. Only a couple of the women in my art class glanced up. The others were too absorbed in their work. I stood at my easel and unpacked my equipment. Mrs Fortune, our tutor, waved a paint-stained rag to acknowledge my arrival. These women didn't know what had happened to me; here, at least, the world was unchanged.

My art class had already saved me, four months ago.

After Sam had gone missing, my family had sunk into constant fighting and weeping. In August, Toby had stepped in and invited us all to travel with him to Italy. So considerate, to take us out of foul air and into fine weather, away from the well-meaning scrutiny of our community.

All four of us on a train, or a boat, red-eyed and fractious, constantly in one another's company.

I'd said to Mama: 'I can't come with you to Italy. I'm enrolled on a course and it lasts all year. I'm studying art.'

It was a complete lie, then. I wasn't studying, didn't even have a tutor. The idea had popped into my mind and dropped out of my mouth in the next instant. Not practised at lying, I had discovered a shocking facility.

I stuck to the lie, and I made it true, and it had saved me, and here I was in my art class. Although today I'd stalled in the doorway.

Ella saw my hesitation. She strode over to me, like a tall storm cloud. 'You're late. I'd given up on you.' She had a low voice, made lower by small cigars, and a languorous tone which was clearly affected but suited her completely.

'Hardly.'

'What are you working on today?'

It was suspicious, like Sam's question, but for different reasons. Ella feared that my devotion to art would waver, that I'd become a 'dabbler': a weak watercolourist, a pencil-portrait sketcher at picnics. As I became unsure of my latest project, she grew concerned.

'I'm making an ivy border for Maimonides,' I said promptly. As proof, I pointed to the spray of ivy hanging from a stand in

front of my easel, too large and gnarled for Ella to argue with.
Since ivy had begun creeping across my bedroom window, I'd
become fascinated by its sneaky tendrils. I'd ripped a piece from
the back wall of my house and brought it to the studio.

'Good,' she said, and meant *you'd better*. She briefly smiled.
I wavered for a moment, tempted to tell her about Sam's return.
But I'd become used to keeping secrets.

'I'm doing hands,' she announced. 'They're ridiculous.' She
wrung her dark brown curls into a tighter knot, ready to paint.
'See you at lunch.'

When I'd first met Ella, I had been entirely adrift. Needing
to find a course of study, knowing only the name of a prestigious
art college, I'd entered their endless corridors of polished wood.
A man in an office told me that although the school accepted
women as students, there was an annual intake, with the entrance
examination months away, and the course beginning the following
spring. No use to me at all.

I sat on a bench in the corridor, staring at the floor and
despairing, until a passer-by halted in front of me. I saw her skirts,
first, and they were the kind that Ruth and I favoured, sweeping
and richly coloured. But when I looked up I saw an unfamiliar
face, like a lady in a Simeon Solomon sketch: a strong jaw and
a penumbra of cocoa-coloured hair.

'Why are you sniffing?' she'd demanded. Her gown had
an ingenious swag hanging down her back which made me, by
contrast, feel like a child playing a game of dressing up.

'I need to study art.' I'd bitten back tears at what I'd have to
endure if I couldn't: bickering in a cramped *pension*, sniping in a
jolting carriage from Naples down to Amalfi.

Ella saw me weeping for my art, and felt my pain.

She'd come to the college that day to find out the details of the
entrance exam, and she understood artistic dedication. She was
already studying elsewhere under a private tutor, Mrs Fortune,

and gave me her details. 'She doesn't take just anyone. You have to be prepared to work. Are you?'

'Absolutely,' I swore. It couldn't be as hard as the journey I was seeking to avoid.

Mrs Fortune was a dramatic Parsi woman in her fifties, with dark hair swept back from an elegant aquiline profile. She tyrannised a fourth-floor attic studio, conveniently close to my house, by Marble Arch. I could see, when I met her, what Ella was aspiring to be. Mrs Fortune had rumoured connections to Indian aristocracy, but her art was her vocation. Mrs Fortune also misattributed my red-rimmed eyes to creative passion, and was glad to take me on. She wrote to Mama explaining that I was cultivating my budding talent (without requiring too much of a demonstration). Did Mama know, Mrs Fortune wrote, what a waste it would be if I blush'd unseen? Dizzy from gratitude, and from climbing the stairs to her attic, I contracted to pay for six months of lessons in advance.

Ella reappeared alongside me at my first lesson. Finding me dry-eyed and hardly knowing one end of a paintbrush from the other, she'd become suspicious of my motives.

'Are you here to try to get married?'

I had been too sunk in my own concerns to parry her in a civil way. 'Why, are you proposing to marry me?'

That had won me an ironic smile. She'd nodded at the other scribbling students. 'Most of them are here for husbands.'

There were no men in the class. 'It doesn't look an ideal place to find a husband.'

'They're here to get *accomplishments* so they can marry well. Mrs Fortune's a brilliant tutor, a proper artist. She's too good for them.' Ella was stretching a canvas as she spoke and I admired her long, agile hands.

'I'm not getting married,' I'd said.

'What, not ever?'

'I don't have any prospects. My sister only became engaged because a man moved in next door.'

Ella yelped with laughter. I was horrified by myself; I'd insulted my mother to a stranger, and used the defining tragedy of my sister's life for a joke. But there was pleasure in making her laugh.

Ella told me she expected to study at the art college where we'd met, to work and earn her living as an artist, and live alone. The fact that I'd already attained that solitary state impressed her. I wondered if she was a New Woman but I knew it would be gauche to ask.

Ella was something else, as well, but I lacked a name for that. Even the questions felt impossible to frame (*Have you always been…? Were you ever…?*). But the something-else inspired me, as well. She lived with a fierce flame, and I put myself in her hands. She told me to go to museums, and exhibitions, and read the reviews. I trotted obligingly round the Grosvenor Gallery and the Egyptian Hall. The fact that I was following instructions fortified me against disapproving matrons who held their purses tighter as I passed, and men who lingered close to me when there was space enough for three.

Wrestling with pastels, splattered with paint, Ella never lost sight of her goal: the entrance exam for the art college where we'd met.

'I suppose you'd have to be very good to study there,' I ventured, once.

'I'm better than nearly everyone.'

'That must be a comfort.'

'A marvellous comfort, thank you *very* much.'

I might have made other friends at the art class; from school, I was used to mixing with girls who weren't of our faith. But the other painters viewed Ella and me with chilliness, giving us the cold shoulder among the water-pots. That nudged us closer together. Ruth had always smoothed my rough edges. With Ruth gone, I sharpened myself on Ella.

Today I didn't know if I'd be able to create at all, as distracted as I was by Sam's return. But I set myself to the task, and the work didn't disdain me. Ivy proved the most absorbing thing to draw. I sketched it half a dozen times, tackling the sheen on the leaves, the detail of the hairy roots.

Mrs Fortune stopped at my easel, gesturing like an orchestral conductor. 'Deepen the colour, Miss Sachs! Deepen the shade! Make it crawl off the paper to seize me!' Mrs Fortune had been encouraging Ella and me in our excesses lately. Possibly because all her other students, the scribblers in light floral dresses, were painting identical watercolour landscapes. I picked up a dark plum pastel stick. Satisfied, Mrs Fortune swept onwards.

The ivy would symbolise the meandering paths of agonising doubt. I was painting Maimonides the rabbi, and his would-be son-in-law. The lad had submitted to being cut into pieces by the rabbi and placed under a glass dome, so as to be made magically immortal. But Maimonides had been paralysed by doubt, midway through the process. He surely shouldn't dabble with immortality. But how could he leave the boy dead? To break his moral stalemate, he had released a cockerel into the room, to spoil the spell.

A fine weird tale, but my own version of it hadn't come off. The rabbi's robes were regal, the cockerel feathers a gleaming black-green, but now I was trying to draw his son-in-law at the foot of the picture, all chopped up. How could one make the viewer feel for him? It would be laughable or disgusting.

Lunchtime was heralded by Ella scrutinising my efforts and pronouncing them tolerable. We sat on a bench in the green square outside the studio, and Ella smoked one of her tiny daring cigars (I stayed upwind). Then both of us ate the bread and cheese we'd brought. I tried to keep my hands inside my coat sleeves as I ate, as the cold could make my fingers stiff for a long time after lunch. I could have just about afforded a tea shop, but I suspected Ella couldn't; for all her sophistication, she lived with her mother, and I believed her father had also passed away. We both scrimped but we scrimped differently. (At least now Toby was looking after my family, Ruth would be eating well in Italy.)

Smoking prevented Ella from talking, and in the lull in our chat, I considered telling her about Sam.

We didn't often share intimacies. I hadn't told Ella about Sam's death for weeks after I met her. I'd wanted to have a place where I didn't think of it, longed to be out from under it.

But this wasn't the same. This was good news, wasn't it? Sam was alive, he was in my house. He refused to go home to Millstone, he didn't know where he'd been – not quite as good. Ella's incredulity would double with each statement. If I told her, would it lighten my burden?

I cleared my throat, and Ella looked in my direction, and she wasn't Ruth. It was truly unfair to tell anyone about Sam's return before we told my sister.

'You're quiet,' Ella accused me. But Ella never looked for motives outside our work. 'What's so interesting about Maimonides and his heap of brisket?'

'I've been worrying about the blood.'

'Why? We can buy some from the meat market.'

'If it looks real, it will be horrible. And if it doesn't, it will be ridiculous.'

'And there are all the unsavoury connotations,' noted Ella.

'Hmm.' I didn't ask. She might smirk at my ignorance.

'A rabbi conducting a murderous magical ritual? I wouldn't want to show it to the public. Too much like the Damascus affair, and all that.'

I wanted to protest but I couldn't deny it. How had I missed the implications?

'Where did you even find such a bizarre story about the Rambam? I thought he did things absolutely by the book. It sounds like a libellous invention.'

I'd read the story in a little pamphlet about folklore from the Middle Ages, by a man called Gaster. I'd known it was unusual, but it had been published by the *Chronicle*, which surely made it legitimate? I'd also been inspired by Wright's painting in the National Gallery, of a dying dove under a bell jar, which I explained to Ella. So many parallel elements: the wild-haired old genius, his delicate experiment, the flapping bird and the weeping daughter...

'You saw a painting about *science*,' Ella asked, 'and decided to draw a *magic spell*?'

'Well, the ivy border will still be useful,' I concluded, trying to sound carelessly confident. 'I could use it for almost any project.'

'Any of your morbid folk tales,' Ella corrected.

This was why I preferred to discuss method, rather than subject. We fundamentally disagreed about folk tales. I believed you could explore any emotion, any theme, with the right myth or story. Particularly as Ella bundled everything together: Norse gods, Greek legends, King Arthur and his knights. Ella called them all a maudlin shambles of throbbing and fighting. Ella particularly loathed the Pre-Raphaelites (which was ironic, given how much she resembled their long-faced heroines). She believed it was modern to scoff at the kind of paintings my father had loved.

'I've wanted to try Thomas the Rhymer,' I said, which was true. And now I was recoiling from Maimonides, it looked more likely.

'Remind me what he did.' Ella never admitted ignorance.

'He went missing for seven years.'

'Oh, yes. Where?'

'He was... trapped.' He was the lover of the fairy queen, but I knew that would attract her ridicule. 'He came back and didn't realise any time had passed. It was only a couple of days, for him.'

'Pfft. Where do you *find* these things?' Ella unwrapped another morsel from her lunch, and bit into it with relish.

Where had we found things, Ruth and I? That was a satisfying question. As children, Mama had read to us from the *Sippurim*, a treasure-box of heroic and mystical tales, translating from German so the words differed a little with each telling. Father had bought us Grimm's tales, and despite some unpleasant surprises, they continued to fascinate. Rose Isaac had been briefly obsessed with making good-luck charms; when her mother found her trove of rabbits' feet and banned the practice, Rose had moved on to crochet. But Ruth and I were incurable. In a conventional tale or an ordinary holiday, we valued anything that would set our spines tingling.

Then, in a musty bookshop when I was twelve, I stumbled on *Folk-lore of the Northern Counties of England*, and Ruth and I realised that these scraps which thrilled us could be gathered up and treated with gravity. We grew greedy. We compiled our own library, snapping up the volumes of Child's *Ballads* one by one. Ruth was mad for tales of premonitions, while I preferred charms for discernment; Mama disapproved of both, but let us amuse ourselves as long as our games weren't morbid. Father indulged us, buying us books, including the pamphlet where I'd stumbled on Maimonides and his cockerel. Father shared the opinion of that author that folk tales were the buried essence of human genius.

Ruth's most recent gift to me, *The Golden Bough*, had been almost too much; tale after tale, rushed over in the author's haste to bring everything into harmony and hierarchy. I preferred the haphazard way I had first encountered the subject, the lack of definitive lore. You had to feel with your fingertips for something that had the ring of truth.

'I find things in all kinds of places,' I told Ella. 'I don't recall, exactly.'

'Well. Inspiration is often a mystery.' That sounded like a concession, but she was scathing about inspiration, as well.

'You never like my inspirations,' I said, unusually peevish.

'I liked your golem!'

I'd liked him too, but it was hard to draw a good picture of an unformed man; it simply looked very like a bad picture of a proper person. I'd lied to Sam about drawing a golem that morning. In fact, I'd drawn it weeks ago and given up.

I noticed Ella was eating fried potato cakes. She caught me staring enviously. 'Do you want one? Won't you be making them yourself?'

Since my family had departed, and I'd stopped attending synagogue, my year had fallen out of joint. Cook might celebrate Hanukkah with latkes, if I prompted her, but Lucy wasn't familiar with the calendar. 'I don't think so.'

'I'd have thought you'd be celebrating more, with your namesake involved.' Ella mimed cutting off the head of Holofernes, another bloody tale which could too easily look comic. 'What part of Thomas the Rhymer would you draw?' Now, that *was* a concession.

'His return. Trying to explain to the people he left that he's not been gone long.'

'Yes. Would you have a crowd scene? You'd be able to draw good reactions, I suppose. People afraid, people doubting…' She stood, dusting crumbs from her skirts.

'Angry, too. And his friends would all have aged.'

'Only seven years.'

'A person can change a lot.' Even in a year, they can change.
They can start to look ill, and dowdy. Or they can go anywhere,
do anything, and not have it show in their face.

Ella called back over her shoulder as we climbed the stairs.
'And you could put columbine all around him in the ivy border.
The flower code, you know? To show that he's lying.'

I started the afternoon well. I set Maimonides aside. Ivy re-posed,
clean rags and water-pots ready, I tried adding dabs of white to
the ivy leaves and then scraping it off, to imitate their greyish
winter sheen.

I thought of Ruth, and whether her wretched year of
mourning could ever be re-figured as a patient year of waiting
for Sam. To buoy myself up, I told myself Mama and Father's
story. They'd been separated for years, Father leaving Frankfurt
to build up his shop in London. Like Jacob labouring to marry
Rachel. When Father was properly established, he'd summoned
Mama to join him.

A happy ending! Father was handsome, wealthy and loving.
But even Ruth and I had wondered, as we grew older, whether
Mama had been patiently waiting, or was surprised by his
summons. Mama had been twenty-three when she married him,
and hadn't seen him since she was seventeen. Their reunion
hadn't ensured happiness in all things: for instance, Mama had
no English at first, and was embarrassed to speak clumsily to the
other young wives of Maida Vale.

I so wanted Ruth to be here. Not to tell her, not to reunite
her with Samuel, but to lean my head on her shoulder and talk
to her about it all.

And then I was crying. I needed a stable thing to hold on
to; my eyes stung too much to see. Groping in front of myself,
I grasped the easel, but I knew the blasted thing wouldn't take

my weight. It would only fall over and alert everyone. I fumbled about and touched the wall behind me.

Every way I'd felt about Samuel dying came back to me. My disbelief at the unfairness, my shock because dashing young lovers don't die.

And now – this was the worst part – I relived those miserable months of family fighting.

At first, everyone had been in confusion. Father's death had been made real by our house filling with serious praying men, but after Sam's accident, everything had been unspoken. There was no shiva, no month of mourning (after a month, we were still hoping Sam might be found) and no grave.

Mama and Ruth had both been distraught. But their sadness had come in waves and the waves were rarely synchronised. Ruth would have a low day, retreating to read with me cosily among the foliage of the library. And Mama would throw open the windows and propose trips to a theatrical comedy. Or Ruth's spirits would have lifted a little, and we'd be chatting over dinner. And Mama would fume and wail: 'I don't know how you can sit there, *laughing*!'

Eventually, Ruth – kind-hearted Ruth, never ever short-tempered – snapped. She shouted and sneered at Mama. Her sarcasm was rough, as she hadn't had much practice. I hid in my room, but I could hear them raging. At that stage, there hadn't even been anything much to disagree about.

Soon, they had plenty to argue over.

When Samuel had been gone for three months, Toby came to visit us. He had been hectically busy in January searching for Sam, then subdued through February, and since March his mood had darkened. Toby asked to speak with Ruth alone, and stayed with her in the library for an hour. She told me, in bed that night, what they'd discussed.

'Toby has been speaking to his rabbi, and to legal men. He

wants—' I knew what she meant at once but I couldn't help her phrase it. Toby wanted to make Samuel dead. 'The legal side will take years.' I winced. 'But the rabbi said we can mourn him, now. And Toby intends to put a notice in the *Chronicle*.'

'Is it horrible?' I was entirely on her side. I was prepared to loathe Toby.

'I hate it. But I can't stay like this for ever.' We clung together. It was monstrous, but it was inevitable.

Mama, when Ruth informed her, disagreed.

Toby had also informed Ruth that he wished to give her investments which would generate a small income – enough for our household to live on, if frugal. Mama argued about that from every angle. It was presumptuous of Ruth to take money from a neighbour. No, it was miserly of Toby, who should treat Ruth like a sister. How could she accept it? How could she not?

The notice of Sam's death was published, and Millstone turned into a house of mourning. On each day of the shiva, Millstone filled with Toby's family and connections, uttering words of consolation, readings and prayers, showing all the sombre kindness of our community. After such long uncertainty, an inundation of grief.

Mama kept her opinions to herself for the week.

Passover was dismal. Lucy polished all the silver, and Cook made matzo ball soup using Mama's family recipe. But by the time we reached the almond puddings, Mama claimed a headache and fled to her room. Later she announced she might take the spa waters at Bad Ischl for her gezunt, to recover her spirits. Ruth told her that even with the new income, we didn't have enough money for that. Mama protested that Ruth *always* bullied her about money.

Ruth cried.

And I longed for silence as an insomniac longs for sleep.

Standing in my art class, in front of my easel but unable

to see it, I felt every emotion all over again. I'd covered the memories up but that had worked like turf on a campfire, keeping in the heat.

Why couldn't I tell my sister? Her suffering over there, me suffering here… It made no sense. Samuel had put an agonising term on telling her: he would first have to recover his memory. But my goodness, when would it return?

This studio was a place to work, a place to master technique, and I couldn't even master myself. Someone bore me up by my elbow and steered me out of the attic studio. I was a flopping doll – I let them move me. Had Mrs Fortune come to help? She must be used to the artistic temperament, or amateur impersonations thereof.

A voice said: 'You'll have to look where you're walking, you'll fall downstairs and kill yourself.' Ella.

In the square outside she mopped my face with her hanky while avoiding my eye. I could have confessed a love affair, or a murder, and she wouldn't have been shocked at all. But my weakness scared her.

'I'm fine now,' I lied.

'Good. Do you need to go home?'

'Best to get back to work.' I considered speaking to her openly. 'I'm sorry, things have been quite horrible. I—'

'Yes, but you'll be fine now, won't you?' She handed me her handkerchief. I would have Lucy launder it. Ella steered me back up the stairs.

I tried a new tack – drawing stone towers, a tall city for Thomas the Rhymer to return to – but it reminded me of my sister, stuck like the Lady of Shalott, half sick of shadows. So I sank myself back into drawing the ivy, over and over. One time I drew it simply, a few swooping green lines. The next time, I scratched every tentacle and furred limb of it. Or swept a great firm line then softened it with feather-strokes until it faded to a shadow.

None of them looked like ivy. All of them looked snagged, snarled, frenzied.

'Not bad,' said Ella as she rinsed her brushes, trying to re-establish our usual cool exchanges after my shameful decline into sentiment. 'Where's our missing man? Does Thomas emerge from the undergrowth?'

I used my tools, I made my judgements, and I drew the ivy.

Little by little, a solution to the problem of Sam came to me.

I saw, after an hour of inking, that Sam and I were in an unspeakably horrible mess, but the mess was also *silly*. Samuel couldn't hide in my house. He couldn't duck behind the curtains for ever, particularly as we'd turned some of the curtains into dresses. Lucy, for goodness' sake, would be sure to notice. She knew Sam, and she might tell her mother, who lived back in the village of Breakwater. I dipped a dark brush in a fresh water-pot and watched the pigment cloud the water. News of Sam's return would spread.

I would give him a week of my silence. Not telling our families, but also not telling Ella, and concealing him as far as I could from Lucy and the servants at Millstone.

Was a week fair? How long might it take for him to get his memory back?

But I knew, really, that a week was all I could endure, whatever his prognosis. A week of him invading my house, which made my skin crawl. A week of lying to my sister by omission, which wrung my guts. Sam would have a week.

It felt awfully hard-hearted. Sam needed sympathy, and I would be giving him an ultimatum. I told myself: *it'll make him work harder*. Even though I didn't know what 'work' or 'harder' meant. Thrashing about with more vigour in the fog.

I resumed another bout with the ivy, dappling it with precise dots of light. Stepping back, I perceived I had done what Mrs Fortune had demanded; the crabbed stems crept off the page.

Then I had my second excellent idea: I myself would find out what had happened to Samuel.

I would do the work of a detective: place advertisements in newspapers, meet and speak with likely individuals. I'd imitate Sherlock Holmes and make sharp deductions. Samuel couldn't have been living in fairyland; he wasn't Thomas the Rhymer. People must have seen him. I was diligent, clever – what couldn't I achieve? I had rid myself of my chaperone and my family, with my own wits, and lived alone for months.

If I could help him find out what he'd been doing, and if it hadn't been anything terrible, he could be reunited with my sister. It wouldn't matter whether he regained his memory or not. Ruth wouldn't mind, would she? His amnesia would be akin to a duelling scar: a painless reminder of a great act of survival.

And if I couldn't find out what he'd been doing, then maybe nobody would be able to trace him from the other direction. Not investigating police, not creditors, not his vengeful cast-off wife.

I simply had to present my plan to Sam, both the ultimatum and the offer. Then in a week's time I could give Ruth the news she deserved.

As I neared home, I saw menorahs in several windows, with two joyful flames dancing. Over at the Isaac house, Leah, the youngest daughter, would be particularly delighting in the glow. In my mind, a possibility danced also: could I bring our family candleholder out of its tissue-paper wrappings and place it in the hall window? Would Sam light it with me, and say the blessings?

The house was dark when I opened the door but I could hear music. High trills and low swoops. No rhythm to it, little experimental bursts like laughter.

Then a tune began to play, a very familiar one. I recalled the words: *The water is wide, I cannot get o'er.* It was a folk song my sister had loved. The tune was simple, and we had improvised harmonies, one of us soaring up to embellish – *and neither have I wings to fly* – or dwindling downwards to enrich while the other carried the melody. Delight flooded me: the family were home, unannounced. My sister was playing the flute. But would she be playing straight after a long journey?

I knew my sister's flute playing. She had a way of blowing, an emphasis, that made it distinctive. Not as recognisable as a voice, but at least as good as a laugh. I could pick her out of a dozen players.

This player wasn't her. The music had longer phrasing, cleaner attack on the notes.

It was Samuel.

Sam had bought Ruth a book of duets, all jigs and reels. They'd played together, chasing one another in canons, competing in jigs. I was sure, now, that I was hearing Sam play.

I waited outside the door of the library. The tune wandered on: *Oh love is handsome, and love is fine, and love is like a gem when new...*

I could have music again, now that Sam was back. For Ruth, their duets had been an ideal pastime: thrilling and passionate but somehow considered genteel, and because they took skill, not money, she could contribute equally to Sam. I'd loved to hear them. Ruth had even kept playing for a little while after Sam's death, but the instrument had cruelly amplified the raggedness of her breath. It had sounded like crying and I'd been glad when it stopped.

I had sorely missed music, without knowing it. I opened the library door.

Samuel was playing one of my sister's flutes. The light of the fire glinted on the silver instrument. Perhaps he and Ruth were playing unwitting duets across the ocean, her tune sad and his hopeful.

As soon as he stopped playing, I marked how dangerous it was.

'You shouldn't,' I said, and he noticed me, surprised.

'Hullo!'

'You shouldn't be playing.'

He held the flute out in front of him, as though he couldn't believe a thing so delightful could cause any trouble.

'What, this?'

'Lucy, the maid. She'll hear.'

'It's all right, she's been out all afternoon.'

'Truly?'

'I've been all over the house, and I haven't seen her. The country maiden's busy being tempted in Modern Babylon.'

I pictured him wandering all over my house, checking on the maid, finding Ruth's flute and playing it. Reading my books, walking in my garden. Taking liberties, assuming intimacies. I couldn't help it: I didn't like it.

Still, I had the plan fixed in my mind which would put an end date to it. I just needed to tell him.

'I went out as well, this morning,' he said, as if he'd noticed my discomfort. 'To stay out of Lucy's way. I walked around Hyde Park. Did you know they're building bonfires?'

That, too, felt like folly and made me twitch with annoyance. 'You might have been seen by people who knew you.'

'Oh no. Big, big park.' He put on his oh-little-sister voice. 'No danger.'

He was wrong. I was always running into the butcher, the baker, friends of my sister. Some of Sam's relatives lived not too far from the park. I'd not met them, but Ruth had been introduced at a dinner; the aunts had been gracious, and the meat had been spiced, and both had intimidated my sister. 'I'll lend you a scarf. To cover your face.'

'I'll do that. Cover whatever needs it, absolutely,' he said, mock penitent. Or was he serious? He was always play-acting. Even when he was sharing his fears of attempted bigamy, it had to be told as a fairy story.

'I'm sorry about the flute,' he said. 'I'll take more care.'

That should have mollified me, but my irritable twitch grew stronger. We'd got off on the wrong foot, and the sun had set with Sam so contradictory that I couldn't ask him to light the menorah with me. But neither could I carry out my homegrown ritual, my wine and my single candle.

'I'm going to the garden,' I told Sam. The path was calling for my feet, even if I couldn't take my charms with me. I went to open the French windows and pulled aside the curtain.

Behind me, Sam rose hurriedly to his feet. I'd forgotten to say *I'm going alone*, and it would have been rude not to escort me.

It wasn't blustery outside as it had been the night before, when he'd arrived. Instead, it was cool and clean. I followed my usual route, trying to find the ritual essence of the walk, despite Sam's presence. The white lake looked pleasingly ethereal, glowing in the dark with the pale gravel paths and the marble benches.

Sam scuffed at some encroaching weeds. 'Are they keeping up the garden, next door at Millstone? Toby did like it neat,' he reminisced. 'Tedious chap.'

'They're keeping it tidy.' I ignored the dig. Sam and Toby's mismatched dispositions had been obvious from when we first met. We came to understand them as inherited. Toby respected and took after their stolid Pa, while Sam was devoted to their onyx-eyed mother ('She always looked so vibrant!'). Too glamorous for grimy London to contain her, their mother had escaped regularly to the Continent. Ruth and I were a duplicitous audience for their stories; Sam's tales were entrancing ('She wore emerald combs in her hair – do you remember, Tobes?') but our slender means made us secretly sympathise with Toby ('Yes, Samuel, and she lost *both* of them in a *music-hall*!').

'Have you always painted?' asked Sam. I was braced in case he intended to mock me, but he continued with apparent sincerity: 'I know you used to draw, and do arty things with Ruth in the library. It's really quite…' He pursed his lips. Like a witch's cottage crossed with a pawnbroker's shop? 'Unique. But you weren't studying art, or anything half so grand.'

'I painted a little.' Very much dabbling. 'I tried to improve – I copied sculptures from the encyclopaedia, but I wasn't serious.'

'You always looked rather serious.'

'Serious about art. Not just painting the same watercolour, over and over. Not being content with the praise of your friends.'

'So it's about being less happy?' He laughed and wandered off on a curving path around the lake.

Ella understood all this already. She was positively fired up by Mrs Fortune's harsh evaluations. This was the first time I'd explained it to an outsider.

Sam called from across the water. 'Will you be showing your work? At exhibitions?'

It was a rather shocking idea. Showing things, showing off. An image came into my mind of a piece of my work – an imaginary ideal piece – hanging in a red-walled gallery. I wanted to do it.

'I'd need to go to college, first.' Back to those wood-panelled corridors where I'd wept from despair. 'There's an entrance examination next Monday.'

'Marvellous! Good luck.'

'Oh, I'm not sure whether I'll sit it.' I was uncertain: should I try for college with Ella this year? Or wait until next year instead? But where would I be next year? What would my family say, when they discovered what I'd done?

'You must! I've every faith in you, and your work.' Sam fell back into step beside me to walk the path again, and we turned two corners before I realised that he hadn't even seen my work. Perhaps he had faith in me, that none of my efforts would be shoddy. No – he didn't know, and I shouldn't be charmed. I wanted to tell him it was no fantasy, and point to the portrait of sorrowing Imogen in our hallway. It had been painted by Rebecca Solomon, and it proved a woman could live by her art. But Rebecca's own family had toppled into scandal; perhaps it proved the opposite.

I realised that if Sam hadn't gone missing then I might never have started to paint. But I could hardly thank him for it.

He sat on a bench and beckoned for me to join him.

As I walked towards him, he lifted something with both hands. He'd brought the flute to the garden. He held it to his mouth; he was about to let the notes out.

I put out my hand, nearly covering his mouth, because I had to stop him quicker than I could form the words. 'Don't! They'll hear!'

He lowered the flute to his knees.

'It wouldn't make *much* noise. And as I said, Lucy's out.'

'Millstone! They might hear you! The staff nearly caught me when I fetched your clothes.'

I looked up at Millstone. There was a dim light in an upper window. The second room I'd searched when I rescued Sam's clothes, the room with a suitcase full of luxuries. 'You see? Someone's in your house. Probably the maid.' A maid with her own transgressions, but not deserving to be startled by a ghost.

'Yes, but she wouldn't think—'

'They might be curious enough to look over the wall,' I said. 'And see you, and telegraph Toby.' I'd spent months avoiding attention, but Sam was incapable of self-restraint. 'You said you didn't want the news to get out. That's why you're here, and not in Millstone.'

He put the flute to one side on the bench. 'Thank you for being so sensible.' He was all solemnity again. I sat by him on the bench and looked out at dark fir trees, dancing. I could capture them in chalk and charcoal, the dark branches and the grey-silver light on them.

Then Sam looked across the garden and said: 'But it's dark, and there are trees between us and them.' Bringing the flute up to his mouth, he played low notes very quietly.

I was becoming accustomed to thinking along two parallel lines: *how can I deny him anything? I'm so glad he's back*. And then, also: *invading my house, defying me, behaving like the lord of the manor*.

Underneath that lay another pair of parallels: the two-faced offer I needed to make to Sam. The ultimatum and the offer, my time limit and my assistance. I waited until the last notes of his music dropped away.

'I'm so glad that you're back,' I quickly said. The dishonesty of the unfinished sentence!

He grinned, a quick flame in his face.

'I'm glad too.' His face fell. 'I shouldn't be.'

'You shouldn't?' Shouldn't be glad, shouldn't be back?

'Of course I should. Silly of me. But it seems a lot of bother for you, for everyone…'

I steeled myself to speak: 'I'm glad you're back but I can't keep you secret from Ruth. I must tell her everything.'

'Even though she's not here?'

'I don't have to lie to her face. But because it's easier for me to lie, it's even worse behaviour. Do you see?'

'No.'

'Well, it *is* worse. So I want to tell her in a week.' I'd drawn a hard line, and I began to soften it. 'I know that's difficult, but she'll feel completely betrayed if she finds out that we knew for a long time.' I had to explain but I was afraid of making him angry.

Why? Sam never got angry. Toby was the angry brother. 'You must understand that.'

'I do.'

'A week would be a compromise – between her being hurt, and you having time to remember.'

That was a lie. She would be hurt no matter how quickly we told her. And Sam might never remember at all. There was no perfect interval where nobody was hurt and everyone was healed.

'I see.'

I rushed on to describe my gift: 'And I could help you. I could try to discover what you did while you were away.'

'How?'

'Ask people around Breakwater. Someone must have seen you. Or place advertisements in the newspapers.'

'Not the papers, too public. It might cause more bother.' More gossip, he meant. More eyes on his family and mine. My candle flame had jumped up, predicting gossip. 'What else could we do?'

I'd laid out all my plans, and he'd dismissed them. I returned to a previous proposal. He'd declined a doctor last night, but that had been for bruises and scratches. Now he had amnesia, a far more serious matter. 'Someone with more experience in conditions of the mind.'

I offered it while in two minds myself, because such a doctor might examine me, too. He might hold that young women are prone to weak nerves. If he uncovered my situation, my family would be whisked back from the Continent.

Sam said: 'What, a mad-doctor? No!'

'But you hurt your head! What if your memory…'

'No. Absolutely not.'

I felt guilty, and thankful. Now I was all out of ideas, while Sam was still looking at me with trust and expectation. 'We could try other ways to help you. There must be…' *Tricks*, I had almost said, but that was a trivial word and I needed to sound methodical, scientific. The flute in his hands made a musical term spring to mind: 'Exercises.'

I watched his hands in his lap. He drummed his fingers on the flute keys, making a tune with slapping ghostly notes.

I'd been so young when I met Sam, and even when he went missing. He probably viewed me as a child. Was I anything more than that? I'd tricked my family. I'd lived alone. But those weren't signs of maturity, but selfishness. I still didn't know what I was going to do, with his amnesia.

'What do you mean by exercises?' asked Sam.

What did I mean? Musical exercises meant running scales up and down, until the memory lived in your fingers and could be fetched back even after a long absence from the instrument. There were art exercises, too, tasks that Mrs Fortune set us. Drawing left-handed, drawing without looking, drawing the same thing over and over in different media.

'We could find activities to help you to recall the past. Try to reach it from different directions. I could help you?' I was babbling again. 'We could experiment.'

'I see. If there's a chance that it might help, we should. Shouldn't we?'

I silently vowed to do my absolute utmost.

'But we shouldn't spend too much time on it. You have important things to do. Your art!'

He hadn't always been this way. He'd been capricious, but not swinging so far between positions, arguing with himself. *Tell your sister; don't tell your sister. Attend to me! I don't want to be any bother.* I saw that if I put a foot wrong, he'd dig himself in to one position, cast the other one onto me, and start arguing with me instead. So I waited for his final verdict.

'When shall we start?'

❦

'Go on. Tell me exactly what to do.'

We were back in the library, thawing after our walk. I cast about desperately for a starting point. What could help him to find his lost memory? A ridiculous, trivial voice came to me: Mama, saying, *Where was the last place you had it?* I stifled a laugh. 'We could begin with questions? Prompts.'

'Yes! No! Wait! We should do this properly. Systematic. How do we record all this?'

There was such optimism that I had to play along, and play up. Clearing my clutter off the big library desk, I fetched sheets of draughtsman's paper, the largest I had, to lay them out on the desktop. Pens, pencils, paperweights, as I did when planning some ambitious project with Ruth. Indeed, we were surrounded by things we'd made together, which had started on this desk as sketches: I could see cushion covers in Berlin wool-work, and an ambitious wall hanging depicting the boyhood of Merlin. That gave me confidence, and arranging the items on the desk gave me time to dream up some questions.

'I'll fetch food,' I offered, to further put off the dread moment of beginning. 'So we needn't stop to eat.'

Lucy was in the kitchen, wearing a clean apron and laying out rows of basins, setting about some project as diligently as I had been upstairs. She nodded at me warily.

'You're home!' I said, and bit my tongue. I shouldn't even have known that she'd been out all afternoon; it was only through Sam that I was aware of it. 'You don't need to work so late,' I added. But I did hope she'd stay out of the way, and not overhear our visitor. It might be better for her to be down here, bustling about, than up in her room, trying to sleep.

'Do you need me, Miss?'

'I came for some food.'

Fresh bread stood on the counter, next to a silver dish holding golden-brown fried fish. Cook had visited during the day, and I hoped hadn't noticed anything amiss. Lucy had already set down her tools and started to carve slices of bread for me. Unnecessarily deferential, but done more neatly than I'd have managed. I fetched my own fish, a great lump. Lucy stared, then cut off four more slices of bread to match. The scale of it was suspicious, and I couldn't request a second plate, so I carried one overloaded platter back upstairs.

The fire was roaring. Sam had piled on more coal. The room felt more homely than it had since my family left. I paused at the library door; it hadn't been improper to close it yesterday, as Sam had been in danger from the cold. But now I'd be closing it to conceal him from Lucy. I did so in a hurry, and felt shabby.

'Hurrah! And you wouldn't have a bottle of beer in the house, would you?' asked Sam.

'Would beer help you?'

'Who knows? Beer has mysterious properties. Imbibers remember things.'

I felt a stab of shame. But he couldn't know about my evening ritual, my daily tipple. I tried to join in his joke. 'Don't they only remember things from the last time they drank?'

'Perhaps I've been drunk for a year... Never mind! I can manage without beer. Now, how shall we organise things?'

The desk appeared less like a craft project and more like a military campaign laid out in a general's tent, the sheets of paper as maps. Seen that way, the fact that they were completely blank didn't bode well. But I'd faced down empty sheets of paper many times; I'd brought out shapes and shade. I pointed at them and dictated. 'That sheet for *since* you've been back, that sheet for *before* the accident, and we can draw connections on to that sheet, which is – what we don't know.' *Your amputated year.*

Sam took up a pen immediately, and began to write the headings in a crisp hand. I cautioned myself: *don't get optimistic.* Sam was a firework, full of energy but the opposite of focused. Suddenly he ripped across the middle of a sheet, crushed half of it up into a ball and tossed it into the fireplace. 'Spelled it all wrong.' I kept an eye on the paper while it burned, dancing about on the coals. Sam wrote the heading out again, more laboriously, then dragged over a chair and sat down, satisfied.

I also pulled up a chair, and sat across from him, to ask the first question.

'Yesterday, where did you wake up?'

'On the lake. I closed my eyes when the ice cracked.' He sounded sheepish, as though I would tell tales against his bravery.

'But I saw you, walking. There was a moment when you were standing up, before you went onto the lake…' The pale smudge of his face had recognised me in the same moment I recognised him. 'You beckoned to me.'

'Wait! You're right! You shook your head.'

I lit up with his enthusiasm. Together, we'd forced back his forgetfulness by a couple of seconds. An easy win.

'What did you see then?'

'You, and the house, across the water, but I forgot it was water. Thought it was marble paving.' Was that relevant? Had he been somewhere made of marble, in a palace, a museum, a bank? I wrote down 'marble floor' on the paper. 'And then…'

He said: 'I saw you. That was why I walked forwards.'

'Can you remember coming up the road to the house, in the dark?'

'Definitely, definitely walking in the dark.'

Wonderful. 'Up *our* road? This road?'

'A long road.'

'Was it cobbled? Were there buildings on either side?'

'Long road, downhill, not cobbled, too dark to tell. That's all.'

Another dimension struck me. How had he got into the garden itself? 'Do you remember coming down the side of my house? That alleyway? It's narrow, there would be leaves underfoot…' That would be memorable, to creep around like a burglar.

He sprang up, rummaged in the sideboard from which our maid had often served him. 'You don't mind, do you?' He returned cradling a glass in each hand. He passed one over to me, and I smelled it, rich and sweet. Brandy. Cook dripped it into boiled fruit puddings in the winter. 'Sorry. Getting a headache. This might help me cogitate.'

It was helping me to cogitate, as well: brandy took up so much less space than wine. I could take a nip to class with me to steady me in the afternoons. To stop me crying. Wasn't there a hip flask, somewhere, that had been a gift to Father?

'Would you care for a glass?' asked Sam.

'Thank you.'

I pulled a spare pad of paper onto my lap and doodled, while Sam drank and chewed on a crust of bread. Obvious symbols grew from my pencil: a huge wall, covered in vegetation and with tendrils working through and around it, to pull it down and wreck it. The art was a sort of charm. I willed it to be effective, then felt childish. I drew Sam instead, beginning a new figure whenever he changed position. A crowd of tiny Samuels.

'Let's go further back,' I said. 'What about our trip to Salisbury Cathedral?'

Sam frowned, and I captured the furrows in his brow. 'That was an age ago. Six months?'

It had been a year and a half ago. I didn't correct him. 'Calling to mind other past events might help your recollection to flow.' And I could tell if there were other moth holes in his memory.

'Oh, that's sensible. Very good. Yes, I recall it.'

'What did the townspeople say to the Bishop of Salisbury?'

It wasn't strictly relevant, only a tease to get his brain working.

He closed his eyes and I drew his eyelids. I knew he was looking back to a May morning in the shadow of that high cathedral, watching women hold oak leaves and dance across the lawns. Good, let him immerse himself in memory. 'Grow something. Growley. No, *grovely*! How could I forget! Grovely, grovely...'

The women had carried an embroidered banner. 'Grovely, grovely, all is grovely, peace and unity.' The bishop said significant words back to them, I forgot what. This exchange gave the townspeople the right to gather wood on church lands all year. It was the kind of ceremony that Ruth and I loved, about ancient forests, old pacts and hardly disguised paganism. The sort of thing Sam loved to discover and take Ruth to visit. We'd watched, walked with dignity round the ancient cloister, then we'd gone to feed ducklings on the river.

'I say, that's not bad. Grovely.' He rolled the word round his mouth, pleased because his memory was working, or because Ruth had been so happy.

The Salisbury trip had been one of our many surprises. Sam would turn up at our door – you could never guess the hour, any time from breakfast to ten at night – dash into the hallway, and bow to me, or Mama, or Ruth. Didn't we look well, and wasn't it a marvellous day? Then he'd fix us with a look.

'Would any of you be available for an adventure?'

He'd explain there were a hundred children dressed as chimney sweeps about to parade through the city. Or he'd located a maypole, or a bonfire, or a figure made of willow about to be thrown from a cliff. And Sam would take us to it. It was exhilarating to be in motion so often, to see and feel what we'd previously experienced through books. Before Sam's arrival, we'd scarcely travelled. Whereas Sam had always been this way, haring off at short notice, sometimes with his mother, to all the capitals of Europe. He'd done so much; Ruth and I had to run to catch up.

As Sam and Ruth became acquainted, we'd travelled often to distant villages, to see well-dressings and bride-blessings and mystery plays and mumming.

His memory was moving now, and I'd nudge it further. I asked, in my most offhand way: 'When you arrived in the garden, had you walked far to get here, last night?'

He grinned. Oh, I was subtle.

'I don't remember…' He looked down at his feet, but he'd trodden the bottom of the lake in his shoes. I'd fetched him a fresh pair from Millstone. No clues down there.

I reached further back for another memory.

'Where did we see the Pope burned in effigy?'

'Oh, blimey. Lewes, on Bonfire Night.' I knew that was unforgettable. His disbelief as the great papal figure collapsed forwards into the red flames. 'I said when we saw it, didn't I: if *we* burned the Pope, they'd hang us as soon as look at us.'

I did remember him saying so, and how our expeditions had been hedged about with wariness. Rural residents viewed our party with curiosity, sometimes hostility, and Toby often made a donation to the nearest village hall to smooth our passage. Sometimes the rooms of a public house would be pronounced 'all booked up' when they were clearly half empty, and one night we'd had no choice but to sit in a railway waiting room until the first train of the morning. I'd felt protected by the brothers' presence, but maybe I should have been more cautious.

I wouldn't trouble Sam with unhappy recollections. I could ask about the opera, or the lectures on dinosaurs (where Toby would be cheery, for once, and ask expert questions). Or the time Sam had hired a sleigh with real reindeer and driven it around the park. I might use those later. But I intended to draw on Sam's deep interest, which he shared with my sister: the old rites and ceremonies of the countryside.

'Where else did we go to see fire rituals?' Sam and Ruth

had spent two autumns courting, and both had been full of fire. Chasing flames in the dark.

'Half a dozen places. Punkie Night, with the turnip lantern faces. Those flaming tar barrels at Ottery St Mary!' A hazardous evening, fire barrels hefted onto the shoulders of men and carried through the crowd.

'Wonderful. Spectacular. And we should all go to Shetland, one day, for the torch procession. Up Helly Aa!'

I'd been right to remind him. He was already relishing the memories and the prospect of travelling with Ruth. And it was bringing him back to himself, his knowledge and his passion.

As I watched him, pleased by his own feat of recollection, I had a quiver of doubt. Had Sam always loved the hidden ways, or had he been clever enough to have discerned Ruth's interest, and made himself into a mirror of it? His library contained a collection of Scottish ballads, and the same volumes of *The Golden Bough* as Ruth had bought for me. But we didn't see his library until weeks after we met, and he'd seen our own collection. Books can be purchased at short notice by comfortable men. He played folk songs on the flute as though he were born to it, but he might have played Mozart until he met us. Before he met us, had he even heard of the Green Man?

I drew Sam as a Green Man himself, ivy spiralling out of his mouth and nose.

'...and now Hyde Park,' he said.

I'd not heard a few words, distracted by doubts. 'Sorry?'

'Bonfires, in the park. I don't know what they're for. The Temperance Society, trying to lure people away from the pubs? It'll be a fine sight when they light them. We should take a turn around them.'

If he'd remade himself to suit Ruth, then it was no matter, I decided. It only showed how lover-like he was.

I dropped my pencil and stretched my fingers. I thought again of playing scales, how the fingers learned the pattern. 'Last night, were you hungry, when you were here? When we were sat here.'

He jumped to his feet, and threw himself into the fireside chair he'd occupied that night. My chair. He hunched himself over and started to shake, and I feared some kind of relapse, but then he asked: 'Like this?' It was a deliberate imitation.

'Yes, and you crossed your arms around yourself.' He'd been half dressed then, but neither of us mentioned that.

Seeing him cross his arms and shiver, half a dozen lines of enquiry sprang into my mind, ways to wake memory: tastes, smells, colours. Sam could handle objects, and tell me what the shapes and surfaces called up, or do tasks with his hands, letting a picture form of when he last performed them.

'I was too confused and cold to be hungry,' he replied. 'But I was hungry as I fell asleep last night...'

'So you'd probably eaten earlier yesterday evening.'

Sam glanced at me in admiration; I caught the shape of his eyebrows with my pencil, extended it into a tendril of ivy.

'What had you eaten?'

'I can't remember.'

'Indoors or outdoors? From a baker or a stall? Or did you sit down and use cutlery?'

'I'm still hungry now, actually. Is there more bread?'

'Yes, but Lucy's in the kitchen. She'll be suspicious if I fetch more.'

'Tell her you were making toast and you burned it all.'

I persisted. 'Do you recall any flavours from yesterday? Even if you don't know where you ate it.'

Incredibly, he nodded.

'There was a taste at the back of my throat – perhaps I'm imagining it.'

'What taste?'

'Like something rotting.'

My questions unearthed no more details about the mysterious taste, only revived Sam's requests for food, so I descended again to the kitchen.

'Don't be moving anything, Miss,' said Lucy, without looking up from her task. Her fingers were weaving methodically, creating a pastry lattice over a pie dish of sliced apples. I stayed well back and looked along the table: there were four sets of bowls and basins, three other identical unfinished pies, a fist-sized lump of pastry next to each.

'I'll help myself,' I reassured her. Best not to ask her about beer, in case she was reporting my tippling to the vicar.

I cut more bread and fish, keeping it well away from her work. I thought of collecting some apples but they were all gone – to be made into pies, I guessed. Rooting around in search of beer, I only discovered signs of slovenly housekeeping. One deep drawer was a bird's nest of twine and corks. Thrust into the back of that drawer was a crumpled envelope. Probably saved to make spills, to light the stove.

The envelope had my name on it, in jagged black ink, with no stamp or address.

I drew it out. It had already been opened. I was sure I'd never seen it before. Whatever it had contained was gone. My brandy-heavy head wasn't sure what to do with it, so I tucked it into the pocket of my dress, then looked around furtively to see if Lucy had noticed.

Lucy was still absorbed in her pastry-rolling. It was restful. Normally when I was around her, my mind scrabbled about, trying to guess her opinion of me. I suspected she scorned me for not being as wealthy, as worldly, as an employer should be. But tonight, her attention was all taken up elsewhere.

'This is all good,' I said, sounding like a duchess opening a charitable establishment. I tried again. 'Why four of them?' It felt like a charm for discrimination: *prick the initials of a different suitor onto each pie case, and see which ones bake and which ones burn.*

'This one's plain,' said Lucy. 'That has rice flour in. Ground almonds in that, and cornflour in that.' She pointed with the rolling pin.

'What does that do?'

'Don't know, do I? Or I wouldn't be trying. I want crisp but crumbly.' Her face wore an expression of determination, flour on her eyebrows.

'Excellent.' Who on earth would eat them all? It was rather impertinent to cook up all my apples for an experiment, but the pies were more productive than my own investigations upstairs. Could we afford it? Well, without Ruth and Mama home, the bills were smaller. 'When will they be ready?'

'Half past ten.'

'Thank you.' My eye fell on a basin of water, with a central melting piece of ice. She was casting a malicious charm; she was using the ice from the lake. 'Where did you get that?' I asked, too sharply.

'Left the bowl outside the back door last night, Miss,' Lucy said. 'And then kept it in the icebox. Cold water's best for pastry.'

'Sorry. I didn't know.'

Lucy silently conveyed that what I didn't know would fill a wheelbarrow. I carried the second round of bread and fish upstairs, unsteadily, and rejoined my conversation with Sam.

He drank. I asked more questions. He said: *Can't remember, don't remember.* Like blunt blows. His amnesia didn't even feel like a wall to climb or demolish. It felt like fog, just as he'd said. The fire in the grate was higher than ever, the room growing stuffy. Sam slumped down in his chair, clutching a cushion to his chest.

He made me keep asking, though. When had he last slept and where? When did he last wash? (I grew hot in the face, I should not have asked that.) When had he last spoken?

'Did I pat any cats that day? Cats of what colour?' He raked at his hair in distress. I stilled my pencil, didn't try to capture that habit on paper.

'Please – forget this, we needn't do it.' Panic plucked at me. We were becoming despondent. It was unsystematic, and I was sweltering. 'We can find another solution.'

Sam slumped back in his chair. 'It was a good idea. Any of those things you asked *could* have been the answer. Or part of the answer.'

But none of them had been.

We returned to the desk to add what we knew to the wretchedly blank sheets of paper. From the sheet of the known present we added meagre lines stretching back to the unknown past. Possible times he had last slept or eaten. His hair must have been cut within a month or so, other fiddling details. I felt a surprising urge to rejoin Lucy in the kitchen, where she was doubtless making more progress with her pies.

'I could feel how much Ruth missed me,' said Sam.

I seized on it. 'Do you mean literally? You felt missed? Samuel. Think.'

His eyes refocused and he straightened up, threw the cushion aside. 'I had this terrible sense of being missed, of people mourning me. I had to stop it. I still have the feeling, it's –' He put his hand to his side. '– sickening.'

'Is there anything else, that comes along with that feeling?' Threshing corn. Turning hops. Walking through an arcade in Paris. Anything, anything…

'Sorry, it's all gone dark.'

I pointed to the join between the far past and the missing year. The accident itself.

'Shall we?'

'Why not.' We settled in our seats.

'You remember Breakwater, and the cottage?'

'Oh! The cottage…' His voice had a pang of pain in it. This was it, the wall in his mind collapsing, the flood of memory – would it be dangerous? 'I hadn't forgotten it, but it hadn't occurred to me. How is it? My little house?' He looked sad in a way that he hadn't even when talking about my sister.

When Sam had first taken us on excursions, it had required exhausting long day trips, or overnight stays at uncertain or unfriendly lodgings. In November Sam had led us to a little whitewashed cottage in a village called Breakwater and announced: 'We're sleeping here tonight!'

We had ducked under black beams to enter a dusty sitting room. The evening sun turned the dust motes golden. Out through the leaded window was a garden, and beyond the garden a river ran. 'Who owns the cottage?' Ruth had asked.

'I do,' said Sam.

Sam told us how sensible he had been to purchase the cottage. Breakwater village had two festivals a year, and using the cottage as a staging post – two hours west of London – would allow us to reach dozens more places by train or bicycle. Nobody could deny us accommodation, and instead we'd have a home away from home.

Toby had been peevish but taciturn. I wondered if the extravagance had annoyed him, or Sam's boasts of security; Toby wouldn't want to speak, in front of my family, of either money or danger. Ruth and I left the brothers to argue and ran into the garden, down to the river at its foot. 'It's south-flowing water!' Ruth had exclaimed. She had memorised all the charms to predict future husbands. I'd dashed back to Mama and begged a loan of her wedding ring. I drew a ribbon from my cuff, to dangle the ring over the water, but when I showed my ingenuity to Ruth she became shy.

'You do it!' she said.

I'd never cared for marital divination. 'No, you. Why not?'

She grabbed the ring from me and took it back to our confused Mama, who'd been assessing the roses.

I suddenly understood. Previously, when we'd tried a charm, the future suitors had been numerous and nebulous. Now, a single candidate had emerged: the young man in the cottage behind us, arguing with his brother. The game was no fun any more.

'Have you been there, to Breakwater?' Sam asked. 'This year?'

I shook my head.

'Tell me again, how did I go missing?'

My throat was tight. I started scribbling once more, using dense little strokes to fill in outlines I'd already drawn, adding layers and layers of shadows to the faces of Sam. Under the eyes, under the nose, under the jaw, and all around his head until the paper distorted.

'It was in the evening. About six o'clock, but it was already dark. Late December.'

'What happened?'

I shouldn't have let him ask questions. His thoughts shouldn't turn in that direction. I gave him the briefest reply: 'You fell while you were standing in the river.'

'Of course! You said it was at midwinter. During the Sully. That was the name, wasn't it? A kind of festival. Beating the water with those big sticks…'

I didn't know if he was prompting himself to remember, or if it had all come back to him just now, and he was feeling the cold and the current.

'And a flood.'

I nodded.

'What happened afterwards?'

What happened to him, we didn't know. What happened to us would hardly help Sam to remember. His hands were writhing again. I saw he'd stopped considering his amnesia. He wanted to know how his family had reacted, what we'd done.

'Well, there were other men who'd been carried away in the flood. Toby came back to shore. He'd fallen, as well, but not been carried off—'

'Poor Toby. Yes.'

'We went back to the cottage.' I didn't tell him that Ruth and I had helped Toby back to the cottage, not vice versa. Stoic, sturdy Toby had been incoherent when he had clambered out of the river. 'When the waters dropped a little, all the men went downriver to look.'

We'd seen the lanterns of the search party from the sitting room of the cottage, each one fuzzy yellow, bobbing along the course of the river. Toby drank whisky and a sedative from the local doctor.

I'd tensed as the weak lights passed the foot of our garden. But nobody stopped, nobody cried out. The river had been noisy that night, rushing and slapping at its banks. I had pictured a piece of human flotsam, chased by the current. Would it catch on a rock or wash up on a bank? Or dangle from a tree's lowest branches when the waters dropped?

'What happened with the search?' Samuel asked.

I angled my sketchbook up, a barrier between us.

'The men went down the river that night. Ten men had been carried off, they found eight of them.' Three of them dead, but no need to tell Sam that now.

'And what did you do afterwards?'

I'd gone up to the room in the cottage which I shared with my sister, under the eaves of the thatched roof. The doctor had also given her a sedative. I was relieved to find her already asleep. I drew the blankets from under her as carefully as I could, and lay down beside her. She was cold. I heard a crack-boom, far off but terrifying, and silently thanked the doctor who had warned us: they would be firing guns over the water, believing that it would bring lost bodies to the surface. In legends the dead reveal themselves gradually and beautifully. Isabella's pot of basil grows lush; the fig tree hiding the murdered Ibn Gabirol puts out wondrous fruit.

Ruth hadn't flinched at the sound of the guns. I fell asleep holding her. I saw that I was falling asleep in a world in which Samuel was missing, and might wake to one in which he was dead, but I was too tired to resist.

If I'd known I would wake to months of Sam being missing, I might have taken the sedative. Bottles of it.

'It's not important,' I told him. 'I should sleep.'

'Right now?'

'I have class tomorrow.'

'Couldn't you skip it?'

'I'm working in clay. I need to finish it before it all dries.'

'Is this another version of your golem friend?'

'Yes.' I thanked my imagination for drawing a neat link between my two lies without my planning it.

'Ha. Young ladies do like having someone to boss around.'

'Look out for Lucy as you go upstairs. Be careful.'

I popped down to check on her myself. The kitchen stairs smelled of butter and cinnamon, but Lucy was gone. Four pies, golden and identical, rested under clean cloths and I didn't dare cut any of them. I turned down the kitchen lamps and peered up into the garden. Lucy was pacing out there, waiting for her creations to cool.

Back in my bedroom, I put my hand in my dress pocket and closed my fingers round the empty envelope I'd discovered in the kitchen drawer. It was almost certainly Lucy's doing, unless I'd hidden it there while sleepwalking. She could have opened it in error, or in mischief. Was she trying to protect her erratic mistress from some bad news? Should I speak to her about it? Must I? I preferred it when we moved like planets in fixed orbits, without intersecting.

I pulled the envelope from my pocket and examined it. Paper, handwriting, no part of it was familiar to me. I stuffed it under my pillow. An old habit, from the oldest kind of charm: *put this beneath your pillow, and the first person you think of on waking...* Or *the first person you see when dreaming...* Ruth and I had often rested our heads on the lumpiest noxious combinations of herbs and tokens, and been scolded by the chamber maid.

But this night I didn't need to wait for dreams. As soon as I withdrew my hand, I had an excellent idea. Interrogating Sam hadn't helped. I'd been wrong to try to startle answers out of him. What if he let the answers grow in their own time? Put them – symbolically, or literally – under his pillow?

The questions came to me quickly, but my nightcap had ruined my penmanship, and it took me a while to copy them laboriously onto fresh paper. Halfway through, I heard a sound in the corridor, footsteps, stopping by my door. It must be Sam, as exhausted as I, coming automatically to this door, believing it to be his own room in Millstone.

Should I call out, or would he realise in time? The door rattled without unlatching. The handle didn't turn. The steps moved on.

I gave Sam ten minutes to find his room and settle in. Then I carried my questions along the corridor. Could I hear him moving, inside the room? I'd rest easier knowing he wasn't roaming the house, half awake. A creaking board, a dragged shoe? I pressed an ear against the door. Rustling? I jerked away again, and slid the paper under the door.

You could reflect on these at your leisure - Judith.
Who was the last person you met (before me)?
When did you last introduce yourself to someone?
When did you last hear music?
When did you last play music?
When did you last dance?

As soon as I pushed the questions past the point of retrieval, I felt I'd been too fanciful. The flute had made me wonder if music could find a fresh channel in his brain. Now it seemed as fruitless as the search for the Northwest Passage.

Back in my room, the other questions I'd written embarrassed me even more. I pitched the paper into the fireplace (where Lucy had made a fire up, although I hadn't asked her to). The fire browned the edges and ate the pages.

A church clock striking reminded me to compose myself, and sleep; I had class the next day. Pulling off my dress I climbed into bed in my chemise, as I lacked the energy to change into a nightgown. That also meant I didn't have to see my bruises, which were probably turning murky green. Lying down, I listened to the wind. A voice carried up from the garden, chatting away. I recognised the speaker, but couldn't hear the words over the wind. Lucy hadn't returned to her baking; she was still standing in the garden, talking to herself. Chuckling to herself, even. A girl alone, laughing her heart out in my garden.

It was an uncanny sound. Particularly after our conversation earlier – civil, almost amiable. And she'd been more methodical than wild while she was cooking. But baking at night, and for nobody? Perhaps she'd become obsessive, and I wasn't the only one heading for a rest cure. She was a country girl, and city life was taking a toll on her nerves.

I should speak to her. Shouldn't I? I didn't know how. With my family gone, was she my responsibility?

Outside, Lucy laughed.

Once, years ago, Father had asked the gardeners to fish in our lake for a lost vase and everything came up except the thing we were looking for.

I slid into sleep.

I didn't dream about the crumpled envelope under my pillow. Instead I dreamed of another person coming up from under the shattered ice of the frozen lake, clawing their way unaided to the shore. It was a woman, and stinking mudwater streamed off her face like a veil and ran down over her body. Maybe she was made of the mud, I couldn't tell. She followed the trail that Sam and I had left, right up through the garden to the house. She placed her hand on the library French windows, and my stomach churned, knowing that she would smash them open.

She had come to take Sam back, and I knew he would go with her.

THURSDAY

Sam was in the kitchen again the next morning, stooped over the stove. My nose was affronted by the smell of smoke.

'What are you doing?'

He shifted a little, revealing a burning spill of paper. 'Morning! This gas stove is an ingenious thing. Ouch!' He shook the spill to extinguish it, and it flared up briefly then burnt out. He placed it beside the stove on a pile of similar half-burned spills. 'I wonder if we have the same one at Millstone?'

If he wanted so desperately to stay secret, he needed to stay out of the servants' spaces. Which he did perfectly well in his own home, but there he could ring a bell when he wanted a coffee with cardamom, or a tiny rosewater cake. 'Where's Lucy?' I demanded.

'She's still in bed, probably. We'll hear her if she comes down here – I can always hide in the garden. Look, I found a pie! Eat some!' He had demolished most of an apple tart, eating it straight from the case with a spoon. The ruined pastry lattice could have been almond or rice flour.

I was conscious that I hadn't changed my clothes, just scrambled back into the same dress this morning. Sam gave no sign that he'd noticed. 'Did you read the new questions I wrote for you?' I asked, cutting a slice for myself and sitting opposite him.

His nose wrinkled. 'They didn't work.' His dismissive tone was hurtful, but unintentional; he was preoccupied with wiping soot from his fingertips. 'What did you try?' Now his firecracker attention had fizzed off in another direction.

'What?'

'You can't have given up straight away. You must have tried all sorts of things!' He was eager, as though I could tell him an adventure out of the *Boy's Own Paper*.

'I said. There was a search.'

'But that was men from the village. I meant *you*, Judith! And Ruth and Toby. You must have wondered, you must have known I might be...' He waved his spoon in widening circles. 'Out there? Somewhere?'

I had to put him off. 'It's not my story to tell. I'm sure that Ruth will want to tell you.'

'Oh. Definitely.' He sipped at a cup of tea. 'So I had the accident in December, and Toby placed that notice in the paper in March? That was awfully quick, to give up on me.'

'It didn't *feel* quick.' I regretted being stung into a sharp reply.

Sam kept on asking, as though my questions last night had unbalanced things and he needed to restore equilibrium by asking a dozen of his own. 'Did Toby see me? When I fell? Did he try to help me?'

Toby hadn't spoken about it, and I hadn't dreamed of asking him. I tried to redirect Sam's attention. 'Do you remember anyone else helping you, that night?'

'If you tell me what Toby did, it might remind me.'

I hated it when he tried to charm me into changing my mind. *Twisty*, Ruth had called it. *I wish he wouldn't be twisty.*

'I have things to do,' I said. 'My class. I'll leave the house unlocked. I'll be home by six.' Why had I said that? Art class ended early in winter, and I could easily be home by four. I was feeling constrained, and buying some leeway. 'But you can't be in the kitchen. Or on the back stairs, anywhere Lucy might see you. You're probably safe in the library.' Lucy mostly kept out of the library, had stopped cleaning the room around the time Ruth and I had hung holly garlands and wreaths of teasel heads along the bookcases.

I left the kitchen before he could argue.

I didn't leave the house, though. Sam's twisting had wormed an idea loose in my mind. He wasn't the only one who could tell me about that night.

I knew someone from the village.

Bracing myself as I climbed the stairs, I reminded myself of my father's efforts. He'd emigrated as a shop assistant, and built up a grocery empire with a hundred staff. I was his daughter, and surely must have inherited some of his talents. On a high wall, in his gilded frame, King Arthur frowned on my cowardice.

I was fortifying myself to question Lucy. Last night's partial success at conversation had been overshadowed by overhearing her strange laughter in the garden. One needs age, authority or practice to deal with servants. Mama had never forgotten she was a shopkeeper's daughter. Other girls' mothers drilled their maids and cajoled their cooks, showing off their gleaming homes at card parties. Mama had been so scared of her own lady's maid that when the time had come, poor Ruth had been the one to sack the girl.

I climbed on up to the servants' attic. I rarely ventured up here, and half expected it to be dusty, but the long corridor was clean and light. Like the kitchen and the guest rooms, it had escaped Ruth and me meddling with its décor, and was painted plain white. I knocked on Lucy's bedroom door and heard scuffling inside.

Lucy came from Breakwater. Lucy had approached Mama

herself, while we were on a visit to Breakwater, and asked if she could work for us as a maid. It had been a timely enquiry. After Father's death, we had been unable to keep up a full house of servants. We had let some of them go (including Mama's lady's maid) and those who remained dropped off one by one, finding the compromise unpalatable. We had resolved to make do with Cook and a couple of maids-of-all-work. And here was Lucy, volunteering, a strong country lass (although more brusque than merry).

Lucy's offer had seemed odd, to me. Her family farm was prosperous – I couldn't estimate the value of cows, but the farm employed several young local men – and while I didn't follow country society, I'd have thought that Lucy wouldn't need to skivvy. But what did I know? I'd seen her down in the village, running after her young siblings, trying to stop them from careering into nettles or out onto stepping stones. Possibly she'd wanted to escape that duty, and her parents' house, and live in the city. I'd raised no objections.

Others hadn't been so stingy with their opinions.

Toby said if we were prepared to take on an untrained girl, why not a Jewish girl from the East End, who needed employment and a trade? The city was full of them, recently arrived, incredibly poor but very hard-working. Toby sat on the boards of a number of relevant charities… Ruth had nodded along. She had cried while reading *Children of the Ghetto*.

Mama said they all had lice and she wouldn't have one in the house. Toby's face went purple.

Sam said Lucy would be fine, if we wanted a bumpkin who'd drop the crockery, be seduced by a cad in a pleasure garden and run off with our spoons. Toby's displeasure exploded all over Sam.

Ruth said Lucy seemed very nice.

We had taken Lucy on as a maid.

Ruth and I had secretly hoped that she would bring rural wise ways into our house. Ideally, she'd arrive with a farthing and a pinch of salt in a handkerchief, and make canny remarks about why the milk kept turning. But Lucy had been disappointingly pragmatic. And not fanciful, at all; I would never have foreseen that city life would disturb her, or that she'd start laughing at nothing.

I hoped she still had her wits. She was now my best connection to the village, and any word about Sam.

The door of the attic bedroom swung open. Lucy wore a white nightgown, reddish hair in a halo. She was surprised and tried to curtsy, and then we both tried to speak.

'Sorry, Miss, I –'

'Thank you for –'

I was happy to yield. 'You first.'

'You want summat?' Lucy had never been truly trained as a maid. She hummed while she cleaned, and spoke to us any old how, because none of my family had corrected her.

'No, no! I don't need you for work. I wanted to ask you…' If I had wanted to build a bridge between us, I should have begun to lay the foundations two years ago. 'Lucy, did you ever hear any news about Sam?'

'What?'

'Samuel Silver, after the night he went missing. Did you hear any reports, or stories?'

'No, Miss.' She shook her head, mystified and appalled, near to closing the door in my face.

'Do you know who was in the search party? The ones who went downriver?'

'Every fit man in the village,' she said sharply. I'd accidentally questioned their honour.

I'd done the wrong thing. It had appeared so simple, to consult a Breakwater girl who was here in the house, whose mother and sister still lived in the village. But for Lucy, she'd had a year to put it out of her mind. My curiosity was morbid and unprompted.

'Why not write to the vicar?' Lucy suggested. 'He can go and talk to the men.'

Of course! But why stop there? Breakwater was a whole village full of witnesses and information. Far better than writing to the vicar, I could visit him, and speak with him directly. Sam had objected to me placing newspaper advertisements, but this would be a far more discreet investigation. I could even take Sam with me! No, that would be dangerous; he'd be recognised by the villagers. But I could return to the river myself and refresh my memories, so I could then prompt Sam's.

'Do you know, I think I'll go to Breakwater,' I told Lucy. 'Today. Shall I take a message to your mother? Or your sister?' Many girls sent their wages home from the city, and I could have carried them safely.

'Oh, don't bother them on my account, Miss.'

I liked that Lucy was keeping her money, and I hoped she'd have fun with it. Her mother had unsettled me, and her sister, Bonnie, was only vaguely known to me as younger and louder. Finer featured, too, although that was a shallow thing to notice. 'Would you like to come with me? I could buy your ticket.'

'No, Miss.' But her manner was a trace more friendly.

My conscience jabbed me further. *Tell Lucy about Sam. Tell her he's here, or she'll find him. He'll terrify her.* I said: 'In fact, would you like a few days off, to visit your family?' To keep her out of the house.

She weighed up my offer – a chance to get away from me – but stood firm. 'No, Miss.'

'Have a couple of days off anyway.' I grubbed in my pocket and closed my hand around some clinking coins. I passed her the whole handful without checking their value, not wanting to appear stingy and embarrassed at playing Lady Bountiful. 'The weather's been so gloomy. You could explore the city a little. There are museums. Or the music halls.' Should I be encouraging her to go to a music hall? I suspected she had more worldly wisdom than I did, and could keep out of harm's way.

Sam's return would be public knowledge in a week's time, or even sooner. I fervently hoped Lucy wouldn't run into him before then. If she could keep out of the house, or he could keep out of her path, all would be well. Should I ask her specifically not to clean the library? Would that make her suspicious of what was happening in there? I turned to go.

'Did you eat any o' the pies, Miss?'

No hiding the ruins left by Sam's spoon. 'Yes! It was delicious. I'll take some with me when I go out. Thank you.'

That pleased her. 'No bother, Miss.'

There was a noise in the room behind her as she closed the door. Perhaps, in her own loneliness, trying to keep herself tethered, she had acquired a kitten.

Coming back downstairs, I saw a white square lying on the hall floor. A letter. The candle-spark prediction had come true. From my sister? Or an invitation from a friend? Leah Isaac had begged me to attend a theatrical recital at her home, last week, and I had written back to put her off. I feared letters from friends' mothers, and an escalation of concern.

No – it bore the same scratchy handwriting as the envelope I'd discovered in the kitchen. Addressed, again, to me.

Ducking into the library, I ripped it open.

Dear Miss Judith. Please tell Mr Silver to send the money that is owed me. A Friend.

Panic rose in me, making me tremble like a will-o'-the-wisp. I would lose myself if I weren't careful.

I calmed myself with logic. Although I'd felt the anger crackling from the letter, its language was formal, and it contained no threat. It pretended to intimacy, but had no claim on me: who was this 'friend'? No friend of mine, I had none. Toby certainly had business friends, and fellows who served with him on charity boards, but none of them would ask me to plead their case with him. Toby's financial arrangements were not my responsibility.

Soon I was cool enough to mock the beastly demand: would Toby have any friends whose handwriting was so poor?

There would be time to consider the letter later. Stowing the letter carefully into the bottom of my satchel of art supplies, I went in search of my father's hip flask.

'You're going to be a bloody holiday sketcher!'

Ella was lecturing me. I'd told her during the morning art class that I wouldn't be coming back for the afternoon session.

'I have business. In a village, away from London.' I clung to my sense that this was the right plan, and tried to make it sound important to avert Ella's scorn.

'Couldn't you do it on Saturday?' Ella resented Saturdays. Her mother didn't like her to paint on the Sabbath. Ella kept the peace and lost the Saturday sunlight, a heavy penalty in the winter months.

'It needs to be done sooner.' I itched to speak to the vicar, and men from the search party, too. Tactfully, not clumsily, as I'd done with poor Lucy.

'Are you drawing nature scenes?' Ella accused. 'Maids a-milking and what-have-you?'

'No.'

'Sun on the duckpond, with adorable ducklings?'

'There's no sun and no ducklings, it's winter!'

'You'll stop coming to class. I'll be all alone in a room full of wilting princesses. I'll be the only one left who gives a fig about technique.'

I had no fondness for the other girls, but I suspected Ella insulted them in part to keep me on her side. I wondered, sometimes, what she would make of Ruth – who would currently be sketching on holiday – and how she'd mischaracterise her kindness. Still, I had no appetite for a fight. 'Actually, I'll be taking the college entrance examination this year.'

I was dizzied by having announced my decision without any planning, and then doubly dizzied as Ella clasped my arm in congratulation. Had I done the right thing? When I said it, it had sounded real. It reminded me of saying to my family, *I am studying art*, and then finding that was true.

'Excellent! We can do a mock examination together.'

I'd let myself in for extra work. 'Good!'

'Well, you definitely can't go off on a country jaunt! Not now!'

'I need to. But I'll take my sketchbook…'

'On your own?' She narrowed her eyes. Was she impressed? Ruth and I had often been troubled on trains. But I'd find someone elderly and respectable and share their carriage.

I cautiously extended an invitation. 'Unless you…'

'Yes, I'll come,' Ella announced. 'I'll draw the church while you do business. There is one, isn't there? Villages have churches.'

We told Mrs Fortune we would be leaving early, and she didn't raise objections, but we still descended the stairs at lunch feeling like truants. Adding to this sense, a woman hailed us from across the small green square.

'Mim! Wait!'

Ella froze.

The woman was older, an immaculate grey jacket enclosing

her with two dozen tiny buttons marching from neck to navel. She strode over briskly, holding out a cloth bag, which Ella managed to accept while still ignoring her.

'You'll be Ella's painting friend,' said the woman who must be Ella's mother. I was fascinated but tried not to stare. She spoke carefully; she might be watching her aitches. I felt sympathy for her, trying not to show up her daughter, and sympathy for Ella, for whom the sheer fact that she had a mother was excruciating. I couldn't satisfy them both, so aimed to be friendly but brief.

'I am, Mrs Leon. It's a pleasure to meet you.'

'I brought Ella's lunch, that she forgot,' her mother observed. 'Are you off somewhere?'

'A sketching tour,' Ella said. She was self-created, a pillar in the desert.

'Marvellous!' Her mother took me by the arm, conspiratorial, and walked me a couple of paces further off. I was so surprised I didn't draw away.

I realised that Ella might fear her mother telling me about her childhood, or asking me to be a friend to her. There wasn't a way to reassure both of them that Ella was doing me a kindness with her friendship. I kept my attention on Mrs Leon's tiny buttons.

'I hope you won't find me impertinent, but Ella told me of your loss. Wait one moment...' She dug into her bag without releasing me, which was a wrestle. 'Take this. I apologise if I mis-speak. But it has meant the *world* to me.'

'Mother!' Ella eavesdropped from a distance.

A pamphlet was thrust into my hand. I decided not to look at it immediately, in case it truly did require an apology. 'Thank you, Mrs Leon.'

'I must be back at the shop,' she said.

Seeing her mother leaving, Ella relented. 'Ma sews at Marshall

& Snelgrove,' she explained to me with some pride. 'What's the work like today, Ma?'

'All coats, this morning! So many people left it too late, and now the weather's changed. But you must excuse me…'

We took an omnibus to Waterloo, and installed ourselves in a compartment on the train. Ella's face opposite me hovered like a moon in the dramatic high collar of her coat. Her mother, the seamstress, must have made it for her, and her wonderful dresses too. It tickled me that the things which marked her as modern had come via such a traditional route. I was glad that Ella's mother was kind to her, and felt a dash of jealousy.

It was the first trip we'd made together. I shouldn't irritate her by sentiment; she could easily become bored with me before it was over. The great arched iron roof absorbed my attention until the train began to groan and move.

'How long will it be?' Ella asked.

'Two hours.'

'Oh, dire. I'll smoke.'

'I'll be sick on you if you do.'

We were alone in the compartment, which occasioned some slight anxiety. Two men peered in, seeking amusement, and then a panting loner with ill intent, but all retreated from Ella's basilisk glare.

I couldn't sketch – the train shook too much – so I resolved to practise looking, instead. I gazed through the window at the grey countryside. Heavy rain had fallen. Rivers had risen, and there were standing pools in all the fields. The smaller ones were frozen white, unpainted patches of canvas in a rural scene. Some fields were gone altogether, and in their place were sheets of earth-coloured water, turning in immense slow spirals. Just like last winter: Ruth and I would be playing word games, but after miles of floods, fall silent at the scale of it. When we took this route in the summer, there were only a few puddles and streams, and the sparkling sun had leapt between them, keeping pace with the train. I sipped from my hip flask to restore some sparkle to the trip.

I imagined my family crossing Italy on a train, seeing baked earth and poplar trees. Ruth and Mama glowing under a brighter sun, Toby keenly regarding the rock formations of the hills. I wanted to be with them. Then I heard Mama arguing over who would sit facing in which direction, Toby chafing at delays, and was a little relieved to be here without them.

Toby and Sam had often squabbled, I recalled, on the way to Breakwater. There had been no obvious reason, as they both enjoyed the village. Toby liked to converse with the vicar, and marched through the woods as though they were a puzzle that needed solving. But on the train he would often be twice as stuffy as usual, demanding to know whether Sam had packed some object or other (in a tone that gave no clue if it would be good or bad). I suppose Toby had often been worrying about Ruth and me, and propriety.

Ella, sitting across the carriage from me, was jumpy from tobacco deprivation. Her agitation increased as the countryside rolled off to the horizon, grass high and miles wide. The sound of the train disguised the size of the silence, but I knew when we got to Breakwater she wouldn't enjoy that, either.

'I brought food.' Prising open the tin I'd brought, I offered Ella a slice of Lucy's pie, and ate a piece myself. It was ambrosian, the fruit melting and the pastry very crumbly (because of rice flour?). Ella devoured it without comment. I felt her mother's pamphlet in my pocket. Out of courtesy, I'd read it when we were apart.

The silence of the countryside struck us as soon as the train chuffed away and left us at Breakwater station. My plans, in order: to quiz the vicar, to contact any of the searchers he might name, and to note the sensations of the village around me. For instance, I must remind Sam that everything smelled sharp and green.

I directed Ella to the steps at the end of the station platform. The village lay beyond and below us, in a valley between grey-green hills, stone cottages dormant under swaying trees. Just as blustery and frosty as it had looked a year ago.

'Take me to the church, then,' Ella demanded.

'Why the church?'

'They're interesting. Religious art interests me. Mrs Fortune said it's essential to experience different traditions.'

Her request was surprising and confusing. There were dozens of churches in the city. Then I thought through the complications: in a busy city church, the congregation might pester Ella. Her visit could reach the ears of her mother. A quieter village church was ideal.

The church was at the top of the village, and I left Ella in the graveyard. Art in public places isn't the same as studio work. You can't take all your best tools, and you can't stay in one spot all day. Because of that, it's best to work quickly. Ella began as an absolute tornado, jotting down the silhouettes of a dozen leaning gravestones.

As soon as Ella was behind me, I took the pamphlet her mother had given me from my bag. 'The Opening Way', the cover said, with an engraving of a hand drawing back a curtain. On the reverse of the paper, the text was all fragments of praise and testimony. The pamphlet was an advertisement for a book. From phrases I picked out while walking (*your questions settled* and particularly *the veil lifted*) I determined that it was a spiritualist text, and that Mrs Leon was attempting to recruit me.

I was glad I hadn't looked at it while Mrs Leon was present. I would have been very snappish. Now I was so wrong-footed I couldn't decide objectively if it had been kind or shabby of her to give it to me. Also, I couldn't square her spiritualism with her dislike of Ella sketching on a Saturday. I thrust it back into my bag to hide it from the Breakwater vicar.

I wandered on down the lane, picking my way around puddles. It was hard not to envision it as a journey backwards in time. On our first visit, Ruth and I had wandered, entranced, round the village, marvelling at the low green-stone houses and wondering how anyone could live in them. It all seemed such hard work: buckets filled from wells, butter churned by hand. A series of ringing notes led us to a blacksmith, and Ruth and I had goggled at him, watching the bellows and the anvil and the muscles, whispering that it could be a hundred years earlier, easily.

It was still an antique scene, but I wasn't tiptoeing with glee this time. Without Ruth, I felt my oddness. A hundred years ago, would there have been any place for Ella and me here, as Jewish girl-artists?

To escape my musings, I walked towards the vicarage as fast as I could. A patch of sludge sent my heel askew. The ground went out from under me. A sickening skid, and I grabbed for a low stone wall.

I hauled myself back to my feet with care. I'd grazed my hand but saved the rest of me. I kept walking, gingerly. The few people out in the street were bundled up and nodded to acknowledge me without recognition, neither hostile nor kind.

The vicarage was a larger cottage than most in Breakwater. The vicar's study had a leaded glass window and I could see him at his desk, distorted, a pink blob under a blond blur. A sudden surge of pleasure; it would be nice to see the vicar.

Then the vicar saw me, and jumped as though I were a ghost.

He swung open the window and called. 'Miss Judith! Is there anything… how lovely to see you! Is anything wrong?'

I wished I'd prepared what I meant to say. To indicate it wasn't an emergency I smiled cheerfully, and he ducked back inside to let me in the front door. It was surprisingly good to see him. I should have written first – no, said a more calculating part of me, it was good to wrong-foot him. He might say more because I'd startled him.

In a moment the door swung open. The vicar must have been an angelic child, but now his blue eyes and his blond mop were incongruous against his face, which was notably more haggard than when I'd last seen him.

'Could I talk with you?'

'With pleasure! Come in, come in. Mind that bundle of – no, don't worry, just step around…'

A large plain cross hung in the hall, another round his neck. He'd always been very well mannered to all of us, Sachs women and Silver brothers. He was an unlooked-for friend, and we wondered if he hankered after educated conversation, or was steering us away from the other villagers to avoid antagonism. He seemed shy about seeming to preach to us, as though it would be bad manners; perhaps he'd attempted to convert someone in the past, and been rapped over the knuckles with *Israel Defended*. So, he never spoke of the Church, and always of fishing with Sam, and Spinoza and palaeontology with Toby. He could recall the categories of extinct animals, but mislaid the details of all worldly matters. His wife had always stood kindly at his elbows and supplied him with place names, dates and people.

He cleared off a chair for me to sit.

'Travelling with Lucy? She's well?'

'I came with a friend, she's sketching in the village. But Lucy's well.'

'What brings you here? Not that you're not welcome. Very much welcome. I'd intended to write.'

How could I explain my business without saying that Sam was home? 'I suppose I came because it's been a year. Since Samuel went missing.'

'I understand. And you had many happy times here.' That confused me – I'd come back today because we'd had one very miserable time here – but the vicar sounded assured. He must have used the phrase often to soothe parishioners in their grief.

'Yes, we did. I wondered if there was any more news.'

'Oh, no. I assure you. We would have contacted you straight away. Nothing untoward, nothing at all.'

Liars over-elaborate. But his way of speaking had always sounded quite high and wandering. His pale eyebrows pressed together. I couldn't ask: are you lying? What are you hiding?

I felt hot frustration. It joined the throb from my hand, and the glow from the sip I'd taken from my hip flask. They all welled up inside me, and tears flowed out.

'Dear Miss Sachs, please let me…' He rang a bell that sat on his desk. Was the bell supposed to turn off my tears? No, his wife would come and comfort me. I liked his wife, and she'd taken a shine to Ruth and me, often inviting the two of us over for meals, allowing Sam and Toby to have a really good squabble on their own. The prospect of seeing her again made me dab my nose with a handkerchief and tidy myself. It would all be fine, I was *taking tea with the vicar*. Ruth and I had giggled at that phrase in the past, it sounded so like a pastime from a Jane Austen novel.

Instead of his wife, a young woman in an apron opened the study door holding a tea tray. We fussed with delicate plates and pieces of shortbread. I felt more self-possessed, but the vicar still frowned. I saw my chance and pressed tenderly on his conscience.

'I feel there's information I don't have. Is it because I'm younger than the others? Did you keep things back from me?'

'No, no. There was no news of Master Silver.'

'And the men who were swept away – after that day, nobody was found?'

'No. Not after that other unfortunate young man. I sent a telegram to the elder Mister Silver straight away about that.'

'Sorry?'

So this was what the vicar looked like when he panicked: throat gulping, lips pallid. He'd intended to offer proof of his honesty and he'd spilled the beans by mistake.

'It's no secret, of course! We did find a young man.'

Wandering, clueless? Could it have been Sam?

'The villagers sent loaves of bread with mercury in them floating downstream. A local nostrum, to find anyone carried away. And they did find one man.'

Dead, then.

'It was…' He turned his head to his side, as if looking to his wife to confirm the date, but she was elsewhere. He tutted and began to flip through a large desk diary. 'Late January. A few miles downstream. He was a tall lad, with dark hair. I sent a communication to Mister Silver as soon as I could.'

'You asked Toby?'

'To visit and perform that sad task.'

Surely the vicar could have identified the body? Identified it as someone other than Sam, at least, so Toby need not have been involved. Sam and the vicar had met dozens of times.

Nausea arrived a moment before I consciously solved the riddle: for the vicar to be unsure, the body would have had to be unrecognisable. In the water for weeks. Parts of him swelling, others dissolving. The close family might know marks by which he could still be recognised. I pressed my hand to my mouth, and only noticed I was doing it when my lips disliked the roughness of my grazed skin. The vicar closed his diary, bundled it away.

'Toby came back here?'

'Mister Silver told me there was no need.'

I could see the winter trees dancing outside the vicar's leaded window. It was as windy as it had been on the night of the Sully. 'But why not?'

'Because it couldn't, couldn't be his brother.'

'Couldn't be…?' He was echoing himself in his agitation, and I doubled the echo.

'I assumed there had been a resolution, which is a mercy, however unhappy.' A glib phrase. He must deliver so much bad news.

No, no resolution. 'Did you find out who he was? The other young man?'

'I did, I did *assume* he was another victim of the floods. We gave him a decent burial.'

He nodded deeply while he made his last comment, to reassure me. Decent? I felt briefly hysterical at the highly indecent idea of Sam, or me, or Ruth being buried in a Christian country churchyard by accident, rather than taking our rightful place in Willesden Cemetery. I calmed myself – there surely wouldn't be many other wandering Jews near Breakwater.

'How are your family, if I may?' he asked.

'Not entirely well. But thank you for asking.'

'Forgive me for not writing. We do get news, from Lucy, naturally.' Was it natural that my maid should be reporting on me? 'But you should know that I keep you all in my thoughts, and pray—' He cut himself off quite neatly. 'Pray *do* give your family my best regards, and Mister Silver. I've not seen him myself since he came here for business, some small matter, I can't recall – just after the accident. I believe it may have been about the use of the cottage.'

'Or the work on the river, I suppose.' Toby had been very proud of his gift to the village, the funds for a new drainage scheme.

'Oh, that was all completed, I believe.' The vicar shook himself a little. 'Most generous, a very charitable act. Mister Silver did take on so much responsibility, for a young man.' The vicar was too polite to say it, but Toby would have been the better elder brother. Sam, by contrast, made a fine prodigal.

The vicar rambled on about the burden of outliving, and how the bereaved always blame themselves. He was in pastoral mode again, rolling out his stock phrases. I wasn't bereaved, but he wasn't to know. 'Particularly other family members. I did reassure Mister Silver that nobody else would have seen it in a bad light, but there's only so much one can do. He is not his brother's keeper. Oh dear, my apologies! I didn't say *that* to him, I assure you.'

He had gone quite red. I wondered if he *had* quoted Cain at poor bereaved Toby. The vicar looked utterly wretched, now. Could I tell him Samuel was alive? No, the news would be round the village within hours.

'Miss Judith, this has been a very trying year for you. Are you keeping well? Some seeming comforts can do us harm. Do you have a good doctor?'

More polished phrases, but they panicked me. He was asking whether I was drunk, or wandering in my mind. Lucy had told tales against me, and now I'd travelled here alone, or with my imaginary sketching friend, to pursue my morbid obsessions. I needed tonics and lukewarm baths. How could I pull him away from this line of reasoning?

I told the vicar hastily that I had a very fine doctor, and that anyway, he'd set my mind at rest. The vicarage room felt cold, when it had always been cosy before.

At the door, he took my hand very sincerely and I guessed he was becoming sentimental over Ruth and me, poor fatherless girls, our mother a shambles. The vicar's wife had mothered us a little – teas, chats and tourist advice mixed in with womanly guidance. But the vicar was too feeble to be a father figure.

'Do please tell your wife that I'm sorry not to have seen her,' I said, a little late for manners.

He blinked. 'I'm afraid my wife passed away in January.'

I stumbled through an apology, a condolence. I didn't ask him how she'd died, but not asking took all my effort, and he read the question in my face.

'She took a chill at the Sully, then pneumonia.'

I pressed his hand again, for lack of words, and left.

The wind was less painful when it was at my back, as I trudged downhill towards the river. I was lost in sadness about that cheerful, bustling woman, the vicar's wife – and how could it be for the vicar, to lose his life companion? And with her, half his memory?

It took me a while, therefore, to note the strangeness in the vicar's account. The tall dead young man in the river. The idea of him dragged me like an undercurrent. Why had Toby not told us when the vicar had contacted him?

Then the graver question crashed over me: why had Toby said the body they'd recovered couldn't be Samuel?

A tall man, with dark hair. There could have been more to the vicar's description, some detail which had clarified it wasn't Sam. But Toby had been desperate. Even if there was the slightest chance…

I should have asked the vicar more questions. I could have been more charming, more gracious, a porcelain guest to match his tea set. Or I could have cried more to rinse the answers out of him. I stood and tussled with myself in the gale, turning back then pressing on again. Ella must have taken shelter in the church by now; she couldn't be sitting in the graveyard. My coat flapped and my grazed hand hurt me. Oh, and I'd meant to ask him about the search parties: who'd been sent, who might know more than they'd told. This had been a vain trip. No, an *arrogant* trip, badly planned. I wasn't Sherlock Holmes; I was barely Watson.

Ahead of me on the road was a woman wrapped in a fine knitted shawl. She loitered to intersect with me. I recognised her as I came closer: Lucy's mother. Her hair was chestnut like her daughter's, weathered into darker brown. Whenever we'd visited, Toby would write to her, and she'd send a girl from their dairy to make up the beds.

'Hullo,' I said. 'Mrs Winscott.'

'Oh! It's you, Miss Sachs.' She glared at me. I suspected she resented my family for poaching Lucy. 'Your family's all gone, then?'

'Yes, they're in Italy.' So Lucy did write home, and she had told her mother about my family's travels.

'Do you write to them?'

'I do when I have an address.'

'You wouldn't worry them though, would you? Not when they're away.'

What was she prodding me to say? 'I'd rather not.'

'Good girl. Have you seen Bonnie? My youngest?'

'No, I'm sorry.'

'Not anywhere?' She sounded vexed. Bonnie was probably late for a farming task where all hands were needed. 'You swear?'

'I've just come down from the vicarage. But I'm walking to the river. I'll look out for her.'

I walked fast to escape Mrs Winscott, and swiftly reached the river.

At the riverbank, I was cheered by the sight of brick embankments, signs of Toby's programme of works. Parts of the riverbed had been dug out deeper (we'd seen great heaps of slimy earth excavated), and stretches of the river had been confined in new brick channels. Toby had told us that higher banks and stronger bridges meant paths and roads would stay passable in winter, enabling local trade. Across the water, I could see the great water meadows which, when we first visited, had been a patchwork of pools and brambles. Today sheep grazed there, on firm ground. This had all been put in place during the summer after we arrived. If nature was a puzzle to city dwellers, in this instance Toby had solved it.

Toby had insisted that he and Sam were in debt to the village – that now they were residents, they had to make a contribution. Sam had teased him: 'Acting the patriarch, Tobes?' Toby had spat back that Breakwater wasn't Sam's playground.

I'd been impressed by Toby's sense of obligation. My father always gave tzedakah, never turned down a charitable appeal, but we'd also never attempted grand philanthropy. Father wasn't selfish, but he hadn't grown up with wealth and he didn't know the rules. Toby, living next door, was from a different world.

I stood on one of the brick banks. There was less vegetation than there had been before the renovations, and the few weeds which had sprung up in summer were dying back. Cow parsley grew chest high but skeletal, and I snapped off a few heads to sketch them later. The brightest thing was the green moss.

I gazed down at the weir. The sound of it, the continuous foaming roar of the water, was mesmerising. Seeing plants in my hands, I had a fear I was becoming Ophelia, preparing to throw myself into the river. But the depths disgusted me, smelling of cow manure and rot. I hoped that the river might reveal a clue or method I'd not foreseen. The weir water was nearly clear, glass sliding over glass. It flowed out and down over the lip of the weir. The curve was smooth but had force behind it. Children, including Lucy's young sibling brood, paddled here, blocking the curve with their legs. The water would fly up in a jet of foam. It would often knock the children over, and Lucy watching from the bank would call them in.

No clues came to me. I kicked at the long grasses on the bank and mocked my own optimism. What could there have been? A magical stick from a memory tree?

An answer came: *There's rosemary, that's for remembrance*. That was Ophelia, again. *Pray, love, remember*. Simplistic, but insistent, and I had no better ideas. Downriver, I could see the garden of our old cottage, the sticks of bare rose bushes. I knew where I could find a rosemary bush.

The small leaded windows of the cottage showed no inhabitants, but I moved as quickly as I could. When I tore off a couple of rosemary stalks, the smell was instantaneous: deep green and medicinal. The sprigs were springy in my fist as I returned to the public path and the river. Now I was a way downstream from the clamouring weir, but the waters still roiled as they passed me. I brought my fist up to my face and opened my fingers, letting the scent open up my head, the memories flood in.

First had come shouts outside the cottage in the dark, then banging at the door. Astonishingly, Sam raced to open it. A whole crew of men had assembled outside, by the sound of it – had the vicar's friendship failed to protect us? – but thankfully, they didn't enter. I strained my ears: they were batting demands at Sam, their accents rough but rounded like Lucy's, and Sam's mellow tones answered them, charming them. It went on for an age, while my heart thundered and I thought of running upstairs to hide. But then both sides erupted into laughter.

Sam bounced back into the sitting room, utterly unharmed.

'Right – they're collecting the men for the Sully. I'm off!' He'd been accepted by the village men, for a night, and I could tell he rated it as a triumph. 'Toby, are you coming? Or are you going to stand on the banks with the children and the girls?'

It was only a mild poke, to ensure his brother would join in. But Ruth had come down to see what the noise was, and caught the tail end of the taunt.

'Sam?'

'My darling! I'm off with the fellows. We have our part to play.'

'But you were going to come with Judith and me, and watch.'

Sam could have turned kind, but doubled down on teasing: 'You can take care of one another, can't you? What, you're not nervous!'

'You said you would.' With their marriage so close, Ruth had become bolder.

Sam wrinkled his nose. 'This is how it's done. Got to stick to the rules, my dear. They're waiting for me!'

The cold crept in from the open door. The local men peered in at Ruth, impatient, slapping their arms around themselves and stomping.

Sam gazed over at me.

Sometimes, it's true, I had stepped in to speak in his favour. I could have done it, clumsily: *do let him go, Ruth, the two of us will have more fun together.* Or more sharply: *he only wants to show off!* But still helping him get his own way: *so let him do whatever foolish thing he's planned...*

I hopped up and fled to the kitchen instead.

I heard Sam relenting and making a little soothing speech to Ruth. I could only hear one word in five, but in short, Ruth had it lucky; he was the one who'd be up to his knees in a freezing river; he'd be envying her the whole time, she should wave to him whenever she could see him. They would, so soon, be together

for ever, and then Ruth would get sick of the sight of him!
Meanwhile, Judith would be perfect company – who could want
more than Judith?

Then he slunk round the kitchen door. He caught my eye
and gave a courtly dip of his head. He must have come to
recruit me to his side, to roll his eyes and ask for sympathy. Or
to apologise to me – that would be more honourable. Then he'd
charge me to take care of my sister and restore her mood, after
he left. He certainly looked abashed. His words to Ruth must
have worked on me, a little, as well, and I was willing to listen.
I wondered how he'd begin his appeal.

The silent moment elongated. He shrugged, and plucked a
bottle of beer from a crate in the corner, and headed out of the
cottage with the men.

I was angrier than his carelessness warranted, scorchingly
angry. The rowdy crowd passed down the side of the cottage, and
phrases could be heard through the kitchen window: 'Poor bloody
girl, shackled to an oaf… Better off without your ungrateful…'
Toby had wrongly judged they were out of earshot, and begun
to berate Sam for his lack of manners. Toby's reprimands had a
lightening effect on me, as though I'd handed him my displeasure,
to carry it away. But I still had to linger a while in the kitchen,
until my blood cooled.

Then Ruth and I layered on every garment we had, and I
muddled myself up in a jumper and let Ruth rescue me. I resented
lifting her spirits when Sam had brought them down, but I also
couldn't leave her low. When we spotted the crowds of people
passing the cottage windows, we stepped out and joined the flow,
shocked by the cold despite our preparations. Lucy came with
us, wrapped up in a clumsy knitted scarf and mittens. Strangers
pressed around us tightly, but I was grateful, because it kept the
chill away. A few torches gave little heat but lit up the angular,
over-reaching trees.

I was in that curious state I often experienced at folk ceremonies: an elated, watchful acceptance. Ruth would tap my arm, ask a question, fret about what she didn't understand. I didn't need to understand. I could tuck a memory away and find out the truth of it later. My teeth began to chatter, and I stuck my hands under my arms. This was the right night; this was the right spot.

Sudden sharp cracks rang out, and I ducked. But the women around us laughed and kept on weaving down the high street. Ruth whispered to me, asking *what was that? Is it dangerous?* I moved my head away from her and pretended not to hear. Lucy had vanished into the crowd, probably to find her sister. I didn't mind. We didn't need a maid tonight.

More cracks, and cries, and the sound of water churning, as loud as a waterfall.

We were near the edge of the river and I couldn't see over the heads of the crowd. Suddenly the vicar and his wife were at our side, clouds of their frozen breath rolling about us. The vicar's wife wrapped Ruth's shawl more carefully under her chin, worried (even though we were entirely swaddled) that our city clothes weren't adequate to the occasion. She wasn't wrong; despite two pairs of socks I couldn't feel my toes. The vicar held his hand out as an invitation, and Ruth and I followed them up onto the bridge. The packed people shuffled aside for him grudgingly, including Lucy and her sister. Bonnie had swathed her head in an embroidered scarlet scarf, which cast her profile as a striking cameo, while the rest of us were like scarecrows in our wrappings. The bridge was one of the new constructions funded by Toby's benevolence, wood beams resting on stone pilings, and a wooden handrail. I pulled my arms in, as tight as I could, and wriggled round to face the water.

There was a riot in the river.

Men stood everywhere across the span of the channel and

downriver for about a hundred yards. Many of them hefted great wooden paddles; you could see them come up, shiny and wet in the lamplight, and then crash down, driven with all the strength of their owner into the water.

Tiny droplets needled my face. We were too close packed for me to lift my arm, to wipe them away.

'Most of them are very old,' the vicar piped up. 'The paddles. They have patterns etched on them. I don't believe I've seen them up close…'

'You haven't seen them, my dear,' his wife confirmed.

'But I believe they're burned into the wood. Now, what is that called…?'

'Pyrography, love?'

Their warbling information was leaching away the mystery of it, so I ignored them, trying instead to hear the shouts of the beaters.

The cheerful violence of it was intoxicating. Men were crashing away next to one another, with paddles and sticks and whatever they could hold. One wielded a cricket bat. I was astonished that each man wasn't felled by the man behind him, in sudden rough slaughter. The water was thrown up in a silvery froth all over the scene. I flinched at the cold rain, pinned in place by the press of the cloud, steam-breath surrounding me.

The vicar's wife nudged me and wriggled enough to press a flask of hot cordial into my hand. It thawed my fingers but I couldn't get it to my mouth.

More cracks rang out. I gasped, and saw the source of the sounds: a couple of men carried long whips and were cracking them over the water, just above the bent backs of their companions.

My eyes, still adapting to the dark, could see the men more and more clearly. The river was up to their thighs, at least, and they were braced against the flow. It must have been extraordinarily painful to stand in that cold current. There was raucous hooting, triumphal singing. That, too, was familiar to me from other folk rites I'd seen. It was so satisfying. It spoke to the ire inside me.

It resembled a scene of work, not celebration. A threshing barn, or a brewery where the hops were shovelled. I saw that for many of them it was a parody of their daily work: the blacksmith beating, the farmer digging.

At that moment, I saw Sam in the middle of them.

He was hefting as much – in shirtsleeves, smiting with a stick. But his 'old' clothes were better than the farmers' Sunday suits. This might be the only hard work he did this year.

Ruth clasped my hand, as she'd seen him too. She seemed to have forgiven him and was now enjoying the sight of him, toiling away. Sam looked up at the bridge and waved and beckoned. Safe for him to concede to us, now we couldn't go down to him.

'You really do like him, don't you?' I asked Ruth. She didn't hear, or heard and didn't answer. I turned my face away from Sam.

The night was a glorious paradox. On one hand, we knew what was happening. Ruth and I had read the right books, understood the great symbolic principles. The men were disciplining the river, to make it work for them for the rest of the year. But, at the same time, why? Why stand in freezing water and beat it with your grandfather's paddle – which the vicar isn't allowed to see – with its mysterious pyrographic design? The Sully had elements which couldn't be abstracted.

I was thrilled to watch without knowing.

When a higher-pitched shouting began, I thought it was part of the ritual.

Behind us, upstream, it intensified to shrieking.

The flood had hurried down from the hills. It had been persistent but not ferocious for most of its journey, gathering strength from every tributary. Coming close to Breakwater, the river narrowed, building the water up and up, making it run faster. By the time it reached our footbridge, it was a stinking, murky wall.

There were screams and I tried to turn, but I was wedged helplessly in place. The bridge was too packed. There was a sudden shove – dozens of people trying to rush off the bridge, all at once. I lost my footing, but I couldn't fall. The crush around me bore me up and squeezed me breathless.

I didn't see the wave at all. I had been looking downstream, unable to turn. If I remembered a sight of it – smooth, dark, rolling – it could only be my imagination.

A roaring crash, and the bridge juddered. Cold smashed into me, striking my whole back. I couldn't gasp; I couldn't expand my chest enough to breathe. I would suffocate.

The crush eased a little and I gulped in air, so thankful. Then cries came from downriver – not ritual shouting, but wailing.

I could breathe because the people crushing me had fallen off the bridge.

With fewer people to hold me up I stumbled. I had a hand on the planks of the bridge and tried to push myself up. A heel came down on my knuckles, agonising until it rolled off again, and I snatched both my hands back. I needed to find Ruth. She was crying, close by me; I recognised her voice despite the clamour of the panicking crowd. I shuffled on my knees, shoving aside strangers, until Ruth's hands reached me and we hauled each other up.

Clutching at one another, we were able to force our way out of the chaos and struggle off the bridge. The fleeing people swept us along towards the village high street.

But Ruth pulled at my arm: 'Sam.'

We went back.

The river was full of lumps of mud, and the water gushed around them. They were the bodies of men labouring to stand, as though they were being born from the ooze, masterless golems. Hands thrust up, found nothing to seize and fell back.

Crawling closer to the shore, they became ruthless. Booted feet trod on bodies and faces. Men using their friends as ladders and bridges.

I rushed to the bank, holding out my hands to them, and they used me, too. Half a dozen slippery hands, one by one, grabbed at my arms and the men hauled themselves ashore.

That was what we saw, then.

Everything else I know, I learned later. That the worst force hadn't hit the men on the weir, as the wave had broken against the footbridge. But the men had all fallen, and ten had been swept away downriver.

The raucous cawing of crows pulled me back to the present. They flapped across the white sky above me, tumbled about by the wind, desperate to perch but blown onwards.

I was shocked by the clarity of my memories. Were Sam's preserved as well, but in a better-locked box? What could I take back to the city to unlock him? There were no postcards of this village, the flat sliding weir.

Not images. I would take back with me true sights, new sensations. Walking into the weeds that grew at the side of the river, I bent over to pick them. I worried at their coarse stems with my thumbnail until they snapped, or ripped them up by the roots, until I had a whole bunch of not-flowers. The yarrow fronds were green and delicate; the ferns were dry amber. It was ridiculous. Would Sam even have noticed the local plants? Would he have touched them? Crumbled dry ferns and crushed seed-heads? But it felt right to pick them.

I carried my bleak bouquet up the street. The vicar had spoken of burdens: responsibility, blame. It hadn't been my fault that Sam fell. But it was my responsibility to try to restore him, now.

As I'd predicted, Ella wasn't in the churchyard. In all our visits to Breakwater I'd never entered the church before, not wanting to worry Mama, or provoke the villagers by trespass. Nobody was here to witness me, but the stiffness of the iron door handle matched my reluctance. As I stepped inside I smelled beeswax polish and snuffed candles. The church was silent except for the scratching of charcoal on paper. Ella was busy, seated in the front pew.

I walked down the main aisle, looking around at the jumble of symbols in the stained-glass windows. A lion and a cow, both holding pens and wearing wings – awkward figures. I inspected the seats, the leaves carved into the wood, striking and rather pagan. Some of my old curiosity returned: where did the church touch edges with rituals like the Sully? Breakwater's vicar embraced the village rites, which was either cowardly of him, or supple.

Ella was drawing an eagle from a carved wooden book-rest. It had a magnificent fierce scowl. Ella masked off sections of her sketch with her hands, to check she had the proportions right. She eased a careful pencil line down over its neck. The bird rather resembled Mrs Fortune. When she saw me she broke off, sensed I had no wish to linger and walked with me to the door.

Outside, the wind caught the pages of Ella's sketchbook and I had to help her pack it away. I envied her sketches of gravestones, candlesticks, ironwork. I had no art, only a book full of vegetation of questionable value. A wasted day and wasted money for the train.

'Did you get what you wanted?' asked Ella.

Dismal memories, no answers, and a new impossible question.

'Oh, absolutely.'

Viewed from the train, there were long spells of dark fields between the pinprick lights from individual farmhouses. I felt quite empty, and longed to see the tight-packed well-lit city.

I sorted the plants I'd gathered, laying them into the back half of my sketchbook. I took the pamphlet Ella's mother had given me, and slotted it in to protect the paper from crushed plant juices. The fattened book barely fitted back into my satchel.

I stood, ignored Ella's quizzical look. It wasn't an outlandish activity, I could have collected them for a nature study, or as a border for poor Maimonides. 'Ella?' I risked mockery to get conversation.

'Mmm?' She was gazing out of the window.

'What would you do if you wanted to remember a thing?'

'Tie a knot in my handkerchief. Write it in my notebook. Write it on my face, but backwards, to see in the mirror in the morning.'

'Something you'd already forgotten.'

'Too late, then, isn't it? I don't know. Try to picture the last place I put it.' She was sing-song, imitating her mother, and mine, and all mothers. 'Retrace my steps.'

I should have brought Sam to Breakwater. I'd judged it too risky, but we could have devised a way to disguise him. The riverbank had been dense with sensations I couldn't describe – bird calls, the way each footstep was unreliable on wet ground. He could have felt that.

'Did you leave something behind in the village? Scatty.'

'No, it's more like…' I searched for a comparison which wouldn't expose me. 'Knowing you saw a painting, but you can only describe the mood of it, or some of the colours. Not what it was, or where it was hanging.'

'I'd draw. Use charcoal. Just make a lot of shapes and see where they took me.'

'The way a medium does automatic writing?'

'Ugh, no.' So she didn't share her mother's hobbies. 'Like a warm-up exercise. Like we've done in class. Move the hand, jog the memory.' Then a greater look of horror came over her face. 'What have you done to your hand?'

My hand lay on the arm of my seat, scraped red in a trail disappearing up my coat sleeve, topped off with a spattering of green plant juice.

'It's fine.' I took it back into my lap.

'You need to look after it! The exam's next week, you can't do it with an *infection*...'

'I'll wash it when we're home.'

I wasn't troubled by my injuries. I was cataloguing all the things that Toby did after Sam's accident. Things I hadn't told Sam about. Toby had sent telegrams to hospitals and the police, written to vicars and mayors all through the county to ask if any strangers had come to their towns and villages. It had been doubly frustrating because Christmas had slowed the mail, and made it unlikely that people would respond. Toby had been so busy.

Or so he'd said.

I was jumping to conclusions. But I couldn't help wondering: how much of that did Toby actually *do*? If he wouldn't come to look at a body – in the right river, looking a little like Sam – then had he made other efforts? Upright Toby, not like twisty Sam. Could I not rely on sober old Toby?

I grew sad at how little I had to offer Samuel. No real news, a few scraps of information, a heap of suspicions. The vicar was anxious, Lucy's mother was demanding, Sam's brother was – what?

I saw street-lamps whizz by, and finally the great bright arches of the terminus. I clung to the hope that because of today's trip, I could ask Sam more vivid questions. *How did it feel when your feet slipped out from under you? Did you scrabble at the mud? When did the water close over your head?*

'I think that Toby may not have told us the truth.'

'Toby?' Sam snorted. 'Toby doesn't have enough imagination to lie!'

We were sitting in the library, with a revived fire driving out the chill of the evening. I was trying to tell Sam about Breakwater without mentioning the dead man in the river, wanting to spare him that. Lucy had taken my hint, and my money, and hadn't been in the house all day, according to Sam. Sam had spread my crushed plants out on the desk, and was haphazardly rearranging them, like cards in a game of patience (which he often played when it was rainy, despite having no aptitude and cheating). I had worried that the plants were an odd gift, but they were quite at home here, matching the dried foliage all round the room, that Ruth and I had brought indoors for decoration. Foliage which might need refreshing, I admitted; the bunches of rowan berries over the window frames were very dusty.

I'd set a plate of bread with pickled cucumber in front of me and I was drawing Sam while eating. It lent me confidence.

'Toby told the vicar to stop looking, in effect,' I explained. 'To call off the search. In January, without speaking to any of us about it.'

'Well, that was weeks afterwards. They wouldn't be able to rescue me then.' Sam grinned. He tugged out one flaking fern from my collection and sent it into the fireplace. It sputtered into flame before it could reach the coals.

'Toby stopped expecting to find you, in any state at all.' I would have to mention the dead man. 'The vicar saw a man who could have been you.' I sketched a lock of Sam's hair curling across one of his ears.

'Did he speak to him?'

'He wasn't alive.'

'He saw a *ghost*?'

'A body.'

'Oh! I see. Yes. People show bodies to vicars.' Sam's amusement drained away. 'He didn't want to see the body that might have been mine. Gah! Jude, this is so confusing.'

I was calling his brother a liar. It could get very confusing indeed.

'Let's be logical,' Sam said. 'He didn't come and look at the body they recovered. Why not?'

I wouldn't slander his brother. There had to be a task to take me away for a couple of minutes, while he reflected. My eyes fell on a wine bottle, standing on a bookshelf. Why not? Walking over, I read the label: Tokay, which could have been white or red, fair or foul, for all I knew.

Would Sam object? When I brought the corkscrew out from the desk drawer, he offered: 'Shall I do that?' He'd abandoned the foliage and settled into a chair by the fire. My chair, but it was ridiculous to object to his adopting it.

'Oh, I'll try. I've seen other people do it.' I watched the corkscrew sink into the cork, as familiar to me as drawing a curtain. I had to use my elbow to hold the bottle while I pulled it, because of the grazed skin on my hand.

'Are you hurt?' Sam asked, and when I ignored him: 'Should you let it stand?'

'How long for?' A delicious smell emanated from the open bottle-neck.

'Twenty minutes?' he suggested.

I would give it ten by the library clock.

'So, what do you think Toby meant by it?' I asked, taking a seat in Ruth's chair, opposite him.

'Maybe Toby knew I was already dead.'

We solemnly contemplated this in silence. Then we both burst out laughing. I covered my face and tried to stop it, then looked back at Sam and saw his shoulders shaking and it set me off again. Horrible-hilarious images filled my mind: Sam, dead, bobbing around and waving to get attention. Sam, being eaten by little river fishes, swatting them away, saying: 'Excuse me, I'm not dead, actually.'

'I mean he *thought* I was dead. He thought he knew I was dead.'

'Yes.' Why would he assume that, though? What had he seen, or thought he'd seen?

That night, Toby had climbed with the others out of the mire. He'd stood, with my help, but his legs would hardly bear him. Toby hadn't thought Sam dead then, I was sure of it. He'd tried to turn back into the river straight away, wanted to join the search himself, until the doctor told him not to be fanciful and gave him the sedative. Toby surely wouldn't have been so frantic to assist if he'd known Sam was dead.

As far as I knew, Toby had received no more information since he saw Sam fall. We'd known that a man long missing is increasingly unlikely to be alive.

When had Toby truly changed his mind? When had he given up?

'Or the opposite,' Sam said. 'He knew I *wasn't* dead.'

When he came ashore, he was terrified Sam might be drowned. Between the Sully and a few weeks later, he had made up his mind, one way or another. I poured myself a glass of wine.

'Perhaps…' I tried not to gulp the wine, bitter and spicy. 'He had news that he kept from the rest of us.'

'Oh, yes. Probably.'

He agreed so easily that it bewildered me.

'He'd have kept it from you to spare you,' he said. 'Toby's an odd beggar but he'd always let someone else off the hook. If he could protect you – and Ruth, naturally – he would.'

But we had all suspected the worst. And the waiting was awful. Why not face the truth? Of course, now that Sam was sitting opposite me, the truth had lost its sting. I made myself nod. 'I see that, yes.' But I didn't see at all.

'I remember you saying he seemed odd, afterwards,' Sam said.

'Odd?' Broken, at first. Restless and frustrated, later.

'Sort of… remorseful?' Had I said that, exactly? 'Maybe you said *secretive*. Or *changeable*. If he was hiding the truth from you, that might explain it.' He leaned forwards, drummed his fingers on the desk, looked at me hungrily. 'Anyway, what should we do now?'

'We might contact the same places Toby wrote to. Police stations and vicarages. We could ask if there was any news.' Would Sam say no? Yesterday, he'd refused to let me place advertisements in the papers, but this was more discreet.

'Yes! You should do that.' No objections, all eagerness. That was what I'd wanted, but I felt a flash of annoyance. He was delighted to let me work, but I had an examination to prepare for. He saw me frown. 'Judith, I can't do it myself, can I? I can't pop up and ask people if they've seen me since I died.'

'I suppose not.' I realised I'd not told him my decision to sit the exam. So he was only half as selfish as he seemed.

He grinned. 'You're brilliant, little detective. Thank you for doing so much.' He reached over to the desk and plucked up the Breakwater plants.

'You're doing the most important part,' I reminded him. 'You're trying to remember.' Wasn't he? How was he trying?

'It's only day one. I've got a week, haven't I?'

I gritted my teeth. The week was the absolute outside limit, not a space for Sam to stretch out and make himself at home. A head of cow parsley, tossed by Sam into the fire, went up in a crackle, and some glowing fragments flew out onto the rug. I stamped them dead. 'How is it? More clear?'

'It still feels like a missing tooth. No, bigger. A missing hand. I need to do it for Ruth, I know. But is it any use?'

'Do the questions help?'

'They're very good questions.' Liar. 'I like it when you help me.' That sounded more sincere. 'I wish I could do more. I can't go anywhere, or help with anything…' He picked up another piece of dry fern and fretted it to flakes between his fingers.

I set aside my sketchbook. I'd pursue the channels tomorrow, sensibly. 'Would you try another experiment?'

Fresh paper covered the library desk. I fetched sticks of charcoal and pencils, the things that most easily made a mark. We built up the fire until the air felt fuzzy.

I explained my plan – Ella's plan, really.

His eyes shone.

'You're a genius. That sounds an excellent idea, Judith, excellent. Sidle around the gap in my memory. How do I do it?'

'You should be relaxed and be able to move your hand easily.' I was making up the rules on the spot, but as I spoke, I felt that reassuring nudge that had guided me through other rituals. How to thread a hagstone on a blade of grass, how to smoothly move a knife and free the apple from its peel. I didn't need to know why a thing would work, to feel when it was right.

Sam brought a dining chair over to the library desk and threw himself down onto it. He was far too alert to be truly relaxed, but I gathered armfuls of cushions and he propped them around himself.

'This is good.' He moved his arm around on the page in experimental swirls.

'Fold your shirt cuffs in,' I advised.

'What?'

'You'll get charcoal on them.' I rolled a stick across the desk to Sam, and he tucked his cuffs away in his jacket sleeves and picked it up.

'So do I just give it a go, or…'

I considered how I might stir up his imagination without directing it.

'Think about a day in Breakwater,' I began. 'It's winter, there are bare trees full of noisy crows, sheep grazing, women wearing shawls.' I would have forgotten half of this if I hadn't revisited.

The movement of his hand startled me. I looked up into his face and he had his eyes closed. He seemed to be listening to me intently.

'The river's ruffled from the wind but it's smooth where it goes over the weir.'

He drew a line, smooth and straight, until it broke into squiggles at the foot of the page.

It was enjoyable to instruct him. But – I reminded myself – I didn't want him following my instructions. I wanted him to uncover things I couldn't know.

'What do you recall about that day?'

He was motionless, but I let the silence settle.

His hand twitched left and right. Small, irritable jerking movements.

A sudden drop, the charcoal moving to another part of the page. Curves: luxurious, winding, curling inside one another.

Staining one of the curves, a little dark mark. Another dot, spreading. The dots joined, turning into a dark spiral.

Suddenly Sam was jabbing the charcoal into the paper, splintering it, smashing the stick to ashes.

'Oh!' Sam gave a startling jolt. He opened his eyes and examined his efforts. 'What do you think all that is?'

'You say first.'

'I don't know. I felt quite happy here, contented, but I don't know why.' He traced the curves. 'And here...' He nudged the pile of ash. 'I felt horrible.'

'Horrible how?'

'As though I'd been utterly shameful, dark and shameful – I wanted to soap my mouth, it was so disgusting. If only I could draw better! You don't know how lucky you are, Judith, being able to make beautiful things.'

The praise was too distracting. I would savour it later. 'But you don't want to create a polished picture. You want to think in images.'

'I don't, though. I've got the artistic equivalent of a tin ear. I think in words.'

'You could write, then.'

'Judith, I could kiss you. How would that work?'

For a moment, I thought: *how would kissing me work?* It wouldn't. Then I understood.

'Try the same thing. But write instead of drawing.' I couldn't think of another way to phrase it. 'Like a medium.'

He didn't understand. 'Mediums? Don't they speak to ghosts? Do they take dictation?'

'They do automatic writing, as well – they put their pen on the paper and wait for inspiration, or dictation, I don't know what.' I could have asked Ella's mother, Mrs Leon.

'Oh, their guides guide them, probably,' Sam said. 'Or the spirits speak to them, and they write great reams of stuff. But we don't want to contact the dead.'

'No! It was only an analogy.'

'Unless you think I'm dead and I need to contact myself.' He dropped his voice: 'Samuel Silver! Am I there? Speak to me!'

'Sam…'

'Samuuuel!' A brocade patchwork lay on the sofa and he pulled it up and over his head, a medium in mystical robes. 'Look, I could be good at this!' When I didn't admire his garb, he flipped the tasselled edge at me.

'Stop it!'

I had snapped at him because I was still irked by Mrs Leon's pamphlet. And I was annoyed by her because I'd considered consulting a medium. During the months when we hadn't been sure if Sam was lost, or worse. A medium, I'd reasoned, might be able to tell us. Ruth and I had dabbled in more ridiculous practices, over the years, and while we'd never really discussed it in terms of belief or truth, we'd felt *things*, intangible things. And we weren't credulous people – we could thoroughly research it, hire the best charlatan. But when I made tentative investigations, I'd experienced it as quite unlike our old hobbies: a world of mystified gabble. None of it felt easy to the hand. I had been aggrieved that there was no solution, and resented myself for being tempted.

'I'm sorry,' I said to Sam.

'I know, it's all tosh. You're much too sensible to want to try that.'

I didn't reply. We hadn't been sensible. In the end, a deciding factor had been Mama's temper; she would have been furious if she'd heard about it. She'd overlooked a lot of our esoteric hobbies, as long as we kept them between ourselves and went to shul, but she had drawn the line at Ruth and I dabbling with the dead.

His face fell. 'Oh, Judith,' he said. 'You didn't, did you? With me?'

'No. Not in the end.'

'Good. I wouldn't have been at home to callers.' He pulled the quilt up round his shoulders. 'Could I keep this? While

I'm still staying here, I mean.' He was changing the subject for my sake.

'Of course, please do.'

'It's only that I'm cold most of the time.'

'There are more blankets in the wardrobe in your room, I think.'

'I saw them, thank you.'

'Put as much coal on the fire as you want,' I said generously, having no idea how I'd afford more if we ran out.

'How should I write?'

'The same way?'

Again the cushions were arranged; again, holding a pencil, his hand idled across a clean sheet of paper. He shut his eyes and began to scribble. Dancing hooks and meaningless curlicues at first. Then words, a small spat-out series of them.

Hated tainted taunted

'Bit pretentious, that,' he murmured.

Ewe yoo yoŭouou

He spun out swoops and loops but they didn't form letters. Then words came:

jill tup rush rash

I watched the point of the pencil hovering, twitching, waited for it to begin again.

'It's no good,' he said, startling me. 'I'm thinking too much, now. I can't not know what I'm writing.'

'Could you distract yourself? Listen to music, or walk around while you write, carry a notebook with you.' My suggestions might have been a little frantic. I didn't want to lose momentum. 'If you tried it when I wasn't here…'

'I don't think it's you, Judith. I think it's me. But I'll try again tomorrow when you're out.'

He looked at the sheet, tapped the words with his index finger as if that would make them yield up meaning.

'What do you think it means?' I asked before he dropped the topic. I had no notions. Mrs Leon might have the expertise to interpret.

He tapped the last line, *rush rash*. 'I've been careless? I suppose I did fall in the river. I'm always clumsy – it made Toby wild!'

I pictured Toby, his fists balled on his hips, in a soaring oration about Sam's faults. When? Of course: we'd been at Ottery St Mary, and a careless gesture from Sam had propelled Toby towards a burning tar barrel.

Sam caught my eye. 'One more try?'

It was different this time. The room was stuffy but vibrated in a new way. Sam's pencil began to jump and dart, faster than the last time. The paper moved around, so Sam pinned it down with his free hand, which crooked his arm around so I couldn't read the words. I watched Sam's face instead, his expression amused at first, then taken aback, then appalled as his hand still scribbled. His lips parted, I swear he blushed.

He shifted his shoulder to further prevent me from seeing. But was it even writing, now? Clawing, a series of graunching downward drags, ripping the paper, scarring the desktop. I shouldn't have begun this. It was too close to a séance, too close to putting Sam in contact with the dead.

But it was working.

An almighty judder ran through him. I heard the lead snap, and the pencil still drag itself to-and-fro dully for a while, until it slowed and halted.

I listened, and watched his chest rise and fall smoothly. He wasn't crying. Slowly, I reached over to take the paper.

Sam crumpled the paper and curled himself around it. 'Don't look!' he told me. Not angry, but as a warning.

'But there might be a sign…' A mysterious symbol or a name that I could build on. I reached out again, more determined this time. Sam sprang up from his chair and turned his back on me. His patchwork cloak blocked my sight, and I was forced to step back or fall. I heard him crumpling the paper into a tight ball, and then the brief puff and roar as he tossed it on the fire.

He stood and hoisted the brocade quilt round his shoulders. He looked flimsy and cold.

'I'll turn in. Goodnight, Judith. Thanks for all your help. I truly mean it.' He tried to catch my eye again. Now he was all contrition. 'We'll be able to tell Ruth soon, yes?' He reached out, his fingers smudged with charcoal, and placed his hand heavily on my shoulder. 'Will you send me more questions?'

'I'll try.'

His feet fell too heavily on the stairs. I tried to make out from his footsteps whether he'd paused at my bedroom door again.

Downstairs, Lucy was laying out another set of bowls and spoons. She looked neat as a pin, as if she was making up for being seen in her bedclothes this morning, and for taking the day off. On the table beside her was one of Cook's recipe books, *An Easy and Economical Guide to Jewish Cookery*, open at 'Remarks on Sweets'. I recalled that the book was dedicated to Baroness de Rothschild, which spoke to its quality, if not its sense of economy.

Lucy must know Sam was in the house, must have been listening out and deliberately avoiding him. I waited for her to bring him up, whether with indignation or astonishment. She only hummed a greeting.

I plucked a jug from a shelf and carried it to the tap, calling over my shoulder to Lucy as it filled. 'I did go to Breakwater. I saw your mother.'

'Oh?'

'She didn't have any messages.'

'She wrote me last week, Miss.'

I turned off the tap and picked up the jug in both hands. 'The pie was absolutely delicious,' I added.

''Course.'

I hadn't expected my compliment to be batted back at me. I tried to expand my praise: 'I'll have more tomorrow. I'm looking forward to it.'

'There be none left.'

How? Even after Sam's depredations, there had been three pies left intact. It wasn't the first time that leftovers had been unaccounted for. Lucy would coax me to try a single slice, and then the whole dish would vanish. I suspected Lucy had a hearty appetite, but adhered to a servant's rule that she couldn't eat until I'd cut the first portion. Or Lucy was poisoning me through her baking. I often felt sick these days. Cakes might be disappearing because Lucy was disposing of the evidence.

'I'll make summat else, though. Go on, tell me what to make.' She gestured at the bowls, the depleted store cupboards.

I had no idea what she wanted me to say. Could she make me latkes, without Cook's help? I recalled we had, in the pantry, an ancient jar of mixed dried fruit. 'I like fruitcake,' I muttered.

'Good!' Her tone said: *that wasn't so hard, was it?* 'I'll make fruitcake.' She turned aside from the *Easy and Economical Guide*, and flipped open the cover of *Enquire Within Upon Everything*, a large and venerable household encyclopaedia.

I sat up in my bed to write questions for Sam, as he'd requested, to salvage a morsel from the day.

Sam had mentioned his 'tin ear' for images. I considered the simplest regular sight, and wrote: *What do you see when you open your eyes in the morning? Think about how much light is in the room. Where is the window?* In case he recalled sleeping in a hay loft.

Then thoughts of Lucy intruded: *Who was the last person you argued with?*

As I wrote, my hand ached where I'd grazed it. Sam had said that last year was like a lost tooth – an uncanny, fleshy thing. So I wrote: *What was the last injury you had?*

Was that too near the knuckle? What had he suffered? Skull cracked, vomiting river water. I considered leaving that question out. But no, it was the ideal question to ask. He might have muscular memories without words, of a fever or a wrenching cough, and then (with my help) he'd be able to see the cottage hospital, or the kind baker's house, in which he recuperated. I must write tomorrow, I reminded myself, to the hospitals, as well as the vicars and the police.

Thinking of Sam sleeping, I thought of flesh, I thought of his fear of a lost wife. *Did you sleep alone?* I didn't add that question to the sheet.

Some questions were too consequential to be asked idly. After Father's death, when Ruth had spoken with our family solicitor, laying out the new conditions of our lives: the income which could not be increased and the expenditures which must be cut. Mama would not come to heel.

'Why should I tolerate this?' asked Mama. 'Why should I not go back to Frankfurt, to my father, who still loves and misses me?'

No mention of taking us with her. The cruel question hung between the three of us.

Then Ruth had replied, 'Why *don't* you go, then?'

I wonder if she had hoped Mama would say: 'Because of you, my dear girls!' Mama was silent. But after that, she kept to her allowance. Two terribly cruel questions, and no answer for either of them.

I thought of Sam's hand, heavy on my shoulder, and the question I wanted to ask him, and wouldn't: *Do you remember how I longed for you?*

I'd wanted him so much. The strangeness of his return had let me press down that knowledge for two days now. But I was all hollowed out, leaving my heart hammering in the empty space of my chest. What had I asked, at the Sully, pushed against Ruth in the crowd? *You really do like him, don't you?* Why had I asked that? Had I been trying – with sarcasm, because I was too raw for sincerity – to find a chink in Ruth's affection? *Do you really like him? If you don't, is there a chance for me?*

But it had been a perverse, impractical passion. No wonder that a day of frustration, not of joy, had recalled it to me now. Wanting him more, I recalled, had made me like him less. I was annoyed at his enthusiasms, his snippet-knowledge of a dozen things. His extravagance. His wild gestures; what a waste of his gorgeous hands, to wave them around imitating an orchestral conductor. (But if he hadn't, I wouldn't have been able to watch them so easily.)

Fortunately, I had kept a sense of proportion. As strongly as I recollected my infatuation, I knew the feeling of shoving it away, over and over. Never speaking about my love, and never writing it down, or creating any object to commemorate it. I hadn't dwelled on it when I was with him because it was too mortifying. I had never brought it to mind when I was with my sister, because it was too disloyal. And I had always been with my sister.

A thing never spoken is unreal. It was true in the tiny pockets of time between putting out the lamp and falling asleep. That was the sole time I allowed myself to think of him. At first, I'd tried to make him speak incredible words, complex explanations, that would make it right for us: 'Your sister has cast me off.' But I'd never heard him speak of serious things, of love. When I put those powerful words into his mouth ('Your sister loves another, and I…'), he'd deliver them like a bad actor.

Instead I pictured him simply standing in my room, where he had never been, and I'd walk over to him and kiss him. I'd even tell him not to speak. Standing next to him, on tiptoe, I imagined what it would feel like to have to tilt my head back to let him kiss me. Sitting beside him, leaning into him, kissing. I only kissed him. I didn't know what else to do.

When he died, that scorched the love out of me. I'd slept with my sister so we could comfort one another. The injunction I'd placed on myself, never to think of him in her presence, now covered my nights as well.

I caught myself wondering: what if he hasn't died? What if he's run away? He'll send for me. He'll say: 'My love for you makes any life with your sister a lie. I could not leave her except by deception, but if you will live with me, two outcasts...' No, he'd never talk that way. 'Look, Judith, I couldn't give her the push. But come and live in Paris with me, we'll get on fantastically.'

I was turning my sister's widowhood into a story, and the happy ending was that I stole her fiancé. I was so ashamed that I stopped thinking about it at all.

Sitting up in bed, I willed my heart to resume its normal rhythm. Had I really been that ruthless, that sensible? Could I do it again? I suspected there were other memories, writhing just beyond my reach, too excruciating to examine.

At least, this time, I'd already set a limit. It would only be a week until our proximity ended. Until then, I wouldn't think of it, wouldn't speak of it. And I wouldn't ask any questions which couldn't be taken back.

I finished my list, folded the paper and it under Sam's door.

Lying in bed, I could hold my body still, but my imagination ranged all around the house. It seized on every clue that Sam had left, that Lucy would stumble across: his handwritten rambles in the library, the patchwork dragged into the wrong room. In the same delirious inventory I noted every sign of impropriety:

doors shut, chairs drawn close together, charcoal fingerprints on my clothes.

On the floor of the hall I saw a trail of prints where I'd scampered from the library with my feet wet and bare. My journeys to fetch cocoa and blankets for Sam were all recorded in lake water. Beside that, another set of marks, more laboriously printed and more clear: Sam's footprints, as he trudged towards the stairs. Bigger than mine, and muddled with mine, they were both a clue and a scandal. The virtuous Imogen, in oils on the wall, cowered away from them. Lucy would surely notice them.

Then I saw, among them, a third set of prints. As small as mine, but steadier, a whole foot solidly planted. These weren't just a trace of water, but mud: thick oozing ochre. Where Sam walked, they walked alongside him. I pictured their two bodies, the mud woman catching up with him, insinuating herself under his arm, until they moved in step. He was weak, so he leaned on her strong limbs of clay. I was bodiless and couldn't help him, confined to an agony of jealousy.

Sam's prints veered away from the route I knew he'd taken. In reality, we'd walked up the stairs together, but here his footprints made a slow circle. The mud woman was steering him back to the door, back to the garden and across the grass. Back into the shallows, past shards of floating ice, embracing as they went down into the darkness.

FRIDAY

Dearest Judith,
Venice is heaven.

My morning headache ground at me. I was dreary after yesterday's experiment and the wave of maudlin memories it had brought me. Too many memories for me, none for Samuel. I again regretted not taking Sam to Breakwater, making him stand by the river.

The letter was a loving hug, a sweet distraction. Snatching it off the mat, I opened it as I left the house and savoured the opening words. Then I couldn't read and walk, so I thrust the letter into my satchel. In Hyde Park, in the foggy distance, I saw great heaped shapes: bonfires, if Sam was right, waiting to be ignited. I'd not tried to find Sam before I left, or Lucy, because I hadn't enough time to be brave. I ran over my plan for the day: art first, then leaving class early again, to come home and write to mayors and vicars, in time for the final post collection.

I reached the square outside Mrs Fortune's studio, sat on a bench and took out my letter from Ruth.

My sister sounded in good spirits.

There are many powerful mysteries here. In a ceremony, each year, a ring is thrown from a boat into the lagoon, to show the city marrying the sea. I *will apply to marry the sea also, unless that would be accounted bigamy! Wouldn't it make a fascinating husband?*

Was that a wistful comment on her spinsterhood? She sent her regards to Mrs Wolfe (who would never receive them) and signed off with a declaration of how she dreamed often of sitting by the fire in the library, her favourite place, with me, her truest companion, which crushed me. My guilt was lessened by the date of the letter. It had been sent days before Sam arrived at our house, so I had still (at the point of writing) deserved her trust.

Ruth had enclosed the gift of a brooch, silver with blue enamel tongues of fire running up it. I pinned it on as I read, garish against my dark red dress. I hadn't worn jewellery in an age. Would it be improper? A year of mourning hadn't yet elapsed, Sam's yahrzeit hadn't passed.

But Sam was alive, and the timetable of mourning no longer applied. I shook my head at how slowly I grasped implications, and at my ridiculous situation. I returned to the letter, and read that Ruth had Venetian glass for me, but it was wrapped in five layers of tissue paper and her bloomers, and she still wasn't sure it would get home in one piece. Tomorrow they planned to visit the Ghetto, a very sombre expedition.

The letter had a postscript running round the edge of the page:

An odd conversation - Toby is worried Lucy will ask you for money, but will not tell me why. He asked me not to mention it to you. Please don't give her any - Toby agrees what we pay her is entirely acceptable.

I was grabbed by an awful fear that Mrs Wolfe had been paying Lucy, and thus Lucy hadn't had her wages for weeks. That brought to mind the other recent letter, the spindly demand that Toby pay his debts (and that I force his hand). But Lucy wouldn't write me an unsigned threatening letter. Would she?

Cutting short my speculation, Ella approached across the square. She was holding a paper bag with her lunch in it, which reminded me to ask after her mother.

'She's fine. I wish she wouldn't pester people.' Ella turned on her heel, and I followed her up the stairs in silence. I shouldn't have let conventional good manners intrude on our bohemian friendship.

As we filled our jars at the communal tap, Ella scrutinised the brooch pinned to my dress. 'Very watery.'

'It's fire.'

'Fire's not blue. It should be running side to side, not up and down. Is your sister collecting? You can get amazing objects in Italy.'

Ruth had mentioned beautiful things in the letter, but to entertain me, not as a shopping list. Half the things she named were famous, or attached to buildings.

'She never has. But she could start,' I said. 'Toby gave her an annuity, so now she has an income. It was generous of him.'

'Not that generous,' Ella said.

'What do you mean?'

'Toby's younger than Sam, yes?'

'Yes.' There had been a period when I'd felt I had to fall in love with Toby. I was the younger sister; he was the younger brother. We were seated together often, thrown on one another's company on outings. I don't know if Toby felt the same pressure. A man never feels as much pressure to marry. He saw me as a child, and I doubt if his brother was as romantically attached to the idea as my sister was. One day Ruth left Toby and me conspicuously alone again, on the garden terrace, and after a long silence I'd said: 'Do you know, I don't expect I shall ever marry.' As airily as I could, apropos of nothing in particular. And Toby had tugged on his beard, and almost levitated with relief, and then we'd talked about trilobites.

'The eldest son tends to inherit more,' Ella told me. 'But now Toby will have his brother's share, too. I should say your sister deserves some of it.'

I stared at my hands, my oil pastels, and tried to ignore her.

Ella continued making impertinent calculations while she sketched. 'I expect their house belonged to Sam. Toby would have enough to live on but not enough to do really interesting things.' She was using their names carelessly, as though she knew them.

'He has a lot of philanthropic commitments,' I said. My hands were clumsy with ill humour.

'I meant travelling, collecting.'

'Toby does collect! He collects fossils. He's been buying them in Italy.' I shouldn't have become engaged in this conversation.

'Well, that shows you. He can buy lots of them now. Lucky man.'

That was the last straw. She was irritable because I'd met her mother (and pardoned her) and I was sorry for it, but I could not let that stand. 'Lucky? Because his brother died?'

Ella had the decency to stay quiet.

I stayed quiet as well, because her words had settled in my low mood and put out horrid little sprouts. Toby was often splenetic about Sam's extravagance. I'd seen that as a matter of principle – Toby was sensible, while Sam was a thoughtless dandy. Ruth and I had sympathised. We'd been patching our own petticoats, asking Cook to make potato soup again, and we'd enshrined thrift as a household deity, to make a virtue of necessity. So we had liked Toby for his prudence. Horrible to imagine, instead,

that Toby was resentful of Sam's position, longing to spend the
money himself.

I thought ahead to the letters I would be writing, that afternoon,
to hospitals and vicars. Bad enough to suspect that Toby had failed
to search for Sam, failed to be diligent. Unimaginable that he'd
failed in his duty because of envy.

'I'm sorry,' Ella said, which I hadn't heard before.

I forgave her. Ella's speculations were nothing to do with Toby
and everything to do with her own life. Her mother couldn't
support her indefinitely, Ella would need to pay own her way, and
that was why she had to be a finer artist than the more comfortable
students. And both work and life would probably be harder for
her than for me, and for all the pastel-gowned girls in our class.
Money would do more for her; it would free her from a lot of
cruelty. Of course she would look at someone like Toby and ask:
where does the money come from? Where does it go?

'When were they going to be married?' she asked, a peace
offering.

'Three weeks after the accident. Everything would have
changed.'

Through the rest of the morning, working on a test piece
in oils, I mused on the depth of that change. My sister installed
as the mistress of Millstone, filling it with colour, flowers and
rich fabrics, relegating Toby's gloomy skeletons to his study. It
would have become a family home, for a different family, Toby
himself relegated to hanger-on, or even moving out. They would
have discussed it, the brothers. They would have reached an
accommodation. Wouldn't they?

As the class ended for lunch, and we tripped down the steps
into the weak white sunlight, I told Ella that business would take
me home that afternoon, and waited for her to berate me for my
lack of purpose.

'Ma's been *sensing a shadow* over you,' she commented instead, rolling her eyes. Holding out another olive branch: *I was rude about your family, here, you can be rude about mine.*

'Do send her my kind regards,' I said.

'Come to my house on Sunday,' Ella offered. 'We can have a trial examination. Ma can feed you up.'

An extraordinary invitation, but what in the world would I be doing, by Sunday, with Sam? 'This business, it may be complex...'

'Well, come if you can.'

It struck me as I travelled home: my sister hadn't written about Samuel.

I had to stop walking and pull out the letter to check. I covered the sheet with my hand, pulling it slowly down over each line, searching for his name. Not one mention of him. Her words of romance were for the sea as a suitor.

I could see a dozen reasons why she might not. She refused to give her melancholy feelings solid form. Or she feared she'd remind *me* of Sam and make *me* sad. That was a brilliantly ridiculous reason, if it was true. I couldn't think of him more than I did, although of course Ruth didn't know that.

Or she was recovering from losing him. In a place with no memories, under a foreign sun, while turquoise canals lapped at the walls of her *pension*. In rooms where she and Sam had never been together, seeing things he'd never spoken of. I felt a pang of pain, because that was what I'd wished for, for her. Yet soon I'd be able to tell her to hurry home. Old affections can become uncanny things. You know you used to feel them, but you try them on and you can't fit into them any more.

I wished another week of misery on her. No, we'd used up a whole day and two nights – she'd have less than a week to wait. If I was to be wretched, she could be wretched too. I wished she would hang on to Samuel. I wished she wouldn't let her love for him become strange to her.

I reread, as I hurried home, the request with which Ruth had concluded her letter.

> We're meeting more people than I'd expected, despite not knowing the language, we have quite a social circle. Could you go over to Millstone and find Toby's cartes de visite and post them to us? Toby says there's a whole pack of them in the drawer of his study desk.

This was very opportune. I needed to know who Toby had written to, who he'd telegraphed, seeking Sam. Now I had permission to trespass – no, I had a direct instruction to rifle through his study and desk.

I stopped off at my own house to fetch the key to Millstone, tucking Ruth's letter in my pocket – I could produce it if I was challenged. The wine I drank in the library was equally fortifying.

On the way out of my house, I heard a brittle whisking sound coming from the conservatory. Lucy was sweeping the mud I had tracked inside. My fears from last night flooded back, and I hurried over to peer at the tiled floor. Were Sam's footprints visible?

The floor was all smears, and nothing could be read in them. Lucy pushed her broom vigorously across that portion of the floor, displeased that I was inspecting her work.

'Excuse me,' I said. 'This is foolish, but you are receiving your wages, aren't you?'

She stopped sweeping and nodded. 'Yes, Miss. Cook gives 'm to me on Fridays.'

'Did she visit today?'

Lucy nodded. 'In and out, Miss. She left a chicken pie.' That was good. But Ruth's warning ran through my mind, not to give Lucy money. There could be an illness in the family; I shouldn't stand by. 'Do you have enough? I don't mean to pry.'

Lucy's expression was positively saucy. She was probably envisioning my family's frugalities: wearing woollen hats in our beds, toasting every old crust. I could tell she was weighing up a joke, then she reconsidered.

'Well enough, thank you, Miss.'

'When I saw your mother yesterday...' I didn't say: *she sounded distressed. Is anything wrong?* We owed no feudal care to her family. But then, if Ruth had been here, she would have been kinder to Lucy. 'She isn't in any difficulty, is she?'

'My sister Bonnie bain't at home.'

That explained why Lucy's mother had asked if I'd seen Bonnie. It was ambiguous, though. Had Bonnie moved amicably out of the family home, or left on bad terms? Maybe Bonnie had obtained a servant's position, like Lucy. Maybe Bonnie had eloped with a disreputable man. 'I'm sorry if that's caused you problems.'

'She'll be well enough, thank you, Miss.' Bonnie could, as far as Lucy's tone suggested, take up residence in a Shoreditch gutter for all her sister cared. 'Oh, I did make your cake, Miss.'

It took me a moment to recall that I had, under duress, requested a fruitcake from Lucy. 'Thank you!'

'A boiled fruitcake, and a Dorset apple cake. Have a slice?'

'I can't, I'm sorry. I'm going next door.'

'Why?'

A rude question, but it was easier to answer than to refuse. 'My sister's asked me to send on some of Toby's things.'

Lucy smiled. I could see her teeth. 'I could do that, if you want, Miss.'

'No need.'

I walked through to the dining room to fetch the key, and Lucy hurried after me.

'Wouldn't bother me, Miss. Really.'

Why were we talking about bother again? Nobody wanted

me to be bothered, or to bother anyone else, as though avoiding bother was the fundamental force which kept the planets in motion. Why would Lucy go to Millstone? To steal? Unworthy suspicion. Simple boredom? A secret passion for Toby? She probably knew where we kept the key, and could go there any day, while I was at class, and I would never know.

I couldn't find the key in the drawer. Opening two others, either side, and finding only cut glass and napkins, I wondered if I'd misplaced it. I wriggled my hand into the first drawer, to reach the far corners, but the space was clogged with folds of linen.

Lucy stepped up beside me. 'Shall I, Miss?' She shoved her hand in and drew the key out straight away. I thanked her. She walked back towards the conservatory, to brush my footprints away. Then it struck me: I'd left the key out yesterday morning for Sam to use.

I could only suspect that the key hadn't been in the drawer while I searched, but in Lucy's apron pocket.

Tiptoeing into Millstone again. In daylight this time. As the front door swung closed I laid my hand on it, making the lock click more softly.

Again, I passed the hallway fossil. It was so ancient I felt obliged to acknowledge it, as one might hail a magpie, but I had no form of words, so I bobbed my head awkwardly as I crossed the hall. Poor venerable thing, about to be dethroned by the specimens Toby was buying in Italy. Toby might fill Millstone with lizards now.

Toby's study was the same room as our library, on the ground floor, but I crept upstairs. I couldn't help it. I'd seen the light glowing in the second bedroom, seen the window lit up when I was speaking with Sam in my own garden. Who'd lit it, maid or thief? I planned to look at that suitcase again, to check for clues – embroidered monograms, a name pencilled inside the cover of a novel. I'd settle the question: did it belong to Sam's mother, or an intruder?

I opened the bedroom door.

The room was transformed.

A rippling silk peacock-coloured shawl, six feet wide, covered the bed. A chemise in a bundle on a chair, a dress thrown over the wardrobe door. A flannel and soap on the washstand, stockings still holding the shape of phantom feet.

Where had everything come from? Who had moved in? Who lived here?

But – I reassured myself – all the things I could see would probably fit into that one battered suitcase that I'd seen under the bed. There was one dress, one set of everything. I recognised the swirls on the scarf, and the sweet-wine smell had insinuated itself everywhere. And there, at one side of the room, was the suitcase itself, flung open.

I peered into the case for identifying items, but saw none, at least on the surface. As the visitor had made herself at home, I felt more like an intruder, and I lacked the nerve to rifle through it. Also, there was a greater chance that she would come back and interrupt me while I searched. I would tell Toby on his return, and leave him to act. I closed the door and hurried back down the stairs.

I'd never before entered Toby's study. The servants had drawn the curtains to stop the light from fading the furnishings, an act which felt optimistic right now, given the weak winter sun. I groped for the desk and lit the lamp. Across the edge of the desk, in a neat row, were a geode with glittering innards and three dark fossils, all egg-sized. So unlike the frivolous profusion in the room upstairs.

I noticed a man's woollen scarf hanging from a hook on the back of the door. I'd take it for Sam. I'd promised him one, to disguise his appearance. I wrapped the scarf round my own neck to keep my hands free.

I opened the drawer Ruth had described. Dozens of images of Toby scowled out at me. He was dressed in his best suit, stood in front of a Grecian pillar. Pity it had been so easy to find Toby's visiting cards – I couldn't dig around the office looking for them, pretending to myself I wasn't prying. I picked out a wad of them, still wrapped in a thin paper band with the printer's name on it, and laid them on one side of the desk, to take away.

Then I pried, shamelessly. Why not? I could find the list of addresses Toby had drawn up last winter, his plan of action. Or correspondence, a sheaf of replies from across the county.

I tugged open another drawer and saw a collage of images, all jumbled up. They were other people's visiting cards. I couldn't read the names in the low light so I dipped in my hand and gathered them up. They were many varieties: photographic and plain, engraved on luxurious card or printed on thinner stock. I dealt them out, a game of patience, until they were all face up, and sorted into types.

The plain but expensive cards were all men's, probably from Toby's synagogue (the Spanish and Portuguese congregation over on Bryanston Street) or the club where he sat in St James. Some were from businessmen, some from lawyers. Perhaps these were the legal men Toby had consulted about formalising Sam's death. They could have advised him on inheritance law as well. No cards from mediums, thank goodness. Toby would never.

The photographic cards were from women. Young wealthy men, even if they don't feel inclined to matrimony, will always be made aware of young ladies. The subjects were elegantly posed, and luminously lit, and they were all very attractive in much the same way. Large eyes and fine brows. Had Toby just kept the pretty ones? I'd not intended to unearth a private preference and felt queasy. None of them resembled Ruth. None of them resembled me. Toby might appreciate beautiful young women as much as he liked ancient fossils. Now he could afford both. That was the kind of thing Ella would say. What if the silky clothes in the upstairs bedroom belonged to a mistress of Toby's, cast off but lingering?

That was an unwholesome train of thought. I kept digging.

The remaining cards, the cheaper, printed ones, bore the names and addresses of houses. Three were located in small villages or towns, and two were in the city, but all the names were bucolic: Oak Lodge and Chapel Spring. One card, for a place called The Larches, had an address near Breakwater, and a subtitle: *A Healthful Place Away from the Smogs of the City*. Were they hotels, where Sam and Toby had stayed while looking for a cottage to purchase?

I squinted to see some even smaller print. *Superior private sanatorium – invalid bedsteads and appliances – private rooms – incurable cases received – terms moderate.*

Not hotels, then. I put the hospital cards on top of the visitors' cards to take away with me.

Why on earth had Toby been researching sanatoriums? My first thought was for Ruth; if she'd declined the trip to Italy, perhaps Toby would have proposed Oak Lodge. Then I heard Sam refusing medical help, protesting against mad-doctors. Had Sam been ill all year – amnesiac, erratic – in one of these *healthful places*?

I started to dig wildly through every drawer in the desk, scraping all Toby's secrets out into the light to examine them. I needed to know, and I might never have the bravery to come back here.

From one drawer, pens spilled out. When I opened another, an object shot to the front of the drawer and hit it with a crack that startled me: a giant marble, a sphere of semi-precious stone. I shuffled through a stack of financial correspondence, anxious but shameless: bank letters detailing property, bills for the renovation of Millstone. Charity calls and charity bills, endless philanthropy.

No hospital bills.

Letters! A letter from a schoolfriend informing him of a marriage, letters setting dates to meet for dinner at his club. No letters from a vicarage, or a mayor or a rural police station. No sign of the great search he said he'd made. No letters from a *superior private sanatorium*. No love letters, either. All dry as dust. I wanted a diary, I wanted him to have spilled his heart onto paper.

Finally, my fingertips found a sheet which was fuzzy from being touched often, and crumpled up. That was unusual, as the rest of the papers were so neatly filed. I drew it out. An envelope, nearly identical to the one sent to me. The same spindly black handwriting, but Toby's name and Millstone's address. It had been sliced open neatly, crumpled up, then smoothed again by the compulsively neat recipient.

I drew out the folded letter without hesitation.

Dear Mister Silver. Please send the money that is owed me. A Friend.

Our Friend was consistent. Our Friend was unhelpful – they'd not signed their name to Toby, either. But they were relying on him knowing who they were.

Of course one doesn't sign blackmail notes. But is it blackmail, if the blackmailer believes they're owed the money?

It was too thorny a problem to consider on the spot, so I stuffed the letter in my pocket and continued searching the drawer.

When I wriggled my hand further and felt to the back, there was a ridged block. A tiny book? I pulled it out. A small stack of visitors' cards, still in their band.

They were Samuel's cards, like the one he'd handed me two

years ago. The same thumbprint face that didn't do him justice.

I put them with the other cards and picked up the whole pile. I extinguished the lamp, and rushed across the room for the door.

And smack, my forehead struck the door-frame. Sparks spattered my vision. I clutched my face and all the cards cascaded to the floor. My eyes kept sparking in the dark and the room tipped – was I fainting? Couldn't swoon here. Couldn't be found sprawled on the floor of Toby's study, surrounded by contraband. I had to stay upright, despite the swaying door-frame, despite my ringing head.

When I had my balance again, I gingerly stooped and clawed at the cards in the dark to retrieve them.

I heaved at the study door and stumbled into the hall. This time, the *Coelophysis* watched me with its stony eye socket, and judged me for stealing. I didn't care.

I wrapped the scarf I'd found more securely round my neck. I locked up Millstone.

Staggering through my own hallway, the *parfait gentil* knights judged me. That stung more than the dinosaur's disapproval. Didn't they see I was trying to be helpful? I kept the key to Millstone in my pocket, rather than replacing it in the drawer where Lucy had retrieved it (or placed it).

I sat in my room, prodding my forehead with my fingers. It was lumpy, a mix of pain and numbness, foreign to me. What a dull, doubt-filled day, ending in injury.

I think I slept.

I woke in the dark, and stumbled down to the library, and he was sprawled in my chair.

'Judith! I expected you home ages ago. I've not seen you all day.'

Sam was bored, Sam had been lonely, without me. He was

surrounded by books. And this house was surrounded by a city! Couldn't Sam find ways to be less bored and lonely?

He waved a finger at me, then at his own forehead. 'Is your face…?'

'It's fine.' Strands of my hair hid the damage from the door. I shouldn't appear unreliable.

'Why are you wearing that scarf? Isn't it Toby's?'

I unwound it from my neck, moving a little stiffly, and passed it over. 'I brought it for you.'

'Thank you! You're so considerate.'

'I've been in Millstone.' I took a seat at the desk, to keep away from his outstretched legs.

'What, my house?'

I bit back a retort: Why not? He'd been in *my* house long enough. I explained about the *cartes de visite*, and the letter from my sister. I didn't mention the sanatorium cards. The idea that Sam had been a patient was so weighty, and the evidence so insubstantial. I'd follow up privately with the hospitals, and then let him know the truth.

'Wonderful! Is she well? How is she?'

'She's very well. You could—' I had been about to offer him the letter to read, but drew back. There wasn't much to it, but it was private. He shouldn't have such easy sight of her, when she couldn't see him at all. Instead, I told him Ruth's movements around the Rialto and the Ghetto, taking a boat up the Grand Canal. The first fresh news he'd had of his betrothed for a year. 'And Toby's been buying fossils,' I concluded.

'Ha! Yes, he'll be like a boy in a sweet shop.'

Ella's comments had left me with a sore spot. I poked at it. 'Does he collect much?'

'Oh, he's got a squirrel's soul. He still owns rocks he picked up when he was a child. I've said to him, don't you ever want to chuck it all out, start fresh? A clean slate is a wonderful thing.'

'But serious things, collector's items…'

'He loves them but he's never owned many. I mean, he couldn't, really. Too poor.' He smirked, looking to me for a response.

Instead, I picked up an apple from the desktop, and bit into it. Who discusses money, and their family, so crudely? And who sneers at his younger brother's constrained circumstances, when only an accident of birth made him richer? (My guilt needled me: *It was what you wanted to know, though, however timidly you asked it.*) Looking out of the French windows, I saw that sunset was long past, and once again we were at odds, and I resolved that I wouldn't ask him to light the Hanukkah candles with me. The wish was too tender, and I wouldn't forgive him if he mocked it.

I felt cruel, for a moment. I could make him acknowledge my generosity, and the insecurity of his own position. 'You've reminded me: do you need anything yourself? Any more money? I could certainly lend you…'

He waved away my offer. 'No need. Got some.'

'How?' Were there coins in his pocket when he came out of the lake? That could be a clue, it could be relevant.

'I can get it if I need it.'

He was forgetting, again, what it meant to be dead. 'You might not be able to go to the bank. Toby might have had to close your account.'

'I've got money elsewhere. In places Toby doesn't know.' He was dismissive. 'Lots of places, lots of names. Best way to do it. Don't worry about me.'

I didn't argue. I had met a friend of my father's once, and he'd reached into his waistcoat pocket and brought out the prettiest pieces of cut glass, which he let me hold. He said, 'I could buy a house with them. Do you know why I don't?' He'd tipped them back into his pocket and patted it. 'Whoosh! I fly away, to another country, if trouble comes. Like a magician.'

Trouble had been coming, recently. Trouble had driven Jews from countries in the east and brought them to London. (*Hard workers*, said Toby. *Vagabonds*, said Mama.) There was always the fear that trouble would grow in England. Toby and Sam's family had been safe for generations. But I understood why Sam might hide his money in many places.

A pip fell from the core of the apple I was eating, and I threw it into the fire. I did it for neatness, and recalled too late that it was a charm to test fidelity. At least Sam didn't know that. The pip fizzled – someone was straying.

Sam had been silent a while, and I noticed him screw the knuckles of one hand into the palm of his other. 'Does she mention me? Ruth?'

I couldn't lie or dodge it. 'No,' I said. 'I'm sorry. It doesn't mean – she might have been trying not to make me sad. Letters are so difficult.'

He closed his eyes and nodded.

'For the best,' he said. It sounded like the inscription on the golden apple in the myth: *for the fairest*. 'She shouldn't be thinking about me, anyway. That's why I'm here, isn't it – it's to make Ruth happy, to stop her from being in pain.' He was swinging back and forth again. Think about me, forget me. Tell Ruth about me, hide me from her. I didn't understand it, and it frightened me. 'She doesn't need me, though. It would be kindest if I just left.'

'Sam, no!'

'I should go away entirely. But then I walk round the garden, when you're not here, and every leaf is a wonder. The wind, the grey sky, even the fog – they're marvels. I do want to stay, so much, I'd do anything to stay…'

I was having to strain to catch his mumbling. I tried a bracing tone. 'Certainly you can stay. You live next door. You've come home. It's sensible that you want to be here, Sam. And we all missed you.'

'You did, didn't you? You missed me.' The thought seemed to give him some peace.

Meanwhile, the concealment – Ruth's letter from Sam, and Sam from Ruth – made me far from peaceful. I resolved not to heap up more secrets, but to share what I'd found. 'Look, look at these.' Pulling out the sanatorium cards, I spread them on the library desk. 'I found them in Toby's study. They're private hospitals. Do you think you may have stayed at one?'

Sam gazed at the cards, and swallowed. 'It could be. These all look very reputable. Trust Toby to set me up right.'

'Toby never mentioned a hospital to us.'

'Perhaps he wanted to spare you and Ruth any pain.'

A very charitable explanation, and I was glad it was his first response. It was a good counterpoint to Ella's cynical conjectures. 'Do you think it's time to let Toby know you're here? Then you can ask him about it directly.' Which would also prevent Toby from lying to my sister while they travelled together.

'No! You promised.'

'Then I'll write to the hospitals. Or telephone, if I can.' Sam didn't forbid me. The cards lay next to the lists and the diagrams and the doodles from our automatic writing experiment. All my elaborate failed efforts. 'Do any of them sound familiar to you?'

Sam laid out the cards like a game of patience. He read the names, he mused, he hummed to himself. One finger like a Ouija board planchette, hovering. Then tapping out a rhythm on one card in particular. The Larches, near Breakwater.

'Maybe that one. Maybe.'

He didn't sound certain, but it was better than nothing at all.

Then, to my surprise, he beamed at me. 'Any more ideas? More exercises to do?'

I didn't know what to suggest. I hadn't devised any more tests or tricks. I'd been concentrating on practical matters.

'Come on,' Sam said. 'We're on the brink of progress, I can

feel it. You'll write to The Larches. Let's throw everything we have at it, and I may recover before they even write back. Let's race them to the finishing line! Let's summon things! Call forth mysteries and... so forth.'

He was humouring me, I suspected. 'We're trying to regain your memory,' I said. 'Not raise spirits.'

'Harrow my brain, then! It's been slumping around all day. Make it sing for its supper.' He saw me giving way and pursued his point. 'Take it up by the scruff of its neck and give it a good shake.'

The truth was, I needed only a little encouragement. The previous evening, watching him draw had felt powerful. There'd been a particular deep vibration in the room. It had gone awry, but a connection had been made. I'd felt, for the first time, for a moment, that success was in our hands rather than in the gift of others. Even if that sense was illusory, I relished it. And Sam wanted it too, he'd asked for it.

I could find some spell in the right line. A charm for truth or memory. Ruth had liked charms for divination – what *would* be – but I'd always preferred charms for discernment – what *had been*, what *was*. I would dig around in our books of folklore.

'I'll find a guide,' I told Sam, and walked to the bookcases. Half of them contained Father's books, in long rows of matching bindings. But the others, all higgledy-piggledy, belonged to Ruth and me, from years of hunting in second-hand bookshops.

The enthusiasm Sam had kindled in me wavered as I pulled down two of my favourite volumes: a thick tome, Thiselton Dyer's *English Folk-lore*, and a pamphlet, *Gleanings from St Martin's Land* by C.L. Nolan. The contents page of the former was divided by topic (*Plants – The Moon – Insects – Reptiles*), not by intended impact. I flicked to the back: the index was more precise, but showed nothing for 'memory', moving straight from 'Measles, charm for' to 'Mice, portend death'. *Gleanings* was no better, each page packed with hallucinatory practices, and nothing fit for purpose. Would

Sam scoff if I advised him to pin feathers to his nightgown, or walk thrice backwards round a church?

I continued to draw down books, one of which shed a peacock feather from between its pages and another a loop of ribbon. I was hardly focusing on the pages now, merely pretending to look. If only I could create a process to suit our needs. Pitch it just right, make it grave and insightful.

I'd invented plenty of rituals in the past, with Ruth and alone, for fun. But had they worked? It couldn't be proved whether they'd altered the world. But they'd certainly changed our minds and our moods. And it was Sam's mind I was seeking to affect. My most recent invention, my evening walk with candle and with wine, had preserved me. Invent it, invest in it, and it will work on your behalf.

What were rituals made of, boiled down to their bones? Fire, water. Trees, land, beasts. Movement and song. Entities to be disciplined or wooed. Gifts and punishments. Contracts and obligations – no, contracts were too transactional, too much a tool of the city. *Affinities*. A soft nudge to tell me when I was moving in the right direction. Suspended disbelief. A voice, a certainty, that only came when I became immersed without interpreting.

Don't think, it said. *Know. Act.*

I closed the book I was holding with a snap. 'I have something.' Better for Sam to believe he was enacting a procedure from a dusty authority. 'Wait here, I need to fetch supplies.'

I ran to the kitchen, opening a dozen cupboards before I saw it: a great earthenware punchbowl. In a changing light the glaze would shimmer between deep brown and dark blue, rough and rural. Ruth had bought it on a visit to a country town, but it had never been used; since the accident, we'd not had visitors. I held it in both hands, with a bottle of wine carried under my arm, jars in both pockets.

Back in the library, I set it on our campaign table. I poured in the wine, the note it made dropping and mellowing as the bowl filled. Sam observed me, amused. It wasn't enough. The bowl would hold three bottles. I hesitated.

'I'll get more,' Sam offered, and bounded off. I cleared distractions away from around the bowl, but laid out the peacock feather and the ribbon at evocative angles. Finally, I pulled up two dining chairs and dimmed the lights.

From the moment Sam returned, we didn't speak. By accident, at first, then deliberately. He poured the new wines at the same time, two red streams joining in the bowl. Then he stowed the bottles under the desk and awaited instruction.

I sprinkled in spices, cinnamon and ginger (and fought the urge to sneeze). But I wasn't making punch, it needed an incongruous ingredient. I pulled a hair from my head and cast it in. Sam caught my eye, and when I nodded, copied me, wincing. I scrabbled around for the remnants of the Breakwater flowers and tossed in some dried seeds.

I pointed to the chair. Sam sat and rested his elbows on the desk, his face in his hands. He gazed into the surface of the wine and frowned.

The smell of the wine and spice was sumptuous. The lip of the bowl cast curved shadows across the liquid. I sat opposite Sam and looked, too. It wasn't unstable enough. Even with the lights lowered, we could see too much detail in the reflection. It was best to summon up unclear images. As if he read my mind, Sam left the desk and the room. I heard him stomp downstairs to the kitchen. (Poor Lucy *must* have heard him by now.)

What could lend the experiment a stronger mood? I sought out Ruth's gramophone, which had been an extravagant gift from Sam, and the much-played discs beside it: *Songs of Scotland, The Girl I Left Behind Me*. I laid *The Wearing of the Green* carefully onto the machine, gave the handle three slow turns and lowered the needle to hear the wistful tune.

As the notes climbed and dropped, I sat in the dark and wondered about poor Mrs Leon. Did she pay money to go to séances, to sit in dim rooms like this and be taken in by cracking tin-lids and apparitions made of cotton? Did she mourn her late husband so deeply?

Sam returned with handfuls of candle stubs. He held their feet to the fire, until their wax melted enough to secure them to a plate. Then he lit their wicks and placed the plate next to the bowl. That felt both naggingly familiar and jarringly inappropriate. The sun set later in Italy than here; Mama might at this moment be lighting candles with love and care in Venice, in a room where the room was full of dancing light, reflecting off the water in the canals. Her voice would mingle with peals of bells from campanili in the dusk. All we had was a high-voiced singer, winding out from the gramophone, mourning his lost home.

The candlelight deepened the shifting shadows. Sam's eyes met mine. The bruise on his forehead was yellow now. He'd leaned in so close, I wondered if he could see my matching bruise, in fresher, darker colours. I turned my eyes back onto the wine, and let the melody lift me.

Images swam into my mind, and in the dim light they had a weird force. I saw a stone wall, as I had drawn it a couple of days ago. A ruined castle or a defensive city wall which had failed. Ivy was growing through and around and over it, so much that it wore a cloak of shiny green scales, but the ivy wasn't prising the blocks apart, the way I'd originally drawn it.

There was a dip in the centre of the wall. It was a window or a well or another deep, implacable hole, although the ivy disguised it. To look into the pitch-black depths of it made me tearful. It had a dreadful gravity, and I'd been so weightless lately. The wall was unsound; the hole was going to bring it down. I saw all this in the surface of the wine: deep, sheer-sided, sick and hidden. I inhaled and the smell of the wine was rotten.

I pulled back and a spasm of coughs shook me.

Sam leapt up and slapped my back. 'All right? I'm not seeing visions. How about you?'

'A thing with a hole in, cracked. Horrible.'

'Gracious!' He squeezed my arm in consolation, then let me go. 'Wish I had your imagination. Let's try again. What if we had a bigger surface? We could use the lake.'

I didn't answer his poor joke. The gramophone music had ended.

'We could scry in the ice.' He wasn't joking. He would go back out onto the ice, and look down into it, and fall through again, and this time he'd drown. 'Come on, Judith.' He scooped up the plate of candles and shadows swung around the half-dark room. An old fear joined the new one – I shouldn't be left alone in the house, I couldn't be trusted with it. I'd set fire to it. We'd both die.

I stepped forward to take the candles from him. He moved them out of my reach, holding them stupidly close to the wall hangings. Bright colours, flaring. I had to stop him, grabbed for the candles, I was pressed up against him. He wrapped his arm around me.

There was a crackling sound, an instant bitter stink. Sam sprang back, I heard the plate of candles clatter to the floor. Then Sam swooped at me like a great bird and everything was airless and black in his hug. Now he was holding me, and *hitting* me, slapping his hand over and over. I felt shiny fabric slide across my forehead. He had smothered me in one of the patchworks and wrapped both arms tight around my head.

'Hell!' I felt his grip ease, then saw light as he lifted off the patchwork, then his anxious eyes. 'Sorry, sorry!'

The reek of burned hair made me shudder. The room was utterly dark. But it wasn't safe, yet. 'Where did the candles fall, Sam? Where are they?'

'They're just behind you. They're all fine! They've gone out.'

I felt him move, point over my shoulder. But at the same time a light gleamed from the opposite direction, near the French windows, down by the floor. Flames were flickering up a wall hanging that Ruth and I had made. I could see tiny orange fire-worms writhing and chewing around the bottom edge, and knew they were the metal threads Ruth had used in the border pattern, super-heated. Gold tongues of fire danced lazily above.

I grabbed up the punchbowl, ready to throw the wine. The heavy liquid sloshed about, made the bowl rock in my hands.

'Wait!' called Sam.

I froze, waited for another command. None came. Wine slopped onto my dress. 'Why?'

He didn't answer, just watched the flames with his eyes glinting. I tried to see what he saw, some reason to delay. The flames marched upwards. A tongue of light touched the central design, the face of Merlin. Sam did not move or speak.

I hefted the whole bowl at the burning wall hanging, heard the pottery crack when it struck.

I stepped in, ready to stamp out the last of the flames, but saw none. Groping my way over to the desk, I lit a lamp.

A tide of wine was flowing across the floor towards my feet. The candle stubs rolled forward on it, their wicks trailing grey lines of smoke. The wine soaked into the carpet as it progressed, and gradually its energy spent itself and the red edge slowed.

I raised my hands gingerly to examine my hair.

'It didn't burn much,' Sam said. 'Forgive me?'

My hair felt more or less the same shape as before. But there were tiny knots all over it, which weren't knots. Cinders. I combed with my fingers and they snagged.

I gazed up at the singed wall hanging. The flames had come perilously close to the garlands Ruth and I had draped along the bookshelves, the poppy heads and pine cones, so much decorative tinder. Then my eyes dropped to the red pool of wine on the cream carpet. I should mop it up.

'All my fault!' Sam said cheerily. As though his taking the blame would have prevented the house from burning.

'It *was* your fault! Why wouldn't you—'

In response I saw in his eyes a flare of irritation. Or excitement, that I'd lost my temper. But when he spoke it was in a formal tone. 'So sorry. I didn't – of course, you're being careful.' He made it sound as though I had been a little too prudish, or over-protective, not to set my house on fire, or my head.

I touched the back of my hair again. I crumbled gritty pieces of ash between my fingers. 'I'm responsible for this house.'

I reached up with both hands and yanked down the wall hanging. While the canvas backing had survived, the squares of cloth were shrivelled brown flakes. The curtain next to it might have taken some damage, but it was deep red and hard to tell if it was charred. I felt absurd sympathy for it; we'd turned its pair into a frock. Imagine surviving our needlecraft, only to be singed? I left it in place. I'd examine it in the morning.

I took my stinking armful of canvas and tried to mop the carpet, kneeling down to press it onto the straggling paths of wine. The cloth grew sodden but the carpet remained pink, and I rolled up the mess of fabric and shoved it under the desk.

Clambering to my feet, wiping my hands on my dress, I told Sam: 'I have to take care of the house.'

He hadn't moved to help me. He looked away, as though to spare me embarrassment. 'Well, precisely. I couldn't help but notice that you're on your own.'

Oh, he was on thin ice, and he knew it. Was he waspish because I hadn't forgiven him immediately? Did he say it just to provoke me?

'Goodnight,' I said, and left the library.

❧

Yes, I was on my own. There was Lucy, obviously, and Sam already knew that my family were gone, so what he really meant was: *you're unmarried, a young woman. Where is your lady's companion? Where is your chaperone?* I went back to my room rather than stay and offer an explanation.

I'd had a chaperone, for a while.

At the very outset, the family refused to leave for Italy without me. Mama said whatever art class I'd enrolled on, I could rejoin when we were back, in the New Year.

I said no.

I'd never disagreed with them before. They were scared of my sudden, blank no. I wouldn't voice any specific discontent, in case they proposed a solution. Ruth said privately to me that I could learn more about art in Italy, which was true. Then Mama said loudly that Ruth wouldn't travel without me, so I was ruining everything for my poor sister. That manipulation was so outrageous that Ruth told Mama she would happily abandon me.

To take the heat from the situation, Toby brokered a deal. I would be left with a paid companion over the autumn and winter. The companion was chosen: Mrs Wolfe, a friend of the family, a widow. She did rather well from chaperoning, staying in houses nicer than her own.

I didn't object at first. I knew that London had a vileness which pressed in like the murky fog. It menaced Ruth and me when we walked in public places. It was made of men's malice and women's whispers and if it knew I was living alone, it would tense its haunches and spring at me. This gentle guardian would keep the vileness away from me.

Mrs Wolfe was no harpy, no dragon. She talked a lot, when I was used to quiet companionship. She required my presence, when Ruth and I were used to wandering out of each other's company.

Certainly, Mama had left undone many things in my upbringing. Mrs Wolfe was too gentle to lecture me but would let out a laugh of surprise. It punctuated my mornings and evenings. Eating breakfast without the maid setting out the silverware? Ha! Reaching for the sugar? Haha! (Why set out the sugar if it wasn't to be eaten?)

I accepted every invitation from the Isaacs, whether it was Leah asking me to recite *Hamlet*, or Rose needing help to untangle her embroidery, although Mrs Wolfe thought that family a little raucous. Art class became a sanctuary. I dawdled home daily, wandering in public parks. I wondered when the vileness would find me. Mrs Wolfe raised her eyebrows at my lateness. Haha! I was on the cusp of dark acts.

But fortune stepped in. After a month, Mrs Wolfe received a letter. Her niece had become a mother, and melancholy had been delivered with the baby. It would be such a kindness and a mitzvah, Mrs Wolfe said over breakfast, to help her family.

'I'll miss you,' I said.

'You funny girl,' said Mrs Wolfe. 'I won't desert you!'

The stifling kindness closed round me. An outright lie could cut me free. It was a larger lie than I'd ever previously considered. Was I sharp enough?

'You know,' I mused, 'Mrs Montague would be happy to come and stay with me.'

'Mrs Montague?'

I sang the praises of Mrs Montague: a lioness of a mother and a fine homemaker. 'Although she's quite strict.'

With that one phrase, I cast Mrs Montague as a rod-of-iron harridan.

Lucy, who was replenishing our tea, glared straight at me. She wasn't stopping me, but she was certainly watching me.

I offered to send two telegrams to arrange things. After art class, I hurried home and waited. By five o'clock, my mother's reply arrived from Florence: Mrs Montague would be ideal. And a telegram from Mrs Montague confirmed that she could join me that same evening.

Mrs Wolfe asked me: was I sure? I was sure. I waved off my chaperone in a hackney cab, and her niece had a great support in a time of trial.

I'd taken the telegrams myself from the boy who delivered them. I fretted that Mrs Wolfe would notice that the telegrams both originated from the same place, but I was ready to persuade her that international telegrams were routed through local offices.

A few shillings had bought my liberty. I was utterly, fearsomely free.

That evening I heard clinks from the dining room. Lucy was working – poor girl, she'd borne Mrs Wolfe's rigorous demands for cleaning. Mrs Wolfe had also required Lucy to Know Her Place: bobbing and ma'am-ing and knocking before entering.

I hurried through to share my relief with Lucy.

The dining table was absurdly long for two people. Lucy had covered it with a pristine white cloth and a pale lace runner. She stood at the foot of the table with a fistful of cutlery. I called the good news.

'Don't bother with that! Not today.' I couldn't keep the triumph from my voice.

Lucy raised her eyebrows, her equivalent of crying *Ha!* She kept hold of the cutlery.

'Mrs Wolfe isn't with us,' I explained. 'She went to be with her niece.'

'For how long, Miss?'

'She isn't coming back. We won't need to set out the silverware any more.'

'Not even on a Friday?' Lucy had grasped the significance of Fridays, but I wanted to dispense with all obstacles.

'We can do without all that.' I swept my hand awkwardly to indicate Lucy's other trials. 'The hall doesn't need to be mopped every day. And you needn't knock before you come into rooms.'

'I never did complain, Miss.' Lucy seemed frozen with wariness. I regarded every item between us, the crystal and the silver, in terms of what she had to wash and polish. I didn't know why she wasn't glad.

Of course, she couldn't risk appearing lazy. I tried to reassure her. 'I know! You've been…' *An excellent worker*, my father's highest praise, stuck in my throat, far too patronising. '…doing all those things.'

'Will there be other guests, Miss?' She'd overheard us discussing Mrs Montague, would be expecting her arrival.

'No, just myself.'

More eyebrows.

I saw suddenly that the threat worked both ways. I could give a bad report of Lucy, but Lucy also could tell tales. Just a note to Mama, and my family would rush home across the continent. I had to persuade Lucy that we'd be happier alone.

'It will be far easier. We can go back to the way it was before.' But there had never been a stable state, not since Lucy had worked for us. Mama gave orders and Ruth countermanded them. Sam pleaded for things and Toby reprimanded him. 'We can find a way that suits us.'

'Cook's already making dinner,' Lucy said.

'I could eat it in the library.' I picked up a knife and fork myself to demonstrate the new, more egalitarian system.

Lucy began to collect in the remaining silverware, to place each piece back in the case. I walked away. I heard a jangle behind me as she dropped a couple of pieces, then cursed.

I'd relieved Lucy of half her work, but she clearly didn't

trust me to keep a home. My strange bohemian friends would turn the place into an opium den. With Mrs Wolfe's warding presence removed, London's vileness would creep in, and our house would be defamed and defiled. Cook would quit; Lucy would be unable to get another position.

I'd drown in the lake. I'd burn the house to the ground.

It was through Lucy's eyes that I first saw my situation and feared madness. Always after that when Lucy looked at me, I felt her judgement. Or I used her presence to judge myself.

That first night without Mrs Wolfe, I scarcely slept. What would happen when my family came home, when the truth came out? The fear squeezed me like a fist in my chest.

I went out into the world, the next day, and kept to my ordinary routine. Around town, strangers gave me sharp looks, in a tea shop and then at an exhibition. Were they worried for my wellbeing, or was it smouldering prejudice? Did they intuit I was a fallen woman? I was too naïve to foresee how I might be accused. There were sins I didn't understand, not only Lancelot and Guinevere, but modern scandals; what had befallen the Solomon siblings, for instance, so that Father had bought their paintings years ago, but then stopped boasting about them?

A gang of young men shouted at me in Hyde Park. While I kept my face fixed I also tried to hear what they said. I couldn't afford to be ignorant.

I hadn't realised how alone I would be. I visited the Isaac sisters, but I couldn't let them into my house, and I feared they'd ask prying questions. Without a companion, I couldn't attend synagogue. It wasn't unusual for a family to miss the weekly service – sometimes Ruth and I would look down from the ladies' gallery, and only see two dozen worshippers below – but the High Holy Days were fast approaching. I knew I'd be expected.

I made an excuse to go along with the Isaacs to Rosh Hashanah in September, to say prayers of penitence, and then home with Leah and Rose to dip apples in honey. For Yom Kippur, I gave the same excuse to a different schoolfriend and attended with her family, joining the froth of women in white gowns flowing down Upper Berkeley Street. We smiled to one another all through the fatiguing day. I wanted to keep hold of the shape of the year, but fasting threw me into a grim gloom, and I had nobody to lighten it. Invitations from family friends continued to arrive, and when I declined them, some letters of mild concern. I wrote back to appease their senders.

I didn't speak to anyone except Ella and Mrs Fortune. My father's store of wine wasn't unfamiliar to me, from family meals and festive days, but I'd never drunk it alone before. I slept late and walked around the house without dressing. I heard my name whispered in crowds. I was heading for the rest cure, or the bolted doors of Colney Hatch asylum.

I put firm rituals in place. No lying in bed in the morning, no more than one glass of wine each evening. I kept myself tethered. I didn't turn into a will-o'-the-wisp.

Samuel didn't ask me about any of this. He only said, in grave tones: *You're on your own*.

I deliberated on his impertinence as I combed cinders from my hair. Couldn't he keep pretending he hadn't noticed? He did it to disturb me, to point out how precarious I was. Each stroke of my comb sent pain through my scalp. Sam was being particularly insulting, as *he* was the chief hazard to my reputation: a man outside my family, an unmarried man, secluded with me in my house.

It was obvious, now: Sam shouldn't be staying here. He'd stayed the first night from necessity, but after that, for the next two nights, he should have found other accommodation. That reflected poorly on him. It suggested he was accustomed to lax habits.

At least I hadn't berated him, or engaged him in an argument. I had done what he lacked the decency to do, and pretended I didn't understand. I set that cold comfort against my hot fury.

I abandoned my hair and climbed into bed, where I read again the card for The Larches. The lamp beside my bed was a brighter light than the library, and I spotted faint pencil marks on its reverse. Rows of numbers. Certainly they were in Toby's handwriting; they resembled the numbers in his dull correspondence. The numbers were in groups of three: *12.10.6, 20.3.3*.

I shuffled the cards. On one card, Toby had taken more care, and written £, *s*, *d* against the three numbers. These were prices, for the hospitals. They seemed dreadfully high, not *terms moderate* at all, but I had no way of knowing if the amount would cover a week's stay or a month's, and with what treatments.

Some couldn't be prices because there were too many pennies. *15.1.92, 11.1.92*.

They had to be dates. Dates when a private room would be available? Dates in mid-January, a month after Sam had been swept away. At the start of January, Toby had still been chasing around the West Country, making enquiries after his brother. Then, later in the month, Toby had grown less frantic, more sombre. In February he had hardly visited Breakwater.

We'd thought, at the time, Toby was moving towards acknowledging Sam's death. But these cards suggested his self-possession came from a different source. Solemn, reliable Toby had deceived us.

I dreamed that night that the lake woman, the mudbride, came into the house and killed my chaperone, strangled her with an unyielding clay grip. She wasn't me, after all. She was far stronger than me and more knowledgeable. It wasn't Sam she wanted, either – she had come to ruin me. She would understand the sidelong glances. I was easily duped; I didn't know enough to avoid danger. Even in my dream, I didn't know what the wrongdoing was, only sensed menace around her like a luxurious perfume, growing powerful as she advanced on me.

She would change as she approached me, turn from clay to flesh, be sweet and human and wrapped in silk. Then tempt me to do some awful, simple thing, and I would do it in all innocence.

SATURDAY

No class, but as soon as I woke, I sat up in bed. I wanted to draw the ivy again, but I never drew on a Saturday. I'd made that decision myself, as a kind of pledge: if I took my art seriously, I should treat it as work, and set it aside for that time. Still, I imagined how I might do it: extending the tendrils, making them reach downwards and sideways across the paper. Holes lay behind the ivy, rotten and unstable. When I moved, flecks of ash from my hair fell onto the bedcovers, and I imagined myself grinding them into paper, what marks they'd make. As I stretched, I kept an ear to the noises of the house but didn't hear Sam moving at all.

This was procrastination. To keep my end of the bargain with Sam, I'd have to begin investigating.

I rose, and retrieved Toby's cards from the library without looking at the mess of pink wine-stains in the corner of the room. Sam had pointed to the card of The Larches, but it had no telephone. It seemed rash to dash off there, hopelessly slow to write a letter and wait for a reply. I told myself that Sam's wavering finger hadn't ruled out the other rest homes. Possibly he'd stayed at more than one of them as he convalesced.

The Havens had a telephone. I quietly left the house, walked to the post office and asked them to connect me. I pictured the telephone ringing in a clean, light room.

The woman who answered sounded northern and personable.

I asked her if The Havens was a private hospital. I was afraid to ask: *are you an asylum?* She offered to send me a printed guide to their services.

'I'm looking for my brother, who went missing last year. He may have lost his memory.'

'How awful,' she said. 'I'm afraid that if he's here, that would be confidential, so the most I could do is ask him to write to you. I'm so sorry.'

'Oh, I'd not considered...' I felt bad about misleading her when my missing person was safely home. But I was also frustrated by her refusal.

'Could you give me his name, and describe him? So I can pass on a message.'

I described him, to preserve the pretence. When she spoke again, her voice was relieved. 'I can tell you this: all the men we've had this year have been older than that. Older than forty, even.'

I hastily called the other homes which had a telephone. One didn't connect, another two claimed confidentiality. Calling in person would have been better. I could have shown Sam's calling card to the staff, and watched their faces.

Since The Larches had no telephone, I resolved to visit them today. As soon as I did, I knew I'd been fooling myself; the trip had been inevitable, from the moment Sam pointed at the card.

After Sam's accident, I'd assumed I'd never go to Breakwater again. Without a word to him, I set off for my second visit there in a week.

Lots of people travelled on the Sabbath: office clerks visiting sweethearts and college men going upriver for boating. It did make me feel a little prickly, when I was already itchy with uncertainty.

A fat rushing river beside the train tracks sparked a more cheerful recollection. A couple of days after Rosh Hashanah Father had read the *Chronicle*. He was scoffing aloud about superstitious practices carried out by the newcomers in the East End. An odd air came over Mama, furtive and purposeful, and she bundled Ruth and me into our coats and out of the house.

'You'll enjoy this,' she said. 'We need to find water.'

We walked to the park first, and studied the pools of the Italian water gardens.

'No, it should be running water,' said Mama.

So we walked on and on, past Buckingham Palace, towards the tower of Big Ben. Mama handed us each a slice of bread. I caught Ruth's eye and shared her confusion. We didn't need to travel so far for ducks: was the bread for kelpies, naiads, mermaids? At Westminster Bridge, Mama led us down steps to the riverside.

'Girls, this is Tashlich!' Mama recited prayers, with a wonderful verse from Micah promising that God would hurl our sins into the depths of the sea. At her urging, we crumbled fragments of bread onto the tea-coloured waters. I hoped my crumbs would be dramatically carried away, but the Thames was sluggish and they circled about. 'And shake!' Mama shook the skirt of her dress and smiled, and Ruth and I shook ourselves in imitation. Tugboats blew their horns and we stood in the shadow of Big Ben, all three of us for once in perfect sympathy.

After that, we went with Mama every year for Tashlich. Mama disapproved of many of our pastimes, but Tashlich felt like a day of shared understanding. We never told Father, in case we had to stop it. The newcomers said their prayers at Tower Hill, only five miles downriver, but they were strangers and we never joined them either.

We'd let the tradition lapse, after Father's death. Why was I dwelling on it now? I was on another mystery mission, feeling optimistic. I'd write to Ruth and ask: *wasn't Tashlich fun? Did you think of it, when you saw Venice marry the sea?* It would fill up a letter, without saying *Sam is alive, come home*, which I couldn't say for another four days. Or *Toby might be lying to you*, which couldn't yet be proved.

The train curled into Breakwater station round the side of a hill. The dip that cradled the village was full of curling sea mist. It had advanced miles inland. I stepped from the station and could only just see across the road. The church tower was a shadow. My destination was two miles beyond the village, so I set out, striding into the whiteness.

The damp air prickled the skin of my face. I made my way down the hill from the station, shuffled along by the river. Everything was made ghostly. People became visible only moments before they knocked into me, then we coughed apologies to one another. At least if I met Mrs Winscott, Lucy's mother, I could pretend not to have seen her.

I had to leave the village on a road I'd never taken before. It was no better than a rough path with hedges either side, and the mist prevented me from anticipating its turns, or dodging the overhanging branches. Within half a mile, my coat was heavy with moisture and my face scratched.

The hedge gave way to a long redbrick wall, the boundary of an estate. After five minutes, the wall curved inwards to a neat set of gates. Wrought iron and standing half open. A plaque on the gatepost announced: *The Larches*.

From what I could see in the mist, The Larches was a modern building. I thought of Breakwater as antique and charming, so this big plain brick block was a shock, squatting in the woods. The long rows of little windows, what did each one hold? An invalid? A mad man?

On a large arched door, another plaque read: *A place of relaxation*. I stood inside the porch and shivered. What if they weren't open? What if they'd closed entirely, and left no more than traces: this sign on the door, their card in Toby's drawer?

I rang anyway. A tall maid opened the door and allowed me into the hall.

The hallway was painted yellow. Cheerful enough, but institutional. The owner had scrutinised every rug and ornament, and said: 'Yes, very nice, but it'll only gather dust.' And then thrown them out. Bare walls, linoleum flooring. My nose twitched with lemon-scented soap.

I felt dizzy and weak, and realised the house was terribly hot. Even here in the hall, there was a fug like a kitchen on wash day. The sick people who lived here needed high temperatures. Was that why Sam was always heaping the coal on the fire, had he become accustomed to heat? Some residents might have tuberculosis. I questioned the wisdom of my visit all over again. I'd make myself ill.

'Are you visiting one of our residents, Miss?'

'No, I wish to speak to the proprietor.' Or was it the matron? Would I need to make an appointment?

The maid – or was she a nurse? – strode off to announce me.

Two corridors ran off from the hallway, one in each direction. Down one of them, a gramophone played harp music. The machine was off kilter; the music sped up and squeaked, then the notes dropped as it slowed, as if the harpist was drunk.

Firm feet on the hall floor, returning, signalled the arrival of the owner. She was an older lady, dressed as plainly as the house was decorated. She ushered me into her office.

I sat across the desk from her, and my soaked coat felt so heavy. In her hot office, my clothes would start steaming.

'What can I do for you, madam?' She had a Dutch accent which gave the words a different rhythm.

I opened my mouth to lie about my missing brother. She might already have careless and unjust opinions of me, and I worried she would smell the brandy on my breath. I tried again, with fewer lies: 'I'm looking for my sister's fiancé. He had an accident on the river, a couple of miles from here, and we believed he had drowned. But now we think he may have recovered, and stayed in a hospital or a home.' And Toby may have tried to hide him, but that was wandering into guesswork.

The owner nodded sedately. 'There are places like this, yes, all along this part of the country. The air is very good.'

'His name was Samuel Silver, and…'

'So sorry, I cannot tell you he was here, or he was not here.'

I said, dully: 'I understand.' My head spun. I'd come all this way, and I'd have to go back with no news and wet clothes. I was angry at Sam, but still desperate for him to think me brilliant and irreplaceable.

'If he was here, he would have been cared for very well.' It was too polished. Like the vicar, she was used to soothing people's fears.

The tall maid showed me back to the hall.

'Will you wait here? Are you being collected?' The young woman had the same homely accent as Lucy. I could see she was confused at the brevity of my visit. My face must have been frightful. She was broad shouldered and good humoured, would be a useful assistant in any accident.

'No, I'm walking back to the station.'

'Dry your coat before you go, Miss? In the hot room, downstairs. Ten minutes would finish it.'

'Thank you so much.'

We were about the same age. This girl was more kind and less canny than the proprietor. I considered what tool would crack her. Should I try to command her, or bribe her?

'I came to see where my brother stayed,' I improvised. 'I couldn't visit when he was here, and now…'

Her face creased with sympathy and I let myself cry. I was a poor detective, but I could try this small manipulation. Even as I shook with sobs, I was asking: *Will it work?* My body cried and my mind watched it, judging it very picturesque. Very much like a weeping woman in a folk song.

I fumbled in my pocket for Sam's card and showed it to her. 'This is Sam,' I said.

She glanced at it. 'Oh, a lovely gentleman,' she said. 'Here for the winter.'

The fluttering in my chest turned to pounding. Could it be a mistake? His face on the card only a finger-smudge, after all, the maid answering out of politeness.

But she nodded in recognition. Lucy would have refused, and seen through this whole shabby trick. 'So unfair.'

Her words were hope and despair, yes and no at the same time. 'What was unfair?'

'A young man, in that state.'

What state? I couldn't ask. And if I asked her when Sam had been here, or where he'd gone after, she'd know I was spying.

I let my tears well up again. 'They won't tell me where they took him,' I sobbed. 'After he left here.' That would cover anything. Burial, recovery, kidnapping. 'They said I was too young…' That might stoke her indignation.

She shook her head. 'I can't say.'

'I know he was in the water for a while,' I said, throwing out a desperate guess.

'Yes,' she said, very gently. 'He wasn't himself.' She meant it as a comfort, that I hadn't really missed seeing him. But it summoned up horrors.

'What do you mean?'

The maid shook her head. 'I'm sorry, I shouldn't have said.'

I pictured Sam in this place, *not himself.* Not able to speak? Not able to smile? Propped up in an institutional bed, and taking the patient's role in endless rituals: cold baths and examinations. The gramophone music down the corridor crackled and began again. I needed this girl to tell me the truth, not make menacing generalisations.

'He was engaged to be married,' I said, a truth to help the truth along.

'What a shame, Miss.'

I tried another angle. 'His brother was very distressed. Mister Toby Silver.'

I waited for the maid's verdict on Toby. Had he been a lovely gentleman, too? Had he seemed compassionate, demanding the best for his brother? Or merely efficient, bundling Sam out of sight?

'It's a sore trial.' No judgement for Toby. Had she even met him? Toby must have arranged Sam's stay here, but had he visited?

'Did you see him, here? Toby?'

'Your coat, Miss?'

The fish had squirmed off my hook. I was unable to cry more; the hothouse had desiccated me. I sat in the hall and waited for my coat to dry. I might have left without it, except that my return ticket was in the coat pocket. I grew increasingly dozy.

I'd tried asking, and I'd tried crying. Why not try sneaking and spying? I had a convincing reason, after all. I was only looking for my coat.

For lack of any other thread to follow, I walked towards the gramophone music. It was far down the left-hand corridor. Every door along the way had a small glass window set in it, showing a bedroom or a ward beyond, with patients sitting or sleeping. Everything was yellow-painted, everything was hot.

The wobbling tune led me eventually to a large lounge. There were clusters of high-winged chairs, facing away from me towards the windows. The windows would normally look out over the hills, I imagined, but all they showed today was mist. A table offered untouched amusements: dominoes and the daily papers. The gramophone stood in the centre.

It struck me that the gramophone shouldn't have been here. I wasn't good at judging what things cost, but the hospital was simple and the gramophone was fancy.

I peered at the manufacturer's mark. It was a Berliner, the same make as Sam's gift to Ruth. My sense of its misplacement came from considering it Ruth's machine. I hate the way manufactured objects cheat your affection: you recognise a toy animal, and you think it's yours, the one you love and have a special name for, but it's a totally different thing. Could Sam have bought it for himself, to enliven his stay? Or could Toby have donated it? In either case, Sam could have heard this lopsided music. It might stir his recollections.

I lifted the needle off the disc to quiet the weird tune. I put the disc away in its paper cover, to protect it from dust and scratches.

As soon as it was in its cover, in my hands, I knew I intended to steal it. I'd take it home to Sam and play it. I hugged it close to my chest. How could I hide it?

'We've got better ones than that,' said a man's voice from behind me. 'If you're going to pinch one.'

I stumbled against the gramophone, startled.

'Didn't mean to scare you,' the man said. I could see him now. He was in the darker part of the room, in a chair with a blanket across his knees. He had a lean face, slightly yellow in tone, but aside from that, his appearance didn't explain his presence here. He could be a hatter or a March hare, or have any disease, including something contagious.

'I'm sorry, I'll put it back.'

'I was teasing! You're not from one of the other rooms, are you?'

'No.'

'What's the story?' He had a shadow of Sam's charm.

'I came looking for my brother-in-law.'

'Did you find him?'

'No.'

'I'd help you, but I've not been here a week myself.' So there was no benefit in interrogating him. 'I'm here for the fresh air. I've only met Ralph.' He pointed to another man, in a chair opposite him, asleep. 'Great conversationalist, Ralph.' The man conveyed that Ralph was the invalid here, not him. Could I quiz him as to the purpose of this place, its specialisms? Did it take incurables? But that was a consequential question.

'It's a good place,' he said, trying to reassure me. 'The nurses talk about you like you're not here, but the food's tolerable. Take that cursed music disc away with you, I've heard it umpteen times. Anything else?'

I looked around the room. I couldn't see anything else which would remind Sam of this place. The sheets were sheets, there was nothing distinctive about the cups. I took a breath, to decline his kind offer.

I smelled soap.

'Yes. Please.' I spotted a small jug and basin set, and picked up the soap. It had the lemony astringent smell that permeated the whole house. 'Can I take this?'

'What's mine is yours, fair lady,' he said. Speaking cost him an effort. 'Get going, though, or Matron will catch us.'

We waved goodbye ungracefully. As I walked back down the corridor I heard a jagged note: a man, crying. It was painful to listen, but the weeper himself sounded in sorrow, not pain. The noise lingered while I strode away. This place might also be a mad-house – put more kindly, a place for the treatment of the mind. The man I'd just met could have been suffering in that regard. Sam could have been treated for amnesia here.

How stupid to come! And how stupidly I'd behaved: asking after a dead man, crying, stealing. The proprietor could ask the Breakwater vicar about me, and then an alienist would be sent to my home. And then confinement, shame and staring at a lemon-painted ceiling myself.

I scurried back to the hall and hid the gramophone record under my seat.

The maid brought me back my coat, roasting hot and only slightly damp. She left me alone to put it on, so she wouldn't be cozened into conversation again.

I fled with my swag and my trove of information.

Down the front path, a wrong turn, and I was lost in the misty gardens of the hospital. Passing a bench, doubling back to take another route, I found myself at the same bench. I realised after a few tries that there were many little paths and many identical benches, so that several residents could take turns round the garden at the same time.

I struck out decisively across the lawn, and nearly fell into the river.

A hand-rail caught me in the stomach, and stopped me from pitching forwards down a steep bank. Below me, the river churned, deep and fast. It must be the Breakwater River, running alongside the road I'd walked up, but a way off, not visible. Then it swooped in closer again to circle around the hospital.

The river frightened me, as though it had deliberately followed me here. But at least it was a landmark in the mist. By keeping The Larches on one hand, and the long line of fencing that marked off the river on the other hand, I was able to find a route out of the gardens. I walked at a fierce pace back through the fog, down the misty road. Now I knew the river was there, I could hear it chuckle behind the hedges.

I caught the train. Sleeping on the journey, I pictured Sam in the river, hair floating like water weed.

Opening the door of my home, I caught myself smiling. I was hurrying to tell Sam grave things. But I was smiling.

The muscles you use to smile have strange properties. There

have been times when I've been unable to sleep, and in the end
I've realised it was the muscles of my face – the *levator labii* and
the *orbicularis oculi*; I had learned the terms while studying portrait
painting – all tensed up with glee or annoyance. When I let my
face go slack, and the emotion drain away, then I've slept.

I went into the library looking appropriately sombre, hoping
the feeling would follow.

Sam wasn't there. The room smelled smoky and appeared
particularly drab, our campaign table pathetic. There was no news
on the big sheets of paper, no recollections plucked from Sam's
foggy brain, no facts rooted out by me. All my new evidence, new
questions, new suspicions, were bundled up inside me.

Someone had tidied a little, Lucy or Sam. The empty
punchbowl had been taken away, as had the plateful of wax. The
charred wall hanging was still bundled under the desk (I stooped
to check) and the pool of wine still stained the carpet.

I poured a small glass of brandy and drank it. I couldn't get
used to it; under the fruity smell it tasted like turpentine. I wanted
to sit in my old chair, but now it felt more like *his* chair, so I paced
around instead and wondered where he was. Walking in the park,
with Toby's scarf disguising his face? Or gone away entirely?

There was a new sheaf of papers on the desk, and I pulled it
over, in case Sam had been working on answers to my questions.
But there were no answers on the sheets of paper.

I brought the lamp closer. There were spindly lines. Curves,
maps of coastlines. No. Bodies, naked bodies.

I was so startled I stood up.

They must have been drawn by Samuel. I couldn't believe he'd
left them on display. They were obscene, imaginary women – or
even women he knew, undressed by his imagination? Did that
one look like Lucy?

Sam, standing behind me, said: 'They're not very good, I'm
afraid.'

I'd heard that tone – proud but fearing criticism – many times from women at Mrs Fortune's studio. It put the sketches in a completely different context. They were his efforts at art.

'I used encyclopaedia entries, the way you told me you did.'

I felt my face turn scarlet. Why had I immediately condemned the sketches? Wasn't I a student of art? Mrs Fortune had needed to argue hard for her students to draw nudes, just as male students could. Ella had told me so.

I re-examined Sam's pictures. The poses, the angles, their serene faces… Clearly they weren't real women. Statues, every one.

'I thought I'd see what you do all day,' he said. 'I know it's not the same. I hope you don't mind.'

I could see in them the same mistakes I'd made a few months ago. I could already see myself giving him advice on the uses of shadow, how to give proportion to a foreshortened limb. But he and I couldn't sit together, tutor and pupil, over a heap of nudes.

'Come outside,' he said. That suggestion wasn't without peril, but it took us further away from his sketches. Before I agreed, I brought out the record from The Larches and placed it on Ruth's gramophone. I hoped it might prompt an immediate recollection, making my disclosure unnecessary. I left the door open so the tune could wind out into the garden. Taking my glass with me I followed Sam out into the dark.

I peered at him, sidelong, and he was grinning so much, I asked: 'You've remembered?'

'No, not yet.' But he didn't stop smiling. He offered me his arm as we walked, but I kept both my hands on my wineglass.

The gardens were so neat, after trekking through the countryside around Breakwater. A little neglected for a city garden, but not out of control. With the music playing, it felt like being in the garden at a dance. It had been an age since I'd been to a proper dance, hosted by a schoolfriend, gawping at her glamorous elder brothers in their beautiful suits. Even when I had danced, it hadn't lived up to my imaginings. I'd anticipated being carried by the music. But I hadn't had enough practice, or my partners had been clumsy. I'd danced with Samuel twice; it had been hilarious. He'd joked I should stand on his shoes and he'd whisk me around the room. Like men do to children.

'I have news,' I said, very quietly. If he didn't hear me, and didn't ask, I could put off telling him for ever.

'What's that?' He sat on our bench.

I told him about the hospital hothouse, up the road from Breakwater. The lemon-painted hallway. I handed him the bar of soap, and he didn't laugh. He sniffed the scent. From indoors, Ruth's gramophone reeled out the tune that might remind him, although Ruth's machine played it smoothly, not in a lopsided rhythm.

I told Sam that he'd been there, at The Larches, probably. Alive, when Toby had let us believe he was dead. I didn't ask: *what was your brother doing?* I didn't suggest any explanation.

I held my tongue and gripped my wineglass.

Was he conjuring up again, in his head, the crisp sheets of a convalescent bed? A yellow room? Delirium, fever, being bathed and discussed as though he wasn't there?

'Poor thing,' Sam said. 'You've been worrying about me all day. All *week*.'

He was examining me. I met his eyes, then had to dip my head.

'It's only been…' I couldn't calculate how long he'd been here. I managed to count forwards, instead, and know that in four days' time – a little less – I could tell Ruth. He'd agreed to it; we'd both promised. I tried to move his attention away from me, back to The Larches and my discoveries. 'I've been worrying because it *is* worrying. It's very strange, because Toby –'

'That *does* all sound strange.' His forehead creased with

concern, but I had a notion that he was relishing the moment, drinking in my interest. The swinging indecision and the self-doubt from yesterday were both gone, and he was all attention. 'Very strange for you.'

'Very strange of *Toby*.'

'I'm sure there's a reason.' I was sure there was a reason, as well, to hide Sam away, but was the reason good enough? Or was it for some hateful motive, like money? I couldn't say that, but Sam must see it. 'Toby probably didn't want to cause you all more distress. It might explain... Every time I think of Toby, it's as though he's angry at me – I know, he was always grumpy. But more so than usual. I've been nervous. I suppose, if I was convalescent – he might have been frustrated, or I might have felt I was letting him down.'

'Nervous about Toby?' Sam had always laughed off Toby's fits of anger.

'Afraid of him.'

His voice was still not entirely serious. He glanced out at the garden as he spoke, as though he were remarking on the shrubs. The music from the inside the house wheezed and failed.

'What?'

'It's been wonderful to stay here, with you. I've felt very rested and safe. That might be because Toby's away. I could never really feel at ease around him, you know? He was always ranting on at me, for one thing or another. You know. The things were never serious, but he got so hopping mad—'

'Sam—'

'I'll mull it over, I swear. And we can look into it. You can investigate it! Just as you promised you would. You're a wonderful detective.' He reached for me and I wasn't quick enough to pull away this time. For a moment his cold hands wrapped around mine. 'Thank you for it. I mean it, Judith. I couldn't have got through these last days without my little detective.'

Sam was relishing this new recollection of his, enjoying the idea of his own fear. He watched me, as if to see whether he'd caught my curiosity.

'I'll leave you to consider, then.' I pulled my hands away, stood and gave him a deep nod or a shallow bow. I placed my wineglass on the bench. Then I paced back up the path. I had to do it carefully because I was unsteady on my feet, and because it was dark, and because I wanted to run and needed to slow myself down.

Once I was inside, I did run. Straight up the staircase, two at a time, and I shut myself in my room.

Samuel still couldn't tell me anything. Despite all the tricks I'd played, the gifts I'd brought him, treasures from his missing life: scenes, scents, tunes. None of it had prompted any real recollections. Just the ghost of his brother's anger, which could have been from any time at all.

Lucky forgetful Sam. Telling him all that, and sitting in the garden in the dark with music, pulling my hand from his, had dislodged another memory in me. I wished it hadn't.

Eighteen months ago, Sam had been teasing us on the train to Breakwater.

'This whole festival is very secret. No, stop smirking, you…'

Toby wasn't smirking. Toby was scowling at Sam, who'd brought us on another unchaperoned trip.

'Where's their mother?' he demanded, as though Ruth and I weren't sitting across the train compartment from them. He was an unchivalrous champion.

'Their mama would have come, but she had a headache,' Sam explained.

'It's not good enough!'

'We'll be married in six months! We're nearly family.'

'You're not married yet! And you're not marrying Judith,' Toby snapped across me.

'You're our chaperone, Tobes,' Sam said sweetly. That was cruel of him. An older man – an *old* man – could chaperone, but Toby was (at least theoretically) an eligible young bachelor.

'Samuel, you're being deliberately stupid.'

'So you're saying you shouldn't be left alone with these young ladies? What a dangerous character you are, Tobes, I never knew.'

Breakwater always made Toby irritable at his brother. Because of the expense of the cottage? Because Sam played the clown more when out of the city? We'd stopped off at Stonehenge to see the midsummer sunrise that morning. Toby had been briefly awed into silence by the monoliths, but he was getting up steam again now.

I watched the steep sides of the cutting as we approached the village, a cool green tunnel. I tried not to let my face show what I was reflecting on. Mrs Leuniger, the wife of our family lawyer, had called unexpectedly two days previously. She'd suggested that Mama stop Ruth and her beau being seen together so often, unescorted.

Mama was happy to relate that the pair had agreed to marry in the winter, as soon as Sam's family affairs had been put in order, and that Ruth had been introduced to Sam's relatives. They were safely on their way to the chuppah. Mrs Leuniger congratulated her joyfully for two whole minutes before returning to her original theme. Ruth should surely be careful, for if any obstacle to their union should arise…

'There's many a slip 'twixt cup and lip!' said Mrs Leuniger. A joke, to accompany the insult. *You are an inadequate mother*, she was saying, *and your daughter's reputation is compromised.*

Listening through the door, I vowed never to tell Ruth about it. It was just before midsummer, and Sam and Ruth would wed just after midwinter. We simply needed to survive six months and the problem would evaporate.

'Hey, you, Miss Judith. No talking about this festival,' Sam commanded. 'Don't even mention its name! We'll be thrown out, driven out of the village. Pay attention.'

I had been paying attention. Not to Sam, but to the gradual slowing of the train. We needed to fetch our luggage down, and Sam was showing off instead.

'I won't mention it,' I said, standing up and taking hold of my own bag (a change of clothes and a box of charcoal).

'Don't even say its name!'

'We won't,' Ruth pledged, hand half-jokingly on her heart. Then, more seriously: 'Was it a bad idea, to come?' She'd been eager for it for weeks, but Sam's talk had sown doubts.

'You'll enjoy it!'

Ruth was placated, but how could Sam know she'd enjoy it? He'd never been to the festival either.

We stepped onto the platform. The vicar and his wife had come to meet us. He offered me a hand down from the carriage, and she kissed me on the cheek. Their noses were sunburned.

'You're all here for the Seething, then?' asked the vicar.

I was wrong-footed. I didn't feel bound by Sam's desire for secrecy, but I certainly wouldn't have instigated a discussion with the vicar. The Seething wasn't a church festival, and its theme, even watered down, was inappropriate (another reason why we should have brought a chaperone).

'Oh! Are we allowed to talk about it?' I asked.

The vicar glanced around us at the empty platform. 'Fair question, Miss Sachs, fair question. I mean to say, Edward the farrier told me you'd be arriving for the Seething. But I may have overlooked some nuances.'

The others were wrestling their larger suitcases from the train, so the vicar, his wife and I hid in the shade.

'Now, you two girls are very welcome to stay at the vicarage,' offered the vicar's wife. She patted my arm. 'We'd be delighted.'

'We'll be fine at the cottage, thank you.'

'Your mama's not with you?' She spoke with the same bright bluntness that Mama's friend had adopted.

I changed the subject. 'Do you have a part to play in the Seething?' Other vicars I'd met had boasted of how they'd brought the local maypole, or solstice dancing, into the church calendar, to the benefit of all. The Seething sounded more difficult for the church to claim.

'No role. I don't normally attend. But I understand it serves a useful purpose. A calming influence.' He stepped over to take Ruth's hat box, and I was left to wonder how a courting ritual could calm anyone.

He persuaded a trap to take our luggage and joined us on the walk to our cottage.

Mrs Winscott had cleaned the cottage and left cake. In the garden, with a slice of sponge, the vicar explained to me: 'The Seething's become a more or less formal commitment, whatever its earlier incarnations. In many ways it keeps people on the straight and narrow. Or rather…' He pinched his cake crumbs into pellets, conscious of the indelicacy of the topic. 'It brings things into the open. There's less ambiguity to exploit.'

Sam cut in. 'So, if I take Miss Sachs to the festival, the whole village knows, and the other young men won't chance their arm with her? Throw their hat into the ring?'

My sister protested at being a 'for instance'.

Even more embarrassed, the vicar tried to draw some lines. 'Let's say it's not as formal, not as *certain* as a betrothal, but after the Seething – well, you can't pretend you don't know who is courting.'

'That's a useful thing,' Toby said.

'Somewhat. It encourages people to take their responsibilities seriously, as well.'

'And what happens to those who don't?' Toby asked. 'The arm-chancers.'

The vicar decided he'd said too much for propriety. 'Oh, just… disapproval.'

'No breach-of-promise cases out here in the countryside, old boy,' Sam said, waving an urbane hand around the garden.

'I was imagining something more rustic,' Toby said.

'It's all just a bit of fun,' Sam insisted. 'Dress up, sprinkle a little water around, drink beer in the sunshine.'

'If there's a chancer, or a jilter, a few young men could turn up at the fellow's cottage,' Toby continued, 'and teach him a lesson.'

The vicar set down his plate. 'I'd never condone that. A general air of disapproval is enough…'

'There's no point if there's no penalty.' Toby's expression was thunderous.

The vicar's wife diverted Toby by asking about Jewish wedding customs, and Toby earnestly talked about balancing our different family traditions, something which seemed not to bother Sam. Sam had not stood on ceremony when proposing to Ruth. He'd asked Mama's permission, but in a rather relaxed fashion, expecting the answer 'yes'. I almost asked Ruth if that was very modern of him, or slapdash. But her engagement changed everything. Before, Ruth and I had stood together against the world. Now, Ruth stood with Sam. I shouldn't ask her to tell tales against him.

When the vicar and his wife left, Sam roared: 'Well, they've taken the fun out of this one, by the sound of it. Church endorsement, no less!'

Ruth said the vicar and his wife were very sweet. She carried the cake plates back into the cottage.

'It's not like the vicar says,' Sam said. 'There's all sorts of shenanigans happening – all over the village, all the time – and he doesn't have a clue. Country girls aren't like you prim city madams.'

Toby leaned over, as though to pick a piece of fluff from Sam's collar, and struck him round the ear without speaking.

Sam's eyes went wide from shock. I fled indoors before he could respond. Ruth and I should have stayed at the vicarage, but I was too ashamed to go running after the offer.

The day wore on and grew no cooler. When the sun dropped, the heat poured back out of the earth. We played cards, waited for a sign and saw none. Just when I might have retreated to my attic bedroom, from outside came raised voices, jeering, fierce laughs. A moment of nerves: had the vicar's wife been trying to protect us from something other than impropriety? Then the yells melted into the sound of high singing.

We stepped into the street. Dusk confused the distances. Ruth fretted, nearly turned back for a hat, but didn't want to miss a moment, and I caught her eye and nodded a reassurance. The villagers were converging, slipping from their houses and joining the flow, moving into the woods alongside the river.

We walked without singing. The tune wasn't hard, although it was in an odd sad key, but I didn't know what it would mean to sing. I didn't mean to imply I was looking for a suitor. I was only watching.

There were too many of us to keep to the track, and I trampled wild garlic in the verge and the sharp smell of it surrounded me. Brambles tore my ankles. The procession disturbed roosting crows, who cried a raucous counterpoint to the plain tune.

A large pool in the wood, near circular, the inhabitants of the village clustered around it. Lamps and torches reflected in it.

A man stood in the pool, holding a horn, scooping up water. He wore a mask: a face of leaves, topped with antlers. I didn't recognise him. Furs were strapped to his legs. A goat-man, a stag-man.

And then everyone sang, and everyone moved.

The tune was a dozen times louder, and most of the villagers were dropping back. No, fighting their way backwards. I saw why

when the first hornful of water was thrown across the crowd.
Shrieks and glee. I saw a thatcher in the front row, who nodded to
his wife. They were old enough that their children were grown.
She grinned back at him and he swung her into his arms, then
staggered with her to the edge of the pool. Cheers encouraged
them. When the man began to lose his footing, the pool dweller,
the antler-man, darted forwards and drenched them.

Not solely for courting couples, then. I hadn't seen the vicar.
I knew he'd be here, though, monitoring the pairings.

The whole clearing fell to negotiation. Couples advanced shyly,
holding hands. A team of boys besieged a single girl – I thought
it was Lucy's sister, Bonnie – and play-acted passion, begging on
their knees while she scorned to even look at them. Bold girls
picked up their swains and took them to be wetted. Several couples
were prodded in, or ducked, and I couldn't tell if it was because
the village wished them good luck, or because of their misdeeds.

I hummed the tune, not knowing the words.

'Why not?' Sam was asking behind me. 'It was you who asked
to come.'

I turned to see, and he was already holding Ruth in his arms,
off the ground.

I was shocked. I shook my head. He should put her down – it
was dangerous – but no, he was a tall man, and strong enough to
carry her securely. She was perfectly safe.

It was the intimacy of it that appalled me. I'd seen them touch
hands, nothing more. Now he had an arm around her waist,
another under her legs.

I shouldn't mind. Not if she didn't mind. Did she?

'I'll keep the worst off you,' Sam assured her.

'I really don't... Judith?' She stretched out her hand to me
for help, for traction against Sam. Our fingers tangled. I had to
step forwards with them, or her arm would have bent backwards.

'Sam, *please*,' she said.

I shouted as I was dragged after them, trying not to let go. I looked around for Toby but all I saw was the crowd, cheering and smiling as we walked. Bonnie was there, still affecting disdain, but by the time I thought of calling to her for help, I'd lost her again.

I couldn't trip him. I couldn't kick him or push him into the water because Ruth might get hurt.

He had to stop at the edge of the pool, and Ruth pulled me close, put her arms round my neck to drag herself out of his embrace. At that moment Sam realised how serious she was, but our bodies were a jigsaw; how could he lower her to the ground without us all falling?

At that moment, blood-warm water slapped across all three of us.

I spat. The pond water trickled down my face. If I opened my eyes, squirming things would invade them. But Ruth had let go of my hand, so I forced myself to look.

What I saw was the man with the antlers, pink tongue stuck out in among the green leaves of his face.

Ruth leaned on me to walk back to the cottage. I didn't look at Sam, because I was still furious at him, and because of another thing. It hadn't been Sam's lack of propriety that had made me heartsick at the water's edge, but my jealousy.

I smuggled cake and sherry to the room I shared with Ruth. Through my mind, questions ran: will Ruth break things off? What would we do, if she didn't marry him after all? She'd been alone with him too much. She wouldn't be respectable. We'd be back where we were before Sam arrived, but worse: three portionless women in a too-big house that Mama refused to sell, getting more impoverished every year. I recalled a dismal conversation, a year before, where Ruth had asked my opinion of 'mixed marriages', speaking like a woman destined for the gallows.

I hadn't known what to reply. Marrying a man who wasn't Jewish was somewhere between unspeakable and impractical; where would one even begin?

When the men returned to the cottage, Toby was ranting, worse than we'd ever heard him. 'That *poor* girl,' he bellowed, several times. He stormed around the ground floor, floorboards creaked as he paced, doors slammed. 'Poor *girls*!' Was I the extra poor girl? Did he know I loved Sam, too? That was dangerous. Sam was a half-hearted voice, trying to jolly Toby out of it, then Sam was silent. I worried that Toby had hit him. Not just a clip to his ear, but a proper crushing fist. Sam moved quicker, but Toby was sturdy.

After everything fell silent, thirst drove me downstairs. I went barefoot in my dressing gown, clutching a porcelain jug in front of me in the dark. There were spots to step so the stairs didn't creak.

'I'm glad you came,' said a low voice from a chair by the fireside. 'Am I forgiven?'

My eyes adjusted further to the dark. Sam was facing the fire. I suddenly knew that he'd taken me for Ruth. If I didn't answer, he'd turn and see me half-dressed. 'It's Judith.'

'Oh! And have *you* forgiven me?'

I hadn't.

'Well, I won't ask you about Ruth. I can't make you play the intermediary!' He'd asked me to do so a dozen times. 'I'll sort things out with her in the morning.'

My heart slithered around. Ruth must forgive him, I must squash my jealousy. We must all return to the sickening normal.

'You should apologise properly.' My audacity surprised me, but I needed to make him understand. This would require more than his usual charm. No use piling on logs if the embers were smothered.

'You sound like Toby.' Sam sank lower in his chair and ranted at the fire. 'Toby doesn't see a damn thing. You know he's given money for all that dredging and building work, down on the river? His grand drainage plan!'

I did. It was a serious and philanthropic scheme, it suited him.

'He means to squeeze the river, keep it on course. Typical! He doesn't understand, not everything runs on tracks. Rivers wander. Things spring up, all over the place, connections flourish, it's cruel to cut them off…'

His hands caressed the air around him, but he still hadn't turned in his chair, and I wondered how much wine he'd drunk. I backed towards the kitchen, felt my way to the tap and fitted the jug under it. The water at Breakwater always tasted so fresh.

'It's *life*, Judith. You understand, don't you?'

Sam was standing at my back.

'Naturally you understand.' I felt him rest his chin on the top of my head, as though I were a child, or a piece of furniture. 'You understand far more than the rest of them. It's all right, you know. The things you feel, I feel the same way.' He settled his hand on my shoulder. His fingers were chill. 'I don't know what I'd do without my little Judith. You're clever. You'll find a way to make it work. A way for everybody who's connected to stay together. Will you tell me how to do it?'

He was murmuring into my hair. He was asking me to solve the one puzzle I couldn't. There was no way for him and me to be together. 'I can't.'

His breath brushed my cheek. 'Then I'll have to find a way myself. Yes! I'll do it. Put it out of your mind, don't waste a moment worrying.'

He was speaking too much and too quickly. When I ran the words back through my mind, they were jumbled. 'Sam, I don't—'

'Judith. I'll *fix* it.' He started stroking me, running his hands down my arms and up over my shoulders again, to soothe himself.

I turned as sharply as I could. The jug of water knocked him, not hard but it startled him and splashed on us both. He jumped

back, or I shoved past him. Leaping up the creaking stairs back
to bed, I threw off my wet dressing gown, and crept back under
the blankets beside Ruth.

So that was how Sam sounded, I thought, when he spoke
about love. Slapdash, offhand, indignant.

The next day, at breakfast, Sam was subdued and attentive.
Ruth seemed content with Toby having chastised Sam, and Sam's
sore head; she ate with them and was perfectly friendly to both.
The betrothal was not called off.

Routine carried me along: packing our clothes and lugging
our cases and calling a lad to fetch a cart for the station. Then
I half dozed, on the train, and accidentally let a question rise in
my mind: what should I do, loving my sister's fiancé, knowing
that he loved me too?

The relief was that the question led nowhere. This new
state was no better than unrequited love. Like a loop of ribbon
tied with a knot, it was no use except to turn round and round
your finger.

I didn't dream, that night, of the woman rising up from the lake.
I saw who that woman was, who I'd feared. She wasn't bewitching,
she had no forbidden knowledge. She was unformed, lumpish,
laughable. She was a thwarted girl with a sinister passion. Who
was making a fraudulent, unjustified claim on Sam's affection?
Who had to be deprived, for the sake of my sister's happiness, and
punished, and expelled?

It had always and only been me.

I woke in the dark, or hadn't slept.

Lighting my lamp, I was surprised by the quantity of bruises
on my arm. Previously green, they'd spread and faded into
sullen mustard. I hurried to lift my chemise and find where they
bloomed all along my ribs, down over my hip. Anywhere I'd

slammed myself against the ground, trying to reach Sam in the lake. And fresh scrapes from Breakwater, on my hand and up my opposite arm. It made me gratified, boastful: *look what I can endure!* Daylight would let me see more, and by then, more stains would have appeared.

The air in the room felt thick with significance, like dust in an unused space. This time I hadn't summoned it, but it still compelled me.

I went back to the library. Lucy had tidied away what I sought, but I discovered them eventually, stacked in a withered heap: the plants I'd brought from Breakwater. I'd brought him flowers! How had I deluded myself that I didn't still want him? Shabby flowers, though. Weeds. Yarrow, I knew from *English Folk-lore*, could be used to dream of your love, but you had to pluck it from a young man's grave.

The velvet air said: *Destroy them. Eat them.* But they were tough, and could be poisonous.

The air said: *Burn them, then.* Don't you ever want to chuck it all out, start fresh?

But the fire in the grate had gone out.

Go to the lake. Get rid of them.

I walked into the garden, which was moon-drained of colour, the long grass flattened by the wind. The air remained thick around me, protecting me from the cold, moving me steadily towards the lake.

The lake had thawed somewhat, with slabs of white ice drifting in the green murk. I came to a standstill, struggling to comprehend. Had I brought Sam back, by wanting him? By missing him, by mourning him? No. I wasn't so important that my desire could seize Sam and drag him here.

Whatever had brought him back, he stayed now for his own reasons, for his own delights.

I tried to turn aside, but the soft nudge insisted that the

lakeside was where I needed to be. Should I throw myself in? No, that was foolish. It was only necessary to throw the flowers.

I watched them drift away on the surface of the water. As soon as I did, the air was thinner. To show no passion, that was good. To want less was the best way to survive. And if I felt anything, never to speak of it. I'd known all this before. I had to relearn those old habits of denial.

Over the wind's low howl, I heard footsteps behind me. I imagined how the fingers would rest on my shoulder, the hands stroke my arms. I spun round, I shoved at the person behind me.

The person I struck was too slight and short to be Sam. With a cry, Lucy was suddenly on her back on the grass.

'I'm sorry.' I held out a hand to her. 'I'm so sorry.' I stooped to help her, but she rolled in the other direction and got up without my assistance.

'Jesus, Miss!'

'I didn't mean to!'

She shook her head slowly. 'Your *face*—'

'I was surprised by you.' That sounded plausible. 'I thought you were someone else.'

'Nobody else out here,' said Lucy, automatically.

Was there any point in the pretence that we didn't have a visitor? But we were both unwilling to relinquish it. 'I know. I'm so sorry.'

I stared up at Millstone. The ghost-light in the bedroom was burning.

'Look,' I said. 'There's a person in Millstone. Do you know who?' Maybe the maids of our two houses talked to one another.

Lucy didn't move an inch. 'Bain't nobody in Millstone, Miss.' The maid at The Larches had cemented my deductions with a word; now Lucy was undermining me, just as easily. Disputing my eyes.

My faculties were failing. It was my fault; I'd courted unreason, all this week. I'd lied to Lucy.

Staring up at the light, I let myself feel everything I could, as fully as I could – the grass under the bare soles of my feet, my aching hands. The wind moaned around us.

The light in Millstone was no less real than anything else. I could not be imagining it.

Hadn't we had this same argument on the night Sam arrived? Both of us trying to convince the other that the garden was empty, that we were alone. I had been hiding Sam. Now Lucy was surely hiding something from me. I should do her the courtesy of allowing it, not pressing her to confession. Even a maid should have some privacy. But not at the expense of my sanity.

'Lucy, I fear for my mind. I fear I am mad. Are you telling me that there is no light, up there, in Millstone?'

Lucy looked up.

'You're right, Miss. There's a light.'

That was enough for me, for now.

SUNDAY

S unday morning, and the first sign of another soul I saw was a letter lying on the floor of the hallway. Not from my sister (a pity) or the blackmailer (a blessing) but in an unfamiliar hand. For privacy and comfort, I ran with it back to my room, and climbed back into the nest of bedclothes I'd just vacated. I ripped open the letter.

It was from the vicar of Breakwater.

> *Dear Miss Sachs, I hope you received the benefit of the bracing air of your last visit and are not cast down by the dark evenings. May nature be a solace to you, as to me; this morning I saw buds on a horse chestnut like tiny lamps in the sunlight!*

I skimmed the remainder.

The vicar offered me support, and enquired after my health. I resented the implication that I was unwell. However, I was fully dressed and curled under a heap of blankets and coats, trying to shiver quietly in case Sam heard me. The vicar wasn't entirely wrong.

There was an odd meandering midsection about recent 'realisations', urging me to judge a man by his best intentions, and consider that 'a kind action can turn to ill ends'. Any family, apparently, 'has its private joys and its hidden faces'. The whole paragraph was mystifying. I surmised that he knew I'd been investigating, and wrote this way to insulate me from whatever I'd uncovered.

I will be visiting London on business this week, the letter informed me. An odd picture, the country vicar in the city, but why not? Trains ran in both directions. *I hope I might call on you in the evening, tomorrow.* He could knock all he liked; I wouldn't answer the door. Maybe I'd stay in my room all evening. I turned over in bed, wrapped the blankets more tightly.

The next paragraph mentioned Lucy's sister, Bonnie, who had *become rather unreliable and wayward.* Wriggling in the bedclothes, I dislodged a coat which tumbled to the floor, buttons rattling on floorboards. I couldn't settle. Like Bonnie, I was an unreliable wayward young woman. The letter asked if I had any news of Bonnie, which took me aback, as I barely knew her – had the vicar quizzed all her closer connections, to no avail? Had Bonnie been kidnapped, or eloped? I would have to ask Lucy.

For the final paragraph the vicar harped on my health again: the perils of excessive grief, the need for companionship and rest.

> *If you wish to lay your burdens on another person, there is a home run by a very good woman near here. I would trust her absolutely with anything medical, or with any other difficulties. You might consider staying for a few days' recuperation, or more. Many ladies of quality do. I would be happy to arrange it and to escort you there from Breakwater. Miss Hansen is excellent and reliable, her card is enclosed.*

I shook the card from the envelope. A card more astonishing than a magician's trick.

It read: *A Healthful Place Away from the Smogs of the City.*

I goggled at it. I would have bet any amount that the vicar

had also recommended The Larches to Toby, nearly a year ago, when Sam had needed lodgings.

'There's some chicken pie left in the larder, Miss. And that apple cake won't keep for ever.'

Hunger had nudged me out of bed and in search of food. The cake Lucy indicated was crusted with demerara, and looked excellent.

'Thank you, Lucy.' Normally I avoided saying her name, as it felt presumptuous, but today I was bold. 'Have you seen anyone entering or leaving Millstone recently?' Last night she had given a little ground, by admitting she saw the light next door. Now she could share what she knew.

'No, Miss.'

'Or any other lights over there? That light, last night, it's not the first I've seen.' I would remind her of her wrongs, of how she had let me think myself mad.

'I've not seen any lights.' She was sticking to the letter of the truth, as though she were under some infuriating specific spell. 'Are you ailing, Miss?'

'I'm quite well, thank you.'

Now her tone was less stubborn, more dejected. 'Your eyes look summat terrible. I do notice things.'

Was Sam one of the things she had noticed? I wished she'd challenged me four days ago when I was optimistic, when I'd resolved to cure Sam's amnesia. Then, I could have assured her that all would soon be well, and asked for her temporary discretion. Now I felt as dubious as Lucy about Sam's presence. I was an unmarried girl living with an unmarried man. And if I couldn't consider him a brother, I couldn't expect the maid to do so either.

Lucy said, almost gently: 'I s'pose it'll be better when your family are home?'

'It will all be different then.'

'But they might not come for months, Miss.'

'No, they'll be back before that.' In less than three full days, I could tell Ruth. Only today, then Monday, then Tuesday. Those were the terms to which Sam had agreed.

In one pocket of my dress, my fingers touched the vicar's letter. 'The vicar at Breakwater wrote,' I told her, to change the topic. 'He asked if I had any news of your sister. Is she missing?'

'Yes, Miss. I told you.'

But Lucy had only said Bonnie was 'not at home'. She clearly didn't wish to elaborate. In the other pocket, I felt the fuzzy paper of the anonymous letter-writer, with their demand for money. In my mind, Lucy was associated with the anonymous notes – she'd opened at least one of them, hidden the envelope in the kitchen drawer. And my sister had warned me, on behalf of Toby, that Lucy might ask me for money.

I took out the anonymous letter, slowly. 'Another worry I've had is this. Have you seen these letters?'

'I don't know about that, Miss.' Lucy marched past me immediately, making to leave the kitchen.

'It says that Toby owes money, you don't know who to?'

'That would be Mister Toby's business.'

But you hid them, so you made yourself part of the business. 'You're sure?'

'It's probably all nonsense! He's a fair man, isn't he?' Lucy turned her back on me, and reached for the doorknob.

From outside, distinct footsteps. Descending the stairs to the kitchen, sharp thuds. Only eight steps, before the walker realised their mistake and stopped dead.

I met Lucy's eyes. She let go of the doorknob.

It was Sam, on the stairs. Would she open the door and confront him? Confront us both?

Lucy pursed her lips, then spoke with marvellous clarity. 'Some people are spoiled, Miss. Some people want everything their own way.' Her voice rose, she was shouting so anyone beyond the door could hear her. 'And they always expect someone else to get them out of trouble!'

No more footsteps. We waited, in any case, and then Lucy opened the door slowly, drawing out the creaking noise.

There was nobody to be seen.

'I'm leaving now,' I said. 'You could take the day off, if you'd like.'

'I don't mean to take advantage, Miss.'

I cut slices off the apple cake and wrapped them in a cloth. 'I won't be home until late.' She could take advantage without me seeing.

If that had been Sam, on the kitchen stairs, I hoped he'd crept onwards to the garden when he heard Lucy. That would keep him nicely out of the way. But he was waiting in the hall.

'Shall we take breakfast out in the conservatory?' he asked. 'Come on, Judith! I've got a surprise for you.'

No, I was leaving the house, I was avoiding him. But I couldn't get past him unless I forced my way. So I let him shoo me along with his elegant hands. And anyway, memories could have come to him since we last spoke. Maybe the information I'd given him – or the smell, or the music – had rattled around in his brain, the way it had rattled in mine, and dislodged the truth. Now I was picturing his memory as a storeroom, with suitcases and baskets and a black locked steamer trunk labelled 'last year'. It would require a crowbar, a lock pick, tools I didn't have. While my own memory was a fragile basket, shedding its contents at the lightest tap.

'Surprise!' Sam grinned. The wrought-iron table in the conservatory was decorated. Sam had picked foliage from the garden and arranged it in a vase. There wasn't much growing: he'd brought teasels and evergreens. I'd thrown away the flowers I'd fetched him, and he'd brought me more. 'It's to say how grateful I am. For having me here, and for all your detective work.'

I tried to say that it was nothing, but stumbled on the words. I knew what I needed to say: *this can't go on. I must break our agreement. You can't live here, and I can't lie. We have to tell my sister. Even though my deadline is only three days away, I can't wait for it. All the wine in the world can't steady me enough for this.*

I was still holding the wrapped pieces of cake in one hand. He reached across the table and took my other hand. His fingers were icy from flower-picking in the garden.

I could press my lips against the back of his hand, the tiny fringe of dark hairs along its outside edge. If I could find out how it felt, then I could draw it with a fine-point pen.

'I swear that whatever happens,' he said, 'I won't forget everything that you've done for me.'

He caught my eyes and wouldn't look away. I squirmed. But I noticed myself squirming, before it showed, and I kept myself still. I let my toes wriggle inside my boots, invisible. If I didn't stop him, I knew he'd carry on telling me how special I was, and how much we shared. He'd pull me closer and wrap his arms around me. I might scream until every pane of glass in the conservatory shattered.

'You're the one who remembered me,' Sam said. 'You've worried about me. You can't imagine.' He still sounded amused, but there was longing in his voice.

'Ruth remembered.'

'Beg pardon?'

Ruth had cried for a month until she exhausted herself and had to be begged to eat. 'Ruth would want the chance to do as much for you. Sam, I know that I promised you a week, to try to recover, but…'

'Do you have plans for today? More investigations? I could come with you!'

I couldn't say the words to break our contract. And what would it achieve to go back on my word? I couldn't send a telegram to my sister today, because the post office would be shut on a Sunday. Surely I could bear three more days. Less than three. I could immerse myself in my art and stay away from him. I snatched my hand back and tried to sound guileless and chatty. 'I'm afraid I'm busy today. I need to go to my friend's house, to practise.'

'Practise?'

'For the college entrance examination. I'm taking it this year, did I not say? Thank you for your encouragement.'

'That's excellent,' he said, but he didn't look pleased. 'When is it?'

'Tomorrow.'

'But Judith, we only have three days,' he said, suddenly full of compassionate concern.

'That's true. Perhaps you could try some more experiments, reflect on The Larches, while I'm gone.' We'd both made promises: I'd told him I'd help him, and offered him a week's grace, but he'd promised to try to remember. I stood and headed for the hallway.

'Judith! Something came back to me last night.'

Those were the only words that could have stopped me. 'What?'

'You know those plants you brought from Breakwater?'

The ones I'd thrown into the lake the previous night. 'Yes?'

'I tried to concentrate on them, feel how *wintry* they were – just stems and husks. They helped me to conjure up that night,' Sam said. 'I remembered the feeling of something pressing against me. Like someone pushing me, quite hard. Pushing me over.' He was murmuring to himself.

'The force of the water?'

'No, before the flood. When I fell, the other lads were still standing.'

'Do you know who it was?' The river had been full of jostling men. It wasn't surprising.

'Someone shorter than me, *strong*. Someone close to me.'

'Standing next to you?'

'Not that kind of close. Someone familiar.'

Ruth and I and the vicar and his wife had all been up on the bridge. He could only mean Toby. I simply couldn't picture it. 'How were they pushing you, where were they touching you?'

'I can't tell you!' He shook his head vigorously. 'Don't be angry with me, Judith. Not like Toby.'

He walked over to me and rested his hands on my shoulders, his face on my hair. He smelled of cologne, the sweet sad scent of winter-blooming bushes and the earth underneath them. He shook a few times. I patted his back, uncertain. Was he crying?

'It will all come right,' I said, and sounded hollow.

He nodded and pulled away from me. 'I'm so sorry, Judith, forgive me. It's such a horrible thing to consider – I can't.'

'It's fine. It will all be fine.' His face didn't show any sign of tears. 'You'll work it out, won't you.'

'Yes.' His eyes lit up.

'But not today. I need to practise for my exam today.'

His smile went cold. 'It's probably not relevant. You know, your mind can play horrible tricks on you.'

I did know that, absolutely I did.

Ella crackled with confined energy inside her little terraced house.

'Is that your friend, Ellie?' her mother called as we climbed the stairs, and I half turned to return her greeting, but Ella called back that we'd speak to her later. I could have invited Ella to my house, to spare her the embarrassment. However, my own embarrassment at cohabiting with my sister's dead fiancé would be greater.

As I passed a bookshelf, mid-stair, a jumble of evocative words leapt out from the spines: *Lights and Shadows*, *Foregleams of Immortality*, *Twixt Two Worlds*.

Ella called, over her shoulder: 'Ma finds her books a comfort. *They explain everything.*'

On the landing, we steered around two student lodgers in their shirtsleeves who were staggering downstairs for breakfast. I lowered my voice. 'Everything about your late father?'

'Ha! My pa's not dead, he moved back in with his sister in Portsea. *Not lost, but gone before…*' I tried not to wince at either the revelation or Ella's bravado. 'No, it explains everything about *me*.' Ella opened the door to her room. 'Spiritualism, reincarnation, all that. If souls can leave bodies, and come back in other bodies, then you can end up with one kind of soul in another kind of body. That's how she makes sense of me, anyway. It's a lot of old flannel but it keeps us on speaking terms.' I wasn't sure how to reply, so I passed her a slice of cake from my bag. 'Oh, tasty!'

Ella's bedroom was not large, but she'd hoisted her bed onto its side against a wall to free up floor space, and the light was good from a big draughty window. The walls were plastered with prints: art, advertising, anatomy.

At least Ella was preoccupied and didn't examine me closely. I was still shuddering whenever I thought of Sam and what he'd hinted. Sam, clinging to me like cobwebs, whispering that Toby had pushed him.

'Read out the examination instructions again,' Ella told me. She fetched water-pots while I read aloud.

'We can draw: a branch of foliage, provided, a life drawing, model provided, or a portrait, from memory. Any materials can be used, and a range will be provided.'

'What do you reckon?'

It all felt trivial. Pointless, compared to the possibility of... what? Sam, holding me? Murder? If I could focus on the art, it might stop me being swept into panic.

'I won't try the foliage,' Ella said.

'Why not?'

'Honestly, what could you do with *leaves*, to make it stand out?'

I considered the judges scrutinising dozens of paintings of greenery. It was optimistic to suppose I could draw dramatic ivy, poignant ivy. Probably, to the viewer, it was still just ivy. 'You're right.'

'Which one, then?'

I was credible at life drawing, but not outstanding. 'The portrait.'

Ella nodded briskly. It was settled. We opened up our folding easels.

'Who will you draw?' Ella asked me.

'A man I know.' I intended to draw Toby. I needed to think about him, and I needed to draw, so it was the logical thing to do. I'd brought chalk and charcoal. I'd draw his face in dark and light – what Sam had called his *little angry face*, his forehead lined and his lips narrowed. I wanted to understand. And I understood things best through my hands and my eyes and my art.

'What about you?'

'Mrs Fortune. I've seen her often enough.'

Her words were offhand but they lined up beside a few other phrases, and certain looks. Ella was in love with Mrs Fortune. I swallowed the usual criticisms that one has of anyone else's beloved. Mrs Fortune was too old, too overbearing. But none of that would make a fig of a difference to Ella, so I nodded, and we settled down to draw.

When a picture you've drawn isn't right, but you can't work out precisely what's wrong, there are tricks you can do. Ella taught me several of them. You can turn it upside down. That sometimes shows you the parts that are obviously askew. You can mask off sections of the picture with your hands.

Usually, it's the proportions. The distance from nose to chin, wall to roof, hill to tree. Things get out of proportion, and even if each element is delightful, the picture goes wrong.

The picture I'd drawn of Toby in my mind was out of proportion, one way or another. He was either an innocent man and I was halfway to accusing him of attempted murder, or he was an attempted murderer and I'd not warned my family or told the police.

I laid out the lines of Toby's head very faintly. I was prepared to take a long time about it. No point in adding the most wonderful textures if the bones of it were wrong.

(Ella was taking the opposite tack, covering the paper in charcoal, then carving out a face from the soot.)

Tracing a link across the forehead, I drew him frowning. The creases of annoyance were etched into his brow even when he was resting, despite his youth. It was unavoidably true that Toby was often angry.

As soon as I'd sketched the depth of his eye sockets, his cheekbones above his beard, I turned the sheet of paper upside down. His chin was wrong, but his furious brow was right.

It seemed likely that Toby had been angry in the river. Toby had been shouting at Sam even as they departed for the Sully. The energy of the river could have spurred Sam on: he could have been joshing Toby for being feeble, splashing him with icy water. That could have made Toby irate.

Turning Toby the right way up again, I used a putty eraser and a pencil to set Toby's chin right.

I started to fill in the shadows around the features. Here,

his mouth. Shaded so it swelled out of the paper. A murderer's mouth? A man's mouth, which I had seen, many times, and could accurately render. I drew it tight-lipped, holding back irritation, or the truth.

How likely was it that Toby had misled us? Known Sam was alive since January, but pretended Sam was dead? I squinted at that. It would make him such an enormous liar.

All right, then, a liar. A habitual liar? I'd never noticed him lie before, but we'd only talked of inconsequential things. How much rain was forecast, the names of fossils. Smudging with my thumb I set his eyes deep: were they showing guilt, or grief? Should I add dark rings underneath? Did Toby have trouble sleeping?

He might have lied if he was certain Sam would never recover. He could have seen it in very literal terms – sparing Ruth the bad news about Sam – and not understood that lying to her was wrong in itself. I could fathom that. But would Toby truly have gone to Italy, leaving Sam in an institution?

Dark dust was ground into each of my fingertips. I'd been circling the most horrible question I needed to ask myself: had Toby killed Sam to inherit from him?

Ella had taught me how to use a mirror to check for mistakes. If a sketch has become too familiar to judge objectively, the reflection gives you back your distance; in its inverted image, the errors spring out.

'Ella, do you have a mirror I can use?'

Ella opened her wardrobe door. Beside three jewel-coloured dresses there was a full-length mirror. I angled my portrait to see its reflection.

The picture was all wrong. The face was one-dimensional, a façade. The shade that was supposed to add depth to Toby's face appeared like rouge. The crimes I had attributed to him weren't sticking, yet.

I needed to dig in and understand the muscles behind his

tight mouth, his frowning brow. What did I really know about Toby? I saw him as I'd first seen him, in our hallway, gazing at the paintings with incomprehension. I could see he judged them fine for girls like Ruth and me. But why would a grown man, my father, collect such fairy tales? He was too courteous to say it aloud.

What did other people think of him? Lucy trusted him to be fair. Ruth was a little daunted by his worthiness. Mama condemned and praised him, depending on her mood. Someone, probably someone close to Lucy, felt he owed them money. It was only Ella who'd suggested he was envious, and she had never met him at all.

I tried again to shade his lowered eyebrows, forehead, mouth, to capture the intensity. When had he been the most angry I'd ever seen him? After the Seething. He was always angry at Breakwater when Mama wasn't there. Did he get on well with Mama? Gosh, no. It was his concern for us, unchaperoned girls. When Sam broke appointments, changed plans, made Ruth sad, Toby grew angry.

If that was true, I reflected, then in Italy Toby wouldn't be angry at all. Sam wasn't there to make Ruth sad, and Mama was there to accompany her.

To accompany my lonely, beautiful sister. A new light from a startling angle: was Toby intending to woo Ruth? Had he nursed a hidden love, and grown to resent Sam? I brushed off the romantic-grotesque idea. He had never been lover-like towards my sister, only steadfast as a lump of granite.

Perhaps it had always been this way: Toby dour but reliable, Sam unreliably charming. Childhood patterns playing out between grown men. Or had their relationship changed since they'd lost their parents? What if, since their deaths, Sam had become more wild, Toby more sober? Perhaps the loss of his parents explained a lot of Toby's anger.

Or – I turned it upside down, I reversed it – his anger explained the loss of his parents.

I fumbled my charcoal and it rolled across the floorboards. 'Don't step on it!' called Ella. 'I'm nearly out of sticks.'

As I picked it up, she continued to regard me, not with annoyance but sympathy. 'You're all right?'

'I'm fine.'

When you do tricks with pictures, you often see what's wrong. On occasion, you find it's even more wrong than you knew. It's past fixing.

Toby's whole family had died, or nearly died, within the last few years, and I'd sent him off to Italy with my own family?

I forced myself to look out of the window, to the rows of terraced rooftops, and take a long breath. I crossed the room, towards the failing light, and regarded my picture. It was laughable. The new shading gave it no depth, only floated like smog across Toby's flat face.

'D'you need some food?' Ella asked me, eyes glued to her own work.

'Thank you.'

'Head downstairs and ask Ma.'

The staircases to the ground floor creaked; I was heard and hailed: 'Come through, dear, you must be starving!'

Mrs Leon had boiled us some eggs. She set out leftover latkes, and slices of challah, and did I like salmon? 'No point in saving it for later.' I was rather overcome, and she mistook my reticence for distaste. 'Lots of lodgers, lots of leftovers, I'm afraid.'

'This is wonderful, I've been eating very dull things.' I washed my hands in the sink.

'How's your picture going?'

I wondered if she'd seen Ella's work and developed a critical eye. 'It's not right, is it?' I asked, holding up my portrait for her.

She gave it an assessing nod. 'Not quite. Looks flimsy.'

'Yes!' My college plans felt foolish.

'I wouldn't say it if you didn't already know it. But Ella said you're good, usually. And you both work so hard. Too hard!'

We both ignored Toby's flimsy face and heaped up chopped boiled eggs on bread.

'I hope you don't mind me saying you don't look in high spirits.' Mrs Leon lowered her tone. 'Are you thinking of someone you've lost?'

Of course she'd steer the conversation back to loved ones *'twixt two worlds*. Her hobby still rather appalled me. But who was more likely to sympathise with my situation than a spiritualist? Who else could understand my interrupted mourning?

'Yes, I am. A young man.' I should have said 'a family member'. It sounded more suggestive than I'd intended.

Mrs Leon poured a cup of tea for me. 'Recently crossed over?'

'It's been a year.'

'Oh, his yahrzeit…' Her sympathy would undo me if I let it in. 'You lit a candle?' It was kind of her to treat me like a legitimate mourner, given that I'd not told her I had any connection to the departed.

'It's not… I don't know the right date.'

That surprised her, but she stuck to her advice. 'Do it tonight. It helps, it really helps.'

It was soothing, to have a stranger speak to me about Sam. To treat his passing as a simple, sad thing. I was abominable, eating her food and taking her sympathy when I didn't deserve it. I didn't need it. Sam was back with me.

'That must be very hard. And he was a good man?'

I almost laughed. He wasn't a good man. Six months separated the Seething and the Sully. Six months of Sam encouraging me, alternating fond looks with teasing. Sam being Sam, but with a very different meaning for me, now. And while I'd managed to master my feelings before, they'd got the upper hand and they shook me.

Six months of my dragging after him, lovelorn, to concerts and festivals and family picnics. Writhing every night, thinking: *he loves me. He mustn't. I can't bear it. He vowed he'd fix it. Will he ask me to run away with him? I'd have to refuse. Will he send me away? Will he tell Ruth?*

The only impossible prospect was that he would do nothing.

And nothing, for six months, Seething to Sully, was exactly what he did.

I stopped expecting anything. I stopped scrutinising him for signs of what he felt. Signs meant nothing. Whether he loved me with a pure flame, or relished my attention like a schoolboy eating jam, the outcome would be the same. He would slither indefinitely away from me.

I'd sat too long without speaking with Mrs Leon, and I'd failed to confirm that Sam was a good man. She was patting my arm. 'Those ones can be the hardest to forget. Is that him?' She pointed to the art.

'No! That's someone in my family.'

Mrs Leon smiled, then gazed past me in surprise. 'It's nearly dark already! Ella gets so annoyed when she loses the light. Would you care to join me?'

Her menorah stood in the window of the front room. I wondered whether Ella would resent being excluded, but Mrs Leon bellowed, 'ELL!' Ella sauntered down the stairs, and listened to the blessings with good grace. Mrs Leon lit the centre candle, and then with it another five lights. In a rush, I realised what harm I'd done to myself, cutting off Ruth and Mama, when I could have spent those evenings with them, and so many other days and feasts. Mrs Leon's voice reciting, then singing, rose and fell with care and joy. This wasn't the same as having my family back, but it filled up some of my hollowness.

Once the blessings and hymn were all done, I noticed that Ella hadn't brought her artistic efforts downstairs, and guessed they had been as unsatisfactory as my own. Without daylight there was no point in either of us attempting another, better sketch. We commiserated bluntly, wished one another better luck the following day, and I set off for home, pondering as I walked.

Was Toby a murderer? I couldn't make it true. I could plan a pretty picture of it, but it would be false and shallow. I'd done the mental equivalent of rubbing through the paper. Suspecting Toby of multiple murders was ridiculous.

I considered Sam instead.

If I went to Sam, this evening, and I agreed with what he'd hinted, what would he say? If I sat with him in the orangery and said, *I think your brother tried to kill you.*

I could almost hear his voice, eager and tender: *That's interesting, that's really fascinating, Judith, my little investigator. Tell me more! Think about me more! You don't know what it means to me, to have you think about me…*

And his huge eyes eating up my responses.

I knew, heart-deep, that I was more afraid of Sam than Toby.

I planned a quiet evening. A silent evening, in fact. I'd tiptoe in, find food and take it to my bedroom, avoiding everyone in my house. If Sam pursued me, I could lie through my door, tell him I was ill. And Lucy wouldn't seek me out, not after this morning's thorny conversations.

As I crept across the hall, I remembered Lucy's melancholy declaration: *I do notice things.*

Into my mind sprang a vision of her and Bonnie, heads bowed in scrutiny, fingers pointing. It had been on the last night

I'd spent in Breakwater, the night of the Sully. I'd forgotten it until I'd visited Breakwater and stood by the glassy weir: Bonnie with her head wrapped in a scarlet scarf, squeezing in next to me in the crowd at the bridge's rail, and Lucy at her side. Both girls ignoring me, looking down instead at the chaos in the river, absolutely intent. They pointed to this man and that, evaluating each fellow's form and vigour, made mocking observations which set them off in peals of laughter. Right up to the moment when the waters hit.

Lucy and Bonnie were witnesses. I'd been trying to discern Toby's character, but either one of them might have seen his actions.

I tiptoed up the stairs to the attic. Two visits in a week. When I knocked, Lucy opened the door a crack.

I tuned my voice to be deferential. 'Lucy, I'm so sorry to disturb you.'

'You could have rung for me,' she said. Strictly true – there were bell pulls in the library, in the hall, even in my bedroom. I'd never rung for her, it felt too imperious, but I was seeing she'd prefer to be summoned than have her territory invaded. And now I would trespass on her kindness and her memory.

'I had a question. A thing that's been concerning me, about Toby, and Sam.'

Lucy closed her eyes for a moment, nearly closed the door on me. 'Miss, you need to stop fretting. You'll drive yourself to distraction.'

It sounded like sympathy, and that felt very raw. But I could get an answer, despite that. I could even follow her lead.

'You're right, I've been full of worries.' She watched me, wary. 'There's one thing I've been worried about in particular. Which I fear has been making me melancholy. Would you help me with it?'

'I don't know what you mean.'

'I've been worrying that Mister Toby might have contributed to Mister Sam's accident.'

Her sympathy evaporated into exasperation. 'You can't keep on and on, worrying at the accident like that! And isn't it against your laws? Gossiping?'

It surprised me that she knew about that prohibition, but she was right. Gossip was like a feather pillow: once shaken out, impossible to take back. But I wasn't the one shaking the pillow. I was desperately trying to gather in the feathers. 'Is there gossip, then?'

'Did you talk to my sister?' Cross with me and cross with Bonnie, her country burr blurred all her words.

'I haven't seen your sister for a year.' Did the whole village know Toby had killed his brother? Did the vicar know? 'Is it true, then? Did Toby push Sam over, when the flood came?'

Lucy threw her head back to scoff. 'No! How did you dream that up?'

'I would be happy,' I said, my throat tight, 'if it were proved ridiculous.'

'Mister Toby was way over on the other side of the river, I saw him. He was right at the edge, hardly got his shoes wet.'

It was the perfect point of truth, my guesswork confirmed by someone entirely practical. 'Honestly?'

'I swear!' Lucy leaned on the door-frame, folded her arms and let the door swing open. Beyond her, the room was empty. 'He was barely paddling. Mister Samuel went in deep, got himself in a girt mess – you were up on the bridge with us? Mister Samuel waved…'

He'd beckoned to Ruth. And then, the flood had come.

'And Mister Toby was over right, on the other side,' Lucy repeated. A picture sharpened in my head of Toby standing in the shallows, loathing the cold water and the flailing paddles, knowing he should make a good show of it, but leaving the work to Sam. 'He waded over after, to where Mister Sam had been, to look for him. He did feel about in the water.' She groped about in front of her in horrible imitation.

'I didn't know that.' How marvellous. 'How awful.'

Toby wasn't a murderer. My sensibilities, in the end, had been right. But only in the way that ivy climbed upwards, wriggling every other way first.

'Did someone tell you he didn't try to help?' demanded Lucy. 'That's slander. Who'd say that?'

'I'm sorry to have disturbed you.'

'Miss, you need to find someone to talk to…'

She began listing authorities again: Father's business friends, a doctor, a rabbi, a rabbi's wife. But I was making my excuses and marching away down the attic corridor, back to the heart of the house.

She was right. I needed to find someone, and talk to him.

I slammed open the door of Sam's bedroom, although I didn't dare cross the threshold. The bed was made, his spare clothes folded in the suitcase. He wasn't lounging there.

He'd hinted that Toby had pushed him over, into the river. It was slanderous.

There were rooms in my house where I'd not been in years. The guest rooms, Mama's small suite, the other attic bedrooms for the dismissed servants. I barged into each of them, dragged down dust sheets, found nobody.

After one circuit of the whole house, I started to suspect him of hiding. Must I open wardrobes, check behind curtains? I'd caught vexation from Lucy, it had given me strength. I needed to find Sam and shake the truth from him.

I paused in the window seat of my room and peered out, hoping to spot him in the garden. Beyond the glass, the ivy.

Beyond the ivy, the moon showed. And between the stems, in the dimness, Sam stood on the garden path. When clouds crossed the moon, he was a crease in the shadows.

He lifted his face but failed to see me. My room wasn't lit, I wouldn't have been visible at the window. Sam paced back towards the house but didn't enter it, taking the path that ran down the side alley and out to the road.

I raced downstairs to follow him.

I burst out into an unusually busy street. Couples and clusters moved south towards the park. I flowed with them, crossing the Bayswater Road and pushing on through the gate lodge, down the carriageway that struck into the heart of the park.

I had lived on the edge of Hyde Park all my life, but that was the daytime park of idlers and carriages and rowing boats on the Serpentine. The park at night was a different animal, and Ruth and I had been sternly warned away from it, fearing robbery and indecency. We took the long way round after the sun set. Except in company with my family, when there was some kind of festivity: a concert on a summer evening, or a winter market with horse-drawn sleighs.

Or tonight, bonfires.

As the crowd jostled restless down the carriageway, I saw our destination. A bonfire had been placed every few hundred feet along the edge of the lake, I could see at least ten of them. The darkness was adorned rather than banished by the orange points of light. We were filing towards the flames.

It was a crowd of smartly dressed people, but also their servants, given the night off. A group of boot boys ran their eyes up and down me and shouted remarks, venomous child-men. Unaccompanied, I could make no retort, so for protection I fell into step alongside a group of women who were comparing notes on thrift and Christmas gifts. But when I came close they drew their skirts in, turning their backs and forcing me to hurry on alone.

The pyres were high. I saw with curiosity that they were built of things natural and unnatural: tree branches, old furniture and packing cases. The flames were beginning doggedly to consume all. The tongues of fire hopped up and up (I thought of them as giant candle charms: *my neighbours had much gossip*), and every few moments, a collapse in the pyre made a sheet of sparks fly up (*I would receive many letters*). Why had these great fires been assembled? What were they for? Was Sam right, that the Temperance people had provided them to lure this crowd away from drinking? It was a lot of burning to save souls, just for one night, and I could see a few of the crowd had brought their bottles with them anyway. Perhaps it had been planned by the hawkers, the roast chestnut sellers doing a great trade along the edges of the path.

It certainly wasn't like a country celebration. It was more dressed up, more tightly buttoned. The dogs that accompanied the crowd weren't working animals but white scraps of wool, carried by ladies. There was no air, yet, of ritual or intensity.

And unlike a country festival, I was not content to follow the crowd.

If Sam had come this way, how would I find him? Was that him, striding out, weaving between the groups of fire-goers? I wove as well, to follow him.

There was no central gathering spot, that I could tell, and the crowd around me turned amicably to walk along parallel to the lake's edge and the blazes. One cannot be entirely tranquil around fire, though, and as soon as the crowd was heated the chatter developed a hectic tone. I felt my right cheek start to burn as we passed the first fire, while the faces around me turned mask-like in the gloaming. As at the Lewes bonfire, and at the Ottery St Mary barrel-burning, I relished the fire and rather feared the crowd.

I wanted Sam here, I wanted him *now*. I demanded his

presence with fresh wrath, stronger than my old aches of hopeless grief or insistent desire.

There he was: silhouetted against the bonfire just ahead of me, black jacket and loping stride. Both of us were walking towards it, and I could easily corner him.

'Samuel.' My voice was sharp. He didn't turn.

I picked up my pace, dodging between clusters of fire-goers to pursue him. I lifted my skirts to keep from tripping, like Janet and her kirtle, hunting for Tam Lin. I needed to drag Sam down but I wasn't here to save him.

As he strolled on and I shoved after him, I became incandescent. I called his name again, and he must have heard me, but didn't break his stride. His profile flashed as he glanced to one side, insouciant. I felt I had been stumbling after him for ever.

Then he stopped in his tracks. He was close to the fire, the wall of heat preventing him from pressing forwards, a lightless silhouette.

'Samuel!' I shouted. 'Liar!'

I expected him to turn at that. I closed the distance between us and reached out, prodded at him with my knuckles, pushing his shoulder blade. He only stirred slightly on his feet, as though the crowd had brushed him.

I jabbed him harder. He rocked on his toes, didn't glance back to see what insignificant thing had jostled him.

'Liar,' I called, at the back of his head. '*Coward.*'

He laughed.

In ballads, people often fly into a frenzy. Passion has never given me wings before. More often it numbs me, freezes me. But Sam's disregard lit me up, and I struck my fist hard on his back. 'Liar! You *lied* to me!'

Someone clutched my shoulder and spun me aside, away from my victim. 'Hey, hey, none of that…'

They couldn't have restrained me, but they had no need.

The man by the fireside had turned, and his amber face was not Sam's face, but that of a perturbed stranger.

'You know that's not me, Judith?' Sam's voice was close up, next to me.

He took my elbow. I pulled my arm free, but we walked together. Best to get away from the crowd who had seen me striking a man. My flare into violence had left me shaking.

'Did you really mistake that man for me?' Sam asked as we walked. 'Were you *shouting* at me, Judith?' He spoke as though I had surprised him with an intricate, unusual gift. When I didn't respond, he nudged me. 'Come on, Judith. What have I done? Why are you so cross?'

'You sound pleased about it.' Pleased that he'd fooled me into considering that Toby might have tried to murder him. Pleased that, beforehand, I'd twisted for months, wondering if I'd be chosen by him.

'I'm dying to know!' he laughed.

I couldn't stay bitter at him. Not in the sense that he had disarmed me – my fury was increasing every moment. But I knew I couldn't show it. Of course a testy confrontation wouldn't pin him down! He was a past master at turning aside wrath. How many times had I seen him sidestep Toby's accusations, laughing his brother red-faced? *Old Tobes, in a tantrum!*

Worse than that, his smile was fascinated. He was revivified by my rage.

'Speak to me, Judith.' Sam wrapped his arm about my shoulders. I was shrugging it off when, beside us, the fire crackled outwards: a jumble of wood sprang at us, tree branches and old chair-legs, all glowing, scattered onto the path and everyone dodged away shrieking.

Sam took the chance to wrap me in both arms.

'Let go. Get *off*,' I said, my face against his chest. He smelled sour and earthy.

'I'm cold! You're warm! Don't be affronted...' His hands, even through my clothes, felt freezing. 'You should have fetched me a coat from Millstone.'

'Stop it.' Tam Lin turned to red-hot iron when Janet embraced him. I was red hot myself, but I knew that would only spur Sam on. I turned to marble instead, to indifferent ice.

I stayed still and silent while I counted ten heartbeats. Then he let me go.

He looked bewildered, more hurt than when I had tried to assault him.

My disregard he hated more than rage. Was that the answer? Might I bring him to heel that way?

It was impossible to interrogate him, or attempt any subtlety, in the midst of these people who might eavesdrop or involve themselves. But only a step or two away, far from the fires, I could see bushes and benches with nobody near them. 'There, let's go there.'

'Absolutely! Whatever you like.' Sam followed me in a docile way. He reached out a hand to touch me, to apologise for having touched me. I snatched my coat sleeve away from him.

The benches were stone, which was bitterly chilly, but we wouldn't be overheard.

I wouldn't sit first, and have him press me. I ignored his *ladies first* gesture and folded my arms until he sat. When he'd settled, and crossed his legs, I chose my own spot, safe at the other end of the bench. In the dimness, his face was hardly visible. I wondered if he'd try his winning smile on me when I couldn't see it.

'It's too cold,' Sam remarked.

'You can go back to the fire, if you like.' I offered it without moving.

'Too cold all the time, I mean. I've been cold for too long.' He wrapped his arms around himself instead, and stamped his feet on the earth.

'It's midwinter. Of course it's cold.' *You're not*, I tried to imply, *especially sensitive*.

'Precisely! We should go away. A balmy place.'

'Do you mean Italy?'

'Perhaps.' He dangled the idea as bait. He thought it was what I longed for most of all: to reunite him with my sister. When I didn't bite, he swerved: 'Or anywhere we can sit out the winter. Come away with me? To the sun?'

He'd said a dozen similar things to me, in the months before he vanished, that made me squirm on his hook. Glances, touches, jokes, attention. That made me hope he might prefer me to Ruth, choose me over Ruth. I longed for that and I dreaded it. But he had never reeled me in.

He was such a careless, charming man. I nearly said: *Oh, I would run away with you, but I have a sister. Do you remember her?* But it would show my heart too much. And he had certainly trained me how to keep a false face and never say my first thought, over those long months. To show only joy to my sister as she planned their wedding. A layer of frost had grown between us, which hadn't melted until after he was gone.

I sidled up to my first grudge. 'Have you seen Lucy, our maid, yet?'

'No! You asked me to dodge her, didn't you? Hasn't been easy. Ducking into doorways, hiding in the garden.'

'We should tell her that you've returned. She half knows already.'

'She's never seen me…'

'Lucy cleans your plates, your clutter. She knows it's not me.'

'Ha! So she's being haunted. Probably the most interesting thing that's happened to her in years.'

He still refused to reveal himself, even to the maid. He would fight to stay secret, *my* secret, rather than return to the world. And he would rather Lucy believe herself mad.

'You're such a selfish man,' I said, lightly, carelessly. 'And such a liar.' I could say it in a teasing way when I couldn't have spoken it sincerely. It was possible to utter any sentiment, if I kept it at arm's length. With a giddy rush I spoke the most horrible thing aloud. 'You lied to me after the Seething, do you recall?'

'Sorry, I don't, not at all.'

'Oh, you said a lot of nonsense about life, and finding a way to be together.'

'I honestly don't recall that. What must you have thought of me? Judith...'

I leaned an inch towards him, felt him lean in to meet me and swayed away again.

'I never thought about it at all! Such an embarrassment, I could tell you didn't mean a word of it. You have such a butterfly mind.'

I heard a pointed cough from the pathway. A trio of women, of middle years, were looking at me with concern but little sympathy. Arguing with a young man, unchaperoned – how brazen. Did they think more poorly of me, or Sam?

I smiled and nodded a greeting to placate them. When they passed on, and I turned back, Sam was walking away towards the fires.

'Too cold, Judith!' he called over his shoulder, trusting the multitude of people would stop me from questioning him. Twisty, slippery man.

The crowd was unstewarded but rules of behaviour had emerged. Groups had fallen into step with one another along the lakeside. A distance from the fire had been agreed: as close as possible, but far enough that sparks wouldn't singe. If this happened next year, people would return to these same routes and flatten the grass again. If it happened for a hundred years, we would tread grooves into the ground.

I walked with the throng but outpaced them, and this time I caught up with Sam easily. Sam smiled airily at me but then tried to stay one step in advance of me, too far for me to shout accusations.

'What is it, what do you want, little Judith?' he asked.

'Lucy has been helpful to me,' I said. 'Very helpful, in fact.'

'That's what maids are for, helping you. Cleaning and polishing and all that *fol de rol*.'

'Lucy helped me today.' I balled my fists in my pockets as I spoke, to keep myself from jabbing him once more. 'She told me where Toby was, in the river, during the Sully. Far over the other side from you. And how he tried to find you, after the flood.'

'Excellent!' Sam didn't pause for a moment.

'Excellent?'

'Well, I couldn't see any of that. I was being drowned.' He threw his head back to look up at the stars. 'Good to have a witness. Toby looked for me? Tried to fish me out? Wonderful! It'll be so good to see him again when he's back.'

There was no sarcasm in his voice, only endless enthusiasm. Inviting me to unite with him in silent admiration for Toby, whom I had been considering a murderer, at Sam's suggestion.

As we were gently but firmly herded onwards, circling the fire, I reminded myself: *you slandered your brother. You told me that he pushed you.*

The crowd brought us close. 'I wonder why you told me Toby was angry at you,' I said.

'Did I? Well, he always was raving at me, wasn't he? Going off like a steam engine…'

Strangers were looking at me again. I tried to speak less loudly. 'I wonder what made you say that he'd pushed you. Was that a joke?'

'Did I say that? *Somebody* pushed me.'

By outdoing him in nonchalance, I'd nettled him. But I still couldn't get the truth from him. Any pressure I put on him, any interest that I showed, energised him.

Breaking from the circling mass, I barged across the flow of people, back out into the dark. I didn't look to see if Sam followed.

It was time to go home, time to get away from the throng. It was long past time for Sam to leave my house. If I couldn't pin him down, could I push him out? It would be a delicate operation, like coaxing a splinter from under my skin. How could I manage it? (Ruth had always helped me with splinters.)

Sam bowled up beside me. I veered away.

'You should stay elsewhere,' I told him, walking faster. 'A hotel.'

This felt much less slippery, more promising, than our previous conversations. The brisk air in my lungs made me more lively.

'What? Don't be silly, Judith!' We were walking towards the Victoria Gate, heading home together after an evening stroll, probably appearing jolly and familial. 'We talked about this. You decided I should stay.'

'But that was when you were wet and covered in mud. You're perfectly well dressed now, you could leave easily.'

'You promised to help me for a week! There's still two days to go.'

That gave me a pang, because he was right, I'd promised. But he'd promised to try to remember, and I had no proof he'd done that. 'I can help you while you stay at a hotel.'

'But why?'

Because my good name is too high a price to pay for your lodgings. But he would turn the accusation personal: *You must be furious with me, Judith, to say such a thing. Aren't we like family?* And of course: *Honi soit qui mal y pense!* He would cast me as the low-minded one.

I chose the blandest phrases: 'It's not appropriate. It looks bad. You shouldn't be here.' That last seemed truer than the rest.

He fell silent for a moment.

'Thank you, Judith. Of course, it's not suitable. I didn't see that. You're so much more thoughtful than I am – you think about me so much…'

His voice had such pleasure in it. It was as though he didn't care what I was thinking, what the outcome was. Threatened disgrace, hinted murder, envious obsession. Just as long as I was preoccupied by him.

'Tomorrow, then. You'll find somewhere to stay tomorrow.' *After which*, I thought, *I will put you out of my mind.*

Such a commonplace phrase but it echoed in my head like a charm, like a great threat. *I will put you out of my house, I will put you out of my mind.* I felt sure it could damage him terribly.

I struck harder with each foot as I walked, outpacing my discomfort. Sam still loped easily ahead of me.

We were coming to the top of the lake, where the big rough-edged Serpentine was constrained into the neat Italian water gardens. I'd seen these stone terraces packed in the summer when the spray of the fountains made the heat more bearable. Tonight, they were almost empty, unable to compete with the spectacle of the fires. A single phosphorescent fountain danced above the large pools.

'We should swim,' Sam said.

'What?'

'We should swim in the Serpentine. Wash off all these misunderstandings.'

He reached up to his throat and yanked off his collar. He kept walking as his hand moved down his chest, impatiently jerking at his cravat.

He broke into a lopsided run while dragging one arm out of his jacket, which hung about his thighs and nearly tripped him. He let it drop to the ground, his shirtsleeves showing pale in the darkness as he ran towards the water.

I scanned the park, desperate for help. I couldn't stop him alone, but could I expect aid from strangers? There were stragglers and I waved to them, called out desperately, pointed to Sam. One pair of men seemed to look my way, but their gaze passed over Sam, and they held their original course. Everyone ignored the sprinting man. I kilted my kirtle once more, and ran after him in earnest.

Sam outran me, of course, but stopped hard at the water's edge. I couldn't see why, until I drew closer: he was fumbling at his chest, delayed not by good sense but by the buttons of his waistcoat and his clumsy cold fingers.

I itched to slap his hands away from their outrageous work. But I also feared to touch him. Now he was half undressed, I couldn't call for help; to draw the attention of the inflamed crowd could only bring danger.

His shirt cuffs flashed white, then his whole shirt, glowing in the darkness. Then he was untucking his shirt tails. 'Come on!' Beckoning to me.

The Serpentine beyond him was glassy and still, a very citified stretch of water. But it was enough to drown a man. In Regent's Park, years back, the frozen lake had broken under the weight of skaters and forty had died. There was a passive power in still water.

'It's not like the lake in our garden, Sam. It's dangerous!' He'd tricked me out of my pretence of indifference.

'It's all the same lake,' Sam said, standing on one leg, pulling off one shoe.

'It's not!' I sounded less than certain because I had never considered it. Both pools might be fed by the same underground river.

'All water's the same water!' called Sam, removing his other shoe and throwing it underarm. Up it sailed and out, curving down to splash into the water.

'Sam, it's freezing.' The water had only looked smooth before, but now I could see lines where thin translucent sheets of ice had been smashed by his shoe.

'Oh, that won't harm us. People swim in the Serpentine on New Year's Day. You know that! You told me that!'

I had. I'd told him, and we'd watched a lot of rituals where people swam, or sang, or burned anything that would burn. That didn't mean that tonight I intended to swim, or sing, or burn.

He spun on his heel and faced me. 'They probably smash up the ice, jump right through it. What a way to start the year! Sluice off the old year, leave it in the water, climb out into the new year. We should do that.'

That made my thoughts frantic. What did he wish to sluice off? What did he need to cleanse? Was it his deception towards me? Leaving my sister? Or disappointing some woman he'd left even more recently, in his null year?

Sam took three steps towards me.

The night air turned suddenly close and soft, enfolding me. As though this whole scene were a ritual, regularly enacted, which I'd only just joined. Sam knew the moves, and I only had to follow him. It was the same heavy texture I'd felt in the hushed expectation of midsummer sunrise at Stonehenge.

I heard the call of the water, a high sweet keening, and it wasn't for me. Sam wanted to be in the water because the water wanted Sam. I'd told myself that the mudbride was my invention, had no existence beyond the fear and desire I felt in dreams. But now she stirred herself in the silt of the lakebed and sang. If this lake was fed by the same springs as our garden, why shouldn't she be here? She could have followed Sam anywhere that water flowed. She could have hidden beneath the smooth weir at Breakwater, or driven the scouring wave that had carried him away. Sam let his shirt flutter to the floor. His skin was not quite as pale as the cotton. Before I could draw back, he had taken my hand. Cold fingers, very strong, tangling with mine, as mine had been tangled with Ruth's at the Seething.

'Come on, Judith,' he said. 'Let's go into the water.'

His fingers tightened and tugged.

I hit him.

I didn't intend to, entirely. But the grazes on my hand stung freshly when he squeezed them, and I wrenched my hands away, and moved with enough force to strike him under the chin.

He reeled away, and I was already running. Having found momentum by accident, I wouldn't waste it.

The park, with my back to the fires, was pitch black and I was off the path. But the grass was trodden down all year by idlers, so I could run without stumbling. My heart thumped as I passed through the park gate. Fast and free, my pounding feet brought back old games and poetry: *I'll put a girdle round about the earth*. I dived into the network of streets, between the comforting lights of houses, and broke my pace but kept on hobbling, walking for a stretch and then racing, urging myself on: *a girdle round the earth, the earth…*

I reached the front door of my house with no footsteps behind me. Secure in the hallway, I locked the door behind me, and the silence of the empty house – the house free of Sam – was wonderful.

But I couldn't lock a man outdoors at midwinter.

I would leave him the key to Millstone. He could go to his own home, and make what explanations he needed to whoever was in residence. I would dig out my long-neglected tools – the jam jar, the candle stub – and place them, with the key, on the garden bench where we'd sat. I didn't intend any sentimental meaning by that; the bench was a flat solid surface. The candle in the jar would burn for a few hours and draw Sam's attention. He wouldn't freeze to death.

As I searched in the kitchen for jar and stub, I reflected that it wasn't in my power to secure my own house. Lucy or her guest could unlock the doors any time they chose.

And then a great knocking came, the front door rattling in its frame.

Lucy was in the hallway before me. She had been closer to the door and more startled. She was holding two plates piled with food, and looking about her in a panic for somewhere to set them down. She dumped them on a hall dresser, and hurried to the door.

I shouted across to her: 'Wait! Don't!' But all her focus was on the banging door.

It had to be Sam, desperate to provoke me. I moved up, behind Lucy, as the door swung open. If she backed away in shock from the revenant on our doorstep, if she swooned, I could catch her.

In the doorway was the vicar of Breakwater, his face a picture of confusion. 'Miss Judith! Shall I call another time?'

I was still carrying the jar, the candle and the Millstone key. I thrust them into my pockets and smoothed my skirt. 'Do come in.'

Lucy glared at me as though I'd betrayed her. Did she dislike the vicar so intensely? He certainly wasn't here at my invitation. He was a spy, and if I didn't handle him deftly, I would be found wanting and hauled away.

'My apologies, I wrote to say I would call on you…' the vicar warbled.

'You said tomorrow.'

'But tomorrow is today! Ah, did my letter only reach you this morning? The post is always overtaxed at Christmas.'

'It's no bother,' I said. 'And Lucy, close the door.' But then I didn't wish to welcome him any further into the house, so we all stood awkwardly in the hall. The vicar removed his gloves, and when Lucy didn't offer to take them, clutched them in both hands.

'I came for selfish reasons,' he said. 'To reassure myself that you were well.'

I tried a laugh. Too stagy, no more of those. 'Ah! Then you should take my pulse, and look at my tongue and so forth.' I was impersonating Ruth, I realised. Gracious Ruth, soothing with one hand, offering cake with the other. Now I had mastered her tone, I could do it all day. 'Mrs Montague has her concerns about my lethargy in the mornings, but the weather has been so gloomy.'

'Mrs Montague…?'

'Is living with me while my family are in Italy. Did I not say as much, when I saw you last?'

I held his eye, so he would not see Lucy's mouth fall open.

I kept holding his eye, willing him to also ignore the smears all down the brass banister, the smuts on the hall rugs. They gave the lie to my story. Mrs Montague would not tolerate a house like this. I wondered how far the vicar was concerned with earthly things, particularly housekeeping. The other rooms were worse, the library bad enough to alert even an unobservant man. I would have to keep him in the hallway. I waved at the two well-loaded plates of food, abandoned by Lucy on the hall dresser. 'You see, we were about to eat. Lucy was bringing us our meal. But I believe Mrs Montague has stopped out at the bonfires.' I had to stop lying. On Lucy's plates, the doorstep slices of bread were clearly not dinner for a young lady and her companion.

'I'm sorry to disturb your meal! A brief word was all I hoped for. Could we discuss privately…'

I wouldn't let him get me alone.

'Oh, please do speak freely,' I said, smiling as much as I dared. He shot a glance at Lucy, but he was a gentleman, and used to speaking in front of servants as though they weren't there.

'I fear you are sinking into melancholy. In an unhealthy way.' Unhealthy melancholy. Unlike the radiant, blooming melancholy which people usually exhibited. I didn't answer. I silently dared the vicar to add: *And you drink*. 'You would indulge my concerns, Miss Judith.'

I made a pensive *moue*, just as false as my former vivacity. 'I'm sorry if I gave you any cause for them. When I visited you, it was close to the anniversary of Mister Silver's accident. My mood has improved over the last day or two.'

'You haven't felt unwell, confused?'

'Not in the slightest. Did you have any other points on which we could reassure you?'

He wasn't happy, but he nodded. 'I wished to have words with Lucy also, if you might spare her.'

Lucy didn't budge. That suited me; I didn't want to leave her alone with him, where she might tell tales about me.

He wrung his poor gloves until the leather squeaked. I realised that while I detained the vicar in the hall, Sam might return from the park, batter the front door and bellow for entry. I needed the vicar to be what he'd never been: brief.

He turned to Lucy. 'I came to speak with you about your sister. You know she's been headstrong lately.'

'Always was.' Lucy glanced around the hall, and I felt it as an echo of my own vigilance. Was she also fearing an interruption?

'Particularly since she was disappointed.'

This was horrid news. 'Disappointment' was a code, meaning that Bonnie had been let down by a man. Had she become a fallen woman? I understood from the papers that spurned girls drowned themselves.

'You would tell me,' the vicar pleaded, 'if you had any news, or had any word from her?'

Lucy nodded, impassive. 'I'd tell Mum.'

'Yes, your mother, yes. She would so love to have the two of you home for Christmas. Although I suppose *you* may be needed here. Or not…' He gazed around the hall, perhaps noting the lack of decorations, trying and failing to picture my home at Christmas.

'But Bonnie! Your mother would love to have Bonnie home for the festivities. And…' The furrows on his brow deepened. 'If you had been offering your sister any help. Or sending money?'

'How could I? Don't know where to send it.'

'Or giving her sustenance.' Now all three of us were gazing around the hall like nervous animals. The vicar's eyes fixed on the plates of food on the dresser. Two plates, prepared by Lucy, and neither of them for me. I'd feared they would show up my lies about Mrs Montague, but they also told a different incriminating story. 'It would be a natural desire, an understandable impulse, to support your sister. But if you were extending a hospitality *not your own…?*'

He looked to me, to see if I had taken his meaning. I remembered Lucy laughing, alone in the garden. Lucy shouting at the kitchen door, with frustration and familiarity: *some people are spoiled.* Trying to turn my eyes away from the lights in Millstone, and conceal the quantities of food that were consumed in this house. We'd been lying to one another; we'd both been held hostage by our unwanted guests.

I composed my features into bland incomprehension.

'A tragic situation,' I said. 'I'm so sorry we can't assist! I hope it can be swiftly resolved.' The vicar gawped at my rebuff, but I felt the heat of Lucy's anger diminish. 'Was there anything else?'

'Miss Judith, I sent you a recommendation: a little way out of our village, a place called The Larches.' He was back to his old theme for a last attempt.

'You did mention it, in your very compassionate letter.'

'It is a most excellent place for rest and recovery. I am a chaplain there, informally.'

That was interesting information. How often would an informal chaplain visit? Would he see every patient?

'I suspect that you might have need of some time outside the city, somewhere calming.' His voice was grave. He was here to transport me to The Larches, to lock me up. *An excellent place for rest*, until my family thundered home to take charge of me.

'I don't believe I have any need of that.'

He shifted from foot to foot. 'Lucy wrote to her mother that you're not quite well.'

It was my turn to stare at Lucy, in outrage and betrayal. But she moved to stand at my side.

Her voice came with wonderful steadiness: 'I was wrong about that, Vicar. I'm sorry that I wrote it to Mum. Miss Judith's been well enough.'

She put her arm through mine, a little familiar for a servant, but appropriate to support a lady in distress. I would not be dragged off easily to a rest home.

I wished to free myself, though, as I couldn't settle the jar in my pocket, and feared it would drop and smash on the hall floor. I tried, one-handed, to rearrange the other matter in my pocket: a handkerchief, some crumpled paper and card.

Then I realised what I had, and the imp of the perverse seized me. This would make him tell the truth, or it would make him leave. I stepped away from Lucy and pulled out the vicar's letter, with the card for The Larches.

'It's a strange coincidence…' I brought out the other card, from Toby's study, also for The Larches. 'This one was in Mister Toby's study, I believe he knew of it too. Which is peculiar, as he was always very robust.'

'And may he continue so,' said the vicar. 'And may you, Miss Judith! I believe I have said all that I came to say.' He thrust his hand into his glove twice but couldn't push the fingers home.

'I do hope it's been a weight off your mind.'

'Indeed. I have some business in town, I'm staying at the Mandeville Hotel, quite close, until next Wednesday. I'll be in the restaurant at two every afternoon, if either of you would like to speak to me.'

Lucy opened the door for him, and closed it behind him. We were alone together, united by our common foe. Would she tell me about Bonnie? Wouldn't it be a great relief to be honest? I knew that it would, for me, to speak about Sam.

'Fancy place, is it?' said Lucy. 'The Mandeville?'

'Rather. It's on Bond Street.'

'Ha! He's only up in town to buy Christmas presents.'

That did put a different complexion on his mission of mercy.

It had been a weird and wearying day, and I couldn't even retire to bed, not straight away. I needed to wait until Lucy wasn't watching me, and leave the key and candle on the bench for Sam. I opened the back door fearfully but he wasn't prowling the garden. The night air turned my sighs to plumes of steam. Stupid to fret about Sam. Fretting was what he wanted. He could have taken me at my word and checked into a hotel, be snug in his own suite by now. Possibly the Mandeville, goodness help us, cheek by jowl with the vicar.

But at last I climbed into bed with a plate of food, stolen from Lucy, and my hip flask. I hunched myself around my knees, dragged the covers and coats up around me, and ate with my fingers and swigged brandy.

I felt shabby. It hadn't been pleasant to see the house through the vicar's eyes. It had lost all prestige, was halfway to being not respectable.

A sad little episode came back to me, from the time between Father dying and our new neighbours arriving. Ruth and I were both growing dreary. In the summer we'd strolled around the city for hours and ticked off plaques and monuments, but winter made that impossible and the entertainments all cost money. So Ruth was very excited when the esteemed Mrs Leuniger invited Ruth to play cards with her. The families of our schoolfriends were around our level, their fortunes sometimes up and sometimes down, but the Leunigers were superior.

'I'm learning a lot just from visiting her,' Ruth told me. 'About how to run a respectable home.'

I silently added: *and how to make a respectable match.*

Then another invitation arrived from Mrs Leuniger's eldest son, Daniel, to visit in the afternoon one Wednesday. Ruth was flabbergasted, and would only discuss the possibility in negatives: he *mustn't* think she was angling for his attention. She insisted I accompany her.

Dan Leuniger half opened the door himself. He was dishevelled, and nonplussed to see me. He let us trail after him to the music room, calling out: 'Ruth Sachs is here! And her sister.'

At the piano were four of his friends, college men with moustaches, not of our people. Two inspected Ruth, while the others were picking out a music-hall song on the keyboard, lurching in and out of sync: '*Cas*ey would *waltz* with a *straw*berry *blonde*, and the band played on…'

There were wineglasses on the piano top, at three in the afternoon.

'I should take your coats,' said Dan Leuniger.

'He'd *glide* 'cross the *floor* with the *girl* he – no, the *girl* he – Davies, you're slow…'

'I should give my respects to your mother, first,' said Ruth steadily.

'She's not in,' said Dan Leuniger, shame making him irritable. 'Won't you let me take your coats?'

'Come on,' called one of the inspecting men. 'Give a fellow a chance to be entertaining.' He sat down and slapped the sofa cushion beside him.

Mrs Leuniger absent, no women guests, no servants. I wasn't worldly wise, but I wasn't foolish.

Dan took Ruth's coat from behind. She grabbed her own

lapels and wouldn't let go. The entertaining man cackled: 'Oho, lively!'

Dan said, 'Come on, won't you just…' His heart wasn't in it, but he couldn't lose face in front of his friends. Ruth stood fast, and Dan cried out and jumped away; he'd caught his thumb on Ruth's brooch-pin. We let ourselves out.

Ruth had been too full of rage to cry, afterwards. She didn't speculate aloud about what hateful habits the college men must have ascribed to her. She had tactfully informed Mrs Leuniger of her son's bad behaviour, and Mrs Leuniger said Ruth should have known better.

'Better than your son?' asked Ruth.

It had all been over in ten minutes, but it had made Ruth sad for weeks because it had reminded her that we were not quite respectable, that we were without protection. As such we were in a double bind: to want anything was to put ourselves in danger. And if someone else wanted us, that was dangerous for us as well.

That double bind came back to me now, full force. I'd wanted Sam and suffered for it. Then Sam had seemed to want me, too, but that was no remedy, and I suffered more. And now Sam wanted me again: needed me to think of him, made excuses to touch me, talked about us going away together. I wasn't patching together a fantasy out of offcuts. He wanted me. But for what?

I eyed the bedroom door – it wasn't enough of a barrier. I'd lost the key to the lock, years ago. A frond of fennel in the keyhole was best for protection, but I had none to hand.

I shook off my bedclothes and went unsteadily to my satchel to find my pastels. I chose a greasy dark green stick. I'd used it to draw a lot of ivy, and it had bowed to the curve of my hand. I slashed a line of colour across the door with it, to remind myself not to answer it if he knocked. A touch of unfamiliarity, enough to stall me. I drew fronds sprouting from it, delicate fennel leaves.

It was gratifying to make such an instant change to the room. The decorations Ruth and I had added may have seemed wild, but we'd mulled over colours for weeks, traced stencil patterns and tested them. We'd never just pulled out a pastel and drawn, straight onto a door, like this! Satisfying thick green lines, gliding across the white gloss paint.

I extended the slash outwards, curled it round, added leaves to it. Then ivy across the keyhole and round each hinge. I worked at making the ivy strong, with many tendrils, gripping tightly. Not a young, pale, pretty plant but an old tough thing, the colour of evergreens. So old it had wormed apart the thing it grew on, and held the fragments together. It matched the ivy that crawled up the back wall of the house, across my window. Holding me in, keeping me up, ivy on both sides of me. I only stopped when I snapped the pastel. I laboriously chased the fragments across the bedroom floor, so as not to grind them into the carpet.

I slumped back into bed, feeling satisfied that I had safely confined myself.

MONDAY

As soon as I saw the polished wood corridors of the college, I feared I might regress to the wreck I'd been the last time I'd visited here, weeping in the corridor, telling Ella's boots *I need to study art.* This time, I wasn't barred, but shown further down the corridor and into a large classroom.

I'd never seen so many serious women in one place. In art galleries and museums they went solo or in pairs, but here was the whole monstrous regiment, holding satchels and radiating impatience. I knew how many places would be made available at the college, and I made a quick count of the room. To succeed, I needed to be more talented than three-quarters of the women here. I doubted that was true. Then I saw Ella across the room, chin defiantly high, which gave me a jolt of determination.

I went to stand with her; we didn't speak, too jittery to be of use to one another.

What if I was accepted, and Ella wasn't? She'd never decline a place to keep me company while I tried again next year. But I was surprised to realise that I wouldn't decline either. Even if we were both fighting for one place. If competing could destroy our association, then it was preferable that it happened now. Because if we both kept painting, this wouldn't be the last time we were set against each other.

A man in an artistic green suit entered the room, bid us good morning and read out instructions. We could attempt:

Foliage (an uninspiring branch of pine); a life drawing (a model stood, bored, wearing a dressing gown); a portrait, from memory.

We were to choose now, and proceed to the room associated with the subject.

I chose, and walked with a crowd of women to a vast, light studio. We showed no camaraderie at having chosen the same task.

Empty easels awaited us, grouped in great rings. I chose one as near to the window as I could get, as the winter sun would be our hourglass. Along the walls of the room were trestles with paints, charcoals, canvases and paper. Others went to fetch their tools. I stood by my easel instead, and pondered who I would paint. Because the person I chose to draw would determine the tools I needed.

I didn't want to draw Toby again. He wasn't a devil or a puzzle; he was just a man with an angry face.

I couldn't draw Ella. She was in the same room, which was definitely cheating. And her character was mostly in her stance and her movements, not her face.

I could draw Ruth. That I could do with oils. Rich colours. I could draw a beautiful woman imprisoned by grief, another limpid-eyed girl in the style of the Pre-Raphaelites. I could draw her as Guinevere, or the Lady of Shalott, or the Blessed Damozel leaning out of heaven, but I wouldn't. I wouldn't turn her misery into a delicacy for other people to enjoy. It was private and a lot of the time it was ugly. Maybe I could capture all that when I was a better artist, but for now, I wouldn't bring another sad beauty into the world.

I could draw Mama in watercolours. Their muted sweetness would suit her well. Why had I never done that? Because I was impatient with her for being pretty and impractical. Unfair of me, because I suspected my father had encouraged her to be that way.

He never foresaw that he might die and she would have to raise us.

I went to fetch charcoal, because I was going to draw Sam. I'd done drafts for it, obsessively, without knowing that I was preparing. I'd learned what worked and what failed. How to capture the angles. I'd seen him so much at close quarters so recently. I absolutely knew I could do it from memory.

It would be dark as ivy, and as confused, and as strong, and have all my mourning and my longing in it. And as well as those year-old emotions, my new fury. I would try to draw the hole in the middle of him, the thing missing behind the façade. And if it wasn't possible to capture what I didn't fully understand, at least I could make him a handsome, heartless chap.

The outline first. Hard to pick one pose because he had always been in motion. I drew him looking over his shoulder at the viewer, as restless as when I'd first met him.

Shading, then: cheekbones, eye sockets, jaw. The shading took, as it hadn't with my attempt to draw Toby, making the contours leap out, suggesting muscle and bone beneath. He didn't look like himself, though, until I drew the fall of his fringe, the cleft in his chin, with all my love and longing.

A quick check, turning him upside down, so I could proceed to the precision work. The line of his mouth. I gave it a quirk at the corner, to suggest we'd been sharing a joke. Or he'd been coaxing me into sharing his joke. Creases around his eyes and a few on his forehead (not as many as Toby, and not ingrained). I noted as I shaded his brows that I was drawing him in a particular tradition of wood-gods, or wine-gods. A dashing, loveable, lying fellow.

The final touch: his eyes, meeting the viewers, bright and fervent. Delicate work. I shaped my putty into a tiny spike to dab clean one spot on each eyeball. Pinpricks of light to make the whole eye shine. A corrupted, captivating man.

I took a step back. It was good, so good I nearly exclaimed.

His expression had the hint of a shared undertaking which meant I would have followed him anywhere.

I pictured again the evening of the Sully. That evening, when he'd quarrelled with Ruth and ducked into the kitchen, I'd thought he might speak to me. He could have taken my hand. I wouldn't have snatched it away. He could have renewed his perplexing vow, to fix things, to make things right. A single word would have kept me loyal to him.

Instead, he'd left without speaking. And I'd realised, as Ruth and I dressed, as the roiling crowd carried us away from the cottage, that Sam was never going to make a decision. He wouldn't brush me off, why would he? He didn't see the need, and he liked my attention. He could seem infinitely promising without promising a thing.

I'd said to my sister: *So, you really like him, then?* I hadn't been asking for my own sake, although in my heart of hearts I'd wanted her to say: *Oh no, you take him off my hands.* I'd been asking because he was silver-tongued, and his eyes were so thrillingly intense. But if he wanted to go out, or stay home, he'd change their plans without asking. And my sister came home from several excursions red-faced and flustered, saying: 'I don't suppose it matters, really. We're nearly a married couple.' And I'd know he'd behaved in a way she'd disliked, in the carriage on the way home. 'It's just a few months until the wedding. It's silly to mind.' I'd hug her, but I wouldn't agree with her.

I didn't want Ruth to turn him down for my sake. I wanted us both to escape him. *So, you really like him?* I'd been trying to tell Ruth it wasn't too late to decline.

Love unspoken is hard to recall. So is anger when it's not given its head. I'd remembered being indignant on Ruth's behalf that night. Now I knew I'd blazed with rage for both of us, so much that I'd felt every strike down into the water, every crack of a whip, as my own. I'd believed, for a second when it hit, that I'd summoned the roaring water.

Despite the other women in the examination room, despite the hush of this unfamiliar scholarly place, I sensed an edge of ritual rising. The air thickened. Above the artists' scratching and shuffling, high flute notes were wandering which I couldn't quite hear. I panicked. Sam had heard me thinking about him, drawing him, I was sure of it. I had opened myself to unreality, hoping it would strengthen my hand, improve my art, but I had let it go too far. I stood between the bonfires and the Serpentine again, and Sam held out his hand in invitation.

I snapped the stick of charcoal between my fingers. I refused him.

Cast him out, sang the high flute notes.

I was surprised that they would be in sympathy with me, and it was heartening.

Turn him down, sang the notes, with triumphal sweetness. *Then cast him out.*

But how could it be done?

Hand him over, they said. To whom? To what authority? A doctor, the vicar, his brother, the law? *Bind him over, hand him over.* Like a child's rhyme and just as nonsensical.

I stepped back from the easel, wiping my fingers on a rag, shaking my head. It had been fine to indulge my obsession, far from home, for this bounded period of time. But now I needed to regain my indifference. I couldn't go home like this – it would be a beacon to Sam, a fire to sustain him. I needed to be cooler.

I ran an assessing, critical eye over the piece. That left cheekbone, a fraction too high. The whole right half of the face needed darkening, which I achieved with some brisk stippling. His ears were out of alignment, but only lightly sketched, so that was a quick fix. I viewed the portrait as an object.

When that was done, when I had him well lit and symmetrical,

I tried to imagine how I'd speak of Sam if I'd never met him, if I'd only seen this sketch of him: *a fairly pleasant fellow. A good enough chap, I suppose.*

A silver bell rang out. An earthly bell, to announce the end of the examination. All around me women lay down their tools and stretched, which banished any air of mystery.

In front of me stood a young man, an assistant. 'Name in the corner?'

I took up a pen and labelled the portrait of Sam with my name. Because it wasn't his face, it was my work. A wonderfully simple erasure.

The assistant came to collect my sheet of paper. *Hand him over.*

I passed the paper to the young man, and he carried Sam away.

Ella tapped me on the shoulder, full of elation. 'Judith? Shall we eat dinner at my house? To celebrate!'

'Your picture was good,' I told her. She'd drawn Mrs Fortune again, staring around herself imperiously, a goddess of war.

'So we should celebrate.'

She was right. We should sit together in a bright place, laugh at our respite and eat like navvies. But then, after the meal, I would have to go home, and I shrank from returning home alone. 'Would you come to my house for dinner?' I asked. We might even light the menorah together, as we had the previous night, if I had enough nerve to ask.

Ella put her arm through mine. The evening was darkening already. 'Lead on.'

It was good to stride through the streets together and chat without the weight of the exam on us. Ella, having relaxed her privacy enough to let me into her house, told me comic stories of her lodgers: frying sausages in their rooms and setting light to their bedding, sending love letters to shop girls.

When we turned into my street, I tensed. The row of white pillars looked so ostentatious. I began to say to Ella: *it's not as grand as it looks*. But our house *was* grand. Too grand for Ruth and Mama and me, these days, but Mama didn't want to leave. Maybe Ruth and I could take in lodgers. Not medical students, but young ladies.

My musing ceased when I saw Millstone, lights on in the upstairs windows.

It pulled me like a magnet. After the exam, I was in the mood to solve mysteries: competent and reckless, a wild combination, and Ella's company spurred me on.

I walked up the front steps and paused. The door was heavy, but were there sounds inside, voices? I turned the handle and the door swung inwards, unlocked. Ella followed me inside.

'This is your house?'

'No.'

Ella dropped her voice. 'Are we trespassing?' She asked as if to say she wouldn't care either way, but would like to know.

'Not quite. I know the person who lives here,' I said. True in both the past and the present. 'I'm allowed to be here.' But my whispering gave the lie to my words.

I paused in the dark hall and stared like a stranger. There were lights on the upstairs landing, and voices. Not speaking, but shouting. Two women's voices, in the middle of a rackety fight.

It was quite horrible to hear. The words weren't audible, from this distance, but the tones were clear: sneering and blame and mockery in theatrical quantities. After a day of tense silence in the exam room, the conflict made my heart start racing, but then Ella chuckled, and that was permission to take it all less seriously. One voice was definitely Lucy, and the other had to be – let's say, the owner of the suitcase and the silk scarves.

I started to climb the stairs.

'Judith!' Ella hissed. 'Really?'

I'd spent too long chasing shadows, and was resolved to see Lucy's visitor in the flesh.

'I won't be a moment.'

'It's not dangerous?'

I shook my head, although I didn't know. Ella followed me up the staircase, both of us dragged by a thread of half-audible insults.

The fighters were still invisible to us – the yells were coming from one of the bedrooms, behind a closed door – but they were evidently very used to arguing. We heard a long list of wrongs, with the other voice waiting to jump into every pause. The first words I clearly heard were: 'You never *bloody* listen to me!' It was Lucy recounting past disagreements, playing both parts: 'And then *you* said, *Oh nooo, it bain't that at all!* And *I* told *you*…' It was intriguing but none of my business, and I considered slinking away.

Then the shouting stopped, replaced by incoherent cries, at least two slaps and someone stumbling, knocking over the fire irons, and I had to intervene.

I flung open the door of the room quickly, to catch the brawlers in the act. The lamplight showed me Lucy knocked down on the hearthrug, Bonnie stood over her. Lucy was grasping at Bonnie's skirts, either to clamber up or to drag her down. Bonnie hauled at her skirts to shake her sister off, then reached down to yank Lucy's hair. Lucy smacked her hand away, Bonnie raised her arm to smack her back.

I was astonished when Ella stepped neatly round me and grabbed Bonnie's wrist. 'Oh, no,' she murmured. 'Probably not that, eh?'

Bonnie shrieked with surprise, and Ella stepped away from her. 'Sorry! No, don't try it again…' She and Bonnie stood with hands half raised, circling one another.

I got my first sight of Bonnie in over a year. She was so like her sister, it was easier to spot the differences than the similarities: chestnut hair a shade redder, eyes larger, mouth more sulky. She was loose-haired and dishevelled, but not bruised and not obviously in pain, disarrayed more from shouting than fighting. The room around her was a lovely chaos of her delicate things, her silk scarves and many-layered petticoats. But she was dressed far more practically, in an army overcoat and stout boots.

She was quite peevish at being discovered. She had recognised me, knew that this meant her eviction.

She scurried. She dodged past Ella, shoved me out the way so hard I rocked back against the door-frame, and ran from the room. I heard her pelt down the stairs. By the time I reached the landing, she'd disappeared up the corridor to the garden.

I ran after her, and heard Ella running after me.

It was properly dark now. Bonnie streamed across the lawn, and I gave chase. She ran in a long curve, aiming at the bushes that led back into my garden. Did she plan to escape up the side of my house?

But she hadn't turned sharply enough. She was running too close to the lake.

I ran harder, to prevent the accident that seemed inevitable. I shouted a warning, which made her turn her head, and trip on the marble kerb.

She felt straight forwards, into the water.

I pictured the dark place under the ice and her hair like water weed. I feared that Sam was dragging everyone down this way, into the hungry mud: my sister would sink in a Venice canal, I'd throw myself into the Thames.

The moonlight showed Bonnie lying face down in the water. But she didn't sink. As I came closer, she pushed herself up with her arms and sucked in air. She was lying on a bed of reeds, sodden but not in danger.

I waded into the crunching shallows. The cold of the water

stabbed my legs. I bent over and helped her; her big coat made it easy to haul her to her feet. She wasn't in half as deep as Sam had been, and I guided her ashore.

It wasn't an irresistible repetition or an inevitable death. Just a cross girl in a wet coat.

'You can bugger off,' she said.

'Come inside,' I told her. 'Get warm.'

There was a face on the floor, a *carte de visite* wedged under the foot of my kitchen chair. When had I dropped it there? Sam's tiny sepia eyes regarded us.

Bonnie pointed to it. 'What's that?' I didn't answer. She picked him up, put him on the table, and swivelled him round with one finger to face her.

After months of solitude, my house was suddenly full of company. I'd made cocoa for the four of us, and left the brandy bottle within reach. I'd intended to be a good host, but now we sat in the seething silence of people who all expected an apology. No apologies were forthcoming, and when I tried to untangle it, I wasn't even sure who should begin. It would be sagacious for Lucy to grovel a little, for sneaking her sister into Millstone. But I could wait for that discussion, so she didn't need to lose face in front of her sister.

Bonnie had changed her wet clothes for a marmalade-coloured dress and plain wool socks, borrowed from Lucy. She was accepting my hospitality and cocoa, all without breaking her scowl. Should I challenge her about the weeks she'd spent skulking around Millstone? And eating my food, which was why Lucy's cooking vanished so quickly? Or ask her to apologise to Lucy, for risking her sister's position?

I should probably apologise to Ella for involving her, but she was the only person enjoying herself, eating cake and drinking cocoa and watching the rest of us frown. I visualised all the thanks and the apologies we owed one another, flowing between us like a confused current.

In the silence, my eye kept snagging on Sam's *carte* in Bonnie's hands. She had pinned down one corner and was flicking it so it spun, his thumbprint face whirling round and round. Heard Lucy tut, heard her about to say *stop that*, and wondered if Bonnie was doing it to annoy her sister. But no, Bonnie was lost in high dudgeon at an older slight than this recent spat. Spinning and spinning the card, proprietorial and resentful.

'Can I keep it?' she asked.

The currents of indebtedness changed direction. The vicar had told me that Bonnie had been 'disappointed' and seeing her here, sending Sam's *carte* into a spin, it was obvious that Sam was the disappointment.

So should she apologise to Ruth, for tempting her fiancé? But when had this happened? My goodness, should I apologise to Bonnie, because my sister had lured Sam away?

An apology seemed an inadequate tool, set against her deepening sulk. I wondered if Sam had ever given Bonnie a print of himself, or a miniature in a locket, or if this was all she had. 'Have as many as you like,' I said to her.

She didn't pocket the card, but she stopped spinning it. In the silence, a tap dripped in the larder.

'What a day,' said Ella. 'May I have another piece of that excellent cake?'

Lucy said to me: 'I never asked her here.'

It was nearly an apology. Now Bonnie could take a turn.

'And I never came here for you! I came because I was owed.' She glowered at me. 'Owed by him next door, not you.'

What did Toby owe her? Another piece connected. I stood and rummaged through the pockets of my satchel, to find a letter addressed to me with black scratchy handwriting.

'This is from you?'

Bonnie nodded. 'Did you ask Mister Silver, then?'

'No, I didn't ask him.'

'Good!' retorted Lucy.

Bonnie recited her well-rehearsed grievance. 'He swore I'd not be worse off. He made me an allowance, and he paid it regular.'

'Toby?'

'No!'

'Samuel? Paid you money?'

'Not much. Not much to him, that is. But it showed he was decent.'

It showed he was despicable! Courting men didn't give girls money. Cads and seducers gave girls money, and never married them at all. Did things work differently in the countryside? All those frivolous clothes in the suitcase: gifts from Sam, or treats she'd bought herself with Sam's pittance?

'He said it was for life,' Bonnie declared.

'But –' I had to say it '– Sam's dead now.'

'*My* life, not his. He should have made provision.'

That was blunt, but was it also a concealment? Was Bonnie's heart bruised? If so, she was hiding it deep under this financial grudge. She wouldn't cry over her loss; she would stubbornly insist on her dues.

I didn't want to cause Bonnie more pain, but I needed to know when it had all happened. Banishing, if I could, the horrible possibility that Sam had wooed Bonnie and Ruth at the same time. 'When did you… Had you parted before the accident?'

Lucy saw my real question, and announced: 'It was all over before Miss Ruth.'

Bonnie shot her sister a quelling look, but then picked up the thread. 'Yes, all done before he met Miss Ruth.'

I was thankful for that small mercy. So presumably Sam had

been travelling in the countryside, and they'd happened to meet, in a brief crossing of their paths, while Sam stayed at a Breakwater inn.

'It was when he first bought the cottage,' said Bonnie.

I sipped my cocoa, so as not to blurt out a correction. Sam had bought the cottage after he met Ruth, bought it *for* Ruth. So we could all explore the countryside together. Drip, drip, went the untended tap. 'When did he buy it?' I asked.

'Three year ago?'

At least six months before Sam and Ruth met. So he hadn't bought the cottage for us, to enable us to see wonders and to keep us safe. He'd laughed off our questions about it, we'd believed he was downplaying his extravagance. Why had Sam bought the cottage? To be within arm's reach of surly country girls?

'What was he doing in Breakwater, then?' I asked.

'Trout fishing,' Lucy replied. 'Mister Toby and him used to come down to Breakwater. Spent all day on the river.'

What a marvellously mundane pursuit for two bachelor brothers.

No wonder Toby had been irascible every time we visited. He'd watched Sam taking his new fiancée to parade in front of his old lover, staying in the same cottage, introducing Ruth to the villagers who'd seen him with Bonnie. *It's not your playground*, he'd told Sam again and again, and those dour lectures on responsibility now felt understated.

Was that why Toby had paid for the repair of the Breakwater riverbanks? To make an apology to the whole village?

'Anyway, I wasn't giving myself airs,' Bonnie protested. It had been unwise to allow her to add brandy to her cocoa. 'There are richer folk who've married worse than our family, and we didn't know how it might be. With him being a Jewish gentleman.'

'Ha!' Ella swallowed her laugh and sent me a sympathetic glance. She wasn't wrong; there was a comic side to this: Sam was a catch, but he was Jewish (so not quite respectable), and the village didn't know what he might do, or who he might marry. Sam had slid around on the social scale of Breakwater, and Bonnie had seen her chance to pin him down.

I felt myself sliding around, too, dislodged by Bonnie's confidence. Ruth had always worried that she wasn't good enough for Sam, with her small funds, her mediocre schooling and her father in trade. That horrible Leuniger party had stolen her self-respect. She'd wondered: was she sweet enough? Beautiful enough, accomplished enough, for Sam?

While Bonnie had been saying to herself: *he could do a lot worse than me.*

I went into the larder to fetch myself food and turn off the dripping tap.

Before I could cut the bread, someone came up behind me in the dark. I was surprised that it was Bonnie, but guessed she'd come to plead her case.

'I wasn't here, I was next door.' Except when the servants might notice her, and she'd stayed here, but we wouldn't harp on that. 'It wasn't her fault, it was all mine.' I understood what she was arguing. 'So Lucy shouldn't have to leave.' Bonnie wanted to ask for clemency, but hadn't done so in front of her sister, hadn't wanted to be caught doing a kind thing.

'No, she shouldn't.' I hadn't considered it properly, but I didn't want to be left alone, and I couldn't imagine another maid would accept the position.

Bonnie had misunderstood me, and continued to make her case: 'You know, people in the village didn't know what to make of them, when they arrived. But I talked everyone round. And I never gave him a bad name, after.' She was telling me she'd behaved graciously and wanted me to do the same. I wished she'd defamed Sam from the rooftops, and that Ruth had heard it.

'I promise that Lucy can stay.'

Bonnie nodded, then reached past me to grab a pear from a bowl of them, perfectly at ease with taking food from my larder. I had to lean aside so she wouldn't brush me. How unlikely it was that all of us, living in this house, hadn't tripped over each another before now. Half of us had been hiding, but it was strange that I hadn't seen more of Bonnie, remarkable that Bonnie and Sam hadn't seen one another.

Bonnie crunched into the pear. The dripping tap sounded its monotonous note. What were the odds that Bonnie hadn't heard Sam? Hadn't known his voice? Maybe Lucy hadn't recognised him, but Bonnie had loved him.

Bonnie had known Sam before Ruth and I. My detective instincts stretched themselves again. What if she'd seen Sam recently, and kept the secret for him?

'Bonnie, after the accident, did you hear anything else?'

'The money stopped. That was all.' She bit the pear again.

'But you didn't hear from people in the village, about Sam…'

'Folk weren't over fond of him.' In that understatement, a whole community simmered. 'But they wouldn't speak ill of the dead.'

The vicar might take Bonnie back to her family; I might not have another chance to ask. 'Sam didn't come to you, after the accident?'

''Course not. How do you mean?' Her face contorted with revulsion. I believed her utterly.

She turned away from me and hurried back to the light and the kitchen table. Another wrong turn in my investigation. Bonnie wasn't the queen of the fairies; she hadn't kept Sam in her kingdom for a year. She was human through and through, the bored daughter of a dairy farmer, and I was no wiser as to the gap in his memory.

I cut some pie for myself and Ella. I tried to turn the tap but it wouldn't shut off, wouldn't stop its infuriating leaden drip. I jerked it open instead.

'Were the two of you awfully serious, then?' I heard Ella ask, back at the kitchen table.

The tap spattered and then a cataract rushed out, so any response was drowned. I wrenched the handle back with all my strength, grinding it shut so the water stopped entirely. It might never turn again, but at least it wouldn't drip.

I rejoined the others, in order to look daggers at Ella, and found Lucy looking daggers at Bonnie. I handed round slices of pie.

I considered Bonnie as I ate, trying to see in her the women I'd feared: Sam's forgotten wholesome country wife, or the treacherous fallen woman who wore silk and perfume, or the mudbride from the lake. She looked weary and ordinary.

Lucy brushed crumbs from her fingers and stood. 'Well, I'm going to bed. You can't stay next door,' she told Bonnie, 'and you can't stay here, and I wish you'd never bloody come.'

'I'm not going home. Mum's in a lather,' Bonnie said, wrinkling her nose, and I sympathised, despite myself. Who would want to return to a house full of quarrels?

'Well, stay here tonight, will you?' I asked. 'I don't want the Millstone staff bothered. And help yourself to whatever you like to eat,' I added, unnecessarily, as Bonnie always had eaten whatever she wanted.

As Ella and I crossed the hall, I listened. No feet on the stairs, no music from the library or the garden.

'Is everywhere freezing, except for the kitchen?' asked Ella.

'My room's better. Well, I can make it better.' Sam the cheater, Sam the jilter of country maidens, would lack the courage to come into my room if Ella was there. I climbed the stairs and Ella followed.

'Were these your father's?' Ella asked, pointing to the paintings around us. 'I can see why you like them.' It was a nicely ambiguous comment. I chose to take it as a compliment. 'How did your father start buying this sort of thing?'

My eye lingered on King Arthur, with all his court. 'He wanted to know England better, and these were some of the parts he liked best.' Or the parts he could reach, and nobody could stop him. No doors could be shut against him. He could read books; he could buy art and learn legends. He could enter England and let England into him. He had made a particular fiction of England, and Ruth and I had grown up in it. It was no less real than anyone else's version, and it was rich and gorgeous. A little too melodramatic for growing girls.

I was looking at the paintings, trying to see them as Ella saw them, and I believe that saved my life.

Had I been walking fast, or taking the stairs two at a time – and Ruth and I had never been disciplined out of our childish scrambling – I would have brought my foot down harder. Put all my weight on the ball of one foot, on that one particular stair. That would have been the end of me.

As it was, my foot fell lightly. The stair was slippery as oil. My foot slid out from under me, and I tumbled backwards. My shoulder slammed into the banister, I couldn't get hold of it. I was falling, helpless, headfirst towards the sharp marble stairs.

Until I was caught. Ella had her arms around me, was bearing me up, halting my fall.

'Whoa!' She was laughing but wincing. 'Can you stand? Quick, I can't carry you!'

I touched the ground with one foot, but my ankle smarted and wouldn't support me. 'Put me down on the floor.' She lowered me to the carpet, and I sat there, awash with shock.

'Take your time,' Ella suggested, rubbing her arms where I'd collided with her.

In the moonlight, I could see a patch of cool colour trickling down the stairs above me. A spillage? I sat up slowly, hypnotised by the blue. I lifted my hand, the one less jarred and sore, to dabble my fingers in it. To find what had made me fall.

The pool of water crumpled under my hand. The pool was a silk shawl, Bonnie's shawl.

Bonnie's carelessness? Bonnie's malice?

Sam's gift, originally. Sam, who scattered things around my house, who wanted me to go away with him.

Up in my room, Ella made me sit by the fire while she set and stoked it. I leaned my back against the bed and examined my ankle. It was resentful but not damaged.

'You're sure you're all right?' Ella asked. 'You're not going to perish on midnight with a cry, like the women in your ballads?'

'I slipped, that's all. But thank you.'

'I could sleep for ever,' Ella said, wrapping herself in a blanket and sitting next to me.

'Rabbi Onias slept for seventy years.' I could already see how I'd paint him, waking white-bearded and surprised. I wished that Father could have seen my work.

'Good man! Good choice! And I like your mural,' she added, pointing to the ivy scrawled across the door and wall. 'Ma won't let me paint straight on the walls, which is silly, because I may be commissioned for murals one day, and I need the practice. I wonder if I could try with chalk?'

'It would still be hard to clean it off.'

'Hmm. I suppose. How about all that, then?'

'What? The examination, or...' I couldn't discuss Sam's profligate affections, not yet.

'Yes, the examination went well, didn't it? Well, mine did, you saw it. How was yours?'

'I don't know. But it wasn't as bad as the one I drew at your house.'

'There's no obstacle to our glorious careers, then!' We had no drink to toast our glorious careers, but Ella produced some more cake she'd hidden in her pockets.

'We'll know by Friday,' I commented, with a mouth full of crumbs.

'Mm. If I don't pass the examination, I'll have to go to technical college, you know,' Ella said. 'To study commercial painting. Ma will make me.'

I knew Ella's opinion of the technical college. Drones without imagination painting flowers on china. It was an unfair judgement, but if I tried to protest at it now she'd know I was pitying her.

'It's a good job you're more talented than everyone,' I said.

'Ma says it's either that or become an art teacher. Showing angelic infants which end of a paintbrush to stick up their nose. But I don't expect they'd allow me, do you?' She sounded more scathing than ever, hurrying over a sore point.

'Oh, you'd be dismissed straight away. For making the pupils too rebellious.' That satisfied her honour. Ella lit up a cigar, and I didn't object. How hard it would be for her. If she failed the exam, might she take another route? Hide herself, and go through other doors, further and faster. But even a glance at her face through the cigar smoke – eyes closed, expression amused and jaw undaunted – made that seem out of the question.

'Would you stay tonight?' I asked. Having made herself vulnerable, she might forget her recent kindness and put on her armour again. But she began to unbutton her boots.

'Yes, why not. Mother sends her kind regards, by the way. She has a suspicion you're haunted.'

'What?'

'You're haunted. You're not unique; she concludes that about quite a few people.'

'How can your mother believe all that? I mean, she's observant...'

'Oh yes. She'll be lighting the candles again this evening.' When we hadn't. Too much had occurred instead.

'But she's consulting with spirits.'

'Consulting? She's having a conversation, from time to time. She's not running a business with them.' Ella hopped off the bed, picked up the bellows and attacked the fire fiercely. Had my question peeved her? 'And what about your mother? She let you get away with all kinds of things. Spells and prophecies…'

'She wasn't happy with a lot of it.' She would sporadically interrogate Ruth and me about being lax in our observations, or wavering in our faith, both of which we strongly denied. 'She drew the line at ghosts – she thought that was particularly bad.' Which could explain why Mrs Leon's hobby shocked me.

'Excessive mourning,' Ella observed, 'is also bad. I've definitely heard our rabbi say that.'

'Who's being excessive?' I sounded as sullen as Bonnie.

'It seems to me there are three people mourning the same man, and that's excessive.' Ella pumped the bellows again, but I hoped more for the joy of seeing the flames flare up than from annoyance. My mourning *wasn't* excessive, I reasoned to myself. Not given the circumstances, the complexity of it all. He died just when I thought I might die myself, from not having him. No, no, be fair, that had been earlier. He died just when I had realised I'd never get him. When I saw that he wouldn't stand by what he'd said to me, when my fury could raise a river.

What had he said to me? *Connections flourish. You understand. I feel the same way.*

I felt my face grow chilly despite the fire, the cold of growing sober, the quiver in the limbs.

He *felt the same way* not about me, but about – who? Bonnie? Had he been actually talking about Bonnie? Or women in general? Love as an abstraction, a naked figure on a monument. What I'd taken for a pledge could have been drunken philosophy.

'He isn't worth it. I never met him and I can say that with utter confidence,' said Ella, slumping back from her efforts with the bellows, and having a little trouble with the consonants of 'utter confidence'.

I considered telling her about Sam's return, I really did. But there were so many layers. Like a gift wrapped in paper, and each layer you took off it became worse and worse. If I told her a little, she wouldn't understand why I was afraid. If I told her everything, I'd sound absurd.

I listened, past the fire's crackle, for footsteps on the stairs. None came.

'Were they serious?' I asked Ella. 'Bonnie and Sam? You asked them, when I was in the pantry…'

I was prying, now, but I had the right, because I'd been generous. I'd been feeding and housing Bonnie, even if I'd not known it. I was opening myself to Ella's ridicule, but the whole night had left me defenceless in that regard.

'There was something local that I couldn't quite follow. She said they went to see things together, or to the "sea thing"?'

'The Seething,' I said.

'Apparently that was quite a coup for Bonnie. It got her hopes up. Other people felt he'd thrown in his lot with the village.'

'It's a festival for courting couples. But…'

Sam didn't know that, I'd begun to say. Sam saw the Seething as a bacchanalia, a wild ancient night without consequence. Instead of defending Sam, I considered how often his ignorance worked to his benefit. When he'd proposed to Ruth in a haphazard way, and Toby had told him off, he'd laughed: 'I didn't know! I've never done it before!'

Ella reached over and squeezed my arm. 'Anyway. Let's get some rest. We'll need to work hard, if we're to be famous.'

So we talked, as we hadn't before, about how famous we would be. Where we'd exhibit and where we'd disdain to show our work

(Ella's notion of fame was as much disdain as opportunity). The fine materials: I admitted I hoped to work with gold leaf, and Ella described canvases six feet square. We considered who'd buy our work – no, who'd *commission* us. I said we'd travel and study in Paris and Amsterdam, and Ella said why not Russia and Japan?

After a good long while of that, Ella sighed, with great force, and I expected her to confide how she felt about Mrs Fortune. I wished she wouldn't. We'd been having such fun, picturing the future. Wasn't it a blessing, the only redeeming part of it, that unrequited love is invisible?

She said: 'You're too thin.'

'For what?'

'You haven't been eating. And your hair needs washing – has it been *burnt*? And I don't suppose you sleep enough. Is Ma right, are you haunted?'

I didn't answer. My ankle ached.

'Or have you gone soft on someone? Even if you have, it shouldn't make you ill.'

She was being deliberately worldly again. What did she know about love? She was in love with her art teacher, and paid to be near her, and never had to take a risk by declaring herself.

'I'll wash my hair then,' I said. 'If people will jump to the wrong conclusions.'

'Come and stay with me and Ma for a while, Ma likes you. Or I could stay here if I had to. You shouldn't be on your own.' She reached out and plucked something from my hair, and handed it to me – a leaf from the bushes in the garden. 'Sleep more! Keep your eyes fresh.'

I pocketed the leaf, conscious to keep my hands from shaking. I'd felt invisible, but of course: she was an artist, she'd been observing me.

She was wrong, though. I wasn't mourning, and I wasn't haunted.

I'd hoped that Ella would sleep alongside me, like Ruth had done. That would have pacified me. But I'd failed to ask her, and she'd assumed otherwise, so she was sleeping in Ruth's room, next door.

At least the house was full of people. I'd put the leaf Ella had handed me under my pillow as a talisman. The pastel sketch of ivy remained thick and oily all across the door. All these were protective, but my mind would not stop roaming around.

Sam the rake, Sam the jilter. *Didn't he lie about everything, anyway?* What more lies might he have told that were yet to emerge? Could I foresee them, and brace myself for them? That he'd never lost his memory, that he'd never loved Ruth, that Toby had not been his brother at all. I lapsed into half sleep and absurd accusations. He was lying about inconceivable things. Lying about having returned, lying about being alive.

I felt my rage escape me and play out unrestrained. I was a fountain of sparks. I wanted to incinerate Sam.

I heard a note, a high vibrating chime that set me on edge. It was dangerous to think deeply about him, to give him the attention he craved.

Sly with sleep, I wondered: if I thought of him, missed him, wanted him, would that bring him here? Let him come. I could call out, and Ella or Bonnie or Lucy would come running and witness him. I would have protection.

I let my memories of him and my longing for him and my outrage wash together in a great miserable lake inside me. *Come back*, I thought. *Come back, and we'll go away together. We'll sit out the winter. Come back, and I'll punish you.* Was he coming? I could hear dogs bark in nearby gardens and late carriages on the road. Maybe his voice, too, but too low to be heard above my breathing, so I held my breath. Could I smell him, earth and cologne?

I snapped open my eyes.

Nobody in the room but me.

A ridiculous vanity, to have thought I could call him like a dog to heel.

I slept, and I woke because there was a light. If it was daylight trickling round the curtain, that meant it was morning already, even though it felt closer to midnight.

But the light was coming from the wrong side of the room.

Then I wondered if I was in Ruth's room, where the bed lay at a different angle to the window. She hadn't left for Italy, and I was keeping her company. The two rooms coexisted for a moment around me. I moved my arm to where Ruth would be lying. It swept clumsily across bare sheets.

I was in my own room. The light was coming from near the doorway.

'Judith?'

I couldn't find my voice, or move my mouth. He'd mistaken our rooms again, and he was as surprised as I.

'You've been hiding away from me all evening,' he said. I tried to reply, but my body was still under the confusion of sleep. 'You promised to help me, but now you're hiding from me.'

I'd been a reckless fool, to think of him and summon him here. The light wavered. He was walking across the room towards me, holding a lamp in his hand.

I managed to tighten my fists on my bedclothes. 'I've helped you. I've tried.'

'You didn't this evening. You weren't even thinking about me.'

That was unfair. I'd been thinking about him and Bonnie for half the night. There had only been a handful of moments, with Ella, when I'd succeeded in thinking of other things.

'We need to go, now,' said Sam.

Why was he so urgent? 'Is there a danger? Is it a fire?'

'No, but I've been terribly worried. And we need to leave now.'

His voice was closer than I expected. He'd put the lamp down and kept closing in on me. I felt the mattress sink and I was dragged towards the dip. Sam had sat on the edge of my bed.

'We can go away together, Judith.'

His voice was elated. I needed to sit up and shout at him, demand to know what he meant. But I was still sluggish. 'I'm not going away with you.' I wouldn't say *we*, I wouldn't say *we can't go away*. Even that would have been disloyal. How often had I imagined him here, in my room? This was a mockery. I made my voice as harsh as I could manage. 'I won't. You offered before and you lied.' I didn't like how pitiful I sounded. 'And it's dark. There's nowhere to go.'

'Of course there is, Judith.' Did he mean the boat train to France? Paris and art with Sam to show me. Sam the *bon vivant*, Sam the liar. 'Wonderful places. Other lands!'

Not Paris, not any ordinary destination. He was beckoning me through the rotten hole in the broken wall, or into the frozen lake. But when I asked myself, *where?*, my vocabulary failed me, or my mind shied away.

'You have to help me,' he said. 'You swore you'd help me.'

My straining fingers brushed the leaf under my pillow, closed around it, and my body was given back to me. I could move freely again. Sam's weight was pulling the mountain of bedclothes off me and I felt the ordinary irritation I'd always felt when Ruth, in her sleep, did the same. I hauled the bedclothes back, and heard him half topple sideways.

'And you promised to find another place to stay. A hotel.' The more I spoke, the easier it was to refuse him. 'This is my home. I'm staying here, and my family will come back here soon.' He needed me so much, I felt it drag at me. But I needed something, too. What? Ah, yes – I needed to get more sleep, and work hard, so Ella and I could be famous. 'I'm not going anywhere with you. I'm going to college, to paint.' My treacherous heart said: *We can talk about this tomorrow*. I may have said it out loud.

Sam said: 'But *you* don't need to go to college.'

That broke the charm entirely.

He said it as he'd said everything else, his voice low and urgent and delighted. *We need to go now! You don't need to go to college!* But it made crystal clear his disregard for what didn't serve him. *You don't need to do the thing you need to do! You need to do the thing I want you to do!* Damn him.

I sat up, clasped the bedclothes to my chest.

'You *will* leave. You will leave *now*.' I forced my will into my words. 'Go. Get out! You should never have come here!'

I felt his weight shift off the bed. Then the lamplight wandered away, as he left. I nearly cried out and changed my mind. I knew we'd never talk about it in the daylight, and he'd never come back by night. He'd never rest on my bed again, I'd never again be so close to him. Close enough to bury my face in his shoulder.

The door clicked shut behind him, and I listened to where his footsteps went. But my shouting had disturbed Ella, next door, and she called back in her sleep, a string of nonsense syllables, then rolled over in Ruth's creaky bed.

In the whole house I could hear no other sound.

TUESDAY

I woke at a knock on my bedroom door. That wouldn't be him, and it was daylight now. I made a noise of assent, and Ella, barefoot, padded into the room.

I rolled over to make space on the bed for her to sit. 'Good morning.'

'I can't face class today. And I'm starved. I'm going to buy a bun and take a turn round the Bond Street galleries on the way home, do you want to come?'

Her agitation was infectious. Listening to her was like drinking coffee.

The mattress sagged under her, and I felt a sudden lurch of fear, reminded of last night.

'Probably all horrid,' Ella chattered on, 'and crowded, but we can see what the popular fellows are turning out these days.'

Last night I'd been fearful, and weak, but then – a spark of satisfaction – I'd sent him away.

But how long would he stay gone?

Ella had fallen silent, and I'd not replied. 'That does sound good…'

'*You* don't sound good. You're not still brooding about last night?'

I froze. Had she heard Sam speaking, when he visited me? But no, she meant yesterday evening, and the kitchen revelations from my uninvited guest. That was why she was babbling me awake, jollying me along. 'A little.'

'Ugh. Could you *try* not to think about it?'

She'd put her finger on my dilemma. I'd tried not to think of Sam, and to put him out of my mind. Two days ago I'd told him to leave this house. Last night I'd sent him out of this room. Did I need to cast him out three times to make it stick? But no, I was the weak spot, I consistently let him back in. My curiosity opened a door to him. Take yesterday evening as proof: I'd gorged myself, I was a glutton for news of him.

'I'll try to think of other things,' I offered. 'Certainly.'

I longed for the clarity of the exam room, that high fluting voice: *Hand him over. Cast him out.*

'Just for one day,' pleaded Ella. 'Put a limit on it.'

That made me indignant, because I'd set a limit from the start. I had promised Sam a week and no more. I tried to tot up the days, but they slithered around in my mind. 'Is it Tuesday?'

'Sleepyhead. Of course it's Tuesday.'

The week was up, the week I'd promised Sam. Our deal was done, and I didn't have to help him any more. I didn't have to *think* about him any more.

Elation flooded me. Then came the echo: but then I'd never know. Round again went my thoughts, a loop of ribbon on busy fingers. I wanted to send him away. I needed to know where he'd been.

'I'm off to Dowdeswell's and Agnew's,' said Ella, swinging her legs off the bed. 'Probably to see at least fourteen boring pictures titled *Winter Scene*. If you're not coming, then will you wash off and eat properly and so forth, after I leave?'

'Probably not.'

'Come and stay with Ma and me. I meant it when I offered. Christmas is so dull, with all the museums closed. And half our lodgers go to visit relatives, you could have one of their rooms.'

An intriguing idea. 'Come on, make me a bargain. Either you look after yourself properly or you have to let Ma look after you.'

'That doesn't sound like a bargain. You get what you want, both ways.'

'Why would I offer you a thing I *didn't* want?' She grinned as she left my room.

She'd been mocking herself. But her joke had some heft to it. Any agreement has obligations and benefits. I was *obliged* to spend one more day assisting Sam, as he'd argued, and thinking of him. I was *permitted* to spend one more day investigating him. Then the obligation was ended, and the permission was revoked.

I rolled back my bedclothes, suddenly eager to be on my feet. I had unpicked the knot in the ribbon. One day, and then no more. That had been our contract. He'd agreed to it. Only one day, and it would be dark by four. Where could I investigate? Whom could I quiz? Where were the loose threads, the stray tendrils I could pull at?

As my optimism reignited, the echo of a rebuke: *Isn't it against your laws? Gossiping?*

That didn't deter me. Instead, it reminded me of a thread that lay within my grasp.

In the kitchen, Bonnie was making short work of a heap of fried eggs and potatoes.

'Good morning! Where's your sister?' I didn't want Lucy to overhear us.

'About.' Bonnie waved her hand to indicate the house as a whole.

'Bonnie, I think you know more about Sam.' I spoke as vaguely as I could, so as not to reveal my ignorance.

'Oh!' A note of recognition. 'Is that why you asked me, had I seen him?'

I pretended I was Ella and set my jaw at a determined angle. 'You tell me.'

'I might.' She spoke with a very indifferent tone, and returned to her eggs. I realised very slowly that she wanted a reward, then that I didn't own anything she wouldn't scorn.

Instead, I attacked. 'I've already done you a favour.' I pointed at the food, and let my hand wave, just as hers had, to encompass the house where she'd been living.

'So?'

'You know, I'm meeting the vicar for tea,' I remarked, emulating her nonchalance. 'I could tell him I've been hearing strange noises, maybe even that I've seen someone in the house…'

'You tell him I'm not here! Keep Luce out of trouble.'

I'd already told him as much, but why give her that information for free? 'I suppose I might. Will you tell me what you know?'

'All right, then! All right. There was one time *he* was in the garden of that cottage.' Bonnie had an aversion to using Sam's name. From disdain for the man, or respect for the dead, or the same sense that I had: that it was best not to draw his attention. '*He* had an argument with Mister Toby.'

Of course he did. I sat down on a kitchen chair.

'It was last winter, just before the Sully. I was round the corner, helping Luce fold the tablecloths. Not eavesdropping.'

I could afford to be generous. 'It's hard not to hear when Toby shouts,' I agreed. 'What was he saying?'

'That he wouldn't let Sam play the devil and disappoint a young lady again.' She relished that, being referred to as a *young lady*, even though the context meant she was a cast-off fallen woman. 'Mister Toby said it would be a disgrace, and he wasn't moving house.'

That dull detail made it clear to me. Sam had been considering delaying the marriage to Ruth – twisting his way out of it. He'd mentioned it to Toby. Put it to him as a proposition, or (more likely) tossed out a careless remark. Toby had shouted at Sam like never before. Toby, bless his little angry face, had said he damn well wasn't going to leave Millstone just because of his brother's roving eye.

Bonnie's mouth showed a joyless smile. This story salved her pride. She hadn't truly been jilted for Ruth, because Ruth couldn't keep hold of Sam either.

'Thank you. That's useful.' I sensed Bonnie wanted me to join in condemning him. 'He was rather unreliable,' I managed.

'Mm. You can't hold with the hare and run with the hounds.'

'What did Sam say in reply?' *Did he mention me, did he say he needed to leave Ruth because he loved me?* I slapped it down, that stubborn flutter of hope and horror.

'I couldn't hear him, not like I could Mister Toby. But they went on for a while. Mister Toby said if that was what Mister Sam was going to do, he should leave and not come back.'

'People say that sort of thing when they're vexed.'

'He told Mister Sam if he couldn't act decent, to go away and not come back.'

That was a far more precise command. 'And did Sam say he would do that?'

'He didn't, but…' She was hinting, and when I didn't pick up the hint, she shrugged. 'He didn't come back, did he?'

'Was that the rumour?' I asked.

'What?'

'Your sister told me not to listen to rumours about Toby and Sam. No, she said *gossip*. Was that the village gossip, that Sam intended to leave my sister?'

'Oh! No. Luce and me heard, but we didn't pass it on. So you'll tell the vicar I'm not here?'

'I will.'

'Make sure he believes you. Don't let go 'til your teeth meet, eh?' An unflattering comparison, but I would rather be a tenacious dog than a love-sick girl.

And I was feeling tenacious this morning. I'd learned something from Bonnie. What might I get out of the vicar? I saw myself in a smart hotel restaurant, presiding over a pot of bohea tea, the man of the cloth opposite me, melting in the steam. I saw myself quizzing him about The Larches. Wringing him for information, on this last day of my investigation. I knew a charm for a loose tooth, wondered if you could convert it to extract the truth from a man.

Bonnie was too hard; I couldn't shift her. But I could use her against someone softer.

I had decided on my next steps and was donning my coat when I heard a cough. Lucy, in the hallway behind me, seemed subdued. I wondered if she'd slept as poorly as I, after she'd stomped off to her bed. She'd told Bonnie to get out of the house, and I'd told Bonnie to stay. I hoped she wouldn't hold that against me.

'Do you want me to go, Miss?' she asked.

'No, I'll be out of your way in a moment.'

Then I realised that she was offering to go not from the hall, but from my employment.

She'd behaved badly, smuggling Bonnie into Millstone. And she'd lied to me. She'd denied things we'd seen and heard because Bonnie was wandering around my house. But a secret guest, I knew, could happen to anyone.

'No! I don't want you to leave. I don't consider you to be in any trouble.'

Lucy sighed deeply, which I took for relief, until she took an equally long breath in, and announced: 'I don't want to work here any more.'

'What? Why not?' She was the one in the wrong, why was she turning on me?

'This bain't a proper place to work.'

I squirmed inwardly. Sam was the problem. Lucy couldn't stay in a house with a man roaming around. 'Not a proper place...?'

'It's hardly a house at all! There's no family, you don't have no visitors. You don't hold dinners. You barely even eat meals!'

That confounded me utterly. It was all true, but why was any of it objectionable? Lucy was paid, she had few rules to follow and copious time to do as she pleased. Was she, at heart, conventional? Should I be bossing her around, making her rise at crack of dawn? 'Does all that matter terribly? Doesn't it make your work easier?'

'No, it makes the work impossible! And if I don't learn to do the work properly, how do I get a better position, somewhere else?'

I gaped at her. Was Lucy ambitious? Applying to be our maid had seemed like the opposite of ambition. I'd wondered why she'd desired it, but satisfied myself with a few easy notions (freedom, pin money, a life in the city).

'I mean, *eventually*,' she said, recovering her manners. 'In a couple of years. I did tell Mum: this is a big house, I can learn to be a cook.'

Cook had been Cook for ever. 'How do you become a cook?'

'You work in a big kitchen, and you learn to make every damn – every blessed thing. Roasts, pastries, puddings, soups, sauces.'

'I see.' You studied at it, you didn't settle for doing the same thing over and over. 'Does it take long?' Had it taken Cook long? I'd not considered her to be ambitious, either.

'Years. And I bain't learnt a thing, not since Mrs Sachs left! You never need work done. And there's no one to show me, Cook's not here, hardly. I never heard of half the food you eat.' That last remark was pure frustration, and I guessed the *Easy and Economical Guide* had not been as helpful as advertised.

I'd assumed I was doing her a favour, by leaving her alone

and living off rye bread and pickles. I'd supposed she'd sleep late and stroll around the city. But she'd wanted to create banquets.

'I didn't know,' I said.

'No reason you should.'

'Is that why you've been baking those things for me?' Test pieces. Sketches for future dishes.

'Had to practise. And had to make things you'd eat. You might be giving me a character, one day, for a position with another family.'

'But it isn't enough, to practise on your own?'

'No! It's not a one-man job. You have to learn to cook for ten at a time, five dishes at once. There's no sense in making you soup and fish *and* roast beef *and* plum pudding, all for one meal, is there?' She enjoyed the disgust on my face. 'You'd hardly nibble a hole in them.'

She was right, but I reasoned she was also culpable: Lucy could have learned more from Cook, even asked her for lessons, if she hadn't been hiding Bonnie in my house. I suspected that when Cook visited, Lucy didn't try to detain her. 'You don't have to leave.'

'I hear you talking to yourself in the evenings, Miss.'

Her voice was low with an embarrassment I didn't understand. Lucy must have known I was talking to Sam. Could she have been unaware of him, still? She'd heard my voice, talking to Sam, but didn't know there was a lower-voiced visitor, talking with me. Just like I'd heard her in the garden, laughing, but not Bonnie, making her laugh. Did she truly think me mad?

I held on to the remnants of my optimism. 'I'll sort it all out soon.'

She sniffed as if to say she would believe it when she saw it. I had a sudden fear that if I left the house, she'd be packed up and gone before I returned, taking Bonnie. And I'd be there alone with Sam.

'Stay for a few days, will you? At least until tomorrow. I give you my word, we'll make arrangements.' I should give her some consideration in return, show her I was trustworthy. 'I'm meeting the vicar for tea, I'll tell him again that I've not seen Bonnie.'

She didn't seem pleased by that either. I wracked my brains for requests she'd made, people she'd wanted me to contact.

'I could ask my family to come home,' I offered. 'You said I should bring them home, didn't you? I'll do that.' Then we'd be a proper house again, or close to it. Mama was an indifferent employer, but she did eat three meals a day and supervise the menus. Perhaps, now Ruth had a small income, we could even entertain visitors.

'But *will* you, Miss?'

She was calling me a liar, and neither of us could quite believe it. She saw everything but she wasn't supposed to say anything. She was a very badly trained maid.

'I swear.' The time had arrived. That had been the final part of the contract with Sam: that I would hold off a week, but then I could summon my sister. It was permitted. It was overdue. I would do it right now, because I wanted to hug my sister as soon as I could.

'I'll send them a telegram today,' I assured Lucy.

At the post office I queued for ten minutes behind people with parcels and cards. Then when I reached the counter, I opened my mouth and shut it again comically.

I ducked to the back of the queue again, for I hadn't considered what to write.

I was permitted to tell my sister about Sam. That had been our agreement. But the same obstacle remained: how could I tell her he was back, when I didn't know where he'd been?

I knew other things. Bonnie spinning Sam's *carte de visite* under her finger. Would I reveal any of that to Ruth? Not by telegram.

I opened my sketchbook and tried to write a message, conscious that words were not my forte.

I have not been well – no, I mustn't scare her.

I have not been myself

I find myself

I gave up on telling what I had been, or what I had found. I asked for what I wanted. *Could you come home soon? There is no emergency but please come home early if you can. I do feel your absence.* I could add another seven words for the same price. *And Mama as well.* Because the telegram would be handed around between them, and it wasn't a lie.

I passed my piece of paper over the counter, and paid for my message. A sudden vision of what it would be like to have them back: conversation, all the time. Arguments, some of the time. Not being free and unregarded. Not being entirely alone.

I had another telegram to send. I scribbled it out and signed it with Bonnie's initials. I felt a glint of guilt, but I'd fed her and sheltered her, and she owed me for that.

On my return, I walked in on Lucy kneading bread. I watched her strong hands, squashing and stretching. Bread took hours to rise and to bake, didn't it? She was planning to stay, at least for long enough to finish the loaf, thank goodness. At least until dusk, when I would have to face Samuel.

'I've done what we spoke about,' I told her. 'I've asked them to come home. My sister should reply to me today or tomorrow.'

Lucy hummed her acknowledgement, but kept kneading in a triplet rhythm: flattening, folding, turning.

'And I'm about to have tea with the vicar.'

Lucy paused, mistrustful, the heel of her hand sinking a pit into the dough. 'You shouldn't go alone. Take someone with you. Your tall friend – is she still here?'

'She's gone.'

'Then I should come, Miss. What if he's called a doctor on you?'

'Like you wanted to?'

'Now, I wouldn't have called the mad-doctors,' Lucy objected. 'Does he know you're coming? There could be anyone waiting. Stay where you are.' She wiped her hands on a cloth and pulled a comb from her apron pocket. 'You're not looking right.'

Lucy seized my hair at the roots in a gesture so practised I knew she'd done it to Bonnie, and every one of her younger sisters. She yanked the comb vigorously through the knots and cinders and it didn't hurt me. I felt a triplet rhythm of tugs and turns, just like the kneading; she was plaiting it deftly, weaving in all my straggling strands. 'I'll clean myself off and come with you. If the hotel's fancy, we should look respectable.'

Not a bad prescription, so I went back to my room, changed back into my dowdy black dress and ran a wet cloth over my face. I located matching gloves and a hat, which I'd often neglected to wear in Breakwater, but the vicar was in my city now and would expect me to observe these niceties. Decently dressed, I crept from the house without alerting Lucy. I'd take my chances alone.

Afternoon tea at the Mandeville was a dizzying spectacle. At the centre was a steaming teapot almost too large to lift, and pastries too tiny to taste. I swallowed three of them before I thought I should have saved them for Lucy, to let her dissect and study them as I would study a Rembrandt.

I shared my thoughts with the vicar. 'Lucy would love these.'

He nodded, but appeared subdued, with an expression like a deflated cherub.

'I'll take her some treats from a bakery instead,' I told him. 'Thank you so much for all this!'

'You've had no reason to be at odds with Lucy?' asked the vicar. 'You've not fallen out?'

'No! Why should I have fallen out with her?'

He sighed. I willed him with all my might to ask me about Bonnie so that I could deny seeing her. 'I worried that she has been helping her sister, Bonnie. And taking certain liberties.'

'Oh! I've not seen anything missing in the house,' I reassured him, deliberately at a slant.

'And you've not noticed odd noises? Voices? Any unaccustomed visitors?'

I let it seem to dawn on me slowly, opening my eyes wide. 'Goodness! No, not at all. Lucy has been quite solitary, and in fact, she often spends the evenings sewing with myself and…' How had I named that imaginary chaperone? 'My companion.' That scene was a little too cosy to be true. I picked up a finger sandwich.

The vicar straightened in his chair but his brows didn't unknit. 'That is good! Good. But I know that you've not been well.'

Thanks to Lucy, my hair was no longer a bonfire, and I knew my face was clean. 'I was a little overwrought. But I've asked my family to return home.' I'd given him a quick victory. I guessed where his weak spots were and pressed on them. 'I'm sorry to have asked so many questions of you, but I still find myself brooding on the past. Despite my companion, and Lucy, I brood. There are things which make no sense.'

'Tragedy often feels senseless.'

I would not let him mollify me with platitudes. 'No, I mean *logical* sense. Things kept from us, about Samuel. My sister and I both find it hard to put it out of our minds.' Forgive me, Ruth, for drafting you to my obsession. 'Because the information we have is simply *wrong*. I feel, if someone would explain, and tell me the reason…'

He uttered some more bloodless comforts with even less conviction. Time to apply pressure from another direction.

'And I've been getting these shocking letters, asking me for money!' I pulled the letter from my pocket and spread it on the pure white tablecloth between us. Spidery ink. Had Bonnie intended them to look sinister, or was it just poor penmanship? I took a sly look at the vicar's green face. Now I could set a clock ticking, as well. 'I shall have to tell Mister Toby, he'll know what to do. When my family comes home, I'll be able to speak with him directly.'

I thought the vicar might choke.

I'd already laid some of the groundwork. I'd kept my telegram short this morning: *I will tell Miss Judith about Samuel Silver at The Larches unless you ask Mr Silver to give me the money he owes me.* Signed with Bonnie's initials, sent this morning, here to the vicar's hotel. I couldn't get more information out of Bonnie, so I'd use her to get information out of others. It was a little unfair to implicate her in blackmail, but she'd given me the idea.

Now I could woo the vicar a little. I knew how seductive it could be to be asked for help, to be told you were wise.

'You've been very much like one of our family. I'm sure you understand so much that you could share.'

'I may do that,' he said. 'I trust I may. Better to grub it out. Better not to let hearsay put down roots!' He was talking himself into it. I'd bent him back and forth with threats and entreaties, reassured and alarmed him, and now he was on the verge of snapping.

This hotel was too cosy, though. I saw through the windows that the day was fading, and knew where I would take him. 'Shall we walk, while we talk? The park is quite close.'

At first I thought I'd miscalculated, as the light outdoors was gorgeous. A rose glow transformed the white stone of Marble Arch. To the west, over Kensington, the sunset sky flared red. The street was packed but the crowds amiably parted for us, perhaps out of respect for the vicar's dog collar.

But the park was as unsettling as I'd intended, all hushed and grey and the trees were stark. Only the passenger plants provided colour, for they were evergreen: ivy, cladding the trunks, but also huge globes of mistletoe perched in the crowns of oak trees.

'Heavens, what is that thing on the edge of the water?' The vicar had spotted a great burned edifice, then another.

'Fires,' I said. As we walked closer, the smell of woodsmoke was phenomenal, savoury and sharp. The pyres were extinguished, each now no more than a few feet of obstinate struts and charred detritus, with grey ash dusting the trampled grass.

'My goodness!'

A series of snaps rang out as children ran past with firecrackers, not yet done with the bonfires' fun.

Walking loosed the vicar's tongue. He babbled, weaving around the beat of our footsteps like the fiddle round the drum at a country dance. He talked about the pools and the park but despite his talk of grubbing out hearsay, he didn't speak of Samuel. It was cruel, I decided, to wait while he fought with his own conscience. I extended a hand to help.

'I know Samuel was in The Larches,' I told him. 'I visited, and spoke to an attendant. But I don't know how he got there.'

'Ah… Mister Samuel stayed at the hospital in January and February.' I was glad I'd not waited. Now he was speaking of Sam, he couldn't seem to stop. 'A farming family came across him the day after the Seething, five miles downstream. They told a police officer, who contacted Mister Toby, not me. Mister Toby asked me about a local hospital, but in a roundabout sort of way. And of course, when that unfortunate young man was brought out of the river during that period, I'd contacted Mister Toby again, not knowing…'

'That Sam was safe, and it couldn't be him.'

'Precisely. But I visit The Larches from time to time, so I came to know that Samuel was there.'

The vicar's voice drooped lower and lower with each sentence. I wondered, would I have to take his arm, to lead him to the explanation before he lost his nerve?

'When did Sam leave, and where did he go?'

'Early March. Mister Samuel was in the garden when he became... when he went missing.'

The ashy ground seemed to spin under me. 'They *lost* him?'

'It is not the fault of that excellent institution! He was one of patients evacuated from the building when a small fire broke out.'

'A fire.'

'A small fire. Mister Silver was helped from the house and left sitting on a bench in the gardens. The nurses did not know he was able to walk unaided, did not believe that he *wished* to leave, but...'

I pictured the routes away from The Larches. Breakwater one way, and I wasn't sure what lay in the other direction. 'Did anyone see which road he took?'

The vicar frowned but answered. 'Well, we do not know if he walked away from The Larches. There is also the river.'

There was also the river. When I'd visited The Larches it had looked deep and fast enough to carry a man away, particularly an invalid. The same river, coming back for a second bite at Samuel. Waiting until he had recovered enough to walk, and then calling him, hands of mud grasping at him...

This was why the vicar looked so sick, had given in so easily to my questions. This was the guilt that had made Toby so erratic. Sam had been found in January, safe through February, and by March he was misplaced again. They had let Sam wander away. They had lost him! And as far as they knew, they'd let him drown again.

I broke away and struck out across the grass. My shadow, running ahead, was twenty feet long. I ran past silver trees, London planes sloughing off pale bark. I pictured Sam sitting on a bench in the gardens at The Larches, as surprised as any other patient by the upheaval. Then Sam standing, letting the blanket over his knees drop to the ground. Tottering forwards, as if compelled, until he reached the rail at the edge of the river. Jumping? Tripping? Falling.

But I knew he *hadn't* drowned.

I'd reached a small copse, four large trees standing together as though to converse. I slipped into their shade, and leaned against a trunk, closing my eyes to concentrate.

In my imagination, I pulled Sam out of his fall, and set him back on the bench. He looks up at the windows of The Larches to check the progress of the fire that he's lit as a distraction. Cries and alarms come from the hospital as staff try to control what he has set loose. Then Sam looks over his shoulder, left and right, to make sure he is unobserved. His legs are fatigued from lack of use, but he marches down the winding lanes as far as Breakwater railway station. Talking his way into a ticket, as a gentleman can – to where? To the city first, to collect funds, and then wherever he chose. Not tired of life – passionate for life! – but tired of responsibilities. Tired of his brother, and of being betrothed. Knowing that to be alive is to accumulate responsibilities. Seeing a chance to make himself appear dead, to escape them.

At that moment, I was sure I'd never know which story was the reality.

Dark birds flapped across the fiery sky, heading to their shared roost. I felt tree bark against my back and wondered how long it would take, if I stood quite still, for ivy to cover me. It would be timid at first, but I'd try not to stir and the tendrils would snag my fingers, the stems would coil confidently around my arms. I'd have a skirt of pale leaves to begin with, then as the ivy saw out a few seasons, a full cloak of shiny bottle-green, veined with white. That mantle would embolden other plants to sprout around my feet, insects to crawl over me. I shouldn't disdain it. Did I deserve better than an age-old oak, or a marker in a cemetery?

'Miss Judith!'

The vicar's voice roused me, and I stepped out from the trees and let him catch up with me.

'Is it a comfort for you, to know?' he asked.

I nodded to dutifully confirm that yes, it was a comfort to know.

'Will you speak to your sister? Need you…?' He hoped I wouldn't make it known.

'I'll consider whether it would set her mind at rest or not.'

I was supposed to thank him. And I was thankful he'd come to London and met me, and hadn't summoned doctors to examine me. He'd spilled so many secrets, but it was hard to feel gratitude when they amounted to nothing at all. He didn't know where Sam had been. I had no better answer than on the night Sam had come back to me.

'There is an omnibus that stops close to here,' I told the vicar. 'It will take you back to your hotel.'

I turned towards the Lancaster Gate. My drab dress felt tight round my heaving ribs. We huddled on the street corner, and I looked everywhere but at the vicar. The last light washed the tops of the trees, catching a few stranded leaves and turning them gold. The fire in the sky was dying. Below it, on the Bayswater Road, a lamplighter made his way from pole to pole.

The vicar would leave, any moment now. My last day of investigation was ending. 'Are there rumours in the village,' I asked, 'about Toby harming Sam?'

I could almost hear Lucy tutting. I waited for the vicar to deny it.

'Mistaken,' he said. 'Of course, mistaken. A few of the villagers consider Toby responsible.' He was implying that they were yokels, misguided, but his voice cracked.

'Why? What did Toby do?'

'He mended the banks at Breakwater.' The vicar explained, in little sad fragments. 'You know, he had banks of brick and stone built all around Breakwater, where they were mud before. You see in the winter, when the waters rise, it wasn't a problem when the natural banks were shallow. They widened gradually, and they absorbed a lot of water. And if the river got terribly high, it simply spilled over into the water meadows. But the new brick courses made that impossible.' He mimed with his hands, holding them angled to show the old banks, then rigid and close for the new. 'When the flood came at midwinter, everything was channelled.' He moved his hands together, staring at the gap. 'Focused.'

This had been Toby's gift to Breakwater, his contribution, now that he was part of the community (his payment for Sam's bad behaviour). To stop the streets in Breakwater from muddying, and to make it easier for the poor to trade and travel. All along the banks, unproductive plants that crept and twined had been hacked back, and the water meadows turned to grazing grounds. But it turned out that the brambles and pools, and the mud itself, were essential. They couldn't be banished without consequence. And the first winter after they were finished, those fresh brick banks had forced the river into a new height and fury, which had swept Sam away.

Toby's gift to Breakwater had killed his brother.

'Is it true?' I asked. 'Aren't there any other explanations?' I still hoped to excuse Toby. I'd had dreams where my rage had raised the waters. When I'd woken, the guilt had been unbearable.

'I have scrutinised it,' the vicar replied. 'I should have done so earlier, before I recommended it. When Mister Silver was looking for a project to benefit the village, I suggested he look to the river.'

The vicar's wife had died from pneumonia caught at the Sully.

It would have taken a very good man not to lay the blame on Toby, and on himself for suggesting the project to Toby.

Toby, I didn't doubt, blamed himself.

The day wouldn't truly end until Samuel arrived. Until I could send him away. I sat in the library, in Ruth's wing-backed chair, and waited. I didn't try to call him, as I had done last night.

I looked around me at every lovely thing Ruth or I had made. My eyes lit on forgotten objects, created years ago, fragments of our old mythologies: a goose egg painted with a phoenix. A miniature clay minotaur patrolled the shelves. It lumbered towards a corkscrew wooden wand made from a particularly tough climbing plant. I'd stripped away the leaves and bark to reveal the spiralling grain.

Tired of staring, I tried to sketch, but I was agitated in every limb. Sam might not be here for hours.

I reflected that I had spent all day trying to get the truth from people, and I hadn't turned to my books.

First, I hauled a great atlas of England out onto the desk and turned the pages to the West Country. There was Breakwater, and there was the road out of town I'd taken to The Larches, with the river a fine blue line, dancing alongside. If Sam had walked down the other road, it would have taken him to a tiny village called Whitley Magna. My restless eyes kept leaping across the locations. Sixpenny Handley, Winterbourne Kingston. Durweston, Shillingstone, Okeford Fitzpaine. Places we'd visited, King's Stag and Long Barrow; I could make a charm by reciting those names.

I turned to the volumes I'd used for bravado when guiding Sam on Friday evening: *English Folk-lore* and *Gleanings*. I cursed them again for jumbling fragments in no good order. I had to pick around in them.

The books offered me charms to prevent family members getting lost: rhymes to recite, bags of herbs to sew up and tuck in a beloved's pocket. Ways to stop men straying (wandering feet, or wandering hearts?) by burying chicken bones under the hearthstone. If those charms hadn't worked, charms to find loved ones who were missing: lost in the woods, or disappeared at sea.

Moved away from charms and spells, into songs and stories, there were plenty of accounts of missing men returning. I was taken back to when Sam had sat dripping in the conservatory: sailors, hunters, long-lost brothers, imposters. Sometimes the missing men brought blessings, sometimes warnings. I carried *English and Scottish Popular Ballads* to my fireside chair to read one tale. A woman's three sons come home, and she makes a meal for them (which they will not eat) and a bed for them (where they sleep quite happily). But they leave before cockcrow, even though she weeps.

Toby's scarf was draped on the arm of the chair, and I wrapped it around my throat. Imperceptibly I had slid from the missing to the dead.

My gaze fell on Ballad 78. I'd read it before, but it had never satisfied me. A woman mourns her lost love. The dead love returns to speak with her, a wonder! But his first words are cruel: *Who sits weeping on my grave and will not let me sleep?*

He has come to admonish his love for excessive mourning. The dead love agrees with Ella, and states it just as crudely, that a twelvemonth and a day is enough time to weep. But does he ask his love to stop for her own benefit, or for his? The versions of the ballad differ. Sometimes the dead lover offers comfort: *Make yourself content, my love, until God calls you away.* Sometimes he delivers news of her doom in a gloating tone: *I am afraid, my pretty maid, your time will not be long.*

I could not imagine the dead lover saying: *don't mourn, you do damage to yourself, don't think of me.* It was all too easy to picture him, sat in the chair across from me, saying: *Tell me you missed me. Think of me more. Love me as much as you did when you lost me.*

I set the book of ballads down on the floor, stretched out my arms and felt my mouth open in a long yawn. It was night-time, and I was done waiting for him. I started to clear the room.

The desk with our plans on it was quickly stripped of material. I would sweep the house to drive out every crumb of him.

I still felt, as I tore the paper, the pull not to give up the search, to stick at it. There were avenues I'd not tried. I could place advertisements, I could visit other vicarages and hospitals, I could interrogate the farmers and nurses. But I put the urge aside, again and again. Like a kitten scrambling from its basket, I turned it round and settled it back. I'd given myself a week, and him a week, and neither of us had tracked down the answer. I held firm.

I felt tears welling in my eyes. But the tears and the weakness were welcome, because they meant I'd given up. Bonnie had been wrong. I wasn't a dog, to hold on until my teeth met. I wasn't Sam's little detective, and I wasn't a questing knight. The way to end this quest was to abandon it. With the weakness came relief.

At the library desk, hands full of papers, I turned to the grate to burn them, but paused. I placed them back on the desk. I sat, and took a sheet, and folded it: some simple symmetrical creasing, and I'd made a small boat. Ruth had taught me how, years ago.

That felt correct. I made another.

I mused, while I worked with my hands, upon Lucy telling tales on me to the vicar, and then lying to retract them. Had it been fair of her, to consider me mad? Even before Sam returned, I'd not been entirely well. I had certainly been lonely. I had felt myself floating away so many times, but I had hauled myself back in, tied myself down again with routines.

I hadn't been talking to myself. Sam had been there.

But what if he hadn't been there at all?

What if madness had come not in strangeness and panic, but friendly and familiar, and pulled up a chair by the fire? Waited for me to catch my breath and soothe my heart, and said: 'Hullo, Judith! Marvellous to see you!'

The vision made me convulse as though I'd drunk neat spirits. I ripped one of the big sheets into squares, and kept folding. The arrows which had connected past and present, cause and effect, were now flowing lines wrapped around hulls. Odd words named the vessels: *jill tup rush rash*. The good ship HMS *Taunted*. My sketchbook yielded up the doodles I'd done of Sam, ripped from the spine. I folded the sheets face down so I'd not have to look him in the eye while I destroyed him. Hands and face quickly became sterns and prows.

I swept the small boats into my skirt, grabbed the corkscrew wood wand from the bookcase and walked out through the French windows. I would cast him out.

At the foot of the garden, the ice of the lake was mostly melted. I crouched down, ready to launch the first boat out onto the water. When Ruth and I had made boats, we'd played at Viking burials. I patted my pockets to find matches, struck one and touched it to the paper sails, watched them catch and flare. I set it on the water and used the twisted wand to nudge it out beyond the reeds, where currents caused by freeze and thaw took it. It floated, and burned, for a surprisingly long time. The colours were mirrored in the surface of the water, lively and beautiful. I sent another, then another.

The heels of my boots were sinking slowly into the wet earth, so I rocked onto the balls of my feet to keep my balance. I imagined being barefoot, spreading my toes out in the mud, letting it well up between them. Being rooted in earth and surrounded by water and not afraid of either.

I said *goodbye, goodbye*, so lightly.

Without hearing him or seeing, I became aware of him. Absolutely, he would come. He'd be late, but he would come while I still thought of him. This was why I needed to thoroughly banish him.

He was sat by the lake, on a stone bench behind me. Dressed as he had been when I'd pulled him out of the water, smiling when I looked up at him.

'Hullo, Judith, dearest.'

I nodded to him and we both watched the boats, watched the tiny sketches of him burning. He knew the game was up, and he was revealed as a philanderer and a deceiver. But he would try one last time to charm me into disbelieving myself.

'Can you forgive me?'

'For which part?'

'Last night? I was ridiculous. Not myself.'

He hated to cause other people pain. Often, because he hated it, he'd deny that he'd done it at all.

'I had this incredible sense of danger. Perhaps it was because of all those things you were saying about Toby.' He turned reproachful. 'You frightened me, Judith.' Or he would blame someone else for causing the problem.

'You're forgiven.' Holding him to account at all would require months of entanglement. I laid my wooden wand beside me on the ground.

I knew he wasn't sure of his pardon because he made no move to touch me. He only smiled at me, and his smile was so lovely. I told myself that I would always remember that about him. I would stop thinking about him, but it was harmless, surely, to keep one memory.

I stood in case Sam reached out and I needed to move away quickly. My legs were aching from crouching so long. 'I don't think those things about Toby any more,' I said, shifting my weight from foot to foot. 'I don't think he tried to hurt you. He was displeased with you, but you know why that was.'

'Oh, he was always…'

'You *know* why.'

'Who pushed me, then?' He wanted my curiosity.

'Someone close to you, you said?'

'Yes.'

'It wasn't me.'

His mouth fell open. He looked quite foolish. 'Judith, I didn't think that for a moment!'

'Didn't you? I was furious with you. Even though it wasn't practically possible, I did sometimes wonder if the flood was my fault. That I'd somehow raised the water.'

There was calculation in his face: if I blamed myself, would it keep me preoccupied with him? Should he reassure me, or stoke my fears?

'But blaming myself was a kind of vanity,' I continued. 'I wasn't alone in being angry at you.'

'What, you think it was one of the village lads?'

It was a good guess: chivalrous young men, holding sticks and bats, taking up Bonnie's cause. They'd called for Sam at the cottage that night, insisted he join them. 'You pledged yourself at the Seething, and brought a different woman to pledge again. Then you threw yourself into the Sully as though you'd done nothing wrong. It was foolhardy to risk that.'

'Judith, if you think one of those ruffians knocked me down…'

'No, no. I don't believe it was a man. Too many witnesses – even the vicar was watching. And I don't think the villagers disliked you that much.' There was anger in Breakwater, but not necessarily in those young men. There was someone more relentless, who didn't let go until her teeth met. Sam had walked into the domain of the mudbride. She'd felt his footsteps on the riverbed, and reared up with limbs of silt, to claim Sam as her own or bring him down. 'It was bold of you to go into the water.'

Sam exhaled sharply. 'You're clever, but you're talking nonsense, Judith.' He liked me to be fascinated, but he didn't see any utility in that line of thought, or maybe there was danger there.

I shrugged. 'When you leave here, I wouldn't go back to Breakwater.'

'Are you sure Toby wasn't plotting something, Judith? I mean, everything you told me sounded so suspicious…' He was turning me back towards my old obsession. 'You thought about it so much…' A hungry quiver went through him. He loved to be thought of; he loved to have me think of him. He'd throw his own brother to the wolves if it kept me thinking about him.

'I imagine Toby did it to spare us false hope, if you didn't recover. Or if you left.' Sam didn't flinch when I said that, so I spun out my story a little further. 'You'd had the accident, nobody knew you were alive. You could have gone to another country – even another city – and we'd never have known.'

'I'd never put you through that. Why would I?' A quick retort but the tone was wrong, almost as though he was trying to imagine himself why he'd done it.

'So you didn't have to marry Ruth.'

'Judith! Did Toby tell you all this? Because you know he's a liar.' He turned his back on me, striding off around the lake, his steps springy with vexation.

I watched him pace to and fro in the moonlight, turning on his heel, raking his hands through his hair. He was truly indignant, truly saddened by every accusation. But he was also putting on a fine display to stop me asking questions. I waited until he tired himself, until the frenzied movement stilled. It took a long while.

I shouted across the lake: 'Why did you come back? Tell me truly.'

'Because I had to. Someone was missing me.' That sounded more honest than what had come before.

'Ruth?'

'I thought it was Ruth. Maybe it was both of you. I came back to let her go, to tell her to let me go…' Didn't he see that his reappearance would make any mourner cling twice as tightly? 'But then, to be here again…' He cast his arm up at the stars, the trees. 'It feels marvellous, you know. I want to stay.'

'So you need someone else to be thinking about you? To be missing you.' I almost felt pity, it was such an impossible requirement. Nobody would hold him in their mind as fervently as a mourning lover. Nobody would love him like someone who had just lost him. If he needed to be so fiercely loved, he was doomed. 'I can't do that.'

'You begged to help me!'

'You made me suspect your own brother of murder!'

He lifted his long hands: *forgive me, you have to forgive me*. He stared about the garden, as though there might be an excuse or an answer in the trees.

I walked towards him, around the water.

'It's all done, now,' I told him as I approached. 'Nobody's thinking of you. Look, I have Ruth's letter. She doesn't mention you at all.' I pulled it from my pocket. To my surprise, he didn't try to take it from me, but shrank away. I moved it slowly from side to side, and he swayed to avoid it. 'She was talking about marriage. Someone who would make a fascinating husband.' She'd spoken about marrying the sea, but the news made Sam writhe. I stepped closer, jabbing the letter towards him, marvelling when he stumbled backwards as though I were holding a burning brand. I was cruel and justified. His legs were an unnatural knot and if I forced him back further, he'd fall. I brought the paper up to his cheek. He jerked his head away. 'She'll come home, soon, and she still won't think of you. You have to leave, for good.'

'I will.'

I knew, in that moment, that I wouldn't give in to him. I wouldn't destroy myself. The river around the stepping stones at Breakwater claims a lot of people, but it has to first unbalance you, then persuade you to throw yourself in. You're safe, if you don't look down.

It was that point of dusk where sight is murky but every sound is piercing and crisp and I could hear him wheeze. I put Ruth's letter back into my pocket.

'Kiss me,' I said. I could risk this. It wasn't a beginning, but another form of dismissal.

He didn't answer.

'You're not Ruth's any more,' I told him. 'You can't be. So why can't you kiss me? Just for a moment.'

'I would, Judith, but my mouth, the taste of it...' His breath had the scent of rotting leaves. I didn't care. 'And you know, it's against the rules.' Mock solemn.

'What rules?'

'Oh, you know – older rules, higher courts. It would be dangerous.' More dangerous than a fire in my library? More dangerous than swimming in an icy lake at night? 'If you kissed me, you'd have to come with me. You know what I am. Don't you? You're clever, Judith!'

But I didn't know. All I really knew was that he'd wanted me, briefly, and now he didn't. Not a chivalrous man. Angry tears flooded my eyes, despite myself.

I craned up, trying to kiss him. A velvet wall stood between us. I pushed into it, and it rebuffed me, like swimming against a strong current or walking in a high wind. I fought it and was deafened by the roaring in my ears.

Sam didn't lift his hand to help me.

I relented and stepped back. 'Goodbye, then.' I had to say it first.

'Must I? Judith?'

I stopped thinking of him. I planned, instead, how to draw a flame reflected in water. I heard him faintly rebuke me while I planned. Chalk and charcoal wouldn't do it. I was cruel, he told me. I considered oil paints, oil pastels, how I'd have to dab and smear them. Forgive me, he begged. I envisioned things beyond my experience, molten enamels, lacquer and gilding, how they'd shine.

With each second, the pattern of lights on the lake shifted, and the boats burnt out. Sam walked off into the dark. Where to? Not down into the water – I'd have seen ripples, heard splashes. And he'd avoided the embrace of water for too long; he wouldn't acquiesce now. But he could have dispersed into the night air like fog.

Or stepped out of the garden, up the side alley, onto the road where he could hail a hansom cab.

By fair means or foul, I'd sent him away.

Another gleam appeared in the surface of the lake, amber and shifting. The lake was reflecting light from the house. For once, that was a cheering sight. It wouldn't be Sam, or Lucy's ghost-guest, making me doubt my sanity. It would be Lucy and Bonnie, eating the bakery treats I'd bought them and making plans.

But this light was too fierce, too red. I turned to identify it.

The French windows of the library were a coruscating gold. Flames licked up against the glass. The library was on fire.

A pale light from a window showed me Lucy and Bonnie were in the attic. They wouldn't hear me shout. I ran to the back door of the house, flung it open without hesitation, and the hallway was thankfully dark. No flames here, yet. But the air was foul and it scoured at my eyes and nose. When I took a deep breath, to call a warning, pinpoints of pain filled my lungs.

I bellowed Lucy's name in the direction of the staircase, twice, so loudly my throat hurt. I listened for a reply. The only sound was crackling, from beyond the half-open library door.

I could run up two flights of stairs to warn Lucy and Bonnie. Or I could go into the library, to slow the destruction. As I tried to decide, all I could think was that Ruth and I had filled the library with tinder. We'd piled every bookcase with holly and pine wreaths.

The library door creaked open further. Toby's scarf was still around my neck, and I wrapped it over my nose and mouth.

I moved into the murky room. The desk was just visible, and the books I'd stacked there. Child's *Ballads* lay open on its back, its pages waving in a hot wind.

Beyond the desk, the far end of the room was alive with fire.

My eyes stung and watered. Why were the flames concentrated in a column, with a white pulsing heart? It was the single remaining curtain, hanging by the French windows. Flames stroked at its edges, rushed and roared at the centre where they had taken hold, but didn't yet extend far beyond it. Smoke clouds rolled towards me, making me woozy.

A gunshot crack – a pane of glass in the French windows had split in the heat. This was too dangerous, I had to leave. Could I carry away any of my possessions, to save them from the blaze? What did I treasure most?

Then my mind leapt ahead: the fire from the curtain would spread. The whole house could burn, with everything I owned, and all that my family owned, too. But at present, the burning column was so slender, so weightless.

I started to move a moment before I understood what I was doing.

Hurtling forwards, head ducked, eyes shut, I told myself I was running towards the garden. I pictured the cool air and the ice lake. This was the quickest route: straight onwards, hurry, run don't think.

I smashed into the wall of heat. Both of my arms wrapped round the flaming fabric, hugging it, slowing me down. It didn't hurt at all and then it was intolerable, my face and my hands ringing with pain. The garden was only three paces away. I pushed on, felt the curtain pole give and the cloth pull free. My shoulder crashed against the French windows and they opened.

Pitching forwards, I hit the ground. That knocked the breath out of me and I lost hold of the curtain. Were my clothes burning? I rolled myself over and over, to smother the flames, until the ground spun and I couldn't tell if I was still moving.

I doubled up where I lay, coughing, then clawed the scarf off my head. The curtain flapped on the lawn a few feet away from me, its leaping flame pouring out sparks (*much gossip, many letters*).

The grass beneath me was stiff with frost. I pressed the seared skin of my face and hands into the coldness.

WEDNESDAY

I cy hands woke me, fingertips dabbing at my face and leaving
sharp chilly dots. Then the fingers pattered across my cheeks
and brow, up to the line of my hair, soothing my stinging skin.

I had been lying on my back, like figure on a mediaeval tomb,
to keep my raw hands and face from touching the bedding.
Resting on my chest, my hands felt white hot and dangerous.
Whoever was stippling cream onto my face, I should warn them
to stay away.

Opening my eyes, I saw my hands wore neat cotton gloves.

'Afternoon, Miss,' said Lucy, sitting on my bed. She took my
hands, plucked off the gloves as gently as she could, which was
agony, and patted cream onto the skin of my fingers and palms.
The cream smelled of lavender and calendula.

'Did you make this?' My voice rasped.

'What? No, I sent Bonnie to Whiteleys. Sit up, drink this.
No doctor?'

'Sorry?'

'You said no doctor, yesterday.'

'Do I need one?'

'Breathe in.' I coughed. 'Stretch out your fingers? Open your
eyes?' She peered into my face, assessing me. 'No, no need, for
now. Sleep some more.' I was too tired to mistrust her prescription.

As I dozed I heard Lucy and Bonnie in the house, laughing,
and sometimes out in the garden, cursing.

That evening, I sat up on my own. My head didn't spin, and my chest didn't ache, so I shuffled downstairs. I managed, unaided and unobserved, to reach the library.

The room was a dark cave. The walls were sooty, and despite the French windows swinging wide open to the garden, the air stank. But the furniture was intact: solid oak, hard to ignite. The books were soot-dusted but not consumed. I saw volumes from my father's collection, and reeled at the thought of everything Sam had tried to take from me.

Sounds from the garden prompted me to carefully cross the room and step outside to the lawns and the light. A heap of charred foliage was piled up on the grass. Lucy and Bonnie stood beside it, wearing sturdy gloves, throwing down armfuls of greenery. I understood the heap was made of all the pine and ivy that Ruth and I had brought into the library. Lucy had a great air of satisfaction at throwing it all out. Under the foliage I could make out the blackened remains of the curtain.

I heard Bonnie's voice, first: 'Do we burn it all?'

'No! Take it down the end of the garden,' Lucy replied. 'Past the old pond.'

I thought of that circle of water, only a dozen strides wide, set within marble kerb stones. It was a pond, truly; we'd been children when we'd thought it a lake.

Lucy turned and saw me. 'Shouldn't you be in bed, Miss?'

'I wanted to see the damage.'

She wrinkled her nose. 'It's not awful. You'll need lads to scrub it down.' Certainly not her job, her tone told me. 'I know two who'll do it, for half a shilling each.'

'Thank you.'

'And you'll need a glazier, and painters.'

'I can find them.' I could use Toby's records to contact the people who painted Millstone when the Silver brothers moved in.

Lucy walked back into the library, calling observations from inside. 'And the rugs are summat awful...' Bonnie followed her sister inside, stomping her feet to drive out the cold.

It had been a shock to see the library as a smoke-stained shell. Soon it would be shocking in another way: a sterile space. I pictured the white rooms of Millstone. I'd been so proud of our house, by contrast, with its character and warmth. What would I do with the library? I could remake it before my family returned. Repaint every curlicue, bring the ivy back indoors. Or I could wait, and when my sister came home, we could make it different.

Ella's offer of lodging became very appealing. I wasn't sure what it would be like to live with Ella and her mother, but I'd avoid the painters trampling around my house, and I'd have company and a routine. I hoped Ella wouldn't resent my fragility, until my burns healed.

I foresaw that if I didn't take any wine with me to Ella's house, I would wake without a headache, and cultivate fewer bruises. Once my burns had healed, provided Leah Isaac still wanted my company, I'd go to her; I'd make a round of visits and show my good spirits to the matriarchs, rejoin the ebb and flow. By the time my family returned I would be serene. I'd never give Mama reason to quiz my old companion Mrs Wolfe about her stay, and Mama wouldn't know I had spent months alone. I felt sure Lucy wouldn't tell, as long as she got her cook's training.

When Lucy came back to the garden, I sketched out my plans to her.

'Sounds right enough,' she said, not concealing her surprise that I was behaving sensibly.

'I'll write to Ella today. I'm sorry I didn't act sooner. I've been living alone for too long.'

'Alone?'

I apologised again, for that. 'Will you stay here? Or spend Christmas at Breakwater? Take as many days as you'd like.'

'I'll think on it, Miss.' Bonnie hadn't re-emerged from the house. I wondered whether Lucy weighed her sister in her calculations, and what Bonnie would do: return home for a scolding, or stay in my house, or run elsewhere entirely.

I tottered back upstairs, and detoured to peer into the room Sam had occupied. There was no trace of him. He must have left wearing the clothes he'd arrived in, as he'd abandoned the ones I'd fetched for him, laid on the neatly made bed. He'd been fastidious, or he hadn't been there at all. I wondered about the notes he'd written, which I'd burned. If I had kept them, if I examined them, would they be blank sheets, or in my own handwriting?

I returned to my bed. I reasoned: if I'd imagined him, he would have kissed me. He'd have said he loved me and kissed me. Because wouldn't I have been kinder to myself?

Then I slept, and after that I didn't think much about him at all.

The following day, a telegram came from my sister:

> *Everyone returning home January 8th. Venice dreary now only fogs forecast and Mama homesick. Planning Spring in Cornwall, will you come?*

Then a letter from Ruth as well, sent earlier and overtaken by her telegram. She mentioned a man, briefly, and said that she hoped I would meet him. How peculiar. He was in Italy; how would I meet him?

Then I realised that Ruth planned to stay in contact with the man when they both returned to this country. I picked at the significance of that. Ruth was coming out of mourning. I wondered if she could remember Sam fondly, now, as strangers had told her she would, which had made her cry when they said it. How would she and her beau manage to see each other? At dances, or afternoon teas? Would I go, too? This man wouldn't, I assume, live next door.

I remembered why Ruth and I had called Sam and Toby's house by that ridiculous name. The first time I saw inside it, I'd politely admired it (while thinking: it's so bare, but they'll make it look better, soon). And Sam said: 'Yes, it's good that it's small, we can shut it up and leave it whenever we want to. Don't you think a man should be free to travel? Any house is a bit of a millstone.'

On Friday, another letter was delivered: the college, inviting me to enrol for the coming academic year. Ella called at the house shortly after. She was unusually tactful, perhaps shocked by my still-healing face; she checked that I'd had good news from the college, before showing off her own invitation. 'What a relief! Now it won't be awkward when you stay.'

'Can I come tomorrow?' I asked.

'Of course. And you know, we could visit Paris before the college term begins, and see the Louvre.'

The college sent me back my portrait of Sam. I hid it in the library in a volume that nobody reads. Years from now, when it's safer to think, it will give me some clue.

What have I been doing?

What have I seen?

ACKNOWLEDGEMENTS

Thanks to all who have given invaluable assistance during the writing of *Unquiet*, including Dan Griliopoulos, Naomi Hetherington, Victor Lesk, Rebecca Levene, Alexandra Mitchell, George Sandison and Max Edwards. My debt is enormous, and my mistakes remain all my own. Massive gratitude to the generous scholars of the nineteenth century, the Gothic and the esoteric, inside and outside academia. Thanks to my reassuring agent Alex Cochran, and Julia Lloyd for the excellent chilling cover. Finally, huge appreciation to my remarkable editor, Daniel Carpenter, who improved things no end, and to all at Titan who have supported the book.

ABOUT THE AUTHOR

E. SAXEY is a queer Londoner who works in universities and volunteers in libraries. Their work has appeared in *Apex Magazine*, *Escape Pod*, *Lightspeed* and *The Best of British Fantasy*. Their first collection of weird short fiction, *Lost in the Archives*, is available from Lethe Press.

A PORTRAIT IN SHADOW

Nicole Jarvis

When Artemisia Gentileschi arrives in Florence seeking
a haven for her art, she faces instant opposition from
the powerful Accademia, self-proclaimed gatekeepers
of Florence's magical art world. As artists create their
masterpieces, they add layer upon layer of magics drawn
from their own life essence, giving each work the power
to heal – or to curse. The all-male Accademia jealously
guards its power and has no place for an ambitious young
woman arriving from Rome under a cloud of scandal.

Haunted by the shadow of her harrowing past
and fighting for every commission, Artemisia begins
winning allies among luminaries such as Galileo Galilei,
the influential Cristina de' Medici and the charming,
wealthy Francesco Maria Maringhi. But not everyone in
Florence wants to see Artemisia succeed, and when an
incendiary preacher turns his ire from Galileo to the art
world, Artemisia must choose between revenge and her
dream of creating a legacy that will span the generations.

ON THE NATURE OF MAGIC
MARIAN WOMACK

'An intricately built tale of history, spiritualism,
and magic; perfect for fans of Susannah Clarke'
A.C. WISE, AUTHOR OF *WENDY, DARLING*

1902. Helena Walton-Cisneros, known for finding
answers to the impossible, has started her own detective
agency. The agency's first uncanny cases are both located
in Paris – itself too much of a coincidence to ignore.

First, two English women claim to have seen the
ghost of Marie Antoinette in the gardens of Versailles.
Then a young woman working at the mysterious
Méliès Star Films studio has disappeared.

As Helena and her colleague Eliza investigate, they
uncover vanishings, impossible illusions, demons in the
Catacombs and connections to the occult. To find the
thread that connects the cases, Helena and Eliza must
accept the natural world is darker, stranger than they
could ever have imagined…

For more fantastic fiction, author events,
exclusive excerpts, competitions, limited editions and more

VISIT OUR WEBSITE
titanbooks.com

LIKE US ON FACEBOOK
facebook.com/titanbooks

FOLLOW US ON TWITTER AND INSTAGRAM
@TitanBooks

EMAIL US
readerfeedback@titanemail.com